THIS
LITTLE
PIGGY

THIS LITTLE PIGGY

DI HEATHER FILSON
BOOK 2

JD KIRK

ZERTEX CRIME

THIS LITTLE PIGGY

ISBN: 978-1-912767-78-6

Published worldwide by Zertex Media Ltd.
This edition published in 2023.

1

www.jdkirk.com
www.zertexmedia.com

ONE

THERE WAS A PRETTY solid chance that Detective Inspector Heather Filson was going to kill someone. She didn't know whose life it was she was going to take yet, but her own was very much still in the running.

She stood at a small, cluttered table in the big gym hall of Kilmarnock Academy, watching lines of disinterested fourth, fifth, and sixth years shuffling their way around the place, urged on by teachers who, by and large, looked equally as bored rigid by the whole experience.

The remnants of last night's Halloween disco were still dotted around the place—a few gruesome decorations in hard-to-reach places that the janny hadn't had a chance to take down yet, and a set of antiquated DJ decks with a pumpkin poster made out of crepe paper hanging from the table they sat on.

Heather met the thousand-yard stare of a woman at another stand. She recognised her from the ambulance service, and they swapped solemn nods across the battlefield of the Kilmarnock Academy Careers Fair.

The whole hall reeked of sweat, stale cigarette smoke, and raging hormones. Although, to be fair, at least two-thirds of that was coming from the uniformed sergeant she'd been paired up with. Wayne something-or-other. Gillespie, maybe.

He was in his mid-thirties, stockily built, with fingertips yellowed by nicotine. He shifted around, fidgeting constantly, like he was agitated about something.

She knew how he felt.

"Is this the police stand?"

Heather looked around, then down into a spotty face that shone with a film of grease. A boy standing around five-foot-nothing looked up at her, bum fluff sprouting from his upper lip.

He clutched a bag of *Wotsits* in one hand, and was dipping in and out of it with the other, refilling his mouth whenever the levels of cheesy mush in there fell below some minimum threshold that only he knew.

Christ, Heather thought. *Here we go.*

"Aye. That's why we wrote it in big letters up the top there," she told the boy, indicating the *Police Scotland* logo perched atop the stand's backboard.

The lad sniffed and nodded, as if quietly congratulating himself on his detective work.

He helped himself to another *Wotsit*.

"And what is it you do, exactly?" he asked.

This caught Heather a little off guard.

There were plenty of exhibitors at the fair whose businesses she didn't understand. She'd seen a sign for 'cloud engineering' on the way in, and had been thoroughly confused until Wayne had explained it was something to do with computers, and she'd immediately zoned out.

But the police? Surely everyone knew what the police did?

"What do you mean?" she asked, seeking clarity on the question.

"Is it murders, an' that?" the lad enquired.

Heather blinked. "What, doing them or solving them?"

"Solving them. I know you don't do them," the boy said.

He glanced around, then stretched up on his tiptoes and whispered, "Aye, no' officially, eh?"

With a knowing wink, he returned to the flats of his feet, briefly scanned the literature on the table, then pointed to the uniformed sergeant.

"Do you get a gun with that costume?"

"It's not a costume, son. It's a uniform," Wayne told him, with a level of weariness Heather fully sympathised with. "And no, you don't get a gun."

The boy made no attempt to hide his disappointment. He tutted, blew out his cheeks, and muttered, "Well, that's shite," below his breath.

"We don't need guns," Wayne said.

The sergeant had seemed even less enthusiastic about the fair than Heather when she'd met him that morning, and his few shreds of positivity had long since left him.

"You get guns in America."

"Aye, well, we don't live in America, do we?"

"Naw. Scotland," the kid said, and he rocked back on his heels like he'd once again demonstrated the full might of his intellect.

Which, all things being equal, he probably had.

"Is that bulletproof?" he asked, indicating the sergeant's stab vest.

"No."

"What if you get shot?"

"You try not to."

"Aye, but what if you do, but?"

"Then it hurts," Wayne snapped.

The boy nodded slowly. His eyes shifted left and right like they were operated by a lever on the back of his head as he considered the response.

"You got any rubbers?" he asked, turning his attention back to Heather.

"What?"

"Rubbers. Aye, no' Rubber Johnnies, I mean. I don't mean 'condoms,'" he clarified, adding air quotes around the word for reasons Heather had no desire to understand. "Just rubbers for pencils."

"No. We don't," Heather told him.

"Keyrings? Or anything cool like that? *McDonald's* was giving away vouchers."

"Vouchers?"

"Aye. Money off. Do you do stuff like that?"

Heather made a mental note to swing by the stand later.

"We're the polis. What kind of voucher would we give you?" Heather asked. "A 'Get out of Jail Free' card?"

"Are they a real thing?"

Heather bit her tongue, then swallowed back the first three responses that popped into her head.

"No. They're not," she eventually said. "Here." She took a cheap plastic pen from a mug and thrust it into the boy's *Wotsit*-coated grasp. "Take that and piss off."

The lad regarded the pen, then recoiled when Heather's instruction finally filtered through to him.

"You can't say that," he told her.

Heather turned to the Uniform at the other end of the table. "Sergeant, can I say that?"

"Aye. Aye, Detective Inspector, you can say that."

Heather shrugged and smiled down at the boy. "Turns out I can, so…"

She *shooed* him away with the back of a hand. For a moment, it looked like he might be ready to stand his ground, but then a team of perky students from Glasgow University caught his eye, and he wandered over to annoy them instead.

"Jesus. Remind me never to have kids," Heather remarked, and the sergeant gave a snort of agreement.

"You met Jaxon, then?"

The voice came from Heather's left. There was something

familiar about it. Something that made her stomach do a flip, and not in a particularly good way.

Toby Pearse, the teacher she had flat-out accused of child murder a few months back, stood smiling at her with his hands in the pockets of his grey Chinos. His light blue shirt pulled tight across his chest, while his tie hung rakishly loose around his neck.

He was just a few years into the latter half of his twenties, and was the kind of teacher Heather would have lusted over when she'd been a pupil at this same school.

Now, just the sight of him made her skin tighten with embarrassment.

He could've pressed charges over what she did. He could've ended her career with one statement.

The fact that he hadn't, meant she owed him. She owed him big time.

And if there was one thing Heather Filson hated, it was being in someone's debt.

"That's Jaxon with an X, by the way," the teacher clarified. "J-A-X-O-N. He's a"—Toby thought for a moment, before settling on—"character."

"Mr Pearse," Heather said, keeping it formal. She clocked a couple of sixth-year girls shooting doe-eyed looks in the young teacher's direction, but he didn't seem to notice. "Nice to see you."

"Is it?" Toby laughed. "You might want to have a word with your face, then, because I'm pretty sure it isn't in agreement."

There was a *crash* from elsewhere in the hall, and a high-pitched voice immediately protested, "I didn't do that! That wasn't me!" before anyone had the temerity to suggest otherwise.

Toby rolled his eyes and sighed, but kept smiling. "Duty calls," he said, then he turned and cut through the crowd to see what damage had been caused.

"He seems like a smarmy prick," Wayne muttered. "Bet he's knobbing half these kids." A look of horror flashed across his face. "Shit. He's not a friend of yours, is he?"

"No. No, not a friend of mine. Barely know him," Heather said. "He was a suspect for a while."

"I bet he fucking was," the sergeant remarked. He patted one of the front pockets of his vest. "Mind if I nip out for a fag? This place is doing my head in, and there's still two hours left of this bloody thing."

"Fire on," Heather told him. "I'll go next."

"You smoke?"

"Not in a while," Heather admitted. "But if it means getting out of here for five minutes, I'll take my chances with the cancer."

Wayne grunted out something that might have been a laugh, then headed for the fire exit. It had been left open to let some cooler air into the hall, and a couple of teachers had been posted by it to stop any of the kids from legging it.

A storm had swept across the country the night before, but despite all the thunder and lightning, the air felt oddly muggy and oppressive, especially for the start of November in Scotland.

Heather suspected that the breeze from the open door was the only thing preventing the whole fair from becoming a powder keg of mayhem and violence.

She watched Wayne go, and then spotted another familiar face in the crowd. A fifteen-year-old girl walked towards her, her bag carried across both shoulders, her school uniform immaculate.

A pair of bright red, thick-framed glasses were perched on the end of her nose, and from the way she kept peering over the top of them to see where she was going, appeared to be hindering her vision rather than helping it.

"Officer," the girl said, as she drew level with the stand.

"Nancy Drew," Heather replied. "Fancy seeing you here."

"It's my school," the girl told her. "Why wouldn't I be here?"

Heather couldn't help but smile. Ace Wurzel had come striding into her life on the same day the DI had met Toby Pearse, and had proven difficult to get rid of. She was what could generously be described as 'an unusual girl,' and while it irritated her immensely, Heather couldn't help but admire Ace's persistence.

"I did not expect to see you here, though," Ace continued. "Is this a punishment of some sort? Did you deliberately flaunt the rules again?"

"No more than usual."

"Did the chief demand your badge, but then relent to your request for twenty-four more hours to catch the perp?"

Heather hesitated. "Not that I noticed."

"Apologies, Officer," Ace said, nodding graciously. "My mother and I have been watching a lot of *Kojak* and *Starsky & Hutch* lately. Heard of them? They're television shows."

"Of course I've heard of them."

Ace pursed her lips and raised her eyebrows in surprise. There was something slightly reproachful to it, as if she thought serving members of the constabulary should be doing better things with their time than watching 70s cop shows.

"I see," she said.

Before she could say anything more, a much taller boy barged past her, using his shoulder to send her stumbling into the table.

"Watch where you're going, *spacker*," he said, and the smaller lad beside him giggled gleefully.

Heather stepped out from behind the stand and stabbed a finger at the gloating wee bastards. "Here. You pair. Come here."

Panic flitted across the smaller boy's face, but the larger of the two just shrugged, his face pulling into a sneer.

"Naw," he said.

Both what he said and how he said it were the exact opposite responses Heather had been hoping for. She took a step to lunge towards him, but Ace blocked her way.

"Don't worry about it, Officer. Darren's just acting out because he tried to have sex with Natasha Bullington from his Chemistry class when they were at his dad's house, but he couldn't maintain an erection."

Darren's face flared burgundy. He almost choked on his own shame.

"What? No! Bollocks! No. Who said that? Did Natasha say…? She's lying! That's not true. I just didn't want to cause she's a fat slag. Did she fucking say that?"

A hand clamped down on the boy's shoulder. Mr Pearse glowered solemnly at him, the slightly mischievous grin of earlier now replaced by a grimace of disappointment.

"Darren. A word."

The teacher met Heather's eye, nodded, then steered Darren away from the table. The boy's smaller sidekick stood frozen to the spot, unsure of his next steps.

Ace came to his rescue.

"You should leave, too," she said, then she pointed over to the *McDonald's* stand. "That way."

"Th-thanks," the lad stammered, and then, spinning on his heels, he was gone.

Heather turned to Ace and peered along the length of her nose at the girl, like she was studying her for the first time.

"That was brutal," the DI said. "Brilliant, but brutal."

"Was it? Did I go too far?" Ace asked. "It's true. I heard Natasha telling Carmen McWilliams at lunch last week."

Heather smirked as she watched Darren being steered out of the hall by Mr Pearse.

"Not too far, no. Just far enough, I'd say," she said. "But what happened? I thought you were the toast of the school. Everyone was cheering for you last time I was here."

Ace frowned, like she was struggling to recall the event that Heather had described.

"Oh. That. No, that didn't last," she said. "Which is fine. I didn't enjoy being the centre of attention."

Her tone, and the bright red glasses, both said otherwise, but Heather chose not to comment.

"Generally, I just sort of blend into the background. As a journalist, it's better that way."

Journalist was stretching it, Heather thought. When they'd first met, Ace was running a true crime podcast called *Crime De La Crime*, which had a subscriber count in the single digits, and two of those had been the girl herself.

Still, her research had proven helpful on the case Heather had been working on at the time. Odd as she was, annoying as she was, lonely as she was, Heather couldn't help but like the girl.

Or, at least, she didn't feel any overtly negative feelings towards her, which more or less ranked her as one of the DI's closest friends.

Christ, that was a scary thought.

"Excuse me, 'scuse me, coming through. Whoops. Sorry. Don't mind me!"

Heather and Ace both turned back in the direction that Darren had recently been led. A meticulously groomed man in his early thirties picked his way through the crowd of pupils, none of whom were making any attempt to get out of his way.

He shot Heather an imploring look, but she just shrugged, then crossed her arms and waited for him to finally reach the table.

"Inconsiderate wee bastards," he whispered, tightening his tie and smoothing down the front of his pastel purple shirt.

"What are you doing here?" Heather asked. Then, for perhaps the first time in her life, she remembered her manners. "Oh. Detective Sergeant Martin Brompton. Marty. This is Nancy Drew."

Ace adjusted her glasses and thrust a hand out for the DS to shake. "Ace Wurzel," she declared. "Of *Crime De La Crime* podcast fame."

Marty shot Heather an uncertain sideways look.

"Just go with it," the DI suggested.

"Charmed," Marty said, shaking the girl's offered hand.

When she released his hand, there was a flimsy business card with the podcast's website address crumpled into his palm.

Ace gave him a clumsy, wildly exaggerated wink, like she'd just pulled off the world's greatest magic trick, before turning back to Heather.

"It was nice to see you again, Officer. I should get going now. I have lots of stands still to visit. I'm told my future might lie out there somewhere." She peered around at the other stands, and didn't look impressed by what she saw. "Personally, I have my doubts, but you never know."

"Good luck," Heather said. She reached into the mug on the table. "Want a pen?"

Ace took the offered pen and regarded it in silence for a few long, contemplative moments.

"No," she decided, handing it back.

With that, she walked off.

A moment later, she returned.

"But thank you for the offer," she said, and then she was gone again.

"Was that the girl from...?" Marty asked.

Heather nodded. "Aye, that was her. What's up? What are you doing here?"

"The Gozer's been trying to get hold of you," Marty told her.

"No, he hasn't," Heather said.

"He bloody has. He's been calling."

"Well, it didn't ring here!" Heather insisted. She took out

her phone and checked the screen. "Shit. No signal. What's wrong? What's happened?"

"Nothing. No disasters. It's just that new lassie's arriving today," Marty reminded her. "From up north. The Gozer wanted you in the office for it. Snecky and Simon are currently drooling over her. I think he wants you to rescue her."

"Aye, well, he wanted me here for this, too. This was all his bloody idea."

"I think he assumed you were going to tell him to ram this up his arse," Marty replied.

He looked around the hall, his lips drawing back over his pearly white teeth in a grimace, his hands wringing together.

"And who'd blame you? Although..." His neck seemed to double in length as he stretched to search the place. "Is that hot teacher around? The one you tried to set up?"

"I didn't try and set him up!" Heather protested.

"Aye, well, you can feel free to try and set him up with me, if you like," Marty told her.

"Aw, shame. I would, but you've missed him. He's just gone," Heather delighted in informing the DS. "I take it you're over your ex cheating on you, then?"

"Cheating? He didn't cheat!"

"I thought you said—"

"*Cheating* implies some sort of romantic entanglement, or a drunken one-night stand," Marty all but shrieked. A few nearby teenagers glanced his way, and the detective begrudgingly lowered his voice to a whisper. "He went out and got himself reamed by eleven different Polish truck drivers."

"Jesus Christ," Heather muttered. "*Eleven*?"

She whistled through her teeth, even though she'd already heard all the gory details at least half a dozen times before, though this was the first time she'd heard them while the DS was sober.

"What, in a row?"

"No! Not in a... He fucking wishes *in a row*. No. Over a few months," Marty fired back. "But still, 'cheating' doesn't really do that justice, does it?"

Heather was forced to concede that no, the word didn't really cover the events that had led directly to the break-up of Marty's marriage.

"Anyway, are you here to take me back up the road, or what?" she asked, changing the subject.

"Oh, I wish! I wish that's why I was here," Marty replied. "But, no." He picked up a stack of fliers from the table and thrust one into the hand of a passing teenager. "I'm here to take your place."

Heather's burst of laughter echoed around the hall. A hundred heads turned in her direction as she thrust her hands in the air and let fly with a joyous, "YES!"

Still grinning, she patted the detective sergeant on the shoulder, then grabbed for the leather jacket she'd left in a heap on the floor beneath the table.

"Nae luck, Marty. They're a shower of wee bastards, by the way. Try and not let them get to you. Wayne'll be back in a minute for backup."

Marty's brow furrowed at mention of the name. "Wayne? Wayne who?"

"Local sergeant. Can't mind his second name. He's alright. I mean, he doesn't smell great, and he's a bit—"

"Behind you," Marty said. His attempt to disguise the words with a cough was admirable, but largely unconvincing.

Heather turned to find the uniformed officer looming there with a face like thunder.

"Sergeant. I was just telling DS Brompton here that..." she began, but the sentence died away when she realised that the sergeant wasn't angry at her.

In her job, you learned to read faces and body language. You became fluent in them, and trusted them more than you trusted the actual words coming out of someone's mouth.

And right now, the sergeant's expression and body language were both saying the same thing.

Something had happened. Something major.

Something bad.

"What is it?" she asked. "What's up?"

Wayne swallowed before replying, like he had to work up the courage to get the words out.

"Sergeant Crier. Tony. You know him?"

Of course she knew him. Everyone in Kilmarnock did, both on the force and off it. He'd been one of the local bobbies for close to thirty years. One of the good ones, too.

"Aye. Why?"

"He had a break-in last night. At home," Wayne said.

"A break-in?" asked Marty. "Is that all? The way you're acting, I thought something—"

"He was at home?" Heather asked, interjecting before Marty could dig himself any deeper. "Tony. He was at home?"

Wayne nodded. "Aye," he said, his voice a croak. "And by the sounds of it, the poor bugger's in a really bad way."

TWO

HOME WAS a fifteen-minute detour she could've done without. Twice that, when you factored in the return trip.

And then there was the time she was going to have to spend in the house. This, as yet, was an unknown quantity.

She hadn't met the new start yet, but she almost felt bad for her. DCI Samuel 'Snecky' Grant and DC Simon Wolfe had been talking about her arrival non-stop since they'd heard the news yesterday. They'd both worked with her before, and while they'd both said that she could be "a wee bit too much," they'd also agreed that she was "fit as fuck."

Heather couldn't imagine much worse than having that pair perving over you on your first day on the job.

Still, the new DC was on her own for now.

Heather took a breath, opened the door of her Audi, then stepped out into the uncharacteristically warm November air.

The carer's car was still there, so that was a good sign. She hadn't quit yet. That was almost three full days. A new record.

The neighbours, Sally and Bob, waved at her as she made her way up the path. Heather's heart sank at first, but the wave was a friendly one, and not a desperate attempt to alert her to the fact her dad was running naked down the street.

She returned the wave, then stopped when she reached the door. Another breath. Another pause. Another moment to prepare herself for what might await her inside.

At last, when she could delay it no longer, she pushed down the handle and was met by the sound of gunfire.

So far, so normal.

She closed the door behind her and padded along the hall, where the light from the TV flickered through a gap in the living room door.

An old black and white war movie played on the screen when she stepped inside. The Nazis were taking a hammering, though the young woman lying on the couch seemed too preoccupied with her phone to notice.

She was facing away from the door, her legs curled up so her knees pointed to the ceiling and her heels almost touched her arse. Her shoes were still on, the soles flat against the cream-coloured fabric.

The chair that Heather's dad, Scott, usually sat in was empty, his tartan blanket scrunched up on the floor beside it.

"What's this?" Heather asked, and the carer launched herself off the couch like the cushions were spring-loaded.

She was young. Most of the ones from the agency were, it seemed. Early twenties, or thereabouts. Bleach had stripped her hair of all its natural colour, and she'd trowelled a mask of orange over her face that made Heather think of the kid with the wet *Wotsits* dust on his fingers.

For someone who'd just been caught out being a lazy bastard, she was quick to go on the offensive.

"Where the bloody hell have you been?" she demanded. The accent was straight from one of the Glasgow schemes, and the sentence contained more attitude than it did syllables. "I totally tried to phone you, like, nine times!"

"Why? What's the matter? Where is he?" Heather asked. "Where's my dad?"

"If you'd've answered your phone, you'd know!" the carer fired back.

"Kelsey!" Heather's voice was an animal growl. And not one of the nicer animals, either. She took a step closer, and the girl's attitude evaporated like morning mist. "Where. Is. My. Dad?"

"He's in the bath," Kelsey said.

"In the bath? He was meant to be going in the bath this morning."

"Aye, I know! Jesus! He did! Now he won't come out, but. I tried, but he won't shift. He's been in there for hours. That's why I was phoning you, but your phone must've been off, or..."

Heather didn't hang around to hear any more. She returned to the hall, took the stairs two at a time, then stopped herself a split-second before she could barge into the bathroom.

She took a moment to compose herself, then raised a hand and knocked on the door.

"Dad? Dad, you alright? It's me."

From beyond the door, there was the sound of water sloshing as the old man moved in the bath.

"That you, Stewie?"

There was a shudder in his voice. He sounded cold. Scared, too, maybe.

Heather's eyes closed, just for a moment.

"No, Dad. It's just me. It's Heather."

A tut.

A sigh.

"Och, you're no bloody good to me. Get your brother, will you? I'm in the scud here. He'll need to give me a hand out."

The carer's voice rose from the foot of the stairs. "That's what he kept saying to me. Kept asking me if I was Stewie, and I'm thinking to myself, like, 'Who the fuck's Stewie?'"

Heather shot her a warning look. "Can you go back into the living room?"

"I've no' been in the living room!" came the reply from the bathroom.

Heather waited for the carer to slink away, then turned back to the door.

"Not you, Dad. I was talking to Kelsey."

Another splash of moving water.

"Who?"

"Kelsey," Heather said, a little louder this time.

"Who's *Kelsey* when she's at home?" asked the voice from beyond the door.

"Did you just shout me there?" asked the one from the hallway below.

Heather turned and shook her head. "For fu— No! I wasn't talking to you."

"Well, who were you talking to, then?" Scott demanded. "Is it Stewie? Get him to come in here, will you? *Stewie!* Stewie, son, come here a minute, will you?"

The reply caught Heather by surprise, the sharpness of it almost drawing blood on the way out of her mouth.

"He's not here, Dad! Alright? Stewie's not here. I'm here. It's just me. You've just got me!"

Silence.

Then, the slow, quiet sloshing of an old man sitting back in the bath.

"Where is he?"

Heather leaned her forehead against the door. She didn't know where her brother was. Nobody did. Nobody had seen him in almost three years.

Until recently, she'd been convinced that an old-school Glasgow gangland boss named Shuggie Cowan had killed him and dumped his body somewhere. Now, though, she wasn't so sure.

Now, there was a chance that he was still alive out there somewhere. That was good, of course. That was great.

And yet, it had all felt much simpler back when he was dead.

"He's out, Dad. He won't be back until later," she said. "So, how about I just come in and help get you out, eh?"

There was no reply, only the faint lapping of water from beyond the door, and the muffled echo of Allied gunfire downstairs.

"Dad?"

"Fine. Fine, come in and give me a hand, then," the old man said. "But shut your eyes before you come in. I'm no' having you catching a flash of ma willy!"

———

Fifteen minutes and a bit of awkwardness later, Scott sat in his favourite chair, in a set of fluffy tartan pyjamas, his thinning grey tufts of blow-dried hair sticking up like the last few strands on a stick of candy floss.

He'd insisted on putting on his favourite socks, the red ones with the hole that his big toe stuck through, and was now watching the old war movie like he'd been glued to it from the very start.

He'd probably seen the bloody thing a hundred times before, of course, so it was no surprise that he could just slip right into the story without missing a beat.

"Haha! Stitch that, ya Nazi bastards!" he cheered. "Didn't see that coming, did ye?"

Heather returned from the kitchen and sat a cup of sugary, milky tea down beside him. He didn't seem to notice, even when she pointed it out to him, and warned him to be careful.

Kelsey, the carer, hovered by the living room door, her jacket draped over an arm like she was about to make her escape.

"I'll just be off, then. If I hurry, I can…"

"Wait. Hang on," Heather said. She opened the door and

nodded for the girl to step into the hallway. "You're meant to be here until two," the DI said, once they were out of Scott's earshot.

He hadn't seemed to be listening, but he had a way of earwigging in when you thought he was completely zoned out.

"Aye, but you're here now," Kelsey said. She gave Heather a quick look up-and-down, as if to double-check the statement was correct. "So can't I just go?"

"No. I'm only here for a minute. I need you to stay on."

"Stay on? How long for? You said until two, and that was it."

"Aye, well, things change," Heather told her, then she bit her lip and attempted to arrange her face into something like a smile. Those didn't sit well with her at the best of times, and it proved to be a struggle. "I really need you to stay for a few more hours. Just until five."

"Five? I said I'd be home by three. I'm meant to be going out."

"Who the fuck goes out at three in the afternoon?" Heather asked.

She still had the smile pinned to her face. The question was meant to sound teasing and light-hearted.

It did not.

"Listen. I can pay you."

Heather took out her wallet and produced a crisp twenty-pound note. Kelsey's expression didn't change.

Another tenner was added as a sweetener to the deal.

One of the carer's overly sculpted eyebrows pricked up, but otherwise, she showed no sign of relenting.

"Jesus Christ. Seriously?" Heather rounded the offer up to forty quid. "That's it. That's your lot."

With a sigh and an exaggerated rolling of the eyes, Kelsey plucked the money from the DI's hand.

"Fine. Five o'clock, then I walk. And if nobody's here, tough shit. I've got places to be."

"Deal," Heather said. It was, she knew, the best one she was going to get. She leaned in closer, and allowed herself one little moment of satisfaction. "But if you put your dirty feet up on my clean couch again, I'll cut the fucking things off at the shins."

THREE

HEATHER MADE it to the Police Scotland HQ at Clyde Gateway in near record time. The M77 was relatively clear, though she'd had to weave around some random branches and other debris brought down by the storm the night before. There was a crew on clean-up, but they were in no hurry, and seemed content to stretch the job so it filled the whole day.

Some flooding on the M74 had caused tailbacks, but she was able to divert off it and reach the station without too much trouble.

The new arrival was sitting at a desk in the MIT office, smiling politely despite DCI Grant and DC Wolfe flanking her on either side. Wolfe was trying to get her to feel his bicep when Heather entered, while Snecky was muttering something about brains being more important than brawn in his nasal Invernesian accent.

The newcomer shot to her feet at the first sight of Heather, like the accused standing before a judge.

The rumours were true, then. The young woman was stunning. Her blonde hair was pulled back into a relaxed ponytail, and her sparkling blue eyes looked like they'd been hand-crafted by a master jeweller.

She had the looks of a Hollywood starlet, and the pang of guilt Heather had felt at abandoning her to these two clowns earlier now returned with armed backup.

"DC, eh…"

She shrugged. She had no idea what the lassie's name was. No point pretending otherwise.

The DC opened her mouth, and Heather almost stepped back at the onslaught of words that came spewing out of it.

"Swanney. DC Swanney. As in the song. You know? The racist one? Forget it, doesn't matter. It's Tammi-Jo. With an I. Not Y. I don't mean like *why*, as in the question. I mean the letter Y. That's not in it. My name, I mean, there's no Y in it. Well, there is at the end. Of the surname. Not my first name. My first name has an I in it. T-A-M-M-I-hyphen-Jo. Just the normal Jo. Well, without the E. J-O."

She swallowed hard, wiped her palms on the front of her light grey trouser suit jacket, then practically ran at the DI to offer her hand.

"Hello. Hi. You're Detective Inspector Filson," Tammi-Jo declared.

Heather cautiously accepted the hand. "Aye. I know. It's written on my driver's licence."

"Ha! That's funny! You're not as scary as you look," the new DC said, then she gasped and shook her head. "That's not what I meant. I meant you're not as scary as they said you looked."

"Who said—"

"No!" The yelp from the detective constable made Heather drop her hand. "I mean, you don't look as scary as they said you were," Tammi-Jo said, then she smiled, pleased that she'd finally got out the right words in roughly the correct order.

"Who said I was scary?" Heather asked.

"Oh, just, you know…" Tammi-Jo swallowed again. "Everyone. Pretty much everyone. More or less."

Snecky, who was still sitting half-draped on the desk by

Tammi-Jo's chair, gave a dismissive wave of a hand. "I don't think she's scary," he announced with a deliberate air of bravado. He pointed to DC Wolfe. "*He* finds her scary."

"No, I don't!" Wolfe insisted.

"Yes, you do. You told me. You said you find her intimidating."

Wolfe rose to his feet, adamantly shaking his head. He had a plummy accent that spoke of his rich upbringing and boarding school education.

"No. No, I said I *might* find her intimidating, but only in a sexual situation."

"What the fuck?!" Heather cried.

DC Wolfe's eyes widened, like he'd suddenly realised that not only had he put his foot in it, but that the 'it' in question was a big pile of dogshite with a bear trap inside.

"No, no, I wasn't saying anything bad, or anything," he insisted. "We were just talking about who we'd—"

The clearing of Snecky's throat and the raising of his eyebrows silenced Simon at once.

But not for long.

"It was just hypothetical. There was nothing creepy about it, or anything," he said, before another look from the DCI finally shut him up.

"Right, well, in that case..." Heather took DC Swanney by the arm and turned her to face the two men. "Hypothetically, Detective Constable, would you shag either of this pair?"

Tammi-Jo let out an audible squeak of discomfort. "Um...?"

"Because I sure as hell wouldn't. DCI Grant there's built like a pencil, and he's probably hung like a five-year-old."

Snecky rose quickly to his feet. "I beg your pardon?!"

"And Simon's just... God. Where do you start? He looks like a witch sculpted a guy out of soft cheese and half brought it to life. It'd be like shagging a lump of Brie."

"You can't say that!" Wolfe protested. "She can't say that!"

Heather held both hands up in a calming gesture. "Come

on, lads. What's the problem? It's just hypothetical. Nothing creepy about it, or anything."

Another throat was cleared. This time, it came from somewhere over Heather's shoulder. She and Tammi-Jo both turned to find Detective Superintendent Gordon MacKenzie—aka, the Gozer—looming behind them.

"Detective Inspector," he said, with a note of reproach. "A word, if I may?"

———

"'It would be like shagging a lump of Brie'? Do I want to know what all that was about?" the Gozer asked, once he'd installed himself in his office chair.

Heather sat without being invited to, and shrugged at him across the desk.

"Probably not, sir, no."

"Good. Thank Christ for that," the Gozer said. He smoothed his shirt over the growing mound of his belly. "One less thing for me to worry about."

"You hear about—"

"Tony Crier? Yes. Yes, I heard." The detective superintendent's expression told tale of the sergeant's current condition. He ran a hand over his balding head and sighed. "He's in the Royal. High Dependency. His son's with him. It's not looking good. We've had SOCOs round at the house doing a sweep. Few bobbies going door to door asking if anyone saw anything."

"We still thinking burglary?" Heather asked. "Officially, I mean?"

"Why wouldn't we be?"

Heather crossed her legs so that one of her *Doc Marten* boots rested on her knee, and picked at the rubber sole. "Hell of a house to hit," she said. "Everyone knew Tony. Everyone knew where he lived."

"Could've been someone from outwith the area," the Gozer suggested. "Or possibly even some Halloween prank gone wrong. They're all bloody *Trick or Treating* these days, aren't they? What's wrong with guising? When did that change?"

"No idea. And, aye, it could've been an incomer. Or, it could've been someone targeting him deliberately."

"Hmm. Yes. That thought had occurred," the detective superintendent replied. "We're running through names, but Tony's either been at his desk or visiting primary schools for the last five years. It's not like he's out there making enemies. I mean, I know Kilmarnock's got its share of problems, but last time I checked, there weren't hordes of disgruntled eight-year-olds going around breaking and entering."

"No," Heather agreed. "Twelve-year-olds, maybe."

The Gozer acknowledged the joke with a single snort, more out of politeness than amusement.

"I'd like to go and see him," the DI announced. "I worked under him for a while, back in the day. He was always good to me. He was always good to everyone."

"Aye, he was that alright."

They sat in silence for a minute, then Heather gave herself a shake.

"We're talking like he's dead. He's a hardy bastard. He'll be fine."

The Gozer nodded and sat back. "Aye, well, give him my best," he said.

"Will do, sir."

Heather got up from the chair, pushed it back under the table, and almost made it out the door.

Almost, but not quite.

"And take our new start, will you?"

Heather groaned inwardly, one hand still clutching the door handle.

"What, to the hospital? She doesn't know him."

She only half-listened to the Gozer's reply. Something about showing the new DC the lie of the land, and keeping her away from Snecky and Wolfe. All very sensible, but not what she wanted to hear.

"I think it's best if—" she began, before the detective superintendent cut her short.

"I disagree. Whatever it is you were about to say, Detective Inspector, I disagree," he told her. "It was not a request. Take DC Swanney out with you. I want her shadowing you for the next few weeks."

"The next few *weeks*?" Heather asked, turning to face him. "You can't be serious?"

"When am I ever not serious, Detective Inspector? She's had a rough few days. She's a new face in an unfamiliar city. For the rest of this month, DC Swanney is entirely your responsibility."

The Gozer smirked. Clearly, he was taking some twisted pleasure from all this.

"Do we understand each other, DI Filson?"

A few months ago, she'd have kept arguing. A few months ago, she'd have fought him tooth and nail, or just turned her back on him and walked out of the office.

But a lot could change in a few months.

Everything you'd ever known about yourself, for one.

"Aye, sir," Heather said. She gave a salute that was entirely sarcastic—she hadn't changed *completely*, after all—then pulled open the door. "I think we understand each other just fine."

FOUR

"SORRY, WHAT?"

Heather blinked, as if waking from a dream, and turned to the detective constable sitting in the car beside her.

They were parked up in the multi-storey that served Glasgow Royal Infirmary, a grand Georgian building that made the car park seem even grimmer by comparison.

"Did you say something?" the DI asked.

Tammi-Jo glanced around like she suspected she was on a TV prank show, and was looking for a hidden camera.

"I said a lot of things," she said. "Like, I've been talking non-stop all the way here. It's a thing I do. I don't mean to, but I can't help it. It just sort of"—she opened her mouth and used her hands to mime a lot of vomit cascading down her front—"*bleurgh* sometimes. I don't do it on purpose, it just sort of happens. Like real vomit, I suppose. People don't generally do that on purpose. Well, bulimics, maybe."

"Right." Heather sucked in her bottom lip and spat it out again. "Sorry, wasn't listening. I'm really good at tuning stuff out."

"Oh," said Tammi-Jo, a little crestfallen. She'd thought she'd been doing quite a good job of breaking the ice and endearing herself to her new DI. "No problem. Well done. That's absolutely fine. It was nothing all that important. I was just asking about your favourite Christmas movie?"

"My what?"

"Christmas movie. What's your favourite? You know, since it's November now, and heading towards Christmas, I thought it would be a fun way of getting to know each other if we both shared our favourite Christmas movies."

Heather pointed to her ear and shrugged apologetically. "Nope. Missed most of that, too."

She slapped her hands on the steering wheel, then turned off the engine. The dying shudder of the car rattled a couple of empty *Red Bull* cans that had been tossed onto the back seat, along with a few sandwich wrappers, crisp packets, and half a *Gregg's* sausage roll, which had turned out to be one of the vegan ones, and so had been rejected out of principle.

"Anyway, here we are. Glasgow Royal Infirmary. Well, the multi-storey car park, anyway, which is about as good as you're getting for now."

Tammi-Jo's smile, which had been fixed on her face throughout the whole car journey, grew wider in confusion. "Sorry?"

"You're staying here," Heather told her, unfastening her seat belt. "I'll only be half an hour or so."

"Uh, but Detective Superintendent Mackenzie said—"

"This isn't a work thing. It's a personal thing," Heather told her, shutting down the DC's objection. "I won't be long. While I'm away, you can just, you know…" She motioned around at the inside of the vehicle. "Guard the car."

"Guard it?" DC Swanney looked worried. "From what?"

"Just, you know, in general," Heather told her, then she pointed at the DC, mimed shooting her, and winked. "Won't be long. If you need me, just, you know"—she thought for a moment—"don't."

And before Tammi-Jo could say anything more, the DI slid out of the car and slammed the door behind her.

———

Christ. He was a mess.

Heather had been braced for the sergeant being in a bad way, but Tony Crier was barely recognisable behind the mask of stitches and swelling. His face was a palette of brooding purples and bloody reds held together by wire. A brace looked like it was keeping his head in place and stopping it from rolling away.

Splints straightened his bloated fingers. Slings supported two of his limbs, one arm and one leg, hoisting them off the bed.

Machines *bleeped* and *whirred* and *wheezed*. Tony's chest was rising and falling, but the movements were shallow, and the medical equipment seemed to be doing much of the heavy lifting.

"Jesus," Heather whispered.

"Burglary gone wrong, they're saying."

Heather noticed the other man in the room for the first time. Ash Crier was twelve years her junior, and while he'd only been on the job for a couple of years, he was polis through and through. Hard not to be when you came from a long line of bobbies that stretched back through the generations.

At first glance, though, most people wouldn't peg him as a police constable. With his big broad shoulders, weathered brow, and shock of ginger hair, he had the look of a farmer about him. Even more so when, like now, he was dressed in a checked shirt and faded jeans.

Just like his old man, Ash had always been an easy guy to like. He was confident without being cocky, charming without being sleazy, and had a relaxed, open smile that helped put people at ease.

Today, though, the smile had abandoned him.

"Aye, so I hear," Heather said.

Ash fidgeted in the hard plastic chair and turned his attention back to the man in the bed.

"That look like it to you?"

It didn't. This wasn't a wrong time, wrong place sort of beating. This had been personal. Directed. If they caught the bastard—*when* they caught the bastard—they'd be pushing for an attempted murder charge. No question.

"I don't know," she said. "Could've been someone off their tits on something. Someone who didn't know what they were doing."

Ash's snort was short and dismissive. "Oh, they knew. They knew exactly what they were doing."

Heather had come here to pay her respects to her old boss. That was all. This wasn't a polis thing, she'd told Tammi-Jo. This was personal.

And yet, she couldn't help but tug on that string.

"What makes you say that?" she asked. "Why would anyone want to hurt your old man?"

Ash didn't look at her. Not even for a moment. Instead, he tapped his fingernails against his bottom teeth like he was considering the question, then shook his head.

"Nothing. No reason. It probably was just a break-in, like everyone's saying."

Heather thought about putting a hand on Ash's shoulder. That's what people did, wasn't it? That was how they showed their support.

But she barely knew him, and he barely knew her, and what good would it do, anyway?

"Knowing him, he'll wake up and tell us who did it," she said. "Even if he didn't see them, the bugger'll crack the case."

Ash didn't see the funny side. "Aye, well, someone better, or—" He stopped himself before he said any more. His jaw clenched, and the fidgeting of his fingers became the cracking of his knuckles. "Someone better."

"They will. We will," Heather assured him. "And when we do, Tony can check the bugger in himself."

The constable didn't even acknowledge the comment. He just sat there, studying the unfamiliar topography of his father's face, his knuckles *popping* one by one.

He was hurting. Of course he was. She sure as hell would've been. She recognised something else in him, too. Rage. Ash wasn't just upset about this, he was angry. The sort of anger, she suspected, that wasn't interested in justice, only revenge.

"You hear there was a constable murdered yesterday?" he asked her out of the blue. "Up north. You hear that?"

Heather shook her head. "No. Hadn't heard," she said, and she wondered how she'd missed it.

"It's getting worse. Out there. Nobody respects the uniform anymore. People treat you like a joke," Ash said, venom packing the spaces between each word. "You've got mouthy wee pricks running riot everywhere. Fucking neds squaring up to you on the street. Bastards like Shuggie Cowan, thinking they run the place, and everyone's too fucking scared to tell them otherwise."

He slapped his hands on his thighs and rubbed them, fingers curled like claws. He blew out his cheeks, and grimaced, like he was struggling with a particularly stubborn bowel movement.

"Wayne's right. It can't go on. They need to start respecting our authority again. All of them. If they were more scared of us, there's no way shite like this would happen."

In theory, Heather liked the idea of people paying her more respect. A world where people tipped their hats to the polis and thanked them for their service certainly held some appeal. But it was a fantasy to think it was ever going to happen.

And it was certainly not going to happen in the greater Glasgow area.

Besides, it would probably bore the arse off her.

"I don't think we want them scared," she reasoned. "I don't think your dad would've wanted that."

Ash's reply was a deep, guttural grunt, and a tightening of his fingers on his thighs. He was studying his unconscious father again, memorising every line.

"Listen, if you need to talk to anyone…" Heather began, before a flurry of movement from the younger man stopped her.

Ash twisted in the chair and glared up at her, his features bunching angrily together like she'd just confessed to being the attacker.

"You don't even know me," he told her. "You barely know him."

"I worked with him for quite a few months."

"Aye, so what? I lived with him for two decades. He's my dad. You don't know anything about him. You don't know anything about either of us."

The ferocity behind the words took Heather by surprise, and she had to perform an emergency override on her usual instinct to bite back and give as good as she got.

The poor guy was upset. He wasn't thinking straight. The last thing he needed was a bollocking from her.

"No," she admitted. "No, I suppose I don't."

She looked over at the man on the bed. Whoever the attacker had been, they'd really gone to town on him. Even if he pulled through this, she suspected it would be a very different Tony Crier who eventually opened his eyes.

"Take care, Ash," she said.

And then, with a final glance at Sergeant Crier, she eased open the door and slipped out into the corridor.

A bear-sized man in an overcoat immediately blocked her path.

"Well, well, well."

Heather looked up to find her former boss, Detective Chief Inspector Jack Logan, peering down at her, one eyebrow raised. He had heavy black bags under his eyes and looked like he hadn't slept in days.

"I had a feeling I might find you here…"

———

Heather wanted to hug him. This was quite an unusual sensation for her. Hugging people—*any* people—was not something she generally felt any desire to do. Quite the opposite, in fact.

The same, she knew, could be said of DCI Logan. Neither of them were particularly tactile people, but she had a feeling that, on this occasion, he might well have been open to it.

But their history made it difficult.

And the fact they were sitting across a table from each other in the hospital's coffee shop didn't help matters, either.

Hugging would've been easier, though. Hugging him would've meant she didn't have to find the right words.

"Jesus, Jack. I'm sorry," she said, once he'd finished explaining what he was doing there. "I had no idea."

DCI Logan blew on his coffee. The cup was a small one, and in his enormous hands, it could've come straight from a doll's tea set.

"Aye. Well. Cheers," he said, raising the cup in thanks. "I was just glad I was able to make it down in time." He shrugged. "I think. I think I'm glad. It's all still a bit up in the air."

"Did he know? That you were there, I mean?" Heather asked.

Logan nodded. "Aye. He knew." He stared into his coffee for a moment, as if just realising the enormity of that fact for the first time. "He knew I was there with him."

There was a hairline crack in his voice. Most other people would've missed it. But then, most other people didn't know the man like she did.

They'd been lovers for a while, back when they were both at their lowest. That had been a mistake, though he'd figured that out long before she had. She could see it now, though.

DCI Jack Logan, at that time in his life, had been a bloody awful romantic partner. When it came to friends, though, there were very few people who could even come close.

"So, what happens now?" she asked, sipping from her cup.

Her timing was all wrong, as Logan had just taken a big bite out of a roll and square sausage, and his mouth was too full for him to reply.

She'd splashed out and bought him breakfast. Even before he'd broken the news about his father, it had been clear he was in need of a cuppa and some hot food.

"God knows," he finally said, forcing down a swallow. "Funeral arrangements. Clearing out his house. All that. Maddie's coming across to help out."

"Your daughter?" Heather's eyebrows arched in surprise. "I thought she wasn't speaking to you?"

"We're working on it," Logan said. "She's married now."

Heather inhaled her coffee the wrong way and had to jam her mouth against the crook of her elbow to cover her coughing fit.

"Jesus Christ," she wheezed. "Married?"

"Aye."

"Bloody hell. You're getting old, Jack," she teased.

"You can say that again," Logan agreed.

He tucked into his roll. Heather sipped on her coffee, saying nothing. Despite the circumstances, she allowed herself a few moments to enjoy being back in his company.

"How's the missus?" she asked, once he'd polished off the grub.

"She's good, aye," Logan replied, picking at a tooth with the nail of a pinkie.

"Tell her I said hello, will you?"

Logan tilted his head left and right, like he was weighing this up. "I think I'll maybe play that by ear."

Heather laughed. "Aye, maybe best," she agreed. And then, because she could wait no longer, she got down to business. "I hear you had some day of it yesterday."

"Aye. Rough one. We lost a constable. Young lad."

"I heard, aye. Sorry." Heather nodded towards the door, indicating the direction they'd walked from. "You know Tony?"

"Not well. Only in passing," Logan said. "Always seemed a decent guy, though."

"Aye, he is. He's a gem," Heather said. "His son's pretty cut up about the whole thing."

"Can you blame him?"

Heather shook her head. She couldn't, of course. He was sitting by the bedside of his badly beaten dad, praying for him to pull through. His anger was entirely understandable.

And yet, it had troubled her. The rawness of it, and the hatred in his eyes had made her uneasy.

Across the table, Logan wiped his mouth with his paper napkin, then scrunched it into a ball and picked up his coffee.

"You met Tammi-Jo yet?" he asked, and Heather was convinced he was smirking at her from behind his tiny cup. "Or, as Bob Hoon affectionately named her, 'the human shite tornado.'"

"God, aye. I've had the pleasure," Heather replied. "She's here, actually. I left her in the car."

Logan's brow furrowed. "You left her *in the car*?"

"Aye. She'll be fine. I cracked a window open. She won't overheat."

The DCI chuckled. "Aye, well, fair warning, expect her to have fiddled with all your buttons and rearranged your glove box by the time you get back. Sitting still's no' really her strong point."

"Great. Now you tell me," Heather replied. "I'm assuming she has some, though? Strong points, I mean? Besides not having to breathe while she's talking?"

"Plenty," Logan confirmed. "She's a good kid. She'll be an asset."

Heather grimaced, unconvinced. "Really? You're not just saying that because you wanted rid of her?"

"I didn't. Wasn't up to me," Logan said. "And aye, she's good. She can't half talk a load of shite, but she's good at her job. She sees the world differently."

"Aye, well, so did Jack the Ripper, but I wouldn't want him on my team." Heather considered this for a few moments. "Mind you, maybe I could swap him for Snecky..."

Logan's phone rang before they could debate the pros and cons of this. He searched his pockets for a while as the people at the closest tables glowered their annoyance.

"It's Maddie," he said, once he'd finally found it. He got to his feet, his chair legs scraping on the polished floor. "I'd better go. She must be here."

"Aye. Course. Go." Heather gave him a nod and a small but heartfelt smile. "And sorry again, Jack."

"Cheers. You take care of yourself," he told her.

And he left without ever getting that hug.

FIVE

HEATHER ARRIVED BACK at the car park, and stopped when her gaze fell on her Audi, and the woman sitting in the passenger seat.

"Oh, great," she muttered, setting off again. "She's been murdered."

Approaching the side window, Heather peered in through the thin film of condensation at DC Swanney.

Tammi-Jo was slumped in the seat, her head lolling forward so it hovered just an inch or two from the dashboard. There were no obvious signs of a violent struggle, and the faint snoring from the detective constable very much stamped a big *case closed* on whether she was alive or dead.

Heather knocked on the window, three hard raps of her knuckles. Tammi-Jo was awake after the first one, erupting back into consciousness with seismic, car-shaking, explosive force.

"You mustn't melt the grandchildren!" she cried, with desperate, frantic emphasis.

Her blue eyes were wide, but still unfocused. A few strands of her hair had snuck loose from her ponytail and hung like curtains on either side of her face.

Her head jerked around in panic as she tried to work out where she was, then she recoiled in fright when she saw Heather grinning in at her through the side window.

"Alright?" Heather asked. "Fall asleep, did we?"

Tammi-Jo's chest heaved as she fought to steady her breathing. "Oh, God. I hope so," she gasped. "Otherwise, we need to go and arrest a *lot* of old people."

By the time Heather had joined her in the car, Tammi-Jo had fixed her hair and managed to come round a bit. Her eyes were no longer like saucers, and her breathing was back under control.

"Sorry. Didn't get any sleep," the DC said. "I was up most of the night. Long day, too. We were in a castle. Big spooky one. DC Neish—do you know DC Neish?—DC Neish thought it was haunted. I don't think it was, though, because I don't believe in ghosts. But then, you don't know, I suppose, do you?"

"I mean—" Heather began, but the detective constable was still in full flow.

"I didn't think I was going to make it. Here, I mean. I don't mean I thought I was going to die. I didn't think I was going to make it to work on time. Which would've been bad for my first day, but I got a ride in a helicopter, so that was good. DCI Logan brought me down. I mean, he was a passenger, too. He didn't fly it, or anything. He's not a pilot."

She paused for almost a whole second while she thought about that.

"I don't think he is, anyway. I'm sure he'd have said. Is he a pilot?"

Heather shook her head. "No."

"No. I didn't think so. He's here, by the way. Somewhere."

"Aye, I know," Heather said. She started the engine. "I saw him."

"You saw him? DCI Logan? Just now?" Tammi-Jo sounded

absolutely thrilled by this, like she was playing a small role in the world's largest coincidence. "How's his dad doing?"

"Not well. He died," Heather said.

"Oh. Yikes. That *is* not well," Tammi-Jo reasoned. "Och. That's a shame. How is he? DCI Logan, I mean, not his dad. We've already established how he's doing."

"Same as usual, pretty much," Heather said.

She checked the clock on the dashboard and was pleasantly surprised to find it was just before three. Still a couple of hours before she had to be back in Kilmarnock to see to her dad.

"There's a thing back at HQ," she announced, checking left and right as she eased the car out of the parking space. "For Tony. A sort of get-together. There'll be a whip-round. You should come. Be good for you to meet people."

"Oh. That sounds nice," Tammi-Jo said.

"Aye, well, don't get your hopes up."

The coast was clear, so Heather put her foot to the floor. The tyres screeched and DC Swanney was thrown back in her seat as the Audi swung onto the exit ramp.

"Because I can almost guarantee it won't be."

———

Heather was not wrong. The gathering back at base was a largely morbid affair, full of long faces and awkward silences. Tony Crier was still alive and kicking, but looking around the room, you'd never know it.

The event was being held in one of the larger briefing rooms. Tony was well thought of, so although the turnout was decent, the size of the room made it feel half-empty.

There were thirty or so people in attendance, from all areas of the force. Uniform made up most of that number, but there were a few faces from CID hovering around a table in the corner, and Snecky and DC Wolfe had even put in an appearance, though they were sitting on their own and seemed largely oblivious to everyone else around them.

Everyone but Tammi-Jo. They waved to her when she and Heather entered, and Simon indicated the empty seat beside him. DC Swanney took a breath and started to head in their direction, but Heather caught her by the arm, shook her head, then led her over to where a familiar face was holding court with a group of uniformed constables.

All male, Heather couldn't help but notice.

She also couldn't help but notice how they all fell silent and shuffled aside at her approach.

"Alright, Sergeant?" Heather said, acknowledging the man who'd been with her on the careers fair stand that morning.

"Detective Inspector." Sergeant Wayne Gillespie gave her a curt, no-nonsense nod in return. "Didn't expect to see you here."

"Why not?"

"Oh, just, you know…" Wayne smiled. It wasn't a pleasant sight, and Heather felt like there was an element of show-boating to it for the benefit of the assembled constables. "It's so rare you lot bother with the likes of us."

Heather frowned. She got the sense that the men around her were studying her. Sizing her up.

"What the hell's that supposed to mean?"

Wayne's smile remained fixed in place. He shrugged. "Just what it says. There's no hidden meaning for you to try and *detect*."

If that wasn't a jibe, it certainly sounded like one. Heather thought she heard sniggering from the other Uniforms, but when she turned to look, they were silent and stony-faced.

"I hear you've been talking to Ash," Heather said.

"I have. He's a good lad. Knows what way the wind's blowing."

There was an intensity to Wayne's reply. Some not-so-subtle hidden meaning.

"And what way's that?" Heather asked.

"Just the winds of change, Detective Inspector. Just the winds of change," the sergeant replied. Something blazed behind his eyes that made Heather uneasy. "Who's your friend?"

"Oh! Hi! Sorry! DC Swanney. Tammi-Jo. I'm new!"

Those men who hadn't already been checking out the new DC now all turned to look at her. Her smile was broad and friendly. Far more so than the ones she got in return.

"Come on, Detective Constable," Heather said, jerking her head back to indicate it was time for them to withdraw. "Let's leave these lads to it."

She marched over to a free table on the opposite side of the room to Snecky and Wolfe. When she glanced back to make sure Tammi-Jo was following, she caught a couple of the constables openly ogling the young DC, and watched as whispers passed between them.

Indicating a chair across the table from her, Heather sat down so she was facing Wayne and the other men, and plastered her annoyance on her face for them all to see.

One by one, they turned back to the sergeant, whatever he was saying apparently now more interesting than Tammi-Jo.

"Well, they seemed nice," the DC said, plonking herself down in the seat.

The same open, affable smile was still fixed to her face, and something about it—everything about it—made Heather want to slap her.

"Seriously? You really think so?"

Tammi-Jo drew in a slow breath through her nose. "My dad always told me that if I don't have anything nice to say about someone, then I shouldn't say anything at all."

"Really?"

The DC nodded. "Especially, if they're a man."

Heather snorted. "Well, that's the first thing we'll be drumming out of you."

"That said,"—Tammi-Jo's eyes darted left and right—"permission to speak freely, ma'am?"

"Don't call me 'ma'am.' And yes. Speak away. You're not in school."

Tammi-Jo leaned closer, her voice dropping into a whisper. "Honestly? No. I don't think they were very nice at all. I think the sergeant was trying to openly defy you to make the constables look up to him. Showing off, sort of thing, and acting *The Big I-Am*. I get the impression they're all unhappy, possibly about what happened to…"

She pointed a finger towards the ceiling and spun it around a few times.

"Tony," Heather said.

"About what happened to Tony, and they're looking to take it out on someone. I'd say the sergeant—Wayne, was it?—is going out of his way to bring on the Mulligrubs."

Heather followed her line of thinking all the way until that last bit.

"The what?"

"The Mulligrubs." Tammi-Jo nodded keenly, like she was egging the DI on, urging her to figure it out.

If she was, it wasn't working.

"Who the fuck are the Mulligrubs?" Heather pointed to the constables. "Are they the Mulligrubs?"

"No! They're not the Mulligrubs. They've *got* the Mulligrubs. The Blue Johnnies," DC Swanney continued.

"The who?"

"The Blue Johnnies."

Heather's temper stirred in her gut. "Stop smiling. What are you talking about? Are you having a breakdown? Is that what's happening here?"

"No! The Mulligrubs and Blue Johnnies. Unhappiness. Discontent. You know, he's getting them riled up, putting them on edge."

"Right. Aye. Could you not have just said that?"

"Sorry," Tammi-Jo said. "Also, he smokes way too much, and I think his wife recently left him." She held up her left hand and waggled her ring finger. "Tan line. Faint, but it's there."

Heather's gaze flitted to the sergeant's fingers, but he was in the grip of a whispered rant, and his hands were flying around all over the place to help hammer home his points.

"Could just be planning going on the pull," Heather countered. "Might've taken it off for that."

It was a test, as much as anything.

"Maybe. But, I doubt it. He'd probably switch it to the other hand, which he didn't," Tammi-Jo said. "And he'd probably want to go home and get changed first before he went trawling the streets for women, or whatever. So, if he did that, his wife might notice that he wasn't wearing the ring, which would make it risky to take it off." She shook her head firmly. "No. I think he was dumped."

The detective constable's sapphire eyes suddenly widened, and she inhaled sharply.

"Unless you think different. I'm not saying I know better than you. If you think it's that, it's probably that. You've got more experience. *Way* more experience! *Way, way* more."

"Alright, steady on!" Heather protested. "I've not got *that* much more. I'm only thirty-six!"

"Exactly! That's more than half my age again!" Tammi-Jo gushed. She reached a hand across the table and laid it on top of Heather's. Then, with absolute sincerity, added, "I can't wait until I'm as experienced as you are."

Heather felt like she should be annoyed by the comment. She wanted to be annoyed by it, in fact. And yet, there had been no malice behind it. Quite the opposite. Tammi-Jo meant what she said. Every word of it.

"Aye, well, don't worry. It'll be here before you know it," Heather assured her, then both detectives turned to look as Wayne's voice rang out across the room.

"What do you think you're doing here?"

A shorter man with reddish-brown hair and a slightly stocky build shuffled uncomfortably just inside the doorway. Heather felt like she'd seen him in uniform before, but he was dressed in civvies now. His already rosy cheeks reddened as all eyes turned to look at him.

"This event is for polis only," Wayne said, and his pack of constables stood in solidarity around him, backing him up.

"I *am* polis, though," the other man replied, though there was a hesitancy to it, like he was only too aware of the potential hidden dangers on the path ahead.

Wayne's snort carried around the briefing room. "No, you're not, *Teddy*. You wish you were, but you aren't. You're just a special. In fact, no. You're not. Sorry. You're a *very* special. Aren't you? That's what you are."

"Jesus Christ," Heather muttered. She wasn't having this.

As she rose to her feet, though, another voice rang out, more or less nailing what she'd been planning to say.

"Oh, grow the fuck up, Wayne."

Once again, heads turned, and all eyes in the room shifted, this time settling on another uniformed officer standing with a smaller group down the far end of the room. He was just a constable—a fairly new one, Heather thought, because she didn't recognise him—but he addressed the senior officer without fear.

"Leave him alone. Come away in, Ted. Get a cuppa."

Wayne's shoes *creaked* as he fully turned to face the openly defiant constable. Heather watched his fingers flexing in and out. A cowboy, readying for a quick-draw shootout.

"What did you say, son?" he demanded. He tapped the stripes on his shoulder. "You need to watch your lip. Let's not forget who outranks who here."

"Good point, well made, *Sarge*," Heather said, getting to her feet.

Everyone's gaze shifted her way now.

This was getting interesting.

"Ted, is it?" she said. She beckoned him over and pointed to the empty seat next to Tammi-Jo. "Come on in. Take a seat."

For a moment, Wayne looked like he might be about to explode, but then he laughed drily, lowered his head, and went back to whispering to his pack. They sniggered as the special constable hurried past them, his head held so high it looked like it might topple backwards right off his neck.

"Thank you. Thanks. You didn't have to do that," he babbled when he joined Heather and Tammi-Jo at their table. "That was very nice of you, um, ma'am?"

"She doesn't like being called that," Tammi-Jo said. "I think it makes her feel old." She held a hand out to the man and almost knocked him onto his arse with a single flash of her smile. "I'm DC Swanney. Tammi-Jo."

"Ted. Campbell. Ted Campbell. And Swanney? Ha! Nice." The special constable swallowed. His eyes were flitting around, like they couldn't deal with the detective constable's radiance for more than a second or so at a time. "Like the river? Well, the song. Is it an actual river? I'm not sure."

Tammi-Jo's blonde eyebrows arched in surprise. "Yes! Like the river. In the song. Exactly! Oh! Settle an argument. Well, not really an argument, more a sort of internal debate. Is it racist?"

"Your name? No. It's..." Ted swallowed again, so hard this time that Heather wondered if his Adam's apple was ever going to reappear. "It's beautiful. Um, your name, I mean. It's nice. It's a good name. *Swanney. Swan's knee.*" He grimaced and shook his head. "I don't know why I said that. Sorry."

Tammi-Jo giggled. Heather wondered if it was too late to side with Wayne after all, and have Ted evicted. One Tammi-Jo was quite enough for any room.

"What was all that about with the sergeant?" she asked, trying to steer the conversation in a less irritating direction. Which, to be fair, would be any of them.

"Oh, him? Nothing," Ted said. He pointed at the chair,

double-checking that he had permission to sit, then lowered himself into it when Heather tipped him the nod. "He thinks it's funny to take the piss because I'm a special constable. You know, like a volunteer?"

"I know what a special constable is," Heather assured him.

Ted's cheeks reddened again. "Right, yes! Of course you do. But, that's what I want. I've got a business. It's doing well. I don't want to be full-time. I'm not in it for the job. I just, I don't know"—he scratched at the back of his head, suddenly self-conscious—"I want to do my bit to help."

"That is lovely," Tammi-Jo said.

Ted's face lit up, like he'd just drawn six numbers on the lottery.

Well, five and the bonus, anyway.

"Really? You think so?" he asked. "Most people think it's a bit cheesy."

"What? No, not at all!"

Heather cleared her throat, then pointed across to one of the other groups. "That guy's a special. Wayne has no problem with him. What aren't you telling us?"

Ted winced, glanced around, then leaned towards the middle of the table and lowered his voice. "Right. OK. Yes. I might have accused Wayne of some shadiness in the past. Throwing his weight around a bit. Think he got a reprimand for it."

Heather directed her attention to the sergeant. He was staring right at her, but looked away when he noticed her watching.

Although, he didn't turn away quickly. He held her eye for a moment, like he was challenging her.

"Also," Ted continued. "I *might* have mentioned to his wife that he was popping round to shag my next-door neighbour before heading home off night shift."

"Of course! That's why there's no ring!" Tammi-Jo cried, and the echo of her voice raced a full lap around the room.

She turned to find most of the other officers looking at her, including Wayne.

Especially Wayne.

The DC quietly cleared her throat. "We're... troubleshooting a phone," she announced. "Think we've worked it out. Got a bit excited. Sorry."

She turned back to Heather and Ted, wiped her hand across her brow to suggest she'd just narrowly averted disaster, then spoke again in a whisper.

"I reckon they bought that. Does it look like they bought it?"

Heather glanced past her to the knot of Uniforms standing in the middle of the floor.

"No," she said. "Not really."

"What if I made my phone ring, and then we all cheered?" Ted suggested. "Would that help?"

Both constables—detective and special—looked across the table to the DI for guidance on the matter. Heather blew out her cheeks and shook her head.

"I'd say that ship has sailed," she told them, and they both struggled to hide their disappointment.

Once again, she tried to steer the conversation in a more sensible direction.

"Who's your friend up the top?" she asked. "The one who stood up for you?"

"Oh, that's Daz. Darryl Hartmann. He's my brother-in-law. Married to my sister. Well, it's not just that. We go way back. Went to school together. That's how I know Tony. Sergeant Crier, I mean. Ash was in the year below Daz and me, but we all used to hang out." He sat back, his face falling, like he suddenly remembered why they were all gathered here. "Poor guy. Both of them, I mean. Tony, too. But it's Ash I'm worried about."

He glanced around the table, and the expression on his face

suggested he was worried he'd said too much. "Have you spoken to him? Ash, I mean?"

"No," Heather lied. "Why?"

There was a stumble. The briefest of pauses. "No reason. Just wondering. I'm worried he's going to take it hard."

"Worried in what way?" Heather asked.

Before Ted could answer, the door to the briefing room opened again.

The Gozer stepped in, and Heather knew. Instantly, she knew. There wasn't an officer there in that room who didn't.

The lines on his face and the curve of his shoulders broke the news to them.

Heather felt her stomach flip.

She watched as a sergeant and a small army of constables all tightened their jaws and clenched their fists.

"Aw," she muttered. "Shite."

SIX

THE RAIN WAS COMING down in sheets by the time Heather and Tammi-Jo pulled up along the street from Tony Crier's house. Or the house that had belonged to him until an hour or so ago, at least.

What would happen to it now, Heather didn't know, though presumably it would go to his son. Tony's wife had died almost seven years ago, right when Ash had been hitting those troublesome teenage years, and they'd had no other children.

It was a wee two-bedroom ex-council house on Knockmarloch Drive. Decent enough for the area, but hardly a palace, and certainly not worth killing your father over. So, sole beneficiary or not, she wasn't looking at Ash as a potential suspect.

Not yet, anyway.

Scene of Crime had already done their bit earlier in the day in anticipation of Tony's condition taking a turn for the worse. Or the worst. From the car, the house looked empty, like it had been deserted for years, the only movement the flapping of the cordon tapes that were strung across the gate and over the door.

Even the constable who stood sheltering from the rain

under the front canopy was statue-like in his stillness. He stared ahead, both hands tucked behind his back, his head lowered in a sign of respectful reverence.

A couple of squad cars were parked along the street, and a female constable peered at the car for a moment as she emerged from a nearby garden. Then, recognising Heather, she gave a wave and moved on to the next gate along.

Heather fished out the key she'd been given for Tony's house, and glanced at the clock on the dash. "Right, twenty-past four. We need to make this quick."

"How come?" Tammi-Jo asked. "Oh, and that might be wrong. The clock. It might be wrong. It is wrong. It's definitely wrong. I pressed a button, and it went a bit haywire, so I tried to get it back to the right time, but it went forwards instead of backwards, and then—"

Heather sat forward in her seat. "Wrong? What are you...? What do you...?" She checked her watch. A yelp of panic burst from her lips. "Shit! *Shit!* It's ten past five!"

DC Swanney nodded solemnly. "Is that good?"

"No! No, it's not good! Why would it be good? Jesus Christ!" Heather started the engine. "I need to get home."

"Home? But..." Tammi-Jo looked towards the house with the fluttering tape. "We're supposed to be going in there, aren't we? For the murder?"

Heather slammed her hands on the wheel. Once. Twice. "Fuuuck!"

Beside her, Tammi-Jo shifted awkwardly in her seat. "I can't help but feel I'm partly responsible for this."

"Partly?!" Heather barked.

The young DC smiled weakly. "Is there anything I can do?"

"Oh, I think you've done quite..." Heather stopped.

She looked at the house.

She looked at the detective constable beside her.

"Actually," she said. "How do you feel about old people?"

———

If Tony's house had seemed empty from the outside, inside it felt positively hollow. Silence seeped from its very fabric, like every molecule of the place was holding its breath, mute with shock over what it had witnessed.

Scene of Crime had been and gone, but stepping mats still lay dotted on the carpets in most of the rooms. Presumably, they were planning on coming back to do a more thorough sweep now that it was officially a murder investigation.

The preliminary report from Aiko Kimoto, head of the forensics team, had only been a page long. The ambulance had been and gone long before she'd arrived at the house, so the scene had already been compromised.

Tony had been found halfway down the stairs, apparently, stark naked and covered in blood. There were traces of it in one of the upstairs bedrooms, and several smears on the banister.

Very little downstairs, though, so the attack had all taken place on the upper floor of the two-storey house.

Heather looked around the living room, feeling like an intruder in Tony's home. She'd been there once before—eight, maybe ten years ago—after he'd broken his arm in a scuffle with a local scally. In a rare moment of empathy and generosity, Heather had brought him a cake.

One she'd bought from *Tesco*, obviously. Baking wasn't really her thing.

It had felt like a home then, even though Tony had been the only one in it at the time. It had been back before Tony's wife had died, but she'd been at work, and Ash had been in school.

There had been some sort of exam on that day, Heather remembered. Tony had cared more about how Ash was doing than he had the broken arm.

But then, that was Tony Crier all over.

The living room had been done over, although not particularly thoroughly. A couple of drawers had been yanked out of a sideboard and tipped onto the floor, but the cupboard doors beneath them were still closed.

A large amethyst geode stood on a circular wooden plinth in the corner of the room, its exposed purple innards a stark contrast to the outer husk of dull grey stone. It was probably the most valuable thing in the entire house, but the weight would have made it a difficult thing to nick.

Tony's 32-inch TV had been toppled over, so it lay on the floor in front of its stand. Notably, it hadn't been nicked, though. The wires were still plugged in at the back, too.

Of course, the telly probably cost a hundred and fifty quid brand new, and that would've been a decade ago. It probably wasn't worth the effort of stealing.

So why knock it over?

The kitchen had suffered a ransacking with a similar light touch. Again, a few drawers had been pulled open, their contents spilled onto the scuffed and faded Lino. A set of wooden handled knives and forks lay scattered across the floor, along with more teaspoons than was reasonable for one person to own.

Some cupboards had been opened. A few plates had been taken out and smashed.

There were crumbs on the worktop, and dirty dishes in the sink, though these were unlikely to be the work of the killer.

The Venetian blinds hanging over the back window were, not to put too fine a point on it, completely fucked. Rows and rows of the thin metal slats were buckled beyond repair, and the whole thing had partially torn away from the fixings on the wall above the window.

With a gloved hand, Heather nudged it aside, revealing the window itself, with its freshly broken frame.

The burglar's entry point.

Allegedly.

Opening the back door, she had a quick check outside. The garden backed onto that of another house. Only a low wooden fence separated them. Easy enough for someone to vault over.

A couple of tents had been set up in the garden—one by the fence and another by the window—to protect some evidence or other from the rain. Footprints, Heather guessed, though she'd find out for sure when Aiko's full report came in.

The rain made staying out there an unappealing prospect, even if the temperature was still uncharacteristically warm for the time of year. Storm Agatha's progress across the country had really put the rest of the weather on the back foot, and it was now trying to figure out what the hell it was meant to be doing.

Although she suspected that wasn't how a meteorologist might explain it.

Even if there had been other evidence out there that the SOCOs had missed, there'd be little chance of retrieving it now, so Heather returned to the kitchen, shut the door, and turned her attention to the rest of the house.

There was nothing else downstairs apart from the hallway, and a tiny bathroom that had been built under the stairs when Tony's wife had been ill. A quick check in there revealed nothing of any interest, and so she turned her attention to the staircase.

The forensics team had marked bloodstains on the carpet with plastic evidence marker tents, each one displaying a little number that would correspond with their notes.

There were six of them on the stairs, numbered 13-18, plus some stickers marking spots and smears on the banister and walls.

Some of the stickers were in the shape of arrows, indicating the direction of spray, or possibly the direction Tony had been moving in when that particular stage of the attack had taken place.

Heather stood there at the foot of the stairs, studying the various blood patterns, and thinking back to the overfilled bag of broken bones and bruises that had comprised the majority of the sergeant's face.

There had been multiple lacerations. A broken nose. Burst lips. There was definitely blood here on the stairs, but not enough. Nowhere near.

Steeling herself, Heather picked her way up the carpeted steps, placing her feet on the mats that Aiko's team had left behind, and taking great care not to touch the handrail or walls on either side.

She found more blood waiting in the bathroom at the top of the stairs. It was around the rim of the toilet and pooled on the floor. Had Tony hit his head on the porcelain? Had the attacker done it?

An evidence marker drew her attention to a bloody hand-print on the Lino. There was no way for her to tell whose it was without running a comparison, but she'd be prepared to bet it was Tony's.

He'd been on his knees here. Either he'd fallen, or been knocked to the floor, most likely smashing his face off the toilet on the way down.

Another plastic tent in the washbasin caught her eye. There was no blood there, though, and nothing to indicate what the SOCOs might have marked.

Water droplets, maybe? There was a hand towel on the floor right beside the basin. Had Tony been washing his hands when he became aware of someone in the house? Had the attack started here, then continued onto the stairs?

Did that fit?

"Maybe," Heather muttered, saying the word out loud in the hope it took the edge off the oppressiveness of the silence.

It didn't.

She left the bathroom, following her train of thought.

He'd got up for a pee during the night. He'd been washing his hands when he heard a noise downstairs.

But he'd been attacked up here. He'd been attacked right there in the bathroom.

So, had the burglar already been upstairs? Had Tony caught him trying to sneak out when he'd opened the door?

Heather sucked in her bottom lip, considering this. It would've come as a shock to find someone standing there, but Tony was polis, and the bathroom door was directly at the top of the stairs.

One push, even a half-hearted one, would've sent an intruder tumbling down to the floor below, especially if he'd already been headed in that direction.

Had the guy been ready and waiting, then? Had he heard Tony having a late-night slash and stood waiting by the door, or barged into the bathroom to launch the attack?

If that was the case, then they weren't dealing with an opportunist. Some random ned would most likely have legged it at the first sign of trouble, not hung around to start a fight.

The thought did nothing to settle Heather's rising sense of dread. A burglary gone wrong was one thing. A targeted attack was something else entirely.

And while someone had made a half-hearted attempt to make it look that way downstairs, she was becoming increasingly convinced that whatever they were dealing with, it wasn't a bungled break-in.

There were three bedrooms upstairs—two decently sized ones, and a smaller box room. Only one door was open, and a quick check behind the other two showed no signs of a search or a struggle. Neither room was exactly tidy, but nor had they been actively trashed.

The smaller of the two rooms seemed to be used mostly for storage now, and was home to a dozen or more supermarket banana boxes all stacked up in three piles. The hole in the sides revealed colourful fabrics and several pairs of women's shoes. Tony's wife's old clothes that he couldn't bear to part with.

The other closed door opened onto what Heather guessed

had once been Ash's bedroom. The *Halo 3* poster was a give-away, faded and tatty as it was.

A desk stood in the corner with a laptop computer sitting on top. A half-filled ashtray and a couple of empty coffee cups beside it told her that Tony had been using the room as a home office.

Heather didn't know much about laptops, but nor did most burglars beyond the fact they were easy to grab and quick to run off with. The fact that this one was still here only added to her growing doubts about the attacker's motive.

She came, at last, to Tony's bedroom. One side of the quilt had been thrown aside, and the exposed sheets were wrinkled and grubby, like they hadn't been changed in several weeks.

The curtains were drawn, though there was a narrow gap running down the middle that let light in.

Something else by the window caught Heather's attention. A short, stocky telescope stood fixed to a tripod, the front lens just inches from the curtains. This in itself wasn't particularly noteworthy—maybe Tony liked looking at the stars—but the downwards angle of it struck her as unusual.

Crossing to it, Heather inched open the curtains, revealing the same back garden she'd stepped out into just a few minutes before. The rain had dropped to a drizzle that dotted the puddle on top of the Scene of Crime tent by the fence.

The angle of the telescope lined it up with the next garden over—the one backing onto Tony's. Heather positioned herself behind it, leaned in closer, and squinted through the eyepiece.

A downstairs window of the neighbouring house appeared before her, magnified by the telescope's lenses. With a bit of effort, Heather could make out the *Barbie* logo on a pink duvet, and a *My Little Pony* poster hanging on the wall.

Heather raised her head, peered at the window over the top of the scope, then went back to looking through the eyepiece.

"What the hell was he looking at?" she wondered aloud.

There was an obvious answer, of course, but she chose not to dwell on it.

Tony was a good guy. One of the best.

There would be a rational explanation beyond the one that immediately came to mind.

Pulling up her phone, she opened the Maps app, found her location, and zoomed out until she could get the name of the next road over. Shortlees Crescent. She couldn't get a house number from the map, but she took a screenshot and pinged it over to Marty for him to look into.

The message had just sent when there was a knock at the front door. A faltering male voice rang out from the foot of the stairs. The on-guard constable, Heather guessed.

"Um, Detective Inspector?"

"Up here. What is it?" Heather shouted back.

"There's somebody out here who'd like a word."

The words 'pot' and 'kettle' came to mind as Heather listened to the ranting of the irate Welshman currently leaning on Tony's garden fence. He was half a head shorter than Heather and in his mid-to-late fifties.

The constable who'd summoned Heather down had introduced him as a neighbour from just down the street, who claimed to have seen someone acting suspiciously the night before.

"He was a right fat bastard, so he was," the man told Heather for the fourth or fifth time. He was far from a waif of a thing himself, boasting a good ten to twelve stone weight advantage over the DI. "Huge, he was. I could see him through the window, just milling about outside. Just a big fat guy standing there."

"Couldn't have been a reflection in the glass?" Heather

asked, the words escaping her mouth before she had a chance to stop them.

"The hell's that meant to mean?" demanded the neighbour, his jowls wobbling as his face contorted in outrage. "I just told you he was a right fat bastard. Huge. Aye, *proper* huge. Ugly bugger, too. Face like a plate of scrambled eggs.

"He was milling about on the street here, walking up and down, so he was. I watched him coming and going, happy as you like. I said to my wife, Roisin, 'Roisin,' I says. 'Look at that big fat fucker walking up and doon oot there,' I says. Up and down, back and forth, so he was."

The neighbour sniffed, shrugged his broad, curved shoulders, and gave a shake of his head.

"Course, she wasn't listening. She never listens. Too busy with her bloody soaps, isn't she? *Emmerdale. Eastenders. Coronation Street.* What's the other one?"

Heather neither knew nor cared. "I don't—"

"*Hollyoaks.* That's it. Have you seen that shite? *Hollyoaks?* What a lot of utter nonsense. When they send a text message, it appears floating in the bloody air beside them for all to see! Have you ever heard such a thing? Absolute horseshit. What are they, wizards?"

Heather glanced back along the path to where the constable on guard was standing, hoping for some slight rolling of the eyes or other acknowledgement. Instead, he continued to stare solemnly ahead, his hands folded crisply behind his back.

She was on her own.

"Can you remember what time you saw him?" she asked the neighbour.

"No. Not really. It was dark, but then it's pitch black from about four o'-bloody-clock these days, isn't it?"

"Can you remember what soap your wife was watching?"

The man's brow formed deep ridges of confusion. "What's that got to do with anything?"

"Well, it might help us pinpoint a time."

"Oh. No, that won't help. She records the bloody things, doesn't she?" He mimed pressing the button on a remote control. "She series links them. Fills the box up, because she never bloody deletes any of them. It was at three percent last week. The storage. On the box. What are you meant to do with a *Sky* box with just three percent storage?"

Heather was starting to think of one or two things she'd quite like to do with it, but refrained from voicing any of them out loud.

"No idea of time at all?" she prompted. "Even a rough one?"

The man blew out his cheeks. It made him look a bit like some sort of African toad.

"If I had to say—if you were twisting my arm, which you are—I'd say from about eight to ten? Thereabouts," he decided, after much consideration. "The bugger was wandering about out here for at least two *Emmerdales* and a *Coronation Street.* Which is how I count time now, by the way. That's what that bastard's done to me over the years. I don't count time in hours and minutes now, I count it in how long it takes Ken bloody Barlow to walk from his living room to his kitchen."

"Sorry to hear that," Heather said. "Can you describe the guy?"

The neighbour opened his mouth and drew in a breath.

"Besides 'fat,' I mean?"

The neighbour deflated again. "I mean, what more do you need?" he asked. "Big fat bugger, ugly as sin. There can't be many of them around."

Heather bit her tongue. Not hard enough to draw blood, but not far off it.

"You'd be surprised," she said.

"No, but we're talking"—he held up a hand, fingers splayed, like he was gesturing off into some great unknown— "fifty stone."

"Nobody's fifty stone," Heather said. "Nobody who's pacing up and down a street, anyway."

"Aren't they? OK, maybe not fifty, then. *Thirty* stone. Does that sound right?"

"I don't know. I didn't see him."

"Fine. We'll say thirty stone, then."

Heather thought of the kitchen window in Tony's house, and the contortion that would've been required to get through it. No four-hundred-pound man was getting through that window without being fired from some sort of trebuchet.

Still, it was something. And, right now, she'd take what she could get.

"Oh, but hang on," the neighbour said. He drew himself up to his full height, which put the top of his head roughly level with the bridge of Heather's nose. "Someone's got that doorbell. The one that watches you."

He squeezed one of his chins between finger and thumb and looked along the street, suddenly deep in thought.

"Oh. God. Who is it now? Who's got it? Who's the one with the doorbell?"

He looked to Heather for her input, but she could only shrug.

"Are you asking me? I've got no idea."

The neighbour tutted. "My brain's addled with too much Phil bloody Mitchell, that's the problem. It's someone, though. It's definitely someone. Someone's definitely got one of them camera doorbells."

He nodded, satisfied, then folded his arms. There was a suggestion of defiance to it, like he was determined she'd be getting nothing more out of him on the matter.

"You want to see the big fat fella for yourself? I suggest you start there."

SEVEN

IT WAS after seven by the time Scene of Crime returned to the house. Heather exchanged pleasantries with Aiko, the team leader, then left them to suit up and get on with it. It was unlikely they'd uncover anything more than they'd already found, though they'd brought in some equipment that would help them get a closer look at the fibres of the carpets, and pick up on any previously undetected blood spots.

Once she'd spoken with them, Heather put in a call to DS Brompton. Marty was still at HQ, sitting at his desk, reading over reports and filling in paperwork. It had been his routine since his break-up, sitting alone in a darkened office, apparently infinitely preferable to sitting alone at home.

As a result, he was delighted at all the extra work Heather called to give him, and sounded genuinely relieved to have something to get his teeth into, even if it was just identifying the owner of an address, and finding out from Uniform who it was on Tony's street that owned a doorbell camera.

Heather didn't ask him to, but she knew Marty would go several steps further. He wouldn't *just* find out who owned the address, he'd get her the full list of occupants. He wouldn't *only* discover who owned the doorbell cam, he'd send her a copy of the footage.

Whatever he could do that would keep him from going home.

Puddles roared against the underside of the Audi as she made her way home, the lights of Kilmarnock's pubs and restaurants reflecting in the water before her tyres tore through them.

Her house was still in one piece when she pulled up outside it. That was something. Trusting the new start to go and babysit her dad had been a bold choice, but it had felt like the only option left to her.

She'd promised to just be an hour or so, given Tammi-Jo instructions to phone her immediately if there was a problem, and then packed her off in a squad car with one of the local constables.

That had been over two hours ago now. There had been no calls. That was either good news, or very, *very* bad.

She stopped at the front door and leaned her head against it for a moment, composing herself. This had become a routine over the past few months—her traditional summoning of strength before stepping into the house, or whichever room she was most likely to find her dad in.

Or, perhaps it was a moment of silent prayer offered up to all the gods she didn't believe in, on the off-chance—in the hope—that she was wrong.

Either way, she indulged it for a few seconds, then readied herself and opened the door.

A blast of music from along the hallway confronted her. It was some old traditional *teuchter* stuff, all fiddles and drums and rousing, enthusiastic accordions.

There was a thud from beyond the door at the far end. Heavy. A cry, sharp and sudden, followed it.

Heather barrelled along the hallway, arms pumping, fists clenched. Her shoulder hit the living room door, throwing it wide, then she stumbled in, mouth open, a shout of, "What the fuck's going on?" ready on her lips.

The scene playing out there silenced her and stopped her in her tracks.

All the furniture in the room had been pushed or dragged aside, and now stood jammed up against the walls.

Heather's dad, Scott, dressed in tracksuit bottoms and a dirty vest, had a big tartan towel fastened around his waist like a kilt. He was laughing uncontrollably as he bounded and leapt from foot to foot, swinging each arm high above his head in turn, like a Highland dancer on some *top-quality* drugs.

Detective Constable Swanney—Tammi-Jo—was mirroring his movements, her face red from exertion and laughter. She danced and jigged on the spot, her blonde hair partly covered by a knitted tea cosy that Heather had never clapped eyes on in her life.

A *whoop* of delight rang out as Scott spotted Heather in the doorway. Tammi-Jo clocked her a second later and immediately stopped dancing, her face somehow finding a way to flush even redder.

"Don't mind me," Heather said, shooting the DC a smile that felt more teasing than she'd intended.

"Come away in! Come away in! Plenty of room!" Scott cried.

He danced towards her, one arm held out, and she relented to a couple of quick spins around the makeshift dance floor. One more dance with her father. Maybe the last.

"You watch your bloody hips, you," she warned, as they swapped arms and swung back in the opposite direction.

"Och, away you go!" he told her. "There's life in the old dog yet!"

As if to prove his point, he unhooked his arm from hers, then shuffled backwards while pointing excitedly at his feet.

"I'm that boy, look! The black lad, with the monkey! Off the telly."

Heather was suddenly fourteen years old again, being routinely embarrassed by her old man's antics. That inner teenager cringed at the sight of him trying to Moonwalk across the living room carpet.

The rest of her almost cried with joy.

"Aye, Michael Jackson's got nothing on you, Auld Yin."

Scott went big for the finale, attempted a spin, then tripped over his own feet.

For a moment, Heather felt the world lurching into slow motion. She saw the panic on his face. Flashed forward to all the possible trajectories the upcoming fall could take him, and imagined the frantic rush to the hospital.

Instead, Scott erupted into laughter as he landed unceremoniously in his armchair. The laughter became a fit of coughing, but it did nothing to dampen his spirits.

"Oh, man! God Almighty! That's the stuff!" he wheezed, once he could talk again.

He looked up at Heather and she felt her stomach tighten as his eyes clouded over and his weathered old brow furrowed in confusion.

She knew that expression. She'd come to know it far too well, in fact, over the past couple of years, as his illness had eaten him away in fits and starts.

Her answer was primed and ready, just waiting to be spoken. *'It's me, Dad. It's Heather.'*

But the question she'd come to dread didn't come this time.

"You no' meant to be at work?" he asked her. "Thought you were meant to be doing some school thing today?" He looked up at DC Swanney. "Heather's a t—"

The word 'teacher' was there on the tip of his tongue. Heather could practically see it. But he fought against it. God love him, he fought it all the way.

"She's in the polis," he said. There was a note of surprise to it, like this was news to him, but then he nodded firmly and said it again with more confidence. "She's in the polis. She's a Detective Chief Inspector!"

Heather didn't bother to correct him on that last part. It had taken weeks for him to get to grips with her promotion, and she was damned if she was putting either of them through that again now that she'd been bumped down a rank.

Tammi-Jo smiled. "Wow! I'd better be on my best behaviour!" she said, which made the old man hoot with laughter again.

"Aye, you better had! She can be a right hard-faced cow!"

"Oi!" Heather protested, but this only made her dad laugh harder. "I rushed back home to see how you were getting on." She glanced around the room, stopping briefly on the detective constable. "Looks like I needn't have bothered my arse."

"Ach, I'm fine. I'm having a ball!" Scott told her. He placed his hands on the arms of his chair and started to wrestle himself out of it. "Have you had lunch? You need lunch. I'll do you your favourite. A wee jam sandwich."

Heather smiled. Jam sandwiches were indeed her favourite, albeit about thirty years previously.

Also, lunch had been hours ago.

"I'm fine. I've already eaten," she said. A lie, but sometimes that was the only way of dissuading him. "What about you? Have you eaten?"

He shrugged and turned to Tammi-Jo, batting the question over to her. The detective constable began to tick through the fingers of her left hand with the index finger of her right.

"Half a sausage supper, three pickled onions, curry sauce, and a mint *Cornetto*," she said. "Not all at once." She winced. "Sort of all at once. It was a bit of an experiment."

Heather assumed the experiment had been her dad's idea, and yet she couldn't shake the feeling that the detective constable may have had a hand in it, too.

"We phoned it in. There was nothing in the fridge," Tammi-Jo continued. "Well, there was stuff. Milk, cheese, and... Well, mostly just milk and cheese, actually. And alcohol. A lot of alcohol."

Heather scratched the back of her head. "Eh, aye, I need to do a shopping. Meant to go this afternoon. But, you know, it's been busy."

"Has there *bin a murrrder*?" Scott asked, ramping up his existing Scottish accent a full two *Connery*s. Maybe even two-and-a-half.

"No. Nothing like that," Heather assured him.

Tammi-Jo's neat eyebrows dipped in confusion, but Heather dismissed the unspoken question with a shake of her head.

Her dad knew Tony Crier well, and Heather was determined to protect this fragile little bubble of happiness for as long as she possibly could. Of late, they hadn't come around all that often.

Meeting DC Swanney's eye, she tipped her head in the direction of the living room door.

"Can I have a quick word?"

Tammi-Jo wrung her hands together and shot a worried look at the stereo. It was still blasting out some traditional folk tune or other, and Scott's hands and feet all tapped along in time with the music.

"Um, yes. Of course."

Heather led the way into the hall. Tammi-Jo was already apologising before the door was closed. "I'm sorry. I'm really sorry. I know he's old, and probably has wooden hips, or whatever, so he could've hurt himself, and I shouldn't have shifted all the furniture, but we got chatting, and he was talking about how he used to love dancing, and OK, yes, I *may* have got a bit carried away, but—"

Heather lunged for her, arms open. Instinctively, Tammi-Jo fired a quick but weighty rabbit-punch that clocked the DI on the tip of her nose.

"Ow! Fuck!" Heather yelped, stumbling backwards.

Cupping her hands over her face, she glowered at Tammi-Jo through eyes blurred with tears. "What the fuck was that for?"

"Sorry, sorry, sorry! I thought you were attacking me!"

"I was going to hug you!" Heather hissed.

"Hug me?" The concept seemed somehow alien to the young DC. "Why do you want to hug me?"

"Well, I don't now!" Heather shot back. "Jesus!"

"Sorry. It was just instinct. I don't usually punch senior officers. I never punch senior officers, actually. I've never done that before. Ever."

Heather checked her hands for blood and was pleased to find none. She wrinkled her nose, then flared her nostrils, checking everything was still working, before fixing Tammi-Jo with a look that would've made Medusa herself avoid eye contact.

"Am I meant to be happy about that?" she asked. "Is that meant to be a compliment? That I'm the first senior officer you've punched in the face?"

"No! I mean, unless you want to…? No. I just… From what everyone said about you, I didn't expect you to be a hugger."

"I'm not. I'm *definitely* not a hugger!" the DI insisted. "I don't hug anyone."

Tammi-Jo eyed her suspiciously. "So, you *were* trying to attack me?"

"What? No! I'm quite tempted to now, but no." Heather tutted and sighed. "I just… I don't generally do emotions. In a proper way, I mean. So I just… I wasn't sure what to… Look, just forget it."

"Forget *what*?" Tammi-Jo asked. She grinned and winked.

"You don't need to point to your eye when you're winking," Heather told her.

"I didn't," the detective constable replied. She winked again. Her index finger was drawn towards the eye as if attached by a length of thread. "Oh. Wait. I did. Wow. Do I always do that? I hope not. That would be weird. Would that be weird? If I always did that?"

She winked and pointed again, this time with even greater emphasis than before.

"Like that. Would that be weird?"

Heather studied the DC's wide-eyed expression. The question, it seemed, was a genuine one.

"Yes. That would be weird," she confirmed, then she ran her hand through her hair and sighed. "Listen, I'm not going to hug you. Ever. Again. But, you know…"

She tilted her head towards the living room door. The music was still playing, and she could hear her dad humming happily along. Granted, he was humming an entirely different tune, but he didn't seem to mind.

Tammi-Jo looked at the door for a moment, then turned back to Heather.

"Know what?"

"Just… you know."

DC Swanney's blue eyes tick-tocked between the detective inspector and the entrance to the living room.

Finally, she shook her head. "No. I'm not sure what…"

"Jesus! Thank you!" Heather spat. "There. That's what I meant. Thank you for keeping an eye on him."

"Oh! That! Pfft!" Tammi-Jo blew a sort of mini raspberry and gave a dismissive wave of a hand. "I had fun. He's a good laugh, your dad. He's got a lot of funny stories. He reminds me of my grandpa. Except, you know, he's alive. I actually had a really good time."

Tiny pinpricks made themselves known behind Heather's eyes. She had no idea how long it had been since she'd cried, but this was as close as she'd come in recent memory.

And, frankly, it was quite close enough.

She looked to the door, feeling the need to point out to the DC that he wasn't always like this. That it wasn't always this easy.

That it was *rarely* this easy.

But he was safe, he was lucid, and he was happy. So, why let cold, stark reality spoil the moment?

"Well, thanks. Again," she said.

It wasn't all she wanted to say to the younger woman. Not even close.

But for now, it would have to do.

"No problem!" Tammi-Jo said. "It's not what I expected from my first day, but then that's what they say, isn't it?"

Heather gave an inquisitive shake of her head. "What is?"

Tammi-Jo looked up towards the ceiling, as if physically searching through her brain to find the correct quote.

"Something about... I don't know. He who fails to prepare should expect the unexpected? Don't judge a book when the green man is flashing?" The DC gave a shrug. "I'm sure someone said something wise that applies, I just don't know what it is."

Heather felt herself smiling, but promptly warned her face to cut it out.

"Anyway, it's good you're back. All my stuff's in your car. I'm going to need that," Tammi-Jo said. "Oh! And since we're having a nice bonding moment—"

"We're not," Heather countered.

"Favourite Christmas movie. Go!"

"I don't have one."

"Ah, come on! Everyone's got a favourite Christmas movie!"

"Nope."

Heather thought back to the tiny rucksack-type bag the detective constable had brought with her from HQ, and jumped on the chance to change the subject.

"Hang on, that one wee bag is all your stuff?"

Tammi-Jo nodded. "Well, it's all the stuff I've got here. The rest is still in Inverness. Someone's going to send it down." A worrying thought troubled her. "At least, I think they are. I'm not sure I actually mentioned it to anyone… I should probably call someone about that tonight, once I get to the hotel."

"Right. Aye. Good idea," Heather said. "Where's the hotel?"

"I'm not sure," Tammi-Jo replied.

"You don't have the address?"

"No, I haven't got the hotel's address," the DC admitted. "Also, I don't have a hotel."

"You haven't booked a hotel?"

"Do you know any? Hotels, I mean? Preferably in walking distance, because I don't have a car," Tammi-Jo said.

There were no hotels within walking distance. None that Heather would knowingly send anyone to, at least.

"Not really. And I can't give you a lift anywhere, because I need to stay with the old man."

"No, of course. Of course! Don't worry about it," Tammi-Jo gushed. "It's fine. I'll find somewhere. Not a problem. Easy-peasey. There's bound to be loads of places. I'll check my phone! My phone will tell me!"

She fumbled in her pocket until she found her mobile, prodded at the darkened screen, then put it away again.

"Nope, that's dead. Didn't charge it last night. I couldn't, since I was stuck in a power cut in a haunted castle. Well, not *haunted* haunted, but sort of. But don't worry about it, it's fine, I'll figure it out."

Heather did something then that she usually wouldn't dream of doing.

She went against her better judgement.

"Look, do you want to stay here tonight? There's a room upstairs."

"Is that Stewie's room?" Tammi-Jo asked.

Heather's hackles rose. She suddenly regretted making the offer, inviting this relative stranger to spend the night in her house.

"Your dad mentioned him," the DC said, sensing Heather's discomfort. "Won't he mind if I stay in his room?"

"Uh, no, he won't mind," Heather replied, after taking a moment to compile a response. "He's not here right now."

"Then, thank you very much, I'll take it!" Tammi-Jo said, beaming from ear to ear. She spat on her hand and thrust it out for the DI to shake. "Put it there!"

Heather looked from the detective constable's grinning face to the offered hand.

"I'm not touching that," she said.

Tammi-Jo nodded, and wiped her palm clean on her jacket. "Good. Regretted it immediately, no idea what got into me," she said. "Pretty disgusted with myself, actually, and if you don't mind, I'd like to suggest we never speak of it again, because people already think I'm weird enough."

Heather thought this over for a moment, before finally nodding.

"OK," she said, then she spat on her hand and held it out. "You've got a deal."

———

Heather returned from putting her dad to bed to find a teenage podcaster sitting in her kitchen in full school uniform.

"She came to the door when you were upstairs," explained an anxious-looking Tammi-Jo. "She said she's a friend of yours."

Heather sighed wearily, crossed her arms, and squinted at Ace Wurzel like she was seeing the girl for the first time. "Nope. No idea who this is."

"Oh!" Tammi-Jo looked between them both. "Well, that's awkward."

"She's joking," Ace said. "I assume. Humour isn't really her strong point, but to be fair, nor is it mine. So, it's possible she isn't joking, and has instead sustained some sort of recent head injury, which would—"

"Jesus, alright, alright! Yes, I was joking!" Heather said,

heading for the fridge. On the way, she passed a sink so crammed full of dirty dishes that the addition of even another piece of cutlery might cause the whole thing to implode.

She really should get around to that at some point.

"I commend you for trying new things, Officer," Ace replied. She produced a mobile phone from the pocket of her school blazer. "But I think 'surly and humourless' is more your thing."

Heather stopped with one hand on the fridge. "Cheers for that," she muttered, then she opened the fridge and was momentarily stunned by its stark emptiness.

Grabbing a snub-nosed bottle of Polish beer, she held it out to Tammi-Jo.

"Drink?"

"No. Thanks. I don't drink," the DC replied. "I mean, I do drink, obviously, or I'd have died of dehydration and organ failure. I don't mean I don't drink *anything*. That would be mad. I mean I don't *drink* drink. I don't *alcohol* drink. Drink alcohol, I mean. Swap those two. I don't drink alcohol. But you should! I mean, you shouldn't necessarily, I'm not encouraging you, I'm just saying, if you want to, you should, and if you don't want to then you shouldn't. No peer pressure here."

She pointed to Ace, mimed a gun firing, then smiled. There was a hint of desperation to it, like she wanted to stop talking but couldn't find the off switch.

"Peer pressure! Don't give in to *peer pressure*," she sang in a slightly breathless whisper, before frowning at herself, shaking her head, and continuing in a normal, if slightly panic-tinted voice. "Right? You know what I'm talking about. Friends don't pressure friends. Not that we're friends. Any of us. I mean, I'd like to be. I definitely don't *dislike* any of you. I'm not against the idea. I just don't know you, you don't know me, I did recently punch one of you in the face, and… Yeah. Yep. Uh-huh." The detective constable nodded firmly. "I'm going to stop talking now."

Heather blinked, the offered bottle still in her hand. "So... that's a no to a beer, then, is it?"

"That's a *no, thank you*," Tammi-Jo said. "But, do you have any milk?"

"You know I've got milk," Heather replied.

"I'll have some milk, please."

Heather took the carton of semi-skimmed milk from the fridge and deposited it on the worktop beside where Tammi-Jo was standing.

"What about you?" she asked, turning to the teenager sitting at the kitchen table. Ace had now produced a small microphone on a stand from somewhere, and was in the process of connecting it to her phone.

"Water, please," the girl said. "From the hot tap."

"For fu..." Heather tutted. "Why? Why the hot tap?"

"I'm conducting an experiment," Ace said. "Don't let it run, though. I don't actually want it warm, just from that tap, please."

Heather almost asked more, before realising that she didn't want to know. She took a glass from the draining board, filled it with cold water from the hot tap, then *clunked* it down in front of the girl.

"What are you doing with that?" the DI asked. "In fact, why are you here?"

"The answer to both those questions is the same, Officer," Ace replied. "So I can interview you concerning the death of one Sergeant Anthony Crier."

"Oh! OK! I see!" Heather said with a level of enthusiasm that made Ace look up from her screen. The Detective Inspector's positivity fell away immediately. "No. Not happening."

Ace tutted and went back to connecting her microphone to her mobile.

"So, you two *do* know each other, then?" Tammi-Jo said.

"Sadly, yes," Heather said.

"Harsh," Ace muttered, still working away.

"DC Swanney, Nancy Drew. Nancy Drew, DC Swanney."

Tammi-Jo eyed the girl suspiciously. "She said her name was Ace Wurzel."

"It is Ace Wurzel," said Ace Wurzel. "She's being facetious. See what I mean about her humour? I'm the founder and host of the Crime De La Crime podcast. I'm sure you've heard of it."

"Nope," Tammi-Jo admitted.

"You're probably not into podcasts," Ace ventured.

"Oh, no. I quite like them. I listen to loads."

Ace pulled her red glasses down her nose enough so she could peer at the detective constable over the top of them, then pushed them back into place.

"Yes, well. It's a competitive sector," she said, then she took a sip of her drink, smacked her lips together a few times, and nodded. "Yes. That's definitely worse."

She looked across the table at Heather just as the DI took a seat.

"Can I have cold now, Officer?"

Heather used the edge of the table to prise the metal cap off the beer bottle, then shrugged.

"If you get up off your arse and get it yourself, aye."

"It's fine, I'm not actually thirsty," Ace told her, then she tapped a big red button on her phone screen and the numbers on a recording timer started ticking up. "Ready?"

Heather reached across the table and prodded the screen, stopping the recording.

"For what?"

Ace tapped the pulsing red button on the mobile's display. The numbers began to count up again.

"For the interview about the death of Sergeant Crier."

Heather leaned over to stop the recording once more, but Ace quickly pressed a button on the side of her phone and the screen went dark.

With a shrug, Heather clamped a hand over the microphone, and pulled the cable out of the back.

"No comment," she said.

"That's rather childish, Officer," Ace told her. "The truth will out. Are you familiar with that phrase? 'The truth will out'?" She turned to look at Tammi-Jo. "Are you familiar with that phrase, Detective Constable?"

"How come she gets 'Detective Constable' and I just get 'Officer'?" Heather asked.

"Don't look at her, I'm not asking her, I'm asking you," Ace said, catching Tammi-Jo's uncertain sideways look at the DI. "Have you heard the phrase?"

"Uh, yes. Yep," Tammi-Jo confirmed. "I've heard it."

Ace sat back in her chair and gestured to her recording equipment, her point apparently proven. "Well, then," she said. "Shall we begin?"

———

The door closed at Ace's back with a *thud* that shook the whole frame.

The girl took a moment to return her microphone to her schoolbag, and zip up her jacket. The rain was off, but the earlier warmth of the wind had been replaced by a harsh, cutting cold.

"Very well, Officer," she said, addressing the empty front garden. "Have it your way. But mark my words, one way or another, the truth will out!"

"What was that?" asked Heather, opening the door again.

Ace shook her head. "Nothing."

Heather regarded her through narrowed eyes for a moment, making it clear that she didn't believe the girl.

"Are you heading straight home?"

"Possibly."

"No, not... Don't say 'possibly,' just go straight..." Heather shut her eyes, sighed, then held up a finger, indicating that the girl should stay put. "Right. Forget it. Wait there," she barked, turning and heading back into the house. "I'll go get my keys and give you a lift. Inevitably, you're going to get yourself murdered at some point, and I'm not having it on my conscience when you do."

Standing on the doorstep, Ace allowed herself a little smile.

"Thank you, Officer," she said, mostly to the half-open door. "I didn't know you cared."

EIGHT

"JESUS, DO YOU EVER LEAVE?"

DS Martin Brompton raised his bleary, bloodshot eyes from his coffee mug and flashed DI Filson a thin, noncommittal sort of smile.

"I'm just dedicated," he said. "Besides, someone has to do some work around here. Oh! And your teacher came back looking for you, by the way. At the school."

Tammi-Jo shot a frown in Heather's direction. "You go to school?"

"No! Of course I don't go to..." She tutted and turned back to Marty, feigning disinterest.

No, not feigning it, damn it. *Being* disinterested. So what if the hot teacher had come looking for her? Who cared? Not her.

"Oh?" she said, overplaying her lack of interest a little. "And?"

"And, we got chatting. Me and him." Marty tucked a tongue into his cheek, held up a slip of paper with a row of digits on it, and waved it back and forth like it was a flag. "And guess who got his number!"

Heather bent to study the writing on the paper, then straightened again.

"That's the number for the school."

"What?" Marty's face fell. He turned the paper around to look at it. "No. Bollocks. It isn't, is it?"

"Yep. Sorry, Marty. Looks like you struck out there, pal."

"The bastard!" Marty muttered, scrunching the page up into a ball. He tossed it towards the wastepaper basket in the corner of the room, then deflated even further when it fell well short.

Heather let out a little laugh. Her first of the day. It had been a rough morning. Her dad, predictably, had been sore from the dancing the night before, and the carer—when she finally turned up—had been so surly and confrontational that she'd come dangerously close to earning herself a slap.

As a result, Heather had set off on the drive north almost an hour after she'd intended, and had spent most of the ride reassuring Tammi-Jo that she wasn't going to get fired on her second day just for being late.

"You're late," announced Snecky, emerging from his office and making a show of looking at his watch. "Both of you."

"We took a drive past the crime scene," Heather lied, *plonking* herself down onto the seat next to Marty's, and indicating for Tammi-Jo to take the one on the DS's other side.

Snecky regarded the detective inspector with suspicion for a few moments, then smacked his lips together.

"Is this true, Detective Constable Swanney?"

Tammi-Jo stopped lowering herself into the chair and straightened in panic. "I, what? Is... Did... True? Is it true?" she babbled. "Is that what you're...? I mean, obviously that's what you're... But is it...? Really, I mean?"

"Those are just noises," Snecky told her. "Is it true? What DI Filson said?"

Tammi-Jo shook her head, swallowed, and flashed Heather an apologetic look.

"No. It's not true," she said in a dry, throaty croak, then she rallied as best she could. "Although, I mean, it's not *untrue*, either!"

Snecky frowned. "What do you mean?"

"OK, no. It is untrue." A pained look crossed her face, and this time she could barely glance at Heather long enough to whisper, "Sorry, sorry, sorry," before sitting down.

"Thanks for that," the DI muttered.

"Well done, Detective Constable," Snecky said, giving the young detective a patronising nod. He folded his arms and fired a smug, self-satisfied smirk in Heather's direction. "You could do with taking a leaf from DC Swanney's book, DI Filson. There's two things I always say. One, 'Honesty is the best policy,' and two, 'Lateness... isn't fair.'"

He winced a little at how that second one sounded. It certainly didn't have the same ring as the first one.

"I've never heard you say either of those things," Heather told him. "Marty, you ever heard him say that?"

"No," Marty admitted. "I've never heard him say any of that."

"Marty's never heard you say any of that, either," Heather said, in case Snecky had somehow missed the detective sergeant's reply.

The DCI's smile lost some of its lustre. He sniffed. "Yes, well, I do. Frequently. So..."

"When?" Heather asked. "Give me one time."

The smile dropped away completely. The DCI's arms fell to his sides.

"Just don't lie to me or be late again, or..." He stabbed a finger at her. It was a warning, although he couldn't quite work out the finer details of what the warning was, so he concluded with a less than confident-sounding, "Alright? We turn up on time, ready to hit the ground running. No excuses."

At that moment, the door to the office opened, and Detective Constable Simon Wolfe entered carrying a three-pack of

Krispy Kreme doughnuts in one hand, and a cardboard tray bearing two takeaway coffee cups in the other.

"Morning, all!" he declared.

"You're late," Heather told him. She checked her watch, just as Snecky had done. "What the hell time do you call this?"

Snecky gave a vague wave of a hand. "It's fine this once."

"No, sir. You're right. You said it yourself, lateness isn't fair," Heather insisted. "You heard him say that, right, Marty?"

"Loud and clear," Marty confirmed. Like Heather, he turned in his chair so he was facing the new arrival. "'Lateness isn't fair,' he said. You know, like he always does?"

DC Wolfe didn't seem the least bit put out by the attention of the other detectives. He strode past them without a word and presented the cardboard tray to the DCI.

"Your coffee, sir, as requested," he announced with a theatrical lowering of his head.

Slightly sheepishly, Snecky plucked one of the cups from the tray, being very careful not to make eye contact with Heather or DS Brompton.

"Doughnut?" Wolfe asked, offering out the rectangular box.

"No. No, I'm fine," Snecky said.

Simon glanced at the box, confused. "But you asked me to pick you one up."

Snecky's tiny moment of hesitation was like music to Heather's ears.

"No, I didn't," he said.

"Yes, you did," Simon insisted, completely failing to pick up on the atmosphere in the room. "You told me to swing by the garage and get you some *Krispy Kreme's* on my way in. You texted me about it at half-three this morning."

"No. I don't know what you're talking about," Snecky said. "Take them away, I don't... Oh, wait, is that a Frankenstein one?"

Simon angled the box so the DCI could see the three

colourful doughnuts through the transparent plastic film on top.

"Yep! Last of the Halloween ones. I got Frankenstein, a pumpkin face, and a big spider."

"I'll have the Frankenstein," Snecky said, then he quickly glanced around at the others. "Since he's already brought it in. Be a shame to waste it."

Simon opened the box, allowing the DCI to remove a slightly stale-looking green and black doughnut from within.

"Speaking of Frankenstein, here's an interesting fact for you," Simon announced to the room at large. "Did you know that Frankenstein isn't the monster? It's actually the name—"

"Yes," Marty said, cutting him short.

"Literally everyone in the world knows that," Heather told him.

"Alright, keep your hair on, I was just saying. And not *everyone* knows."

With the other two doughnuts in one hand and his coffee in the other, Simon walked around to the desk opposite where Tammi-Jo was sitting, and installed himself in his chair.

"Did you know?" he asked, nodding at his fellow DC.

"Yes," Tammi-Jo confirmed. "I thought you were going to say that Mary Shelley kept her husband's calcified heart on her desk after he died. I always thought that was pretty interesting."

Simon made a show of licking the tops of both doughnuts to mark them as his own, then prised the lid off his coffee and began the process of tipping six sachets of sugar onto the milky froth on top.

"Who the fuck's Mary Shelley?" he asked.

Tammi-Jo opened her mouth to reply, but Marty put a hand on her arm and shook his head, indicating that it wasn't worth it.

"Forget it. Right, then," DC Wolfe said, tearing open another sugar packet. "What have I missed?"

———

The recap didn't take long. Everyone in the room had rattled off everything they knew about the case, but because this didn't yet amount to very much, it was over in no time.

Tammi-Jo had enthusiastically volunteered to start a Big Board where they could gather all the information they had collected so far, and then had deflated slightly when Snecky had shot the idea down.

"That might be how Jack Logan does things," he'd said. "But I fly by my own rules here."

Tammi-Jo was reasonably confident that wasn't how the phrase was supposed to go, but she hadn't drawn attention to the fact, and had instead just gone back to feeling completely out of place, while the conversation continued to flow around her.

Tony Crier had been discovered halfway down his stairs by the woman who came in once a week to do his ironing. She'd turned up just after nine, and when she couldn't get an answer at the front, had used a spare key she had access to and entered the house.

Once inside, she'd seen the mess, then put in a call to 999. She'd been talking to the operator when she spotted what she'd thought was Tony's body on the staircase.

"He was facing down the way, apparently," Marty said. "Like he'd been crawling or sliding head first, trying to get to the bottom."

Trying to get help, Heather thought, and she'd zoned out for a few moments while she imagined what the sergeant must've been going through in those moments.

Talk of the blood pattern had dragged her attention back. Aiko's Scene of Crime team had come to similar conclusions to Heather. The initial attack had happened in the bathroom, but it had continued on the landing at the top of the stairs.

The SOCOs also believed that the intruder had entered

through the kitchen window. The back door had been closed by the time they got there, but the woman who'd come to do Tony's ironing had insisted it had been standing open when she arrived and found the body.

She had access to a key to the front door, and swore she'd seen the back door open when she'd looked along the hallway. It was possible that the paramedics had shut it while attending the scene.

If she was telling the truth, it suggested that whoever had been in in the house during the night had made a hasty exit.

"Sounds like a pretty open and shut case to me," Snecky declared. "Burglar breaks in to rob the place, gets disturbed, lashes out, then legs it empty-handed."

He shoved the last piece of his doughnut in his mouth and dusted his hands together to indicate he was done with both it and the investigation.

"Case closed," he said, the words having to work their way around the mouthful of semi-masticated pastry and gooey red jam.

"Except it's not, is it?" Heather pointed out. "We haven't got anyone for it."

Snecky shrugged. "It'll be some local bam. We'll put the feelers out. Knock a few heads together. Shake the tree and the shite's sure to fall out."

Heather wasn't buying it, though. It didn't fit.

"Nothing was taken," she said, gesturing to one of the many colour-coded printouts Marty had provided her with as soon as the briefing started.

"Nothing was taken *that we know of*," DC Wolfe corrected.

"Yes! Thank you, Simon," Snecky said, pointing to the detective constable, who immediately broke into a big, triumphant grin. "Nothing was taken *that we know of*. For all we know, he had a big suitcase full of money under the bed that's now vamoosed."

To her annoyance, Heather had no choice but to concede

that one. By definition, it was difficult to tell if something had been taken because it was no longer there.

"OK, fine. It doesn't look like it, though," she said, hanging onto the argument for as long as she could. "Also, how could Tony have 'disturbed' a burglar while he was having a piss?"

"Maybe he pissed dead loud?" DC Wolfe suggested. He chewed thoughtfully on what was at least his second doughnut of the day, and quite possibly his third or fourth. "Or maybe the attacker was a woman, and he pissed on the seat!"

His smile widened further. Clearly, he was pleased with the remark. His gaze flitted between Heather and Tammi-Jo.

"Because youse hate that, don't you? Guys pissing on the seat. Youse proper hate that."

"Please don't try and pretend that a woman's ever been in your bathroom, Simon," Heather told him. "And it was Tony's house. Why would a burglar care about how loud he was pissing?"

Tammi-Jo shifted in her seat and cautiously raised a hand to just below shoulder height.

When nobody appeared to notice, she added a quiet, "Um..." for good measure.

This did the trick. Heather turned her way, tutted, then ordered her to put her hand down.

"If you've got something to say, just say it. You don't need permission," the DI told her.

"Right. No. Yes. Sorry. I won't ask permission again." A flicker of doubt temporarily creased her delicate features. "For anything, or just...? No. For questions. Obviously, not for anything. I need permission for other stuff, clearly. I don't just get to make the rules! I'm not the boss, you're the boss."

"No, *I'm* the boss," Snecky protested, prodding himself in the centre of the chest. "Me."

"Right! Yes! Obviously, you're the *boss* boss, but it seems like she's—"

"What were you going to say?" Heather demanded.

"Oh! Yes! What if it wasn't him?"

The others sat in silence, waiting for more.

"What are you talking about?" Marty asked, when no more came.

"Having a pee, I mean," Tammi-Jo clarified. "What if it wasn't Sergeant Crier having a pee? What if it was the attacker? What if Sergeant Crier heard someone in the bathroom, went to investigate, then the attack started? I mean, probably not, probably stupid of me to even think it, but I just wondered… Could that be it?"

It was feasible, Heather had to admit. According to the preliminary report from forensics, all of the blood they'd been able to identify so far had been Tony's. So, if he'd disturbed someone in the bathroom, they'd very quickly got the upper hand.

"Does it matter?" asked Wolfe. "Do we care who was pissing at the time? Is that important?"

"No. I mean, probably not," Tammi-Jo said. "And it's probably wrong. Completely wrong. Although…"

Snecky polished off the last dregs of his coffee and let out an almost imperceptible sigh of impatience. "Although *what*, Detective Constable?"

Tammi-Jo glanced briefly at Heather, then very quickly looked away again.

"I was just thinking, if you hadn't gone there to rob him, but to hurt him or kill him, and you wanted to make it look like an accident, you could go flush his toilet."

Across the desk, Wolfe burped. "Scuse," he said, before blowing the fetid air off to the side in what he presumably considered to be an act of politeness. "What are you on about? Why would you flush his toilet?"

"Because he'd hear it," Heather said, joining the dots.

"Yes! Exactly!" said Tammi-Jo. "You're the attacker. You break in, flush the toilet, he hears it and comes to check, opens the bathroom door—"

"And you shove him down the stairs," Heather concluded. She sat back in her chair, contemplating this.

"But nobody shoved him down the stairs," Snecky pointed out. "The blood was in the bathroom."

"Maybe they underestimated him," Marty suggested. "Maybe they didn't expect him to be so ready for them."

"Oh, come on," DC Wolfe said with a derisory snort. "He was, like, sixty-odd. What's a sixty-odd guy going to do?"

"He was fifty-seven," Heather corrected. "And he could do plenty."

"Aye, well, clearly not enough, considering he got his head panned in," Wolfe replied.

"No pun intended," Snecky added, before the look on Heather's face pointed out the error of his ways. "Sorry, that was just out of me before I could stop it."

"I don't get it," Wolfe said.

"Toilet pan. Head panned in," Snecky explained.

Understanding lit up the DC's face like a sunrise. "Oh! Gotcha!"

"Jesus Christ," Heather muttered, massaging her temples with the index and middle fingers of both hands.

She steered the conversation away from the actual attack and on to some of the other details. The man spotted wandering around outside Tony's house was of particular interest, but Marty hadn't yet been able to track down any footage.

Uniform had identified two houses with doorbell cameras, but the owner of one property was away on holiday, and the other was proving difficult to get hold of. Marty promised to get it to her as soon as he could, even if that meant driving to Kilmarnock and ripping the cameras right off the walls himself.

"What about the house across the back?" Heather asked. "Anything on that?"

"It's an ex-council house. I've put in a request to the Council Tax department for info on who's living there, but I haven't heard anything back yet," the DS told her. "I can follow up again after this."

"Please," Heather told him. "I want to know who's living there."

"Why? What's the story?" Snecky enquired. "What's the big deal with the neighbours?"

Heather thought of the telescope, the focus fixed on what was clearly a little girl's bedroom.

The scope was close enough to the window that it could potentially have been noticed from across the adjoining gardens. Spotted by the girl, maybe.

Or by a protective parent.

"It looks like the guy crossed their garden and jumped the fence. They might have seen something," Heather said.

Technically, this wasn't her second lie of the day to the DCI. That genuinely was one of the reasons she wanted to find out who lived in the house. It just wasn't the *only* reason.

"What's this about a pen?"

DC Wolfe held up a printout and waved it, as if drawing attention to the fact that he'd actually been reading it.

"Says here they found a pen."

"On the floor in the bedroom, yeah," Marty confirmed.

Wolfe took a slurp of coffee, then wiped a spillage off his chin with the back of a hand. "So? What's the big deal? It's a pen. There's loads of pens in my house. Must be"—his eyes went glassy for a moment while he ran some numbers—"thirty pens. What's the story with this one?"

The question had been aimed at Snecky. The DCI drew in a breath like he was going to reply, studied his own printout for a moment, then peered at Marty.

"DS Brompton, explain it to the detective constable, will you?" he urged, with an affectation of weariness that was so see-through it was essentially invisible.

"Right. Yes, sir, no bother," Marty said. "It's part of a set."

Across the table, Simon frowned. "What, a pen set?"

"Notebook and pen," Marty clarified. "One of them clip-on ones that attaches to a notebook."

Simon looked from Marty to Snecky and back again, clearly still not grasping it. "Eh?"

"The notebook was missing. Was it? Is that it?" Tammi-Jo gushed. "They found the pen, but not the notebook? Is that it? I bet that's it."

Marty touched the end of his nose with one index finger and pointed to the young DC with the other. "Bingo. Prize to the new girl."

"There's a prize?" Tammi-Jo gasped, then she blushed and shook her head. "No. Obviously. Not an actual prize, just a figure of speech. Right? Right."

"Jesus."

Heather grabbed the hole punch from her drawer, leaned past Marty, and *clunked* it down on Tammi-Jo's desk.

"There. Congratulations. Treasure it always." She turned to Marty. "They can't find the notebook?"

"Nope."

"And they found the pen in the bedroom?"

"Yep."

Heather's chair creaked as she leaned back. She twisted her hips, making the revolving mechanism beneath the seat turn back and forth.

"That mean something to you?" Snecky asked.

"No. Nothing," Heather replied. She got to her feet, checking her watch. "Do we reckon the PM will be done yet?"

"Should be," Marty confirmed. "Ozzy was at it from about four this morning, according to the thirty-odd emails he sent to the inbox complaining about it."

"That'll serve him right to piss off golfing half the bloody week," Heather said. She gestured around the room, then met Snecky's eye. "We done here for now?"

The DCI sniffed indignantly. "Well, I hadn't dismissed anyone yet..."

"But we're done, aye?" Heather said, her body language making it very clear that she was itching to get going. "We can get the Incident Room set up while I'm out, get someone from Uniform on exhibits, and be ready for when I get back."

Snecky sprang to his feet. "Oh, we *can*, can we? Who's giving the orders here, exactly?"

Heather's nostrils flared, but she was able to keep her temper in check. "OK. Over to you, *sir*. What should we be doing, then?"

The Detective Chief Inspector started drawing himself up to his full height, but didn't even have the conviction to finish.

"I mean, *that*, obviously," he mumbled. "It's just I should've been the one to say it."

"Fine. I'll go, and you can be the one to say it then," Heather replied, turning and heading for the door.

The clearing of Snecky's throat stopped her. When she turned back, he was standing behind Tammi-Jo's chair, pointing directly down at the top of the detective constable's angelic blonde hair.

"Sorry, Heather," he said, and his smirk almost earned him a mouthful of expletives. "Aren't you forgetting someone?"

NINE

THE UNIFORM they walked by in the corridor was familiar. Not in the way that most of them were familiar—Heather had reached an age where the faces of most of the constables blurred together into one homogeneous, far too young-looking mass—but in a specific way that told her she'd interacted with him recently.

The way his gaze lingered on her and Tammi-Jo as they passed each other only backed that feeling up.

She was half a dozen paces further along the corridor when it struck her.

"Wait. You're that guy from yesterday," Heather said, turning and calling to the constable. "At Tony's... thing. Downstairs."

The constable stopped, though it took him a few more steps. When he turned, it was clear from his face and the twitches of his body language that he'd rather be on his way.

"You're the one who stood up for that Special. For..."

"Ted," Tammi-Jo said. She smiled along the corridor at the uniformed officer. "Daz, wasn't it?"

"Uh, aye. Yes. I mean, yes, *ma'am*."

"Oh! No! I'm not a ma'am! I'm way too young to be a

ma'am!" the DC replied, before jabbing a thumb in Heather's direction. "She's a ma'am, though. She's definitely a ma'am."

"I'm not a ma'am. Don't call me ma'am," Heather instructed.

The constable had nothing really to say to any of that, so he just smiled vaguely and nodded his understanding.

"That was nice of you," Tammi-Jo said. "To stand up for your friend like that."

"Well, you've got to do what you've got to do. He's family," Daz said. "And, I mean, he's a friend of Ash's. We both are. It was only right he was there." He shifted his weight between the balls of his feet, then glanced back over his shoulder at the door he'd been headed for. "Have you seen him, by the way?"

"Who, Ted?"

"Ash. I've been trying to get hold of him since yesterday."

The constable was worried. More so than Heather would've expected, which meant he knew something she didn't.

"No. Why?"

"It's just…" The constable looked over his shoulder again, like he was expecting to find somebody there listening in. "Nothing. Just wanted to pass on my sympathies, ma'am."

"Don't call me ma'am," Heather said, as if on autopilot. "There's a lot to deal with after someone dies. He's probably just busy. Unless you've got some reason to think otherwise?"

The hesitation lasted a beat too long. "No. There's nothing. I just wanted to check in and see if he needed anything."

"Aw," Tammi-Jo said, and the light streaming in through a nearby window turned her blonde hair into an angelic glow. "That's so nice. He's lucky to have a friend like you."

"Eh, aye," said Daz, clearly uncomfortable with the compliment. "Thanks. If you see him, can you tell him I'm looking for him?"

"Will do," Heather said.

She nodded, and had just started to turn when Daz blurted, "It's Wayne!"

"Sorry?" the DI asked.

"Wayne. Sergeant Gillespie, I mean. Ash has been listening to him. Like, a lot."

Heather found herself taking a step closer. "So? Why's that a problem?"

"What? No. Nothing. Not a problem," Daz replied. His eyes darted around again. The man wasn't just worried, he was afraid. "It's just... Wayne's been saying a lot of daft stuff."

"What kind of daft stuff?" Heather asked, when no more information was forthcoming.

Daz scratched at his head, and Heather got the impression that he was regretting opening his mouth. There was no chance she was letting him back out now, though.

"What's he been saying?" she demanded.

Daz let out a breath. "Just that people need to start paying us more respect. That we, Uniforms, I mean, are out there on the front line, dealing with all the shit of the day. He reckons the force has got too soft, and that we should be out there cracking heads. Seems to have a beef with Shuggie Cowan's guys, in particular."

If that was all, Heather wasn't too worried. She's heard dozens of officers—mainly men, but by no means exclusively—state pretty much that same point of view over the years, convinced that things had been better in the old days when you could clip an annoying teenager around the ear, and throw your weight around if some local scally needed bringing down a peg or two.

And, to be fair, she saw the appeal in it. Less time spent on red tape and paperwork, and more time spent throwing arseholes down the stairs, sounded like a bit of a dream come true as far as she was concerned.

But only if she was the one identifying said arseholes and doing all the throwing. That was the only way it could work.

She'd stand toe-to-toe and fight anyone else attempting it,

because she couldn't trust that sort of power in anyone else's hands.

Which she knew meant she probably shouldn't trust it in her own, either.

"Lot of people think that way," Heather said.

"Aye, I know, but that's all they do. Think. Sure, they might moan about it. We've all moaned about it," Daz said. He stole another backwards glance over his shoulder. "But I get the feeling that Wayne's out to do a lot more than that."

TEN

DR OSCAR 'OZZY' Osgood was up there among the most unpleasant people that Heather had ever met. Which, considering her profession and life experience, was really saying something.

Unlike the catalogue of rapists, child molesters, and murderers she'd dealt with, though, Ozzy hadn't actually done anything *too* bad. Not that she was aware of, at least.

He was an educated, intelligent, highly commended member of the UK's forensic pathology community.

He was also, it was widely agreed, an arsehole.

Osgood was only too aware of that fact, too. He delighted in it, taking real joy from his own arseholery that he was apparently unable to find in any other aspect of his life.

Pathology was the man's career, but being a complete dick was his lifelong passion.

Heather had detested him from the very first moment they were introduced, and he had treated her with the same disdain and contempt that he treated everyone else.

Over the years, though, their stance on each other had gradually softened. While he remained largely insufferable, and their every interaction felt like a fresh declaration of war, she'd found herself at first tolerating him, then almost enjoying being in his company.

For his part, Ozzy had continually tried to berate and belittle her at every turn, but the insults were much more mellow now, and some of the more cutting comments were sometimes even at his own expense.

In contrast to how he spoke to Snecky or Wolfe, say, and you'd think that the DI and the pathologist were practically best buddies.

"Well, what do we have here?" Ozzy asked, tilting his head back and peering at Heather and Tammi-Jo down his long, crooked nose. "Is this a *Cagney & Lacey* reboot? If so, I have to say, I can't see it being a ratings winner."

He was tall, with a sculpted quiff of dark grey hair, and a skeletal frame that stooped slightly to the left. There was a downwards pull to one side of his face from a stroke he'd suffered in his late twenties and which, rumour had it, had really launched his whole 'insufferable arsehole' persona into top gear.

He had a limp that came and went with no discernible pattern. Some days, it was barely noticeable. Others, like today, had him supporting himself on an elegant black walking stick with a silver skull grip.

If you were going to be the creepy old guy who cut open dead people for a living, he'd once told Heather, you might as well do it in style.

And he did. When not working at the slab, he dressed in one of three suits, all identical aside from the colours, which ranged from an Autumnal brown to a brooding black, via the ash-grey pinstripe number he was wearing now, which seemed to be his preferred choice.

His shoes were handmade, with a thick sole and Cuban heel that added another inch or two to his already impressive height.

Heather had once told him he resembled what she thought

Death himself would look like in human form. It was one of the only times she'd seen the man smile.

"Detective Constable Swanney, Dr Oscar Osgood. Ozzy to his"—Heather stopped short of using the word 'friends,' and concluded with a clumsy—"people who know him."

"Hi! Hello! Howdy!" Tammi-Jo blurted. She moved to shake his hand, spotted his rubber gloves, then turned the movement into a friendly wave. "Hey there! Nice to meet you, Ozzy. Ozzy. *Ozzy.* That's fun to say."

Ozzy took a pair of narrow spectacles from his waistcoat pocket, perched them on the end of his nose, and looked the DC up and down before turning to Heather.

"Explain," he urged, pointing a gloved finger in Tammi-Jo's direction.

"She's new," Heather told him.

"Oh?"

Dr Osgood gave the DC another once over, then turned and looked at the double doors leading through to the mortuary.

When he faced front again, his mouth was twisted into a thin, wicked smile.

"How new, exactly?"

———

If Ozzy had been hoping to disturb the young detective constable, he was sorely disappointed. Tammi-Jo watched in wide-eyed fascination as the sheet was pulled back to reveal the naked, scarred body of the late Sergeant Tony Crier.

He had already been cut open, checked out, and stitched back together with the pathologist's usual fastidious care. For a man who seemed to hold most of the living in complete contempt, Dr Osgood really seemed to have a soft spot for the dead, and treated them with a level of respect that he rarely afforded those still shuffling around above ground.

"That's neat," Tammi-Jo said. "The stitches, I mean. They're well done. I don't mean him being dead is *neat*. You know, like cool? I'm not saying that. Please don't think I'm saying that. I'm just saying—"

"Maybe stop saying it?" Heather suggested.

"Right, yep. Ten-four, Big Chief. Over and out," the DC babbled, then she snapped off a quick salute and mimed zipping her mouth shut, securing it with a padlock, and finally throwing away the key.

Dr Osgood, who had already been disappointed by the lack of horrified screaming or vomiting from the detective constable, now regarded her like something he'd found on the sole of his shoe.

"Good Lord. You can't half talk some shite."

Inexplicably, Tammi-Jo chose to take this as a compliment, and replied with a toothy smile and a double thumbs-up.

This only frustrated the pathologist more. He exhaled through his long, dramatic nose and shook his head in mild disgust.

"Unbelievable."

"What have you got for us?" Heather asked, impatient to get going.

She was surprised and secretly a little impressed by the young DC's lack of horrified reaction when the body had been uncovered. Tammi-Jo wouldn't have been the first junior detective to throw up, faint, or—on one particularly noteworthy occasion—explosively shit themselves at the sight of a recently reassembled corpse.

DC Swanney had taken it in her stride, though, which either meant that she was far more cut out for the job than Heather's initial instincts might suggest, or she was a psychopath.

Although, those two things were not necessarily mutually exclusive.

"Good idea. Get you out of here as quickly as possible," Ozzy said. "Well, as is very much plain to see, the victim sustained multiple blunt force injuries, primarily to the head and upper torso, although by no means exclusively."

"From the beating," Heather muttered.

"Well, yes. Obviously. Unless he recently fell out of a helicopter and tumbled down a steep hill, I'm putting it down to the beating," Ozzy said, then he glared at her to make it clear he didn't appreciate the interruption. "There was significant cerebral edema, or swelling of the brain, which was a direct result of the repeated impacts. Contusions on the brain tissue indicated he suffered a traumatic brain injury."

"We think his head might've been smashed off the edge of a toilet."

"That might do it, yes. And it explains how his nose came to be forced back into the skull."

"Jesus," Heather whispered, and for a moment she felt the urge to take hold of the dead man's hand. Professionalism and stoicism stopped her.

"So, the brain injury was the cause of death?" Tammi-Jo asked, her invisible mouth-lock already forgotten.

"Hold your horses, not so fast," Ozzy told her. "I'm getting to that."

"Get to it quicker," Heather said, and there was an edge to her voice that made the pathologist dial down the theatre of his presentation a little.

"Cardiac arrest," he announced. "The brain injury was a factor, but he died from a cardiac arrest."

Heather looked from the pathologist to his patient lying on the slab.

"Heart attack?"

"Not a heart attack. Cardiac arrest. There's a difference, Detective Inspector."

Ozzy rocked back on his heels, like the DI had just fallen

into some carefully set trap. Heather groaned, feeling a lesson coming on.

"A heart attack, or *myocardial infarction*, is when blood flow to a part of the heart muscle is blocked, usually by a blood clot in a furred artery," the pathologist explained. "What he suffered was a *cardiac arrest*, which means his heart abruptly stopped working.

"The severe pain and stress from injuries such as his, combined with the likely release of certain chemicals from the injured cells—catecholamines, cytokines, even potassium—can stimulate the heart in a way that causes arrhythmias."

"Irregular heartbeats," Heather said.

"Exactly. In this instance, the arrhythmia produced was, sadly, a rhythm of death."

"That'd be a great book title," Tammi-Jo said, then she winced, shook her head, and forced herself to shut up again.

"It would, actually, yes. *Rhythm of Death*." Ozzy patted his pockets, searching for a notebook. When he couldn't find one, he pointed to Heather. "Text me that, will you? I might use it for my next book."

Tammi-Jo let out a gasp. "You write books?! Proper books? Like, with pages?"

"Yes. Didn't DI Filson mention?"

Heather didn't have time to listen to Ozzy gloating about his latest medical-based crime thriller novel. They didn't sell very well, but the last one had been positively reviewed in *The Sunday Telegraph* a year or so back, and he'd only just stopped going on about it.

Heather shook her head. "No, I didn't mention. So, that's it? Cardiac arrest. That's the cause of death?"

"It's what will be going on the certificate, yes," Ozzy confirmed. "But would it have happened without the beating? I very much doubt that. The physical trauma, the body's inflammatory response, coupled with internal bleeding, reduced oxygen supply to vital organs, and the brain injury, all contributed. It created a perfect storm, which is what caused his heart to stop. The heart itself was in pretty good shape. Far better condition than his liver, anyway."

Heather nodded. "Aye, well, that's to be expected. Tony did like a drink, right enough."

"Hm. Yes. Probably less keen on the cancer, I'd have thought."

It was only then that Heather realised how intently she'd been staring at the dead man's face. She tore her eyes away from it now and looked across the table to where Ozzy once again wore that *I know something you don't* face.

"Cancer?"

"Riddled with it," the pathologist confirmed. "Liver, pancreas. Some signs in the outer lining of the stomach."

"God. Did he know?"

"Yes. I pulled his notes. He'd been given six months a few weeks back. Personally, having seen the inside of him, that feels incredibly optimistic."

"Was he being treated for it?" Heather asked.

"There aren't a lot of viable treatments for 'impending certain death,' in my experience," the pathologist replied. "According to the notes, there was talk of palliative care, but nothing decided."

"How long would you have given him?" Tammi-Jo asked. "Now that you've looked inside and seen all the gubbins, I mean?"

Ozzy sniffed and stared up at the ceiling for a moment. Tammi-Jo looked worried, like she might have somehow offended the man.

It became clear that he was just considering the question when he nodded and lowered his gaze to meet hers.

"Not six months. Half that, maybe. If he was lucky. It's surprising he was as fit as he was. At that progression, most people would be bedbound."

Heather felt an odd little fluttering of pride at that. Her old sergeant was one of the nicest, friendliest, and warmest men she'd ever known, but he had a stubborn streak a mile wide. If he thought he was right on something, he'd fight for it every step of the way.

And that's what he'd been doing, fighting for his life, until some bastard had come along and beaten what little he had left right out of him.

Heather's phone buzzed in her pocket, notifying her of a message from DS Marty Brompton. She stared at the message for a moment, confused by it.

Found your foot...

"Found my foot?"

One of Tammi-Jo's eyes narrowed while the other grew larger. "Sorry?"

"Message from Marty," Heather said, tapping on the notification.

"Oh. Did you lose a foot?" Tammi-Jo asked. "I mean, not one of your own feet, obviously. Well, not obviously, they do amazing prosthetics these days, don't they, but why would—?"

"It was cut off," Heather said.

"Wow." Tammi-Jo's eyes crept down to floor level. "Which one?"

Heather tutted. "The message. Not my foot. The notification was cut off. Footage. He found my footage."

"Right! Yes! That makes more sense," the DC said. "Of the man the neighbour saw outside the house?"

"Don't you two mind me," Ozzy said. He pulled the cover back over Tony Crier's body with an indignant flick. "Just you have your conversations while I'm in the middle of explaining things to you. That's fine."

But Heather wasn't listening. Instead, her eyebrows were moving closer and closer together as she watched the grainy, silent footage on the screen.

The images weren't very clear, but they were good enough to tell her everything she needed to know.

"Oh, God," she groaned, watching an obese man shuffling back and forth on the street outside Tony's house. "You have got to be kidding me."

ELEVEN

"THE PIG AND BICYCLE?" Tammi-Jo said, ducking so she could look through Heather's side window. "Why's it called that?"

"I don't know. It's a pub. Why are any of them called anything?"

The question confused the young DC. "Well, so people know what one you're talking about. If they didn't have names, and you just said, 'Let's meet at the pub,' how would anyone know where to go?"

Heather tutted. Her seatbelt snaked across her chest as she unfastened it. "That's not what I meant. I meant where do the names for any pubs come from? They're just names."

"Actually, they've usually got a story behind them, like—"

"I don't care," Heather told her.

"No, OK, but I'm just saying, the name must come from somewhere."

"It's got a bike inside it and a statue of a pig. Alright? That's where the name's from."

Tammi-Jo was visibly taken aback by this. "A statue of a pig?"

"Yes. In the hall."

"Just a normal pig?"

Heather sighed and shook her head. "No. It's got a hat on."

"It's got a hat on?!"

There was a *click* as the detective constable hurriedly unfastened her belt.

"Hold on, what are you doing?" Heather demanded.

"I'm coming in!"

"Why?"

Tammi-Jo looked at her like she'd lost her mind. "To see the pig."

"No, you're not. You're staying here."

"No, but—"

"That's an order. I'm not pissing about," Heather warned. "Whatever happens, you stay here."

Tammi-Jo was unable to hide her disappointment, but responded by clicking her belt back into place.

"What do you mean, 'whatever happens?'" she asked. "What do you expect to happen?"

Heather looked across the street at the pub. One of the big windows was boarded up. Looked recent, too. Someone had some balls on them to smash a window of this place.

The area was embracing gentrification, with new cafes, coffee shops, and even a vegan restaurant run by bearded men in checked shirts and leather waistcoats. Presumably fake ones.

The Pig & Bicycle, however, remained steadfastly stuck in the past. It was an old-school working men's pub where punters could rely on getting cheap beer, shite food, and blood on their clothes come a Friday and Saturday night.

Back in the days when shipbuilding had been at the heart of the city, it had been a thriving hub, close to the banks of the Clyde. Now, though, most of the 'working men' who visited the place worked in some capacity or other for its owner, and while their line of work was more lucrative than knocking together a cargo ship, it was far less honest.

"I don't know," Heather admitted. She gripped the handle of her door. "But whatever it is, stay here until I get back."

Without waiting for confirmation, she opened the door, stepped out onto the mostly deserted street, and headed for the pub's front entrance.

The heavy wooden external doors were often shut tight, regardless of the time of day, while some shadiness or other took place inside.

Today, though, was one of those occasions when the place was open to the public. Although, the public by and large had the good sense not to go anywhere near it.

If only Heather could say the same.

She stopped just outside the pub, under the flickering glow of one of the lights that illuminated the sign. It was the middle of the day, but a layer of grey cloud hung over the city, choking out the light until only the last gasps of it made it through.

A quick glance back at the car confirmed that Tammi-Jo had stayed put. Heather's gaze trailed up the scabby frontage of the building on the opposite side of the road to the pub. The gentrification of the area hadn't yet extended to the row of flats that overlooked the street. Most of them sat empty, following a demolition order that had been put in place, but half a dozen of the residents refused to leave, so work hadn't yet started, and quite likely never would.

Heather turned back to the pub's front doors. It had been a few months since Heather had last set eyes on Shuggie Cowan. He'd given her a dossier of information on her brother, Stewie, which she'd hoped might shine some light on what had happened to him.

So far, none of the leads she'd followed up had panned out, though, and she was no closer to finding Stewie than before.

Heather glanced back at the car again to make sure Tammi-Jo was still there. The detective constable had clearly been watching her, because she quickly turned away and pretended to be very interested in the sun visor of the Audi the moment Heather looked in her direction.

Steeling herself, the DI stepped over the threshold of the pub and made her way along the short corridor towards the set of double doors at the end.

Halfway there, she passed the foot of the staircase that led to the pool room above. A cheerful fibreglass pig stood at the bottom, a spatula in one hand, and a chef's hat balanced on top of his head.

Heather rapped it on the snout, strode past it, then stopped and sighed.

Taking out her mobile, she snapped off a photo of the statue, then returned the phone to her pocket and continued through into the bar.

The place was as dead as it always was, and even gloomier than usual, thanks to the boarded-up window. A lanky barman leaned on the bar, idly flicking through a copy of *The Sun*. A lesser-known track by *Genesis* hissed and crackled from the speakers of the pub's ancient stereo system.

The landlord himself sat at his usual table, two glasses of some cheap whisky or other placed before him.

It had only been a few months, but Cowan had changed. His thinning hair was no longer dyed an unnatural shade of black, and he'd instead taken to embracing his natural grey.

Paradoxically, it made him look younger, although the fact that he'd lost a little bit of weight didn't hurt, either.

His skin was as saggy and pock-marked as ever, and yet there was a dash of colour to it that hadn't been there before, as if life was slowly returning to some once-dead cadaver.

Even the swastika scar he'd been given during a spell in prison was less obvious. Sure, it was right there on his forehead, but the edges seemed less fiery and raw than they usually looked.

He smiled at Heather as she entered, and gestured to the drink positioned in front of the chair across from him.

"You're later than I expected," he said. His voice had the same gruff rasp as before, but there was a lightness to that now, too, like he was sharing a joke with an old friend.

The very thought made Heather's skin crawl. God help the man if that's what he thought they were.

"What do you mean?" she demanded. "Why were you expecting me?"

He gestured again at the drink, and the chair next to it. "Take a seat. Take the weight off. Have a drink, on me."

"I'm driving."

"You can't sit down because you're driving?"

There was a twinkle in the bastard's eye. Heather was sure of it. His hair and skin care regimen weren't the only things different about Shuggie Cowan.

Heather pulled the chair out slowly, scraping the legs on the old wooden floor. The noise was annoying enough to make the barman scowl at her from across the room, but Shuggie just held eye contact, a satisfied wee smirk sculpting the corners of his bloated lips.

He said nothing until she'd sat, then picked up his glass and nodded his approval. "There. That's better, isn't it?"

He raised the glass in a salute to her, then knocked it back in one. He grimaced at the taste of the cheap firewater, then waggled his glass in the barman's direction to indicate he wanted a refill.

"How did you know I was coming?" Heather asked.

Shuggie gave a noncommittal sort of grunt. "I have my ways. As you know."

Heather knew there was no point in questioning him further on that. Cowan got his information from a wide variety of sources, including, it was suspected, from within the walls of Police Scotland itself. He certainly wasn't going to give them up now, and especially not to her.

"Right, well then, you know why I'm here?" she asked.

"Well, I hoped it might be you popping in for a social visit,"

Shuggie said. "Been a while since we last chatted, you and me."

Another drink was placed in front of him, and the empty glass taken away. Shuggie and Heather held eye contact throughout, neither one acknowledging the barman's presence.

"How's the old man?" Shuggie asked. "He still"—he tapped the side of his head a couple of times—"away with the fairies?"

Heather's reply was a growl of modulated menace. "That's none of your business. Where is he?"

"What, your dad? He hasn't gone wandering off again, has he?" He leaned closer as he picked up his glass. "Or do you mean Stewie? He still not turned up?"

"Gonad," Heather growled. "Where's Gonad?"

"No idea. Sorry."

"You're lying," Heather shot back. "He was in Kilmarnock last night. Outside Tony Crier's place."

"I heard about poor Tony. Terrible business," Shuggie said, but there was something mocking about his tone. "My condolences to his friends and family."

"I'll be sure to pass that on. Why was Gonad there?"

Shuggie grunted. "What am I, the fat fucker's keeper?"

"More or less, aye. Gonad's a lazy bastard. Left to his own devices, he'd be headfirst in a KFC family bucket. But he wasn't. He was pacing up and down outside the home of a Police Scotland sergeant who was later found beaten to death."

"I heard he died in hospital."

"Irrelevant. Answer the question."

Shuggie's lips drew back over his teeth in a grin. "That wasn't a question."

Heather banged her fist on the table. Whisky sloshed up the walls of her untouched glass and splashed onto the scuffed wooden tabletop.

"Why was Gonad there? Tell me," she demanded. "You owe me that much."

Shuggie's jovial air popped like a bubble. The smile dropped from his face, and suddenly she was face to face with the Shuggie Cowan she'd only heard rumour of. The Shuggie Cowan of twenty years ago. Forty.

She'd always known he was dangerous, but in the same way an ancient, half-blind, mostly toothless lion was dangerous. You didn't want to stick your head in its mouth, but it didn't have the energy to chase you down.

He was a dinosaur, clinging to the past, praying that some extinction-level event wasn't going to come along and wipe out everything he'd ever known.

He and this pub were a perfect match, both of them relics from days gone by, unable or unwilling to fit in with the changing world around them.

Shuggie Cowan had always been a bit of a joke.

But nobody was laughing now.

"I owe you that much?" The words came hissed through his gritted teeth. "I don't owe you fuck all, girl. Maybe I do. Maybe I owe you a fucking hiding, in fact. Maybe I owe your old man a late-night visit with a couple of big lads and a pair of fucking bolt cutters. Aye. That feels more like it. That feels more like *what I owe you*."

He picked up his drink and knocked it back in one. His hand gripped the glass so firmly that his knuckles were white. Heather half expected the container to shatter in his grip.

Clearly, she'd hit a nerve.

"You want to know why Gonad was there? Fine. You should know," the gangster growled. "Your man, your sergeant? Let's just say he wasn't whiter than white."

Heather shook her head. Tony Crier was as straight up as they came.

"Bollocks. You're lying."

Shuggie shrugged. The movement was sharp. Aggressive. Heather could almost hear the rage whooshing through his veins. She didn't think she'd ever seen him this angry before, and she had no idea what had kicked it off.

"Am I? Believe what you fucking like. And no, before you ask, Gonad didn't kill him. He didn't even speak to him. He just made his presence felt outside. Made it clear to your man that we knew where to find him. Showed him that if he didn't cut his shit out, we'd be on him."

"What do you mean, 'his shit'? What are you saying? That Tony was on the take?"

"What? Christ, no. How's that my problem? The man needs to make a living, and your lot pays fuck all," Shuggie said. "I'm not going into details. We were just asked to provide a wee reminder that his whereabouts were well known."

"And, so, what? Gonad just walked up and down outside his house for a bit? I'm not buying it. What sort of warning is that?"

"He'd already been spoken to. Gonad was just, what do you call it? For emphasis. A big fat fucking full stop on the whole thing."

"Who already spoke to him?" Heather asked.

Cowan snorted. "Oh, what? You want me to tell you so your lot can kick the shit out of him, an' all?"

Heather was unable to hide her confusion. "What? What are you talking about?"

"Oh, come on, Detective Inspector," Shuggie said. "Don't tell me you don't know?"

Heather hated when the bastard knew something she didn't. There was no point in trying to bluff it out, though.

"Know what?"

Shuggie's reply was a lone, ominous drone.

"That some of your boys have been getting a wee bit out of hand. Getting a bit carried away with themselves." His chair groaned as he shifted his weight forward. "Which is why I'm being forced to take steps. I want you to know that. That everything that happens next—any *unpleasantness*—the blame for it lies on your side, not mine."

A creeping sense of unease tingled across the nape of Heather's neck. "What are you talking about? I don't understand."

Shuggie's hand shot across the table like a striking cobra. Heather jumped with fright, her chair legs scraping backwards across the floor.

The gangster snatched the DI's glass, and knocked back what was left of the liquid in one big gulp.

"You pricks want a war?" he hissed through the fiery aftermath. "I'll give you a fucking war."

———

Tammi-Jo had almost managed to fix the clock on Heather's dashboard. The time was more or less right, fast by just a few minutes.

Assuming twenty-seven counted as 'a few.'

She thought she could probably get the time closer, but it was the date that was the problem. Today was the second of November, but the car now thought it was the sixth of January.

It also thought the year was forty-six years in the future.

"Wow, these things are so complicated," the detective constable muttered, stabbing at another couple of buttons and holding them down.

The screen flashed. The date shot up, the numbers birling around, years spinning rapidly into decades before she could whip her hands away.

"Oh... knickers," she muttered, before some movement out on the street drew her attention away from the clock.

Two black Range Rovers had pulled up outside the pub, and a surprising number of large men had disembarked from both—six from one vehicle, seven from the other.

"God. What were they doing, sitting on one another's

knee?" Tammi-Jo whispered as she looked the men over, searching for weapons.

She couldn't see any, though they were all big enough that they probably didn't need any.

One of them turned her way and clocked her watching. He was a muscular twenty-something with a shaved head, dressed in black. Although, that pretty much described all of them.

He nudged one of his clones and nodded towards the parked Audi. Tammi-Jo found herself smiling and waving, then she immediately tried to sink straight through her seat when the two men who'd seen her stepped out onto the road and approached Heather's car.

"Ooh, that's not good," she mumbled.

After a moment, a face appeared at the passenger side window. The other man—the one who'd spotted her first, she thought, though they were so similar it was hard to be sure— stood directly in front of the car with his arms folded, blocking the way.

Up close, she could see that the man at her window was older than the others. Approaching the upper end of his thirties, maybe, or even early forties. His stubble was flecked by spots of grey, and he wore the wrinkles of a man who frowned on a professional basis.

She could also see that he was wearing a black tie, but it was camouflaged against the matching black shirt. It made him look a bit like a waiter, although she doubted *The Pig & Bicycle* offered a table service menu.

It took her three attempts to find the button that rolled the window down. She tried to bring it down halfway, but it retracted all the way into the door, leaving her face to face with the man in black.

"Alright, Princess?" he said. He was English. London, she thought. His eyes searched her face, appraising her. From the way his mouth puckered, it was clear that he liked what he saw. "Well, well, you're a pretty little thing, ain'tcha?"

He gripped the door at the bottom of the open window frame. The plastic trim creaked beneath the force of his fingers. He leaned in closer, and the smell of cigarette smoke on his breath hit Tammi-Jo in the face.

"You tell your Uncle Billy, what's a pretty thing like you doing out here all on your lonesome?"

Tammi-Jo's blue eyes widened. "My Uncle Billy?"

"Yeah." The man by the door grinned at her. "You tell your Uncle Billy."

"I don't... What, phone him? He'll probably be at work."

It was the turn of the man to look confused. "You what?"

"My Uncle Billy. He'll be working. He works in a bank. NatWest, I think. Can't remember. I don't think he's going to want to be interrupted."

"No. No, what are you...? What the fuck are you on about? *I'm* your Uncle Billy."

"You're not," Tammi-Jo told him. "He's shorter, better looking, and he doesn't smoke."

She produced her warrant card and smiled sweetly up at him. "Now, do you mind not touching the car? I don't know her that well, but I've got a feeling that my detective inspector *really* won't appreciate you putting your hands on it."

The Police ID didn't have the effect Tammi-Jo had been hoping for. The man in the window barely glanced at it, and seemed to relish it as some sort of challenge.

"Oh, yeah?" he asked, bringing his face closer to the car.

She could see the yellow scum on his teeth, and the way the vein in his temple pulsed.

"And what do you reckon she'd have to say if I put my hands on *you*?"

———

Heather hated that she'd shown fear. Most people who'd heard of Shuggie Cowan—which was most of central Scotland—had the sense to be wary of him.

But she'd jumped back. She'd retreated in panic. It would take her a while to shake off the shame of that.

"Nobody wants a war, Shuggie," she assured him.

"It's not me you need to be telling that to," the gangster replied. "I'm just defending my interests. There'll be no more broken bones or broken windows under my watch."

Before Heather could question him any further, she heard the creaking of a floorboard at the foot of the stairs. The sound was loud, the cause of it heavy.

She turned in her chair and, through the frosted glass of the inner door, saw the bulky mass of a man waddling quickly towards the exit.

"Fuck," Shuggie hissed below his breath.

Heather launched herself away from the table, sending her chair toppling to the floor.

"Gonad!" she bellowed, racing after the fleeing fat man.

She reached the inner doors just as Gonad's blurred outline went thundering out onto the street. Hauling the doors open, she went hurtling along the corridor.

"Get back here!" she roared, skidding out onto the street.

She found herself surrounded by a forest of six-foot-plus skinheads.

"Out the fucking road," she barked, pushing through them.

Thirty yards down the street, and moving at an impressive rate of knots for a man his size, Gonad fired a worried look over his shoulder, then went stumbling across a street, earning himself an angry blare from a car horn.

Heather set off at a sprint, powering away from *The Pig & Bicycle*, and the small army of skinheads assembled outside.

In the passenger seat of the Audi, Tammi-Jo watched the detective inspector break into a run, then turned to the man still blocking her door.

"You need to step aside, sir," she told him. When he just smiled at her, she raised her volume and clipped her tone. "Out of the way. Now."

"Oh, yeah?" the man in black purred. "And what if I—?"

He yelped as Tammi-Jo caught him by the tie and pulled hard, smashing his face against the top of the Audi's door frame. She repeated the process two more times for good measure, then released her grip on the tie. He stumbled back, howling in pain, blood gushing from his burst nose.

The car door slammed into him as the DC threw it wide. It struck him like a battering ram and he stumbled backwards for several big paces, frantically trying to keep his balance, before gravity took its toll and deposited him unceremoniously on the pavement.

"Sorry, sorry, sorry!" the DC cried, leaping out of the vehicle. She started to run, then turned back to the man lying on the ground. "Oh, and please don't move from there, you're under arrest."

She pointed two fingers at her eyes, then directed them to the shocked-looking younger man still standing in front of the Audi, letting him know she'd be watching him.

And then, as tyres screeched, and another horn blared further along the road, Tammi-Jo kicked off her shoes, tossed them in through the open window of the car, and ran.

TWELVE

DC SIMON WOLFE almost spilled his coffee at the sight of the gelatinous man-mountain being led along the corridor towards the interview rooms. He had seen Gonad once before in his life, but that was nowhere near enough to acclimatise someone to the experience. You needed to be exposed to the man a good six or seven times before his size no longer took your breath away.

His real name was Stevie Ross, but he'd earned the nickname in high school, which was when he'd first had the misfortune to start physically resembling a man's testicle. He was fat enough to be almost round, had thick, wiry black hair in all the wrong places, and veins pulsed below his sagging skin whenever he was excited or under great stress.

Considering that walking up a shallow incline counted as 'great stress' for a man of his size, Gonad's veins were currently engorged with the thick red jelly of his blood. A sheen of oily sweat oozed from his pores and tainted the air around him with a pungently sour tang.

The chase had started well for him, panic lending his legs an almost superhuman burst of strength and speed that had carried him a full hundred yards away from *The Pig & Bicycle,* before biology and physics had both simultaneously kicked in and he'd fallen, face first, onto the road.

A minibus full of pensioners had come dangerously close to driving straight over him, though fortunately for both Gonad and the physical integrity of the bus itself, the driver had managed to stop in the nick of time.

By the time Heather caught up, the wheezing Gonad lay surrounded by a gaggle of angry eighty-somethings, and a few whacks from handbags and pokes from brollies had only added to his misery.

Once she'd ushered the OAPs back onto their bus, she and Tammi-Jo had worked together to first turn Gonad over, then get him back to his feet. The second part had proved to be impossible, though, and when a couple of Shuggie's men in black had turned up, Heather had put them to work.

The man that Tammi-Jo had assaulted—or 'restrained' as she described it—was nowhere to be seen when they returned to the car with their wheezing, shuffling prisoner.

The DC had suggested she should go into the pub to try and find him, but Heather had shown her the photo of the fibreglass pig, and she'd been content to leave it at that.

It was only when they'd got Gonad loaded into the back of her car that Heather had asked the question that had been bothering her since she'd helped roll him onto his back.

"What the hell happened to you?"

Squashed into the back seat, the bruised and bloodied suspect met her eye in the rearview mirror, and shrugged his rounded shoulders.

"No comment."

He'd continued that same approach all the way back to the station, refusing to respond to any of their questions, even the ones asking if he wanted the window open a bit, and whether or not he was thirsty.

His commitment to the whole 'no comment' bit told Heather a lot more than he had probably intended. Gonad wasn't the sharpest knife in the drawer. He was barely the sharpest spoon in the drawer, and was more of a 'sharpest sausage down the back of the fridge,' type of guy.

Basically, he was as thick as mince. Getting him to understand an instruction was difficult, but once you had—once he'd somehow got all the steps involved locked in place in his head —getting him to deviate from it was next to impossible.

This wasn't Gonad refusing to comment. He wouldn't have the sense to decide that on his own. This was Shuggie Cowan ordering him to keep his mouth shut.

And if Shuggie had taken the time and gone to all the effort to drill the order into him, Gonad had to know something.

Heather was going to find out what. Stubborn or not, if she couldn't outsmart a man with both the appearance and intellect of a reproductive gland, she had no business being in the job.

"Fucking hell," DC Wolfe muttered, as Heather and Tammi-Jo led the sweating Gonad past him. The detective looked the suspect up and down. "What's the story here?"

"No comment," Gonad wheezed in his dense North East accent.

Dense being the operative word.

"He wasn't talking to you," Heather said.

Gonad squirmed under the weight of her stare, as if he thought she might be expecting a response to that remark

"No comment?" he said, though this one sounded more like a question than a statement.

Heather sighed. "Forget it. I'm taking him into interview room six."

"Four," DC Wolfe corrected.

"No, *six*," Heather stressed. "It's bigger. More room for the smell to spread out."

Wolfe slurped at his coffee and shook his head. "Nope. Four." He gestured along the corridor with his mug. "His solicitor's already in there."

"That was quick," Tammi-Jo remarked.

Heather gritted her teeth. Cowan must've got straight on to his lawyer the moment she left the pub, knowing full well that Gonad wasn't going to get away. Shuggie's lawyers were good. Terrible people, but good at their jobs. She'd hoped to get half an hour or so free and clear with Gonad before they stuck their noses in.

Plus, interview room four was tiny, and the extractor fan didn't work.

Time, then, for a power play. She gave Gonad a shove on the back, urging him to start walking again.

"Well, we'll be in six," she told Wolfe. "If he wants to come and join us, tell him he's more than welcome."

THIRTEEN

"MILLIE WATSON?"

"Here, Miss."

"Edward Williams?"

"Here, Miss."

"Enough with the silly voices, Edward."

The reply wobbled between a deep baritone and a finger-nails-down-the-blackboard squeak. "This is my proper voice, but!"

As one of the oldest teachers at Kilmarnock Academy, Mrs Hawkes really should've grasped the whole concept of puberty by that point in her career, and the physical effects it had on boys of a certain age.

Instead, she peered along the length of her classroom to where a spotty-faced oik with a daft haircut stared indignantly back at her.

Of course, that wasn't much of a descriptor. They were all spotty-faced oiks with daft haircuts. That had been one of the only constants of her career.

Well, that and the tedium.

"Good luck with that," she muttered, then her eyes flitted back to the list of names on her register. "Alison Wurzel?"

There was no response. Mrs Hawkes tutted.

"*Ace* Wurzel," she said, with a derisory, patronising sort of air that would not have gone unnoticed by the girl it was aimed at, were it not for the fact that she'd failed to turn up to class.

"She's not here, Miss," said a boy from the back.

The teacher flicked her gaze at the empty chair where the girl usually sat.

"Where is she?"

"Dunno, Miss."

There was a snigger from up the back. "Maybe she's got herself kidnapped again."

Another boy let out a cackle. "Haha! Imagine! Who'd want to kidnap her, though?"

"Leave her alone."

Edward's voice started strong, then peaked into a mouse-like squeak, before becoming the drone of a tuba, all within the space of three short words.

A collective *ooooh* went around the class.

"What, do you fancy her?" demanded a girl with tumbling blonde curls.

"You trying to shag her, or something?" teased another.

"Alright, alright, that is enough!" Mrs Hawkes barked.

She pointed a crooked finger around at the pupils in general, lingering a little longer on some of the known trouble-makers. She always hated the first lesson back after lunch. The little shits were all buzzing on sugar, or on a high from the *wacky baccy* that she knew some of them were smoking.

It came a close third on her list of worst lesson periods of the day, hot on the heels of first period, but well below the period immediately after morning break.

Once things had settled down, she looked back at her page, marked a cross in a box next to the final name on the list, then begrudgingly began the lesson.

———

It was at times like these that Ace wondered if she should have considered a career in video journalism instead of audio. She loved the podcast medium, but felt it was going to be difficult to effectively convey what she was currently seeing.

How would she describe it for her listeners?

'A spray of blood'? No, too vanilla and on the nose.

'A visual echo of death's grand overture'? Too flowery. Also, she wasn't convinced it made sense.

'The lifeblood of Sergeant Anthony Crier, spilled in anger by an assailant yet unknown'?

Now she was onto something. Yes, that would do it.

She took a photo of the bloodstain on the wall by the stairs, though, just in case she needed the visual for later. She'd print it out for her Wonderwall.

It was quite a grandiose name to give the area of her bedroom wall where she pinned up the evidence she collected, she knew, but *grandiose* was right up her street.

Ace knew, of course, that she shouldn't be here. The guard was no longer posted out front, but there was still crime scene tape across the front door and the entrance to the back garden.

There was definitely an argument to be made that she should've gone back to school after lunch. She'd be hard-pressed to offer an explanation as to why she hadn't, at least not one that anyone would've agreed with.

Even her mother, who was generally supportive of her endeavours, even if she didn't understand most of them, would not be happy that her only daughter was currently an illegal intruder on a murder scene when she should've had her nose buried in a textbook.

If she was forced to argue her point, she'd say that she wasn't missing much, because Mrs Hawkes often nodded off during afternoon classes, which really limited the learning opportunities available.

And, more importantly, this was likely her only chance of gaining access to the property, now that the forensics people had left, but the clean-up team had yet to come in. She had a small window of opportunity to assess the scene of the crime and gather up what evidence she could. What sort of investigative journalist would she be if she didn't jump at that chance? The front door hadn't even been locked! So, that was practically an invitation for her to come in and look around.

And besides, the police had been and gone. Presumably, they already had what they were looking for, so it wasn't like she would be contaminating the scene. She'd be in and out in just a few minutes. No one would even know she'd been there.

She took a few more photographs of the bloodstains on the wall from the foot of the stairs, then decided to have a snoop around the ground floor first.

Ace opened the door to the living room, and immediately came face to face with a man in police uniform. He squatted by the fireplace, twisting himself so one hand was jammed up the chimney.

"Oh. Hello," Ace said. And then, in a tone that managed to suggest the police officer was in the wrong, added, "I really did not expect anyone to be in here."

The uniformed man pulled a soot-stained arm out of the chimney and leapt to his feet.

"Who are you, and what the hell do you think you're doing?" he barked.

Ace raised an index finger.

She opened her mouth.

And then, when her brain failed to come up with an appropriate answer, she turned on her heel and ran.

FOURTEEN

HEATHER HAD ENCOUNTERED this solicitor before. She couldn't remember his name, or even the exact details of their previous meeting, but as soon as he entered the room she felt the bile rising at the back of her throat.

It was his movements she remembered, the preciseness of them. He moved as if powered by some intricate clockwork mechanism, hand-built by artisans somewhere in the Swiss Alps. Every movement he made, from the nod of acknowledgement to the opening of his briefcase, was slow, and calculated, and painstakingly deliberate.

He spoke like a late-night Radio 4 presenter talking to their cat, his soothing tones like syrup to the ears.

"Apologies all. I was led to believe the interview would be taking place in another room. Please, permit me a moment to ready myself."

"No comment," said Gonad, then he crossed his enormous arms and sat back, pleased with himself for sticking to the script.

The solicitor didn't bat an eyelid. He didn't seem to blink at all, in fact. Maybe, when the Swiss engineers had been putting him together, Heather thought, they'd given him those baby doll eyelids that only closed when he laid down.

"Tea? Coffee?" asked Tammi-Jo, already rising to her feet.

It was becoming apparent that sitting still was not one of the DC's strong points. While they'd waited for the solicitor to arrive, she'd fidgeted in her seat, clicked the top of her pen somewhere in the region of six hundred times, and drawn a small family of ducks at the top of a notebook page.

And then, below that, the extended family.

"Hm?" The solicitor gazed blankly at her, his face not so much as hinting at what was going on inside his head.

"Tea? Coffee?" Tammi-Jo said again, then she looked at Heather with a single line of concern creasing her smooth forehead. "That's what people drink, isn't it?"

"What do you mean 'people'?" Heather asked.

"No. Thank you," the solicitor said, the mechanism in his brain finally coming to a decision. "I have my own water."

With great care, like it was a container of unstable liquid explosives, he removed a featureless grey bottle from his briefcase, set it on the table in front of him, and then spent a few seconds making incremental adjustments to it until its positioning was *just so*.

"It's got added electrolytes," he said, once he was happy with the bottle's placement.

"Of course it does," Heather remarked.

"OK. Mr, um, Gonad?" Tammi-Jo asked.

"Ross," the solicitor corrected. "It's Mr Ross."

"Oh. Yes. Sorry. Tea? Coffee?"

"No comment," Gonad replied.

"Sit down, Detective Constable," Heather instructed.

Her eyes continued to follow the meticulous movements of the lawyer as he lined up his pens and notepad on the table in front of him. He was actually quite fascinating to watch. Give those engineers another few years to tune him up, Heather thought, and he might almost pass for human.

"Now, then. There we are," he said, satisfied that everything was in the right place. "Harold Grout. I'm Mr Ross's legal counsel."

He half rose to his feet and extended a hand across the table for the detectives to shake. Tammi-Jo reached for it, but a sideways glance from Heather made her draw back.

"Come now, Officers. We're all friends here," Grout insisted. He kept the hand held out for several more seconds, then nodded technically and sat down again. "Very well. We'll do it your way."

He clasped his hands in front of him with the same machined precision as the rest of his movements. Heather could almost hear the cogs in his face *whirring* as the corners of his mouth raised into a thin, carefully calculated smile.

"You have absolutely no justification for bringing my client in for questioning. None whatsoever."

"He was caught on camera at a crime scene," Heather replied.

"No."

"I'm sorry?"

"He was caught on camera *near* a crime scene. There is no evidence to suggest that he was involved with the incident that took place, either directly or indirectly."

Heather glanced from lawyer to client and back again. It was early days, but she already didn't like the way the interview was going. "We just want to know if he can tell us anything."

"I see. And that was worth chasing him into the street, was it? That was worth almost getting him killed?"

"How did he know about that?" Tammi-Jo asked, but both the DI and the solicitor ignored the question.

"Let us be open and honest, Detective Inspector, you know full well that Mr Ross was not behind the attack. The intruder gained access via a window, I believe?"

He gestured to Gonad like he was presenting the booby prize in a particularly cruel game show.

"I'd say the evidence speaks for itself."

The bastard knew about the window. He probably knew as much about the case as she did. One of Shuggie's informants had no doubt spilled everything.

Any decent lawyer would've refused the information. Most dodgy ones would take it all on board, but keep it to themselves.

But Grout was being brazen with it. He was privy to illegally obtained information, and he didn't care if the detectives knew it.

Heather almost respected his brass neck. His legal knowledge made him formidable. His connections made him untouchable.

"You have personal history with Mr Ross. Isn't that right, Detective Inspector?"

Tammi-Jo gasped. "God! Ew." She flashed an apologetic smile at Gonad. "Sorry, I didn't mean—"

"Not like that!" Heather hissed. "Jesus!"

"My client very kindly refused to press charges a few months back after you manipulated him into aiding you in breaking the law. Correct?"

Heather said nothing. She just stared across the table at the soulless bastard in the expensive suit, feeling the sudden weight of Tammi-Jo's gaze on her.

"One might argue that, despite this, you have a vendetta against Mr Ross. Attempting to frame him. Chasing him into oncoming traffic. That goes far beyond even harassment, Detective Inspector. That sounds like a targeted campaign by you against my client. And now, you bring him in here, with no justification, so you can what? Accuse him of murdering a well-regarded serving police officer?"

"That's not why he's here," Heather insisted. "We just want to talk to him."

"You could have talked to him somewhere else, but you chose to arrest him and bring him in here."

"He ran away."

"Yes. Well. After how you've treated him, can you really blame him?"

Heather sighed. She *really* didn't like how this was going now. She shifted her gaze from the solicitor to Gonad, studying him.

His face was a mess. Granted, it was always a mess—often, it had *Nutella* on it—but today, it was far worse than usual, thanks to all the bruising and swelling. The tips of a few sutures were just visible between the rolls of a couple of chins, the stitches poking out like the legs of spiders that had become stuck down there, and were now fighting for air.

Gonad looked blankly at the centre of the table, then sensed the detective's gaze on him. He sat up a little straighter, mumbled a, "No comment," in case he'd just been asked a question, then smiled hopefully at his solicitor like a child seeking the approval of a fickle parent.

When the approval failed to come, he sunk back down in his chair again, and fumbled anxiously with his sausage-like fingers.

"What happened, Gonad?" Heather asked, and the note of concern in her voice made him raise his eyes to meet hers. "Who did this to you?"

Gonad's fingers wrestled one another on the tabletop.

"No comment," he said.

Heather checked her watch. "Interview terminated at one-twenty-seven PM." She stretched over to Tammi-Jo's side of the table and pressed the button that stopped the official recording.

"Off the record. Just between us, Gonad. What happened? Who did this to you?"

Grout took his briefcase from the floor and placed it on the desk. With a *clunk*, both clasps sprang open.

"My client is done answering questions."

"He didn't actually answer any," Tammi-Jo pointed out.

Heather ignored them both. "Was it one of our guys? Is that what happened, Gonad? Did one of our lot do this?"

Gonad's tongue flitted across his lips like a fast-moving slug, then rolled around inside his mouth, pushing out cheeks ravaged by both violence and poor dietary decisions.

He opened his mouth to reply, and Heather leaned in closer, sensing he was going to say something different this time. That he was actually going to give her something to work with.

Before a word could emerge, though, his gaze crept to the mirror on the wall across the room. It lingered there for a moment, and Heather couldn't tell if the man-mountain was staring at his own reflection, or imagining someone on the other side of the glass.

When he turned back, his expression was as blank as before.

"No comment."

Grout had finished returning everything to his briefcase, and closed it with a firm, definitive *click*.

"And that, as they say, is that," he announced, rising from his chair. "This was a pleasure, Officers. But, ideally, let's not do it again anytime soon."

———

A Big Board, Tammi-Jo had suggested, would make keeping track of things so much easier. A Big Board, in her limited experience, helped keep everyone focused.

"You have a notebook. We all have notebooks," Snecky pointed out. "Think of it like your own personal Big Board that you can carry with you. That makes it better, doesn't it?"

Tammi-Jo started to reply, pointing out that they could all still write in their individual notes, but having one central repository of information would *surely* reduce the chances of anyone accidentally—

It was at this point that DCI Grant had ordered her to immediately stop talking. There would be no boards in his Incident Room, thank you very much, big or otherwise.

He had taken centre stage before his assembled audience of detectives. DC Wolfe sat closest to him, his chair angled so he was partly facing the rest of the group, like he straddled the worlds of both performer and audience. DS Marty Brompton and Tammi-Jo had both brought their chairs over, and had done their best to comply when Snecky had instructed them to form a semi-circle.

It wasn't an easy task for just two of them, but Heather had sat on her desk, refusing to get involved in the arrangement of the chairs.

Snecky now stood with his hands clasped in front of his crotch, and his head slightly lowered. He looked like he was either praying, or about to start singing, 'My Heart Will Go On,' from the Titanic soundtrack. Heather couldn't tell which, but for everyone's sake—particularly his own—she hoped it wasn't the latter.

"Well," the DCI began. "Here we are." He raised his head to look around at the team. "How are we all doing? Given the circumstances?"

Wolfe looked up at him, frowning. "What circumstances?"

Snecky tutted, his solemn air already crumbling away. "The… What's his name? The dead fella. Sergeant…"

"Crier," Marty said.

"Yes. Thank you. Exactly. Him! We're all upset about it," Snecky ranted. "And so, I'm just… I'm just being… what do you call it?"

"A dick?" Heather guessed.

"Compassionate!" Snecky shot back. "I'm considering everyone's feelings. It's an emotional time. We lost one of our own. We lost a good man in Sergeant…"

He winced. This time, nobody rushed to help him out. The strain showed on his face as he grasped for the name, and for a moment it looked like he might be about to rupture something.

"Crier!" he said, with a gasp of relief. "Sergeant Crier. Sergeant Crier. He was a good man. Sergeant Crier. One of the best. And he was one of us! One of the good guys. So, please, Simon, let's show him a bit of bloody respect, eh?"

Wolfe took a long slurp from his ever-present coffee mug and nodded. "Sorry, sir."

"Actually…" Heather gritted her teeth, like she was fighting herself, trying to stop the words getting out. "I heard rumour that maybe Tony wasn't as much of a good guy as we thought."

"Tony?" Snecky appeared momentarily confused, then he clicked his fingers. "Crier. Sergeant Tony Crier. Of course. We all knew his name." He pinched his chin between finger and thumb and nodded. "Go on."

"It's probably nothing. He's probably just playing mind games, but Shuggie Cowan reckons he was dirty."

Marty turned in his chair. "Tony was dirty? Tony Crier? I can't see it."

"No, nor me. I just don't get what Cowan would stand to gain from lying about it."

"Could be protecting that fat lad," Wolfe ventured.

Heather shook her head. "He doesn't give a shit about Gonad. And why would Tony being on the take have anything to do with him, anyway?"

DC Wolfe took another noisy slurp from his mug. "I mean, I don't know. I can't think of everything myself."

"We should bring in his son," Snecky suggested. "Talk to him, see what he knows. If his old man was on the take, he'd know about it."

"Or he might not," Marty said.

"Or he might not. Granted, yes, he might not, but it's worth a try," the DCI replied. "Simon, bring him in."

"Simon, don't you dare," Heather countered. She met

Snecky's questioning gaze. "Ash is dealing with enough. Until we know more, we keep him in the dark."

The DCI folded his arms. "I firmly disagree."

Heather bit her tongue before she could voice the first response that sprang to mind. That wouldn't help.

Nor would the second response, and the third one that came to mind would likely have got her fired.

She was no longer the boss. She couldn't just throw her weight around. She had to play it smarter.

"Well, whatever you think, sir," she said. "The buck stops with you, after all."

Marty, realising immediately what was happening, lowered his head to hide his smile.

"Exactly! Thank you, Detective Inspector. I'm glad we're finally starting to understand the pecking order," Snecky crowed. He turned to address DC Wolfe, then turned back to Heather. "Why did you say it like that?"

"Like what?"

"'The buck stops with you.'"

Heather shrugged. "Well, it does. You're the boss. For better or worse. I mean, aye, if we pull Ash in and get a result, then brilliant. Well done. If we blow it, though? If he's involved, but plays dumb and denies it all, and then knows that we're onto him?" She winced. "Oof. That's going to take some explaining to the Gozer."

"Bank accounts."

Tammi-Jo's interjection caught everyone off guard. They all turned to her, and their attention made her cheeks blush red.

"I'm sorry?" Snecky asked.

"I was just thinking, sir, bank accounts. Sergeant Crier's. Couldn't we do a check of those to see if there were any large deposits made? It could give us something we could use when interviewing his son."

The DCI snorted. DC Wolfe rolled his eyes and shook his head.

"He's hardly likely to pay it into the bank, is he?" Snecky said. "He's far more likely to keep it in his house."

"Except it wasn't found in his house, sir. Scene of Crime would have mentioned it," Tammi-Jo replied. "I mean, unless they have mentioned it, and I just haven't seen it? If we had some sort of place to put all the information…"

She mimed pressing a hand against a large, flat, vertical surface.

"Did they mention anything like that?" Snecky asked the room at large.

"What, a big bag of money? No," Marty replied. "They didn't mention that."

"Maybe the burglar took it?" Wolfe suggested. "Since he doesn't seem to have nicked anything else."

"I don't think it was a burglar," Heather said.

Snecky tutted. "Oh, here we go. So, what was it, then, if not a break-in? Hmm? We're all ears, Detective Inspector."

Heather's fingers wrapped around the stapler on her desk. Her aim was pretty decent. If she tried hard enough, she could clonk the fucker right between the eyes from here.

But, no. Enjoyable as it would be, it wouldn't help anyone.

"Don't know yet," she admitted. "But, I'm working on it." She hopped down from the desk and jabbed a thumb in the direction of the door. "Want me to go bring Ash in, and we can see what he knows? I can let the Gozer know on the way out."

Snecky bit his bottom lip. He rubbed the palms of his hands against the sides of his trousers like they were suddenly itchy.

Finally, he turned his attention to Tammi-Jo. "Bank accounts, you say? Yes. That might be worth a quick look first. Get on that, will you?"

"Of course," Tammi-Jo said. "Although… I'm not actually sure how to go about it. I mean, presumably, I phone someone? At the bank? But do we know what bank? There are quite a lot of them. TSB. Bank of Scotland. *Royal* Bank of Scotland."

She looked to Heather for help, but the DI just raised her eyebrows and shook her head.

"Clydesdale," DC Wolfe volunteered.

"No," said Snecky. "That's been taken over. It's Virgin Money now."

Wolfe let out a little snort. "Heh. *Virgin.*"

"I'll do it!" Marty announced. There was a snap to his tone, like he'd been one more bank name away from losing the rag. "I can find out."

"Oh. Phew!" Tammi-Jo said, wiping a hand across her forehead. "Thanks. I had a feeling that could have gone terribly wrong. I can help, though, if you want. I can help you out. Do you want me to help?"

"Eh, no," Marty replied. "I'm fine. Honestly. I've got it under control." He struggled against a smirk. "You stick with helping DI Filson."

"Aye-aye, sir!" Tammi-Jo said, her smile dazzling as she snapped off a salute. "I'll stick to her like glue."

"Please," Heather said. "Don't do that."

She told them about the rest of what Shuggie Cowan had said to her, about some of 'their lot' throwing their weight around, and the threat of an imminent war. It was discussed, then set aside. Shuggie was too long in the tooth to go to war against the police. Even for a slippery bastard like him.

Snecky made a note to discuss it with the Gozer. If Uniform was running riot, then that was above the detectives' pay grades.

"You talked to the iron woman yet?" Snecky asked.

The way Tammi-Jo's head perked up excitedly made Heather rush to clarify. "The woman who did Tony's ironing. And no, not yet. I'm going to do it on the way home. You get anywhere with that address yet?"

"The neighbour? No. Weirdly," Marty told her. "It's owned by a limited company based in Malta. *MB Property.* Seems to be a property rental business, but from what I can find out, it only owns this one house."

"What about council tax? Leccy bills?"

"Drawing a blank. All registered to the company."

"Has anyone spoken to them yet? In the door to door?"

"No one's been home," the DS replied. "So not yet, no."

Snecky crossed his arms, clearly feeling left out. "What's the big deal, anyway? What's so important about the neighbour?"

"Nothing," Heather said. No way she was telling them about the telescope trained on a young girl's bedroom. Not yet. Not until she knew more. "It's just possible they saw something."

"Well, it seems like the buggers are never home, so I wouldn't go counting my chickens," the DI warned.

There was some more discussion on the post-mortem results, Tony's cancer, and then decisions had to be made regarding the investigation's next steps.

Marty would dig into the bank accounts and try to find evidence that Tony had been on the take. Heather very much hoped he didn't find any.

Wolfe would have a few of the known local burglars brought in to see if any of them had gone back to their old ways, or heard anything about the break-in.

That one was Snecky's idea. Heather still wasn't buying the botched burglary story, but there was no point in trying to steer the DCI away from his chosen course of action.

Besides, it would keep him out of her hair.

It had also given her an idea of her own. Shuggie Cowan wasn't the only one who knew about all the shady shite going down. There was someone else who had his ear to the ground, too.

And, she knew, he would be far less of a challenge to break.

FIFTEEN

THE BLADE in his hand was glossy and slick with blood. It meandered along the curved cutting edge, droplets spilling one by one onto the faded vinyl floor.

"Conn? You've got a visitor."

No response.

"Christ's sake. *Conn!*"

Conny Byrne turned sharply, the knife still clutched in one hand, while the fingers of the other yanked an AirPod from one ear.

"Sorry?" he asked in a heavy Irish accent. He adjusted his blue hairnet. "Did you say something?"

The duty manager, a thirty-something woman with an eating disorder that had whittled her away to almost nothing, stepped aside to let one of the chefs pass by.

"I said, you've got a visitor," she said, and her displeasure about this fact was written all over the bony right angles of her face.

"A visitor?" Conn asked. He placed the knife in the dishwasher alongside the others. "Who the hell would be coming here to see me?"

———

"Ah, shite, no, no. Nope. Not doing this," Conn said, pulling a crisp about-turn towards the back door of the restaurant.

"Aye, you are," Heather told him. "Unless you want us to go in there and tell your boss about some of your past exploits."

"You can't! Don't do that! No. I just got this job!" Conn turned back to her, and there was genuine panic in his eyes.

He was a good-looking young lad. Too handsome for his own good, sometimes. Those looks and that winning smile of his had landed him in a lot of bother over the years, most lately beneath the boot of one Shuggie Cowan.

Of course, Heather looked at him differently these days, ever since she'd been subjected to the *OnlyFans* video that Conn had reluctantly appeared in alongside a geriatric dressed as a much-loved *Disney* character. That sort of thing could really change your impressions of a person.

"I've gone straight now. I'm not into anything dodgy, I swear," he insisted.

He stumbled over the last few words and stopped talking completely when, standing among the overfilled bin bags and damp cardboard boxes gathered around the restaurant's rear entrance, he saw DC Swanney.

Were he a cartoon character, Heather thought, his tongue would have rolled all the way out and down to the floor, and his eyes would've immediately become throbbing pink love hearts. As he wasn't, though, he just stood there staring, a look of genuine shock on his face, like he was having some sort of profound religious experience.

Or possibly a haemorrhage of some description.

"What?" he asked, as if responding to something that no one had actually said. "No, not... I mean... Who is...? How did...?"

Heather sighed. "Detective Constable Swanney, Conn

Byrne. Conn's a regular pain in my arse, and... What, Conn? An associate? An employee? A lackey of Karina Novikov."

Tammi-Jo nodded sagely. "I see," she said, then her confidence fell away. "I don't know who that is."

"I'm not. Not anymore," Conn said, tearing his eyes away from the DC long enough to respond to Heather's remark. "After what happened, I quit."

"You quit?"

"Yeah."

Heather zipped her leather jacket up a little higher. The rain was off, but the narrow alleyway at the back of the row of eateries was acting like a wind tunnel, blasting them with gusts of cold air.

"What, you just handed in your notice to a Russian gangster, and she accepted it, did she?"

"Pretty much," Conn said. "She seemed alright with it."

"Aye, well, you always struck me as a bit of a useless bastard," Heather told him. "No great loss to her, I suppose."

"I'm not," Conn said, aiming the denial at Tammi-Jo. "I was good. I was really good."

"At what?" Heather asked. "What were you doing for her, exactly?"

Conn almost walked right into it. The reply made it all the way to his mouth, but never quite managed to emerge.

"No comment," he said.

"Jesus, not you, too?" Heather said.

A seagull swooped down from one of the rooftops and splashed into a puddle beside her. Its beady eyes examined the bin bags for a moment, then it strutted towards the closest one and pecked at it with an inquisitive beak.

"What do you know about what happened in Kilmarnock yesterday?" Heather asked.

"Nothing. Why? What happened in Kilmarnock yesterday?"

Heather stamped a foot. It made Conn jump in fright, and

sent the seagull flapping frantically into the air, a chunk of something bloody and gristly dangling from its mouth.

"Let's not play games, Conn. You're a nosy wee bastard. You hear things." Heather took a step closer. She and the lad were about the same height, but she may as well have towered above him. "You can share those things with me here, or you can do it at the station. It's your call."

"No, don't. I can't lose this job. And I don't know anything about nothing, I mean it."

Heather sighed through her gritted teeth. "Fine. Station it is," she said, grabbing him by the arm.

"I don't know anything! Please, I need this job."

Before Heather could drag him away, Tammi-Jo stepped into their path. "Please, Conn. If there's anything you can tell us, even just a little thing, even just something that might not seem important, then it would really help us out. We'd *really* appreciate it."

The detective constable swept a loose strand of blonde hair back over her ear.

"*I'd* really appreciate it."

Holding onto him, Heather felt the precise moment that the young man's legs turned to jelly. He babbled out something that wasn't quite a word, but was more than just a noise, then swallowed hard and tried again.

"I mean…" He groaned. "I take it you're talking about that copper who was killed?"

Heather released her grip on his arm. "Go on."

"I don't know much. Nothing really," he said.

"Anything would be a big help," Tammi-Jo told him, and when the DC smiled, Heather felt it safest to grab Conn by the arm again, if only to stop him falling over. "Even the slightest little thing."

Conn scratched at the back of his head. He looked tormented, his sense of loyalty and self-preservation locked in battle with his surging levels of testosterone.

"I don't know how true it is, right? It's just something I heard."

"Well, come on, then. Spit it out," Heather told him. "We haven't got all day."

Conn took a deep breath. It was a bold move, considering they were surrounded by festering restaurant garbage, and his face almost immediately registered his regret.

"Mickey Buttfuck," he announced.

The tip of Heather's tongue flitted across her lips. Her eyebrows rose.

"I'm sorry?"

"Mickey Buttfuck," Conn said again, putting real emphasis on the surname this time.

Heather's eyebrows changed direction until they were nestled at either side of the top of her nose.

"What's that? It's not another *Mingey Mouse* thing, is it? Oh, Conn, you've not been making yourself the filling in a Mickey and Minnie sandwich, have you?" Heather asked. "What are you going to do next, get reamed by the *Rescue Rangers*?"

"No! It's not..." Conn shot DC Swanney a sideways look. "It's nothing like that. Mickey Buttfuck is some ex-gangster guy. He's an old mate of Shuggie's, I think."

"Shuggie doesn't have friends."

"Well, whatever they are, I think they go way back."

"Never heard of him," Heather replied.

"No, well, he's from down south somewhere. London or something. And he's keeping a low profile, isn't he? Lost a lot of money a while back, did some time. He's out now, though, and trying to keep his nose clean, so he moved up here."

"To Glasgow?" Heather asked.

"I don't know where, exactly. I've not been invited to one of his dinner parties, have I? I just know he's up around here somewhere."

"Right. And?"

"And what?" Conn asked.

"And what the hell's 'Mickey Buttfuck' got to do with anything? And why's he called... In fact, no. Don't answer that."

"I don't know," Conn said. "I just heard the name mentioned. Connected to what happened, I mean. In Killie. It might be nothing. It probably is. It's probably not even worth bothering with. And that's all I know, I swear."

A thought struck him then. Heather could watch it dawning on him by the way his face changed. He turned to Tammi-Jo, who had been scribbling notes in her pad.

"But, eh, maybe you should give me your number, in case I think of anything else. Something might pop in there during the night, and I could give you a call to—"

"Aye, nice try, Casanova," Heather said. She gestured to the door behind him. "Away you go and get back to your dishes."

"But what if I remember something? Or hear more?" Conn asked. "I should probably take a number, and I don't want to be bothering a DI...?"

Heather slapped a hand against his chest, then pinned a business card there with one finger.

"It's not a bother, Conn. If you think of anything, you feel free to give this number a ring, day or night, and someone will be happy to listen to you."

Conn took the card, stared forlornly at the 0131 number printed on it, then slipped it into the pocket of his dirty chef's jacket.

"Eh, yeah. OK. Will do," he mumbled.

"Thanks again for all your help," Tammi-Jo said, beaming radiantly at him. "I really do appreciate it."

Conn perked up at that. "Right. OK! Great! Well, maybe—"

Heather pulled open the door at his back. "Goodbye, Conn," she said. "Time you fucked off."

The lad's face fell again. With a sigh, and a final lingering look at DC Swanney, he turned and trudged back inside the restaurant.

Heather let the door swing closed behind him, then turned to Tammi-Jo. "You did all that on purpose, didn't you? You absolutely knew what you were doing there."

The detective constable blinked her brilliant blue eyes and hooked that troublesome strand of stray hair back over her ear again.

"I'm sorry, Detective Inspector," she said, with an impenetrable level of innocence. "I don't know *what* you could be talking about..."

SIXTEEN

"WHO'S MICKEY BUTTFUCK?" Heather demanded, striding through the muscled knot of henchmen until she was standing over Shuggie Cowan's favourite table, glaring down at the bastard.

"Just you come on in, Detective Inspector," Shuggie told her. "I'm glad you're here, actually. Kevin here would like to lodge a complaint against one of your officers."

Heather followed the nod of the gangster's head and found herself gazing up into the blackened eyes and squint nose of a man in his late thirties.

"Some blonde piece, the boys tell me. Wee lassie. Smashed his face in, with no provocation whatsoever."

There was some sniggering from the other men. The ratio of red to blue in Kevin's bruising shifted ever so slightly towards the former.

"You know anything about that, Detective Inspector?"

"Nope, not a clue," Heather said. "Mickey Buttfuck. Who is he?"

Shuggie shrugged. "Nope," he said, a smile playing across his lips. "Not a clue."

"Fine. Maybe your daughter's heard of him. Maybe I'll go

pay her a visit. Bring her in even, if she plays dumb. Hope she can arrange a babysitter."

The silence that fell was so heavy it had almost a physical heft to it. All humour drained from Cowan's expression, leaving only a cold, narrow-eyed stare.

"You lot," he said, addressing it to his men, but not looking at them. "Fuck off. You know what you're doing."

Nobody breathed a word. As one, they turned and shuffled away, filing out through the front door and onto the street outside.

For a moment, Heather worried she shouldn't have left Tammi-Jo sitting out there alone again, but by the sounds of things, she'd handled herself pretty admirably last time.

Besides, Shuggie's goons had been given an order. They wouldn't risk deviating from that.

She just wished she knew what the order was.

"You don't come in here and start threatening my family. Alright?" the gangster said.

To Heather's surprise, there was no venom behind his words. He spoke them almost matter-of-factly. This wasn't a threat, she realised, it was a cold, hard statement of fact.

"Then tell me who he is," Heather urged.

Shuggie's chair let out a low, ominous creak as he adjusted his not-inconsiderable weight.

"He's someone with concerns."

"Concerns? About what?"

"About the welfare of his daughter."

Heather hesitated as a row of dots all joined up in her head.

A telescope.

A *Barbie* quilt.

MB Property.

"What do you mean?" she asked.

Shuggie rolled his tongue around inside his mouth. It made a horrible, wet, clicking sound that made Heather's nostrils flare in disgust.

"He's a decent lad. Got himself into a bit of bother down south. Came up here to start fresh. Him, his missus, and his little girl. Cute wee button of a thing."

"Surprised he's got a kid with a name like that," Heather said when Cowan fell silent again.

Shuggie snorted a half-laugh. "I mean, I don't the know the origins. I've never asked. But women have arses, too."

"Aye, but they don't usually produce weans out of them," Heather replied. She nodded to him, urging him to continue. "Go on."

"Right. Aye. So, he's out the back one day. Couple of days back. Minding his own business. It's late on. He's sitting out, watching the sun going down, having a drink while the wife puts the wee one to bed."

Shuggie leaned forwards and lowered his voice a little, like he was getting to the good part of his story.

"And what does he see? Someone watching. Someone spying from a nearby window. Some dirty nonce bastard staring right into that cute wee button's bedroom window while she's getting changed. Standing there watching, tugging himself off."

Heather raised a sceptical eyebrow. "How would he know he was tugging himself off?"

"Well, what else would he be doing? Dirty fucking nonce like that. Trying to get a read of her bedtime story? No. Wanking." Shuggie shook his head in contempt and stabbed a finger against the top of the table. "You know it and I know it. He'd have been knocking one out and loving every bloody minute of it."

His face contorted into a scowl, and he drained the dregs from an already empty glass on the table like he was trying to wash a dirty taste away.

"So, anyway, Mickey daren't go round and kick off. Not with his record. Not with him trying to keep his nose clean and stay out of trouble. So, he asks me if I'll have a word. Make my presence felt, sort of thing."

"You and him must've been tight," Heather said. "For him to ask a favour like that."

"Oh, no. Not at all. Slippery wee bastard. Don't trust him as far as I could throw him, although I could probably fucking launch him pretty far."

"So, why come to you?"

"Because I owe him for a spot of trouble I caused him a while back. And because he knows my stance on nonces," Shuggie said. "He knows how I feel about those who prey on little kiddies. But, then, my thoughts on that particular subject should come as no surprise to you, of all people, Detective Inspector."

Heather chewed at a piece of loose skin on her bottom lip, considering her response.

"Aye. I do know, Shuggie. And I know how far you'd go to punish someone you thought fit that bill."

"Oh, no, you really don't," Shuggie told her, and his voice was a low, hollow-sounding rasp. "You've got no idea how far I'd go. No idea the things I'd do."

He left that hanging there in the air between them for a moment, then punctured the tension with a slap on his thigh and a big, beaming smile.

"But in this case, I just had Gonad have a word, then wander up and down outside his house for a couple of hours, making it clear that he was being watched. The spy had become"—uncertainty flashed across the gangster's face—"the spyee."

"That's not a thing," Heather told him. "Do you have a number for the guy?"

"For Mickey Buttfuck?" Shuggie snorted. "Aye, I've got three." He sat back in his chair, crossed his arms over his broad chest, and smirked. "But there's not a fucking chance I'm giving any of them to you."

SEVENTEEN

CONSTABLE DARRYL HARTMANN shut off the engine of his squad car and opened the door just a crack. The low, squat, white building in front of him stood shuttered and silent, the pockmarked car park beside it devoid of any vehicles.

He radioed back to base, letting them know he was on the scene, but that there was no sign of the reported ned action, and if the alarm had been ringing, it had stopped now.

"Just give it a quick check-over," the voice on the radio instructed. "Might as well belt-and-braces it."

Daz confirmed that he'd take a look, then climbed out of the car and pulled on his cap.

The Molendinar Community Centre was a council-owned building on the north side of Blackhill, one of Glasgow's less affluent areas. The folks running the place were doing good work in the area, by all accounts, but that wouldn't deter any of the local bams from breaking in and smashing the place up.

If anything, it'd only encourage some of them.

He had a quick look around before leaving the immediate vicinity of the car. There were streets here where just wearing a high-vis vest would be enough to get you into trouble, regardless of whether you were actually on the force or not.

The community centre was tucked away out of sight, too. If there did turn out to be a squad of neds hanging around out the back of the place and they all kicked off, he'd be on his own.

Just to be on the safe side, he took out his baton and held it ready by his side.

His footsteps crunched on the patches of grass and weeds that had forced their way through the cracks in the car park's tarmac. That suited him fine. He wasn't interested in stealth. If he was stealthy, he might surprise them, and the last thing you ever wanted to do was startle a gaggle of wild neds.

If they were there, better to let them know he was coming. With a bit of luck, they'd do a runner, and he could stand shaking his fist at them until they were safely no longer his problem.

Of course, the ideal situation would be to find there was nobody there at all. That was the dream. The call had come in just as he'd finished taking a statement from a woman around the corner. Someone had been shitting on her doorstep for weeks, and she'd finally had enough.

She'd collected it in bags—clear plastic freezer bags with a zip-lock top—which she'd proceeded to hand him as evidence. There were fourteen bags in total, the shapes and sizes of the contents covering almost the entire spectrum of the Bristol Stool Chart.

Daz had tried to contest that the 'samples' she'd gathered may not have been human, until she'd showed him a couple with big dauds of dirty bog roll pressed into them, and he'd been forced to concede the point.

It was her ex-husband, she reckoned. He'd always been a clarty bastard, and this sort of thing would be right up his street.

He lived in Galashiels now—a three-hour round trip by car

—so it would be a hell of a commute just to take a dump on a doorstep, but the woman was adamant that this wouldn't dissuade him in the slightest.

He'd eventually taken away the collected evidence in a big Asda Bag for Life, which she'd made him pay her the thirty pence for. He'd happily done it just to get out of there.

The call had come just as he'd locked the big bag of shite in the boot of the car. He was less than two minutes away, so he'd driven past the community centre a couple of times to suss it out, then had pulled in when it seemed unlikely that backup would be needed.

Of course, you never knew for sure. A place might look safe enough, but you never knew who might be lurking inside. Or how many.

His fingers adjusted their grip on his baton. He noisily cleared his throat as he approached the corner of the building. A few more steps and he'd get a clear view of the back, and of anyone who might be lurking there.

A few breaths were taken to loosen the knot of dread in his stomach, then Daz stepped around the corner into full view.

"Oh, thank Christ," he whispered, finding the back of the building clear. There were some scattered fag ends and a couple of empty *Buckie* bottles—clear signs of some recent ned action—but the coast, for now, was clear.

The shutters on the rear windows were solid, too. Nobody had tried to force them. Or, if they had, they hadn't tried hard enough.

Daz raised a hand and patted the wall, like he was clapping a well-mannered horse.

He retracted and holstered his baton, put a thumb to the button of his radio, and turned to head back to the car.

A blade slid up beneath his stab-proof vest. Sharp. Sudden. Tearing upwards through his bowel and into his stomach.

It twisted. Wrenched. Pulled free with a sickening *shlurp*.

Daz heard something wet and heavy splattering onto the

ground. He raised his arms to defend himself, but they were already weakening, the pain pulling him down, dragging him to the floor.

He was on his knees. On his hands. The wet ground warm against his palms.

It was only when he felt the fingers grabbing at his hair that he realised he'd lost his hat.

Where was his hat? He needed his hat.

Daz's head was yanked back. The edge of the blade was pressed against his throat, though it was too sharp, and he was already too far gone to feel it.

A voice hissed in his ear. Harsh. Cruel.

"Not such a big man now, are you, *pig*?"

And then, the knife slid sideways. A line of red appeared across pale flesh.

And what remained of Constable Darryl Hartmann pooled as a dark puddle on the broken, uneven ground.

EIGHTEEN

SURE ENOUGH, Tammi-Jo was safe and sound when Heather returned to the car, although she had adjusted her seat a little too far back and was now struggling to get it back into a comfortable position.

The electric motor in the mechanism *whirred* quietly in short little spurts, and the Detective Constable narrated the whole process below her breath as Heather called up the contact on her phone and tapped DS Marty Brompton's name.

There was a crackle as the audio transferred to the Audi's speaker system, and a ringing sound filled the car. Heather shot Tammi-Jo a sideways look, and watched as the DC folded herself a few inches too far forward.

"Nope. That's not it, either," Tammi-Jo muttered.

The ringing ended, and Marty's voice chirped an enthusiastic, "Hello!"

"Marty. It's me."

"Aye, I know. Your name comes up," the detective sergeant reminded her. "What's up?"

Tammi-Jo's chair jerked sharply backwards, making her grab for the dashboard.

Heather did her best to ignore her.

"You heard of a Mickey Buttfuck?" she asked.

"No! But I'm all ears," Marty replied.

She filled him in on what she knew, and agreed when he'd expressed his doubts about Tony Crier having an interest in prepubescent girls.

But then...

"He had a telescope," she said. "In his bedroom. You could see a girl's bedroom through it."

The silence lasted so long that Heather started to think the call had dropped. Marty's reply came just before she could ask if he was still there.

"Bloody hell."

"Aye. Anyway, find out what you can, will you? And try and keep Snecky out of it for now."

"Of course," the DS replied. Keeping DCI Grant out of the loop until absolutely necessary had pretty much become standard practice for him and the DI. If it wasn't for DC Wolfe, Snecky would rarely get to hear about anything.

"How are the interviews going?"

"What interviews?" Marty asked.

Heather glanced at DC Swanney, who was now struggling at a forty-five-degree angle, then back to the stereo. The bursts of *whirring* from the seat's motor continued.

"We were meant to be rounding up some of the local scallywags. The ones with previous," Heather reminded the DS.

"Oh. Yeah. Sorry. Uniform's out doing them now. Snecky thought it would be a better use of resources to have them handle the first round of interviews, then we could read them over and see if we want anyone else brought in for a follow-up."

"So, he couldn't be arsed doing it," Heather translated.

"Basically, yes. Though, to be fair, we're not exactly brimming with staff."

"Suppose not," Heather conceded. She checked the clock on the dashboard. Then, having been burned once before, checked her watch. "Right, I need to head back down the road if I'm going to talk to the ironing woman. You got everything in hand?"

"As always."

"Don't pull another all-nighter," the DI told him. "That's an order. I'll let you know what I hear from this woman, but then we'll regroup in the morning. Alright?"

It was for her own sake, she knew, that she said that. Once, she'd have been the one insisting that everyone stay late with her while they worked a case. Eighteen-hour days had not been uncommon and had rarely been optional.

But now, with her dad, those hours didn't work for her. Suddenly, she was all about the work-life balance.

She'd say it was a big change in her, but it really wasn't. Her needs came first then, and they came first now. It was just the needs themselves that were different.

She concluded, as she so often did, that she was a massive piece of shit.

"Whatever you say, boss," Marty replied.

After some brief farewells, Heather started the engine, just as Tammi-Jo let out a joyful little cheer.

"I've got it!" she said, her chair now fully upright again. A line formed on her brow, and she reached for the controls again. "Although, actually—"

"Leave it!" Heather barked, and the DC whipped her hand away from the controls like they were toxic to the touch. "You got a hotel sorted yet?"

"Yes!" Tammi-Jo replied, with an enthusiasm that waned as quickly as it had risen. "No, I mean. I mean, no. I haven't."

"Why did you say yes, then?"

"Because I knew there was something I was supposed to be doing, but I'd forgotten what it was. I was like, 'Yes! That's what it is,' but I can see how you might have thought I meant, "Yes! I've booked a hotel.' Which, I haven't. Though, I meant to."

"But you forgot."

"But I forgot," the DC confirmed. She smiled sheepishly, then looked up and down the street, turning in her seat so she could see. "Are there hotels?"

Heather frowned. "What, in Glasgow?"

"Yes. I mean, obviously there must be some. I'm assuming. But do you know any?"

Something occurred to Heather then. A question popped into her head that she had never thought to ask anyone before.

"Have you...? You have been to Glasgow before, aye?"

"Of course!" Tammi-Jo laughed.

"Right. Good. Thank God," Heather said, relaxing back into her seat.

"We went to see a panto. At a theatre. There were people in it off the telly!"

Heather stared back at her for a few long, silent seconds. "Right," she eventually said. "And when was this?"

"Ooh. I must've been..." Tammi-Jo bit her bottom lip in concentration. She stared ahead along the street, like she was peering back through the mists of time. "Eight?"

"You were eight?" Heather asked.

"About that."

"And that's the only time you've been here? That's the only time in your life you've been to Glasgow?"

"Are we including now?"

Heather's reply was quite emphatic. "No. We're not including now."

"Then yes," Tammi-Jo said. "Just that one time. But, I'm told the panto was very good. I don't remember much about it myself, but from what I hear, it was a big hit."

Once again, Heather was momentarily lost for words. They'd sent her a detective constable with no experience of Glasgow. Literally none.

There was no way this was ending well.

"Great!" was all she could think to say. "Well, I'm glad it wasn't a complete waste of time, then."

"Wait, no!" Tammi-Jo cried, sitting forward. "That's not true!"

"What, was it rubbish? They usually are."

"No, I mean about me visiting Glasgow!"

"Oh?" Heather brightened a little.

Tammi-Jo nodded happily. "I was *six*, not eight!"

"Right. Aye. Fair enough." Heather checked her mirrors and clicked on her indicator. "Listen, if you want, you can crash at mine again tonight, and find somewhere tomorrow. But I need to go see the ironing woman first."

Tammi-Jo considered the offer. "Will I have to sit in the car again? Or can I come in?"

Heather pulled the car away from the kerb. "Fine, you can come in," she conceded. "But only to stop you pissing about with all my buttons."

———

"Holy moly!" Tammi-Jo remarked, as Heather pulled her Audi onto the driveway of a sprawling detached house a couple of miles to the northwest of Killie. "I'm guessing there must be some pretty good money in ironing."

The car's headlights picked out the details of the house in the gathering autumnal darkness.

It was an old grey stone number, with a double garage at one side, and a modern wood and glass extension sticking out from the other in a way that was almost, but not quite, all the way tasteful. It had been set back from the road that connected Kilmarnock and Kilmaurs, and sat surrounded by fields on all sides.

A small van was parked in front of the garage, an 'Iron Woman' logo on the side confirming that they had come to the right place.

"Aye, but is it worth it?" Heather asked. "I mean, I barely iron my own stuff. Can't imagine doing some other bugger's."

"My dad did all my ironing," Tammi-Jo said. "He liked it. Said he used to do it in the army. And, I suppose, if you're going to take a habit from the army away with you, ironing's probably quite a good one. Better than, you know, machine-gunning people to death, anyway."

Heather tilted her head left and right, weighing up which of the two struck her as worse.

"I don't know if he *did* machine-gun anyone," Tammi-Jo said. "I'm just saying, in general, if you're going to take any habit away from your military service, it might as well be one that has some practical use beyond mass murder or—Oh, we're going? Is that us going, is it?"

She unclipped her belt and scrambled to catch up with Heather, who was already striding up the gravel drive in the direction of the house.

"I didn't know we were going yet!"

She caught up with Heather just as the DI rang the doorbell. Inside the house, a series of bells chimed grandiosely.

"Even that sounds expensive," Tammi-Jo whispered.

"Yeah," Heather said, watching the door.

They waited.

Tammi-Jo grinned. "Imagine it's little people."

Heather sighed, then turned to look at her. "What?" she asked flatly.

"Ringing the bells. Inside. Imagine it's little people."

The smile on her face suggested this was the most joyous thought she'd ever had. Heather, however, did not share her appreciation for it.

"It's a doorbell. It's not little people."

"I mean, no, obviously. I know it's not *actually* little people. But imagine it was."

"Like dwarfs?"

Tammi-Jo shook her head. "Smaller. Borrowers. No, bigger than Borrowers. What's between a dwarf and a Borrower?"

Heather didn't even bother trying to answer that. Instead, she turned back to the door and peered through the frosted glass.

"Oompa Loompa, maybe?" Tammi-Jo mused.

There was no sign of movement from inside. Heather knocked this time, really putting some welly behind it. The harsh rat-a-tat-tat stung her knuckles.

Another sound rang out from over on their right. It was the high-pitched squeak of a push-up garage door opening. A woman with a wild mop of silver hair leaned out just enough so only her head was visible.

"Can I help you?" she asked.

There was no attitude behind it, or even any sense of authority. The woman sounded so uncertain that Heather wondered if this was even her house. Maybe she was a cleaner, or something, giving the place a tidy-up while the owners were out.

"We're looking for…" Heather wished she'd bothered to learn the woman's name. "Um, the ironing woman."

"The Iron Woman," the lady in the garage corrected, then she stepped out, revealing a black and white dress and pinafore combo that skirted quite close to a 'saucy maid' outfit, but stopped just within the realms of decency.

She seemed self-conscious about the outfit, and pulled down on the hem, trying to lengthen it.

There was a bandage on her forearm, crisp and white, like it had only recently been applied. When she realised that Heather had spotted it, she tucked both arms behind her back.

"Who are you?" she asked.

Heather held up her ID. "Detective Inspector Filson. This is Detective Constable Swanney."

"Is this about Mr Crier?"

"It is," Heather confirmed. She returned her warrant card to the inside pocket of her leather jacket. "You mind if we ask you a few questions?"

The Iron Woman glanced along the driveway. Heather's car had blocked in the van. If the woman wanted to do a runner, she'd be doing it on foot.

"OK. If you have to," she said. She beckoned to them, indicating that they should join her in the garage. "But it'll have to be quick. I've got a lot to get through."

NINETEEN

ACE STOOD at the garden gate for a few moments, running through a few alternative routes that her upcoming conversation might take. A few of them ended badly, so that wasn't good. Some ended in a fairly neutral way, and one—just one— worked out well for her.

That one involved her being asked to join the official police investigation team in an advisory capacity and was, she reluctantly had to admit, the least likely outcome of them all.

Still, anything was possible.

Just probably not that.

"Right," she whispered, opening the gate. "Knock. Wait. Ask if there are any plans to arrest me, then go from there. Yes. Right. Knock, wait, ask. Knock, wait, ask."

She repeated it like a mantra all the way up the path until she reached the door.

She knocked.

She waited.

So far, so good.

She waited a bit longer.

Then a bit longer, still.

This wasn't part of the plan. In the plan, Heather was at

home. If she wasn't, then the plan was ruined. It would have fallen at the very first hurdle.

It was going off script, but Ace decided to knock again. Knocking again, she decided, wasn't an alteration of the plan, it was a reset.

She knocked.

She waited.

This time, she heard a sound from within. That was encouraging.

A moment later, she saw movement through the door's frosted glass.

OK, this was good. This was better. Knocking again had been completely the right call.

"Knock, wait, ask. Knock, wait, ask," she whispered.

The door handle turned. She started to speak even before the door was open.

"I need to know, Officer, if you have any plans to—"

The figure standing there was not DI Heather Filson. It was an old man in grotty pyjamas, who gazed down at her in a way that didn't seem to be all the way present in the moment. Ace was dimly aware that this was the DI's father.

"Are you the woman?" he asked.

Ace didn't feel she had all the necessary information to answer the question.

"Am I which woman?"

"The woman. The one who does my breakfast."

"Breakfast? It's almost five PM. Breakfast was hours ago."

Heather's father looked worried by this news. "Did I already have it?"

"I have no idea."

Scott slid a hand up under his pyjama top and scratched at his belly. His eyes were studying Ace's face, searching it like he was hunting for something familiar to latch onto. Something that would tell him who this stranger was.

"Are you the woman?" he asked again. "She was meant to

be here. Are you the woman?" He looked away, unable to hold her eye. "I need the shower. I need someone to help me in the shower. There's a mess."

Ace decided not to delve too deeply into that remark.

"OK, three things. One, I am not 'the woman.' Sorry about that. Two, I'm fifteen, so it would be inappropriate for me to help you into the shower, regardless of the size or amount of mess involved. In fact, more so, because of that. But, three…"

She looked back over her shoulder, like she could see right through the row of houses standing across from Heather's front door.

"Luckily for both of us, I may have a much better idea."

TWENTY

THE IRON WOMAN had not been exaggerating when she said she had a lot to get through. The garage was lined along the two longest walls with basket after basket of crumpled clothing waiting to be pressed.

At the back of the converted space, a dozen or more large canvas bags were filled with much neater and more carefully folded garments, and thirty or forty shirts and dresses hung from a rack behind them.

A large ironing board had been set up in the middle of the room, with another couple standing folded and propped up against a side wall.

An iron sat on a stand on top of the board, the water inside lightly hissing and popping as it turned to steam.

A second iron stood upright on the draining board of a little sink, like an understudy waiting in the wings for its chance to shine.

There were a couple of hooks affixed to one of the walls, presumably for storing ironing boards.

"That's a lot of clothes," Heather remarked, as the garage door was pulled shut behind them. The smell of forest pine detergent made the place smell fresh and clean. "I take it business is good?"

"Yes. It is. Thank you," the woman confirmed. Her eyes flitted left and right, her gaze darting anxiously between both detectives. "I'm very busy. I doubt I know anything. I don't think I can help. I don't know anything."

"That's fine," Heather told her. She could see that the woman was wound tight, her defences raised. Handle this the wrong way, and she might well completely clam up. "It's just checking a few details for our records. That's all."

"Oh. Right. Well, as long as it's quick…" She gestured around at the stacks of ironing waiting to be done, and there was a squeak of desperation in her voice. "It just keeps piling up. Never-ending."

"Rather you than me," Heather said. "I can't iron to save my life."

She looked down at the front of the black shirt she had been wearing for the past two days, and realised she needn't have bothered announcing that fact, given the already very visible evidence.

"Oh, I never bother with my own stuff," the woman replied. "Too much hassle."

"They say that, don't they?" Tammi-Jo said, inserting herself into the conversation. "If you do something professionally, the last thing you want to do when you're done working is the same thing again. Like, chefs. A lot of them don't want to cook at home. Same with painters and decorators, or…"

She fell silent, racking her brain for another example.

"Anyway," Heather began, turning back to the Iron Woman.

"Proctologists," Tammi-Jo announced, triumphantly.

"*Anyway*," Heather stressed. "Sorry, I don't know your name. I've just got you down as 'The Iron Woman.'"

"Ha! That's fair enough. That's all I really am. But it's Selma. Selma Baird."

Selma. That was it. Heather remembered seeing it in the notes now.

Selma Baird, thirty-something. Six?

She looked older than that. A decade or more.

Her makeup was partly to blame. She'd layered it on thick, like she was hiding behind it.

Or maybe hiding something under it.

"What happened to your arm?" Heather asked.

Selma didn't so much as glance at the bandage before replying. "Burned it. It happens. One of the downsides of this job." She forced a smile that felt like it was entirely for the detectives' benefit. "Well, that and the actual job itself. That's a pretty big downside. But it pays the bills. Just."

"Big house to pay bills on," Heather said. "You on your own?"

"Since I kicked my husband out, yes," Selma replied, though there was a microscopic pause before the answer came. "Eighteen months shot of the bastard now. I fought for the house to spite him. Though, with the mortgage, the bills, and the council tax, I'm not actually sure who got the last laugh."

Heather checked to make sure that Tammi-Jo had her notebook out, then dove into the questioning.

"I believe you were doing some ironing for Tony Crier?"

The name struck the other woman like a slap across the face. Her cheeks paled, and she swallowed before nodding a reply.

"Yes. Just a wee bundle once a week. Not much. Bedsheets every month or so, but otherwise just shirts and trousers, really."

"You do those at his?"

"Yes. Sometimes. Not always. Sometimes I bring it here, but when it's only a small amount, sometimes it's easier to just rattle through it there," Selma explained. "And I think he likes the company."

"And what about yesterday? Were you going round to iron there?"

"Uh, no. Not yesterday. I was dropping off a couple of bags."

"Right. Got you," Heather said. "And you just normally walk in, do you?"

Selma blinked rapidly like the realisation that she might be a suspect had suddenly hit her.

"Not always, no. But he works odd hours sometimes, so he leaves a key under one of them rocks in the garden. Not a fake one. He didn't see the point when he had actual proper rocks. He keeps it under the big one. I didn't get an answer, so I got the key and let myself in."

She picked at the edge of her bandage and took a deep breath, clearly working up to something.

"How is he? Mr Crier? How is he doing now? What are they saying?"

She didn't know. She hadn't heard. Heather paid very close attention to the woman's reaction.

"I'm afraid he didn't make it."

The bandaged arm raised, shaking. A hand covered her mouth and nose, like she couldn't bear anyone seeing it.

"Oh, God. Oh, no. Oh, no."

The hand clamped across her mouth. Heather recognised the panic in the woman's eyes, and quickly side-stepped, clearing the path to the sink.

Selma bolted, her insides heaving, forcing the contents of her stomach up through her throat, through her mouth, through her fingers. One of the nearby baskets caught some of the spray, staining the garments piled up on top.

And then, with a *splatter*, her half-digested breakfast was deposited unceremoniously into the sink.

While Selma continued to boak and retch over the sink, Heather took the opportunity to have a better look around. There was a solid-looking door leading from the garage into the house, and a small window at the back of the space that let a bit of light in. Three metal bars ran horizontally across it, so anyone trying to break in would have their work cut out for them.

Between that and the camera affixed up near the ceiling at the back wall, it was clear that Selma had concerns about security. Then again, there were probably thousands of pounds worth of clothes in here, so it made sense.

The floor was concrete, but some rubberised tiles had been laid across part of it to form a pathway from one end of the garage to the other.

Now that she was looking more closely, Heather could see there was a washing machine and a tumble drier right up the back of the room, half-hidden behind the racks of shirts and dresses.

Other than that, though, there wasn't much to report. The place was clearly used for ironing, and not a whole lot else.

Over by the sink, Selma straightened, wiped her face on a threadbare towel, then turned on the tap.

Nothing happened.

"Oh, not now," she croaked, giving the tap a waggle back and forth. "Please, not now."

"Everything alright?" Heather asked.

The smell of the vomit had already started to lace the air, overpowering the pine-fresh scent of the detergent.

It wasn't a big problem—one thing you rapidly got used to in the police was the smell of other people's puke—but she'd rather not be breathing it in if it could be avoided.

"The water's off. It, uh, it does that sometimes," Selma explained. "I've been meaning to get it fixed for ages."

"You have a dog," Tammi-Jo said.

It was more of a statement than a question, and came so out of the blue that the other two women both turned to look at her.

"No," Selma said, though she looked a little uncertain on the matter. "I don't."

"Oh! Right!" The detective constable pointed to a metal bowl on the floor with a dribble of water left at the bottom. "It's just, I saw that…"

Selma stared at the bowl like it was a smoking gun in her hand. It took her a few seconds to offer a response.

"Oh. That. No. A couple of my clients, when they're dropping a load off, they have their dogs with them. It gets hot in here with the machines on, so I put out some water."

"The dogs come in?" Heather asked.

Selma's smile was tissue-thin. "Sometimes. Not often. I keep them away from the clothes. I know some people have allergies, so it wouldn't be… I keep them away."

"Fine." Heather shrugged. "Aye, sure. Not a problem for me."

The aroma of *L'eau d'Vomette* was really starting to spread out from the sink now. Any minute now, it would hit the back of her throat, and switch from a smell to a taste.

Time to crack on, then.

"Can you tell me what happened when you got to Tony Crier's house?" Heather asked.

But then, before she could answer, Selma's whole body started to vibrate, starting with the shoulders and rapidly working its way down. The Iron Woman buried her face in her hands and barely managed to squeeze a few words out through her breathless, throaty sobs.

"Oh, I have to say it. I have to tell you! I can't keep lying!"

Heather and Tammi-Jo swapped looks. Despite the smell of sick, the DI took a step closer.

"Tell us what, Selma?" she prompted. "What is it you want to say?"

There were a few more sniffles. A low, pained groan.

And then, through a gap in her fingers, her wide, bloodshot

eyes met Heather's. "I did something," she whispered. "I did something terrible."

"OK. OK, I'm sure it's fine," Heather said, like she was talking someone down off a ledge. "Whatever it is, we can deal with it, alright?"

The bandage caught her eye. A scratch, maybe? A bruise where Tony had held her?

She was small enough to get in through the window. If Tony saw a woman at the top of his stairs, he'd be less likely to lash out, giving her time to attack.

And coming back to the scene in the morning, compromising it like that, would explain any DNA discoveries.

But could she do that amount of damage to a man? Heather doubted she had it in her, let alone the physical strength it would take.

Maybe, if she was angry enough, if she had a strong enough motivation.

"I took money."

The remark derailed the DI's train of thought. She shot a look at Tammi-Jo, who seemed equally as surprised.

"What? What money?" Heather asked.

Selma sucked in an unsteady sob. "Off the mantelpiece. He usually leaves it out for me. Thirty pounds. It was there. I saw it when I was waiting for the ambulance, and I just... I took it. I lifted it. I went and lifted it, even when he was lying there! I just took it!"

"Is that it?" Heather asked. "You took thirty quid?"

If Selma heard her, she didn't let on. She ran across to the opposite wall, where a handbag had been carefully tucked in against the skirting. Snatching it up, she rummaged inside until she found a small handful of banknotes.

"There. That's it. I shouldn't have touched it, I'm sorry, I'm so sorry, but he usually leaves it out for me, and I knew it was mine, and I shouldn't have taken it, but I did, and now..."

Her throat closed over and shame burned its mark on her

face. Through tears and trailing snot, she forced the money into Heather's hands, then staggered back, like she was about to collapse.

"I'm sorry. I'm so, so sorry!" she squeaked. She inhaled shakily, building up to asking the question she was almost too afraid to. "What happens now? Do I need to go to jail? I've never done anything like that before, I promise, and I know I shouldn't have. I *know* I shouldn't have, but I did. I did. I took it."

"Whoa, whoa. Calm down. Nobody's going to jail," Heather assured her.

"But I took the money! Off the mantlepiece, I took the money!"

"Yeah. We got that bit. And while, yeah, it was a bit of a shitty thing to do, ultimately? In the grand scheme of things? I couldn't give a shit."

The bluntness of the response immediately made Selma stop sobbing.

"Look, you feel bad enough about it already," Heather continued. "We'll need to hang onto it for now in case it's needed as evidence, but as far as I'm concerned, it's your money. All being well, you'll get it back."

Selma shook her head. "I don't want it. I don't want it back."

"OK, well, whatever," Heather said. "The point is, it doesn't matter. We don't care. All we care about is finding out what happened to Tony. That's all that matters right now. Right?"

Selma sniffed, wiped her eyes on her sleeve, then nodded. "Right. Of course. Yes."

"Good," Heather said. She gestured to the garage door, the choking smell of fresh vomit becoming too much to bear. "Now, how about we crack this open and get some air in here, then you can take us through everything from the beginning?"

TWENTY-ONE

TED CAMPBELL MISSED THE 80S. Which, given that he hadn't been born until 1995, was quite a feat. His parents had both instilled a love of power ballads and New Romanticism in him, though, and the opening chords to *Saint Elmo's Fire* never failed to set a blaze in his belly and force him to whip out the old air guitar.

Sadly, as he was currently doing fifty along the M8, the air guitar wasn't an option. He settled for tapping along with his fingertips, until the chorus kicked in and he had no option but to belt it out at the top of his lungs.

He screeched out the "Saint Elmo's" bit along with the track, then found himself wailing the "Fire" part solo when the sound from the stereo cut off.

A moment later, it was replaced by the *burring* of his phone.

Ted never liked his calls being broadcast over the car stereo. You never knew who might be listening in, although admittedly it was less of an issue while travelling at high speed along a three-lane stretch of motorway.

Still, habit made him search the dashboard until he found his Bluetooth headset. One-handed, he fumbled it on, then tapped the button to answer the call.

"Yo!" he said. "What's up, sis?"

He listened. His fingers, which had still been tapping along to the now-imagined drumbeat in his head, slowed, then stopped.

"Wait, hold on. Hold on. Calm down, calm down," he urged. "Take a breath. What's happened? What's wrong?"

He listened again. His face fell, though he tried not to let it show in his voice.

"It'll be nothing. It'll be fine. It's going to be fine," he said. "No, no, you're not. I mean, yes, you *are* being an idiot, but don't worry about it. It's allowed."

He checked his mirrors, then clocked his watch.

"I'm about twenty minutes away from yours. I'll come round, and we'll get to the bottom of it, alright? But I bet he'll be back before I get there. And if he is, I'll hold Maisie, while you give him hell. Alright?" He smiled. "Alright. OK. It'll be fine. I'll see you soon."

He ended the call. The music returned, but he switched it off, his heart no longer in it.

A knot of dread formed low down in his gut.

"Shit," Ted whispered, then he clicked his indicators, slid out into the fast lane, and put the pedal all the way to the floor.

———

"Is this Mickey BF's house?" Tammi-Jo asked, as Heather pulled the Audi up outside an unremarkable semi-detached house on what could have been any old Kilmarnock street.

"Yeah, this is... Wait. What did you call him?" Heather asked, tapping on the handbrake and turning to the detective constable.

"Mickey BF."

"But that's not his name. His name's not 'Mickey BF.'"

"I don't like swearing," the DC explained. "I mean, I don't mind other people doing it, that's totally fine, I just don't like doing it myself. It feels... I don't want to say 'scummy,' because I don't mean that, though it does a bit, but that's not what I'm saying, I'm just... It's not for me."

Heather adjusted herself in her seat so her back was supported by the inside of the driver's side door. "Say it," she urged. "Say his name."

"Mickey BF."

"No. Say it properly."

Tammi-Jo's nose crinkled, and her mouth puckered up like she'd just bitten into a lemon.

"Mickey..."

"Go on," Heather urged. "You can do it."

"I don't want to do it."

"Just say it!"

"Mickey Bumfudge!" the DC yelped.

A grimace worked its way slowly down Heather's face. "Jesus," she muttered. "I think that might actually be worse."

"It felt worse," Tammi-Jo agreed. "Coming out, it felt worse."

"Then say it properly."

Tammi-Jo's tongue moved around inside her mouth, as if shaping the air into the necessary sounds and syllables.

But then, with a nervous sideways glance, she said, "No. I'm not going to. Sorry."

"Right. Try that again without the apology."

"What?"

Heather's voice raised. "Say it again! Tell me no, but don't apologise!"

"No! No, I'm not going to say the name," Tammi-Jo cried. "I don't want to, so I won't! So... there!"

"Finally!" Heather said.

Tammi-Jo blinked. "You're not angry?"

"No. Jesus. Listen, I'm your boss. I'm not your master. No one is. A lot of people in this job are going to act like they are. They're going to ask you to do things that make you uncomfortable. But you don't have to do them." A flicker of doubt crossed her face. "I mean, sometimes you might, you know, because of the nature of the job, and everything. It can get pretty ropey at times. But..."

Heather looked out of the front window, as if searching for the lost thread of the point she was trying to make.

"Sometimes you don't have to do them. So, you know, don't let anyone force you into those. But *do* do the ones that you need to do. You know what I'm saying?"

Tammi-Jo nodded slowly, but it quite quickly deviated into a sideways shake of the head. "Not really," she admitted. "I mean, I thought I did at the start, and then it sort of got a bit confusing in the middle. Well, from the middle onwards, really. How will I know which ones are which?"

Heather shrugged. "Don't know. I'm still working that out," she said. "You want to see if Mickey Bumfudge is home?"

The DC's eyes widened. "I can come?"

"Yeah, what the hell. You can tag along," Heather said, opening the door. "As long as you promise not to talk."

———

Heather needn't have worried. Knocking on Mickey's front door brought no response from within, and a quick check of the handle revealed the place was locked up tight.

For a fleeting moment, Heather considered a window. Had the detective constable not been with her, she may very well have tried one or two of them.

Instead, she went around to the back of the house, where the tents in Tony Crier's garden were still set up and clear to see. The pink curtains of the little girl's bedroom were still open, and the *Barbie* bedspread looked pristine, like it hadn't yet been slept in.

From there, Heather looked up at the window to Tony's bedroom, and caught a glint of light reflecting off the telescope lens. Would she have noticed it had she not been looking? She wasn't sure. But it was definitely visible now that she was.

"Someone's a heavy smoker," Tammi-Jo remarked.

Heather turned to the DC and followed her gaze. There were dozens of discarded cigarette ends trampled into the wet grass. A couple of beer bottles had been forgotten by the back door, standing upright in the corner where the step met the wall.

They'd been half filled with fag ends, and then rainwater had filled them up to the top. They looked like a particularly disgusting arts and crafts project.

A quick check of the wheelie bins revealed several more bottles, though these were mercifully empty.

"Two people, actually," Tammi-Jo said, squatting to better examine the discarded butts. "Two different types, anyway. Of cigarettes, I mean, not two different types of people. Though, they probably were. Unless they were twins."

"I doubt they were twins," Heather mumbled, contemplating the finding.

"No. Different shoe sizes," the DC continued. "I'd say, a ten, and an... eight? The ten mostly stands still, but the eight does a lot of pacing about."

She looked up to find Heather staring at her, and smiled nervously.

"I mean, I could be wrong. Obviously. But the mud. You can see the prints in the mud. Of course, it could just be the same person with different shoes, because the sizes aren't always accurate, are they? In some shops, I'm a five, and in some, I'm a four. Same with jeans. And dresses. Everything, in fact. Maybe not socks. But—"

Heather employed her trick of tuning out the detective constable's rambling. It was, she reckoned, going to be an invaluable ability to have in the coming weeks and months.

Two people, smoking and drinking, one standing still, the

other pacing. Men, probably, looking at the prints. One of them almost certainly an ex-con with gangland ties.

Out here.

In front of the little girl's window.

Directly in view of Tony Crier's bedroom.

"What if he wasn't looking at the kid?" Heather posited. "What if he was spying on Mickey and whoever he was talking to?"

"They probably wouldn't like that," Tammi-Jo suggested.

"Aye. That's an understatement."

Before she could think any further on the subject, a movement caught her eye. A face, pale white, shifted in the shadows of Tony Crier's bedroom.

"Fuck!" Heather hissed. She set off at a sprint for the fence, shouting to Tammi-Jo as she vaulted it. "Get the car. Get around front!"

If the DC replied, Heather didn't hear it. She was already halfway across Tony's garden, racing for the back door.

She found it unlocked, went stumbling across the kitchen, and skidded out into the hall just in time to meet a man in police uniform coming down the stairs.

"Ash. Jesus Christ!" Heather hissed. "What the hell are you doing here? You shouldn't be in here."

Tony's son stood half in shadow. It hooded his eyes and cast most of his face in darkness. "It's my dad's house. I grew up here."

"I know, but—"

"Can I not even come to my dad's house? In fact, it's *my* house now. Can I not even come to my own house?"

"It's a crime scene, Ash. You know that. We're polis. There are rules." Heather looked past him up the stairs. "What were you doing up there, anyway?"

The reply made him sound like a surly teenager. "Nothing."

"Nothing? You were in your dad's room."

"So?"

"So, you shouldn't be!" Heather said with a venom that made it clear she was already tiring of his attitude.

Murdered dad or no murdered dad, she wasn't letting him away with being a dick.

She jabbed a thumb in the direction of the living room. "Get down here, *Constable*," she said, in a not-too-subtle reminder of exactly what the pecking order was. "You and I have got some catching up to do."

The front door flew open, and the DI spun around, fists raising. A breathless, sweating Tammi-Jo all but collapsed into her arms.

"Made it! Made it! I'm here!" the detective constable wheezed. She looked from Heather to the constable on the stairs, then swept away a strand of hair that had become stuck to the sheen of her forehead. "Everything alright?"

"It's fine," Heather told her. She looked past her through the open door to the street beyond. "Where's the car?"

Tammi-Jo bent over with her hands on her thighs, sucking in air.

"You didn't give me the keys, so I ran round."

"You ran round?" Heather glanced outside again. "What, the long way?"

The DC nodded. Her mouth pulled wide as she inhaled, and a hand clutched at a stitch that was now developing in her left side. "By the road."

Heather glanced backwards up the stairs at Ash, but he was too cast in shadow for her to be able to see if he was as dumbfounded by this as she was.

"That's, like, quarter of a mile," Heather told the DC. "You could've just run around the house."

For a moment, the only sound in the hallway was Tammi-Jo's ragged breathing.

Eventually, she stood up straighter, her hand falling away from her aching side.

"I mean, yes, in hindsight, I could have done that," she admitted.

She and Heather both turned to the stairs as Ash came thumping down them, still very much in moody teenager mode.

"DC Swanney, this is Ash Crier."

"That must hurt," Tammi-Jo said. "Crying ash, it must... Actually, no, I shouldn't have said that out loud. Sorry." A smile lit up her face when the constable reached the bottom step. "I'm DC Swanney. You know, like the..."

The sentence trailed off as Ash strode between them and disappeared into the living room.

"River," she concluded, after a pause. Lowering her voice, she leaned closer to DI Filson. "Someone's put on their grumpy trousers this morning. I hope it wasn't the 'crying ash' thing. That just came out."

Heather blew out her cheeks. "Whatever. Listen, leave this one to me." She took her keys from her pocket and tossed them over to the DC, who caught them one-handed and looked *tremendously* pleased by that fact. "Go get the car and bring it round front."

"Ten-four!" Tammi-Jo said. She turned for the front door, twirling the keys around one finger.

"That way," Heather said, indicating the back door. "Just go that way."

"Oh! Right! Yes! Much quicker," Tammi-Jo replied.

Then, limping slightly and holding her side, she headed down the hallway, through the kitchen, and into the garden beyond.

Heather waited for her to leave, then ran a hand down her face, whispered a, "Right," and joined Constable Crier in the living room.

She found him sitting in the room's only armchair, a couple of feet from the sparkling purple geode that stood on its round wooden plinth in the far corner.

There was a local newspaper draped across the arm of the chair, and several of the loose pages had slid out onto the floor.

Had Heather not lowered her gaze to look at them, she might never have noticed the handprint on the carpet by the empty fireplace.

It was black, like someone had left it after touching the coal in the grate. An attempt had been made to rub it away, which would make it useless for prints, even if it hadn't been on the rough fabric of the carpet.

Still, it could be significant.

"What's that?" she asked, pointing to the mark. "Was that you?"

Ash's gaze flitted down to the floor. "No."

"It wasn't there before. Last time I was here, I mean. It wasn't there."

Ash sighed. "Well, it's there now."

"Drop the attitude, Ash," Heather warned. "I know you're upset, and that gets you a bit of leeway, but it's not a free pass to be an arsehole."

"Upset?" Ash shuffled forward in the seat. "You think I'm upset? I'm not. I'm fucking raging. I mean, what are you doing? What are you actually doing to find out who did this?"

"We're doing everything we can."

"No. But you're not, though. Because you know who did it. We all know who did it."

Heather raised her eyebrows, inviting him to continue.

"That fat fuck."

Heather continued to wait, like she was hearing this information for the first time. Yes, he was a copper, but he was also a grieving relative.

And grieving relatives could do some really stupid things.

"Stevie Ross. Gonad. You know him," Ash said. "He works for your pal. Shuggie Cowan."

"Cowan's not my pal," Heather shot back.

"Ha! That's not what I've been hearing. What we've all been hearing."

An icy shiver ran the length of the DI's spine. "Oh, aye? And what have you been hearing, exactly?"

Ash shrugged. "This and that."

"Did you miss the 'exactly,' part of that question, Constable?"

For a moment, Ash didn't respond, but then he placed both hands on the curved arms of the chair and rose to his feet.

He was younger than Heather. A little taller, but not much. He puffed out his chest like he was lining himself up for a square go, and something in his eyes made the DI question her chances of victory.

"Let's just say, you should be careful of who you share your secrets with," he told her. His eyes darted left and right, staring into each of hers in turn. "And if you can't get justice for what they did to my old man, there are plenty of us who can."

He let that sink in for a moment, then barged past her, one of his shoulders clipping hers so she was forced to spin around on the spot to stop herself losing her balance.

"Was it you?" she asked. "Who attacked Gonad? Was it you?"

Ash stopped. When he looked back over his shoulder, there was something almost maniacal about his smile. "Come on, Detective Inspector. We're polis, remember? There are rules." He looked her up and down. "Pretty rich, coming from you."

A wave of nausea bubbled up from Heather's stomach.

Did he know? Did he know what Shuggie had done?

What she'd *let* him do?

There was a metallic *chink* as Ash dropped his keys onto the floor.

"See yourself out when you're done," he told her.

And with that, and the slamming of the door, he was gone.

TWENTY-TWO

HEATHER HIT the brakes of the Audi more firmly than intended, and Tammi-Jo let out a little, "Wargh!" as she was slung forward in the seat.

"Shit. What now?" Heather groaned. She threw open the car door and jumped out, leaving the engine running. "What is it?" she shouted to the teenage girl sitting on her front step. The door was open behind her, showing the empty hallway of the house. "What are you doing here? What's going on?"

"Ah. Officer," replied Ace Wurzel. She closed the notebook she'd been writing in, tucked it under her arm, and got to her feet. "It's nothing to be alarmed about. It's just your father."

"Shit!" Heather was already past the girl, powering her way up the hall. "Dad? Dad, it's me? It's Heather!"

She barged through into the living room to find the old man swaddled in his usual tartan blanket, a Rich Tea biscuit poised above a steaming mug of tea that sat on a fold-out wooden lap tray that Heather had never seen before.

A plate on the tray, empty aside from a scattering of crumbs, suggested he was already a few biscuits deep.

"Aye. Well done," he said, tearing his eyes from the telly

long enough to shoot her a scathing look. "Do you announce yourself like that everywhere you go?"

"No, I— What the fuck's that meant to mean?" Heather asked, then she shook her head. "Forget it. What's going on?"

The flickering lights of the TV had captured his attention again. Even the biscuit remained stationary above the cup, patiently waiting for its inevitable dunking.

A floorboard creaked behind Heather. She turned, expecting to find Ace or Tammi-Jo standing there. Instead, a plump, cheerful-looking woman stood there, peeling off a pair of bright yellow gloves with an elastic *snap*.

Ace's mum. Christ, what was her name?

Heather opened her mouth and, to her relief, the name emerged all on its own.

"Cathy?" She looked around. "What are you doing here? Where's Kelsey?"

"Who's Kelsey?" Cathy asked, neatly tucking one rubber glove inside the other and folding them together. "Is she 'that bloody girl'? If so, she left."

"Left? What do you mean? When?"

Cathy shrugged. "No idea. Early, by the sounds of it. From what I can gather, your dad was on his own most of the day."

At that, all of Heather's worry immediately converted itself into rage. "For fuck's… I don't believe that bitch!"

"Language!" Scott grunted.

This seemed to activate his brain enough for him to finally dunk the biscuit into his tea.

He held it in a little too long, but didn't seem to notice when the dunked half failed to re-emerge, and he seemed content to crunch away at the dry part while continuing to stare at the TV.

Heather could only imagine the shock he was going to get when he drank all the way to the bottom of the cup.

Entertaining a thought as it was, it did nothing to curb her rage. She pointed out into the hall, and Cathy took the hint, stepping aside and letting the DI lead the way into the kitchen.

"What happened?" Heather demanded, with a curtness that even she realised was out of line. "Sorry, I'm not... I know you're not the bad guy here, I just... What's going on?"

Cathy smiled and batted the apology away. She clicked the kettle on like she'd been doing it for years, then wiped an invisible speck of dirt off the counter before replying.

"Ace came round here looking for you. Don't ask me what for, she wouldn't tell me," Cathy explained. "Your dad was... He was a bit confused. He'd, uh, he'd had an accident. You know?"

Heather set her jaw and gave a single nod. She knew. Only too well.

"So, obviously she didn't want to deal with it herself."

"There's supposed to be someone here," Heather insisted. "There *was* someone here. I'm going to kill her. I swear to God, I'm going to find her, and I'm going to kill her. This is so out of order!"

"It's not your fault."

Something about the way the other woman said the words made Heather's breath catch at the back of her throat. She stared at her in mute silence, too stunned to reply.

Cathy was only seven or eight years older than she was, and while she lacked any real air of authority whatsoever, there was something knowing about her, like she'd seen more of the world than most.

"I know you think it is. But, it isn't. None of this is."

Heather felt a now-irritatingly familiar prickling sensation at the back of her eyes.

Jesus. What was happening to her?

"Ace tells me you're on your own with him," Cathy continued. "That can't be easy."

Heather looked away. At the ceiling. At the door. At the kettle rolling towards the boil.

Anywhere but at the woman with the eyes so full of sympathy.

She didn't want to reply, either, but the words came crawling out through her narrowing throat.

"I used to have someone else. But it's just me now." She rallied, letting her anger push all other emotion away. "And there should be that fucking carer. She's supposed to stay with him until five!"

"It's half-six," Cathy said, but there was no accusation behind the words, only kindness and concern.

Heather scratched at her head, running her fingers back and forth through the greasy tangle of her hair.

"Shit," she muttered, then she pulled the hand down her face and turned away, leaning on the worktop. "I'm messing it up. I don't know what to do."

"Ha!"

The laugh took Heather by surprise. She looked back over her shoulder to find Cathy folding a kitchen cloth into a neat rectangle.

"Sorry, I know it's not funny. It's just… the number of times I've said those same words myself." She sighed, but it was good-natured. "But eventually, I got tired of it. Berating myself for my failings. I decided *no more*."

She draped the cloth over the curved back of the mixer tap, and Heather noticed for the first time that the sink was no longer stacked full of dirty dishes.

"You know what my husband said to me the day he left? Ace's dad? The day he walked out and left us, I broke down. At his feet. Literally at his feet. I broke down and asked what I was supposed to do. How was I supposed to cope without him? Ace was really acting out back then, panic attacks, melt-downs, you name it."

Cathy crossed her arms and leaned against the worktop. It was her turn to look away now. She fixed her gaze on a random spot on the kitchen floor and kept it there.

"So I begged him. I pleaded with him to stay. Told him I couldn't do it without him. And you know what he said?"

She looked up then. Heather shook her head.

"He looked me in the eye—dead in the eye—and told me, 'You'll figure it out.' That's what he told me. I'd figure it out," Cathy said. "And then, that was him. He left."

"I'm sorry," Heather said.

"Oh, don't be," Cathy said. Her smile returned, but she gave her eyes a wipe with the corner of a sleeve. "He was an arsehole. We're better off without him." She sniffed and straightened her back. "And we did. We are. We're figuring it out. It's not always easy. It's *rarely* easy. But we're getting there. And so will you."

Heather smiled back, but it was a thin-lipped thing with very little to hold it in place. "How?" she asked.

The kettle clicked off. Neither woman reached for it.

"I can help. Monday to Friday, at least. Ace is at school most of the day, and she can either fend for herself or come here until you get back."

"What?" Heather shook her head. "No. No, that's not... I can't..."

"I'm a trained nurse. Bit rusty, maybe, and some of my qualifications will have lapsed, but if that's not a problem for you, then it isn't for me."

"No, it's not... I can't ask you to do that."

Cathy crossed to her. Heather looked down at her hands as the other woman took them in her own.

"You aren't asking me. I'm offering. But if you *were* asking, I'd be saying exactly the same," Cathy told her. That smile of hers broadened, softening all the lines of her face. "You saved my daughter's life, Heather. More than that, you've inspired her. You've breathed life into her in a way that I couldn't. She goes out now. She went to a birthday party last week."

Cathy pulled an exaggerated wince and shrugged. "I mean, she hated every minute of it, but she went. A few months ago, before she met you, that would've been unheard of. God, it'd have been unheard of for her to be invited in the first place. But she went. Because of you."

Heather frowned and shook her head, not quite getting it.

"She stands up for herself. That's new, too," Cathy continued. "I know she probably seemed sure of herself when you met her, but she wasn't. Not remotely. You know how many times she came home from school and cried? I don't. I lost count. They all blur into one after a while."

Cathy's voice cracked then, but her smile only grew. Her fingers tightened on Heather's hands, squeezing them. "She doesn't cry now. 'Detective Inspector Heather Filson doesn't care what people think of her. Why should I?'"

The sob that had been building at the back of Heather's throat escaped as a single note of laughter. She looked down at her hands before Cathy could see her watering eyes.

"So, whether you like it or not, Detective Inspector Heather Filson, I'm helping you," Cathy insisted, and she made no attempt to hide her own tears. "Because you've done more for me than you will *ever* know."

It took Heather three full clearings of her throat before she was able to speak. Even then, she didn't dare look up.

"I'll pay you. What I was paying the carers."

"You don't have to—"

Heather raised her head and shook it emphatically. "I do. No, I do. I have to. It's the only way I can do it."

Cathy gave her hands one last squeeze, then relinquished her grip on them.

"OK. If that's what you need to do, fine. I won't pretend it won't come in handy."

"Podcasting equipment not cheap?" Heather asked.

That was good. Crack a joke. Push all that emotion back down where it belonged.

"Oh, you can say that again. Laptop, microphone, headphones. New headphones because she lost the first lot. New microphone because the first one was the wrong kind."

Cathy rolled her eyes as she crossed to the kettle and poured water into a blue and white teapot that Heather hadn't even been aware they owned.

"Did you know there are different kinds of microphones? I didn't. I do now, of course, having sat through a three-hour bloody lecture on all the ins and outs of them from herself."

She placed the lid on the pot, picked it up, and gave it a gentle shoogle to encourage the tea bags to get to work. As she did, she looked over at the kitchen door. Heather could just hear Ace and Tammi-Jo talking, but couldn't quite make out the words. By the sounds of things, though, they were still in the front garden.

"You know what I like about you, Heather?"

"Is it my winning smile and charm?"

Another joke. Another step away from her feelings. Yes, this was good.

"Haha. No. Not that," Cathy replied, perhaps just a little too quickly for even Heather's liking. "It's that you've never asked. Most people ask."

"Ask what?"

"You've never asked what's wrong with her."

Heather opened the fridge beside her and took out a snub-nosed bottle of beer. She shrugged as she cracked the top off with the edge of the kitchen worktop.

"I didn't realise anything was," she said, then she took a swig. The cold liquid soothed her aching throat. "And I hope you told all those people to mind their own fucking business."

"Ha! No. Sadly not. That's not really me. Although, well... Once, actually."

Heather smirked behind her beer. "Satisfying, right?"

Cathy laughed and blew out her cheeks. "Oh, you've got no idea. One of the top ten moments of my life, easy."

"Aye, well. Maybe you should do it more often."

Cathy looked horrified by the suggestion, but then her expression thawed, and her smile crept back across her face. "Do you know what?" she said, taking a couple of mugs from a cupboard. "Maybe I will."

She poured tea into both mugs, added just a splash of milk from a small jug that Heather was also sure she'd never seen before, then picked the mugs up by the handles.

"Now, I'm going to go bring this to your dad, since the last one is bound to be about nine-tenths biscuit by this point. We'll have a chat. Get to know each other a bit. I'll let you explain the arrangement to him when you're ready."

"Thank you," Heather said, and she immediately felt her throat tightening up again.

Fuck.

Cathy stopped on the way to the door. "I tell you what. Let's make a deal. See, if we were to keep saying thanks to one another, I'd never stop. I'd literally be here all day, and you'd probably murder me within the hour."

"That's being generous," Heather said.

"Nobody wants that. So, we don't, OK? That's the deal. We don't thank one another, me and you. We just take it as read and get on with it. How does that sound?"

Heather raised her bottle. Cathy brought up her mug, and they *clinked.*

"Right. Good. All sorted, then," Cathy said.

She almost made it to the door this time, but Heather felt compelled to offer a warning.

"He seems pretty good tonight. But he isn't always. It's only fair you know. It can get hard. It does get hard."

Cathy considered the DI's words for a few moments, then shrugged. "Doesn't everything?"

TWENTY-THREE

TEN MINUTES after Cathy had gone through with the tea, Heather sat across the kitchen table from Ace, listening to a thudding from the room above.

"What the hell is she doing up there?" the DI wondered, shooting a concerned look at the ceiling.

Stewie's room had remained mostly undisturbed since his disappearance. He'd only been here on and off in the months leading up to it, but when Heather moved back in and found that Scott hadn't touched the place, something told her to leave well enough alone.

Tammi-Jo, it seemed, hadn't got the same memo.

"I'd say moving a bed," Ace replied. "Is there a bed?"

"Yeah."

"Then she's moving a bed. That's what my money's on."

The thumping stopped. A door opened. Ace's eyebrows crept up her forehead until they were above the rim of her red-framed glasses.

"Do we have a bet?"

"No," Heather said, just as a slightly breathless Tammi-Jo returned to the kitchen.

Ace pointed an accusatory finger at the detective constable. "Were you moving a bed?"

"What? Oh. Um, a bit. Yes. Just out from the wall a little bit." She winced and tried to judge the expression on Heather's face. "Is that OK? It's just a bit."

"It's fine," Heather said.

It wasn't.

"I don't care," she insisted.

She did.

Tammi-Jo smiled, relieved, and scraped her hair back into a much looser ponytail than she'd worn it in during the day.

She'd only been upstairs for a few minutes but had already changed into a pale blue velour jogging suit that was completely shapeless, yet still made her look more feminine than Heather could ever aspire to.

Or *would* ever aspire to, at least.

"Is it OK if I get some water?"

"No," Heather said.

Tammi-Jo appeared momentarily alarmed, but then held her head high and crossed to the sink. "I'm getting some water."

"Better," Heather told her.

"In fact, you know what?" Tammi-Jo changed direction and headed for the fridge. "I'm having some ice-cold semi-skimmed."

"Just call it milk," Heather told her.

Tammi-Jo took the bottle from the fridge and waggled it defiantly at the Detective Inspector. "Ice cold semi-skimmed, baby!"

She unscrewed the top, brought the bottle towards her mouth, then lowered it again and shook her head. "No. Shouldn't do that. I should put it in a glass, shouldn't I? I mean, that would've looked quite cool. Me going, 'Ice-cold semi-skimmed, baby!' and then just, like, chugging the whole thing. But germs. And it's, like, two full litres of milk. I might die if I chugged all that in one go. Should I get a glass? I'll get a glass."

She stepped towards three different kitchen cabinets, one after the other, then turned to Heather.

"Do you have glasses? Where are the glasses?"

Heather sipped her beer and leaned an elbow on the back of her chair. "You tell me, Detective."

DC Swanney considered the various cupboards and cabinets. As she did, the top of the milk bottle drifted absent-mindedly towards her mouth again, before she realised what she was doing and set it down on the worktop.

"That one," she said, crossing to one of the high cabinets and pulling the door open.

A mass of mismatched drinking glasses stood assembled on the shelves.

"Nice!" she said, helping herself to a half-pint tumbler.

"What gave it away?" Heather asked.

Tammi-Jo shrugged as she poured milk into the glass. "Don't know. It just felt right. It just sort of made sense, like, spatially. Do you know what I mean?"

"Nope."

She turned back to face the teenager sitting across from her. Ace was grinning from ear to ear.

"What are you so happy about?"

"This. Us. Look at us," Ace said. "Three female crime investigators gathered together. We're like a neurodivergent *Charlie's Angels*."

"What do you mean?" Heather demanded. "I'm not neurodivergent."

Ace snorted. "Oh, please, Officer. I'm autistic, she's ADHD, and you're clearly a sociopath."

Tammi-Jo pulled out a chair and joined them at the table. "What's *Charlie's Angels*?" she asked.

Heather spluttered on her beer. "Jesus Christ. How old are you?"

"She's older than I am," Ace pointed out. "So it's not age, it's ignorance."

"It's a film," Heather explained, which earned a tut of annoyance from the teenager.

"It's a TV series," Ace corrected.

"No, it's definitely a film," Heather insisted. "What's-her-name is in it. The kid from E.T."

Tammi-Jo raised a crooked finger and steered it in Heather's direction. "Elliot?" she asked, in a croaky alien voice.

Heather slapped the finger away. "No. The girl."

"Drew Barrymore," Ace said.

"Yes! She's in it."

"She's in the terrible movie adaptations, yes. Some of them, anyway. But it was a TV series back in the 70s."

"Oh." Heather took a sip of her beer. "Before my time."

"Well, obviously it was before my time, too," Ace replied. "So, again, it's not age, it's ignorance."

They sat in silence for a few moments. It quickly proved too much for Tammi-Jo to bear.

"Why were we talking about *Charlie's Angels* again?"

"Ace wants to be an investigator," Heather said.

"Oh!" The Detective Constable brightened considerably. "You want to join the police?"

"Ha! No. God, no," Ace said. "The police are mostly grunts and morons."

Tammi-Jo shot Heather a sideways look, but the DI didn't seem to be in a hurry to disagree.

"Oh. Right."

"Present company excluded, of course. I mean, probably, I don't know you very well," Ace said. "But you did find those glasses, and if DI Filson likes you, then I should give you a chance."

"Who said I like her?" Heather asked, with a note of objection in her tone.

"Please, Officer. You're literally letting her live in your

house. I mean, I don't generally read people well, but that one's coming in pretty loud and clear."

"Temporarily. I'm temporarily letting her live in my house," Heather said, but even she had to admit it was a pretty weak comeback.

"Question," Ace announced. She interlocked her fingers on the table in front of her, indicating that the chit-chat was over and things were now getting serious. "What would happen if, as part of my investigation into the murder of Sergeant Tony Crier—"

"An investigation which had better not exist for your sake," Heather said.

"What would happen if, during that investigation, I was to gain entry to the victim's house and attempt to gather evidence?"

Heather paused with her bottle halfway to her mouth. She set it down on the table with a *clunk*. "Is this a theoretical question?"

"No, it's a hypothetical question," Ace corrected.

"Isn't that the same thing?" Tammi-Jo asked.

"No. A theoretical question would be a question that only exists *in theory*. This question *literally* exists, but it concerns a hypothetical scenario."

Tammi-Jo took a drink of her milk. "Right. I see. And what's a *rhetorical* question again?"

Ace felt it only right not to answer that one. Instead, she turned her attention back to Heather, who stared at her through narrowed eyes.

"What would happen in the scenario you describe is you'd be arrested," Heather told her. "You'd be arrested and charged with interfering in an ongoing murder investigation."

"Even though I'm fifteen?"

"Yep."

"And you'd do it, would you? If you caught me in the act?"

"I'd have no choice," Heather said. "So don't, alright? Don't go sticking your nose in. Stay out of it. You're not really Nancy Drew."

"I understand that."

"I'm not sure you do, though," Heather said. "You treat this like it's all a game. But a man died. A good man. And it's not like in the books. You can't go snooping around with a big magnifying glass, finding footprints, or leather gloves, or... God. I don't know. A business card conveniently dropped by the killer."

The slamming of Tammi-Jo's glass on the table effectively derailed the conversation.

"Oh! Wait!" the DC cried. She fished around in the pockets of her jogging suit, then slapped a rectangle of orange card down in front of Heather. "I found that."

Heather looked at the card. The edges were crumpled, and one of the corners bore some black debris that had most likely been scraped from under a fingernail.

A purple logo that looked like a stylised eye stared out from the front of the card.

"It was down the side of the bed when I moved it," Tammi-Jo said, but Heather was barely listening.

She knew that card. She knew that logo.

"Eyedol," she mumbled.

"What's that?" Ace asked. She reached for the card, but Heather stabbed a finger down on it, pinning it there like a dead butterfly to a board.

"It's a nightclub."

"In Killie?"

Heather picked up the card and turned it over. A mobile phone number had been written on the back in red pen.

"In Glasgow," she muttered.

"Oh." Ace sounded faintly disgusted by that.

"Bosco Maximuke used to own it."

"Who's that?" Ace asked. "Is that a friend of yours?"

Heather gave the card a flick with a finger, as if it was the ear of some annoying wee toerag.

"No," she said. "Very much not."

Ace sniffed haughtily. "Well, I have to say, they're being very frivolous with their card production costs. That's needlessly thick card stock. That wouldn't be cheap. I make my cards on my printer at home."

Heather unlocked her phone and punched the number into her contacts, marking the name as 'Eyedol card' followed by a couple of question marks.

"Aye, well, your cards are so thin they curl up in your hand like one of them little fish," Heather said, placing her phone down on the table.

"What little fish?" Ace asked.

"Goldfish?" Tammi-Jo guessed.

"No—"

"Guppies?" The DC turned to Ace. "Or, what's Nemo again?"

"Clownfish" Ace replied.

"Jesus Christ, no. I don't mean a real fish!" Heather snapped.

"Nemo's not real," Tammi-Jo said.

"For fu—" Heather held a hand flat and poked her finger against the palm. "One of the wee red paper things that curls up. It tells your fortune or... I don't fucking know what it does."

"Oh! Like you get in Christmas crackers!" Tammi-Jo cried. "Sort of thin red plasticky stuff? Rolls itself up?"

"Yes!"

The DC sat back, nodding happily. "I know the ones," she said. "What about them?"

Heather opened her mouth to reply, but then realised she'd completely lost the thread of the conversation.

"Now, I can't remember. Doesn't matter," she said.

She looked at the business card again, then slipped it into her wallet behind her driver's licence.

That done, she knocked back the rest of her beer, and pointed across the table with the neck of the empty bottle.

"My point is, stay away from Tony's house. Or else."

Ace tapped her thumbs together. She wrinkled her nose in an attempt to reposition her glasses.

"Of course, Officer," she finally replied. "Whatever you say."

———

Heather shut the door to Scott's bedroom and held onto the handle, like she was afraid he'd pull it open from the other side.

The door muted his ranting a little, though not by much. He'd called her every name under the sun when she'd been trying to wrestle him into bed. She was a slut, a whore, a home wrecker, a liar, and a thief.

And a disappointment, of course. He'd really gone to town on that part.

She was robbing from her mother, he'd told her, despite the fact she'd been dead for years. He was going to get his daughter on her, he'd said. His daughter would sort her out. She was in the polis.

When Heather had tried to make him realise who she was, he'd got angry and lashed out. The scratches on her forearms wouldn't leave a permanent scar, but they'd show up as burning red welts for a day or two.

"You're a dirty, no-good, fucking *liar!*" came a shout from the room beyond the door.

Heather held her breath, listening, and then let herself relax a little when she heard the creaking of springs, the rustling of covers, and a low muttering from the old man in the bed.

She checked her watch. It was barely nine o'clock, but that

last half-hour of dementia-related chaos had seemed to drag on forever. It felt closer to midnight now, and exhaustion leadened Heather's bones.

A soft knock from Stevie's room stopped her halfway along the hall. It was a one-off sound, like someone had tapped the wall a single time with a small hammer.

Heather listened at the door. She could hear DC Swanney shuffling around on the carpet. There may have been some light whispering involved, but it was hard to say for sure.

Heather knocked on the door, and the shuffling became a hurried, frantic thudding of footsteps.

"Hang on! Coming!"

The door was pulled open just enough for Tammi-Jo's head to be forced through the gap, like Jack Nicholson in *The Shining*, albeit with less of a murderous look in her eyes.

"Hi. Hello!" the DC said. "Is, uh, is everything OK?"

"Aye. You?" Heather asked.

"Fine! Yep. All A-OK in here, Daddy-o!" She winced. "Mummy-o? No, that's worse. All fine, though."

Heather's eyes narrowed. "You're being weird."

"Maybe you're being weird. You ever think of that?" Tammi-Jo's eyes darted to the door of Scott's room. "Is your dad alright?" she asked. "He sounded…"

"Mental?"

"I was going to say he sounded upset."

"Oh, aye. He was that, too," Heather said. "And yeah, he's fine. Well, no, obviously not fine, but this isn't that unusual."

The look of pity on the younger detective's face snapped Heather back to the matter at hand.

"What are you up to?"

"Up to?" Tammi-Jo asked. Heather assumed it was supposed to sound casual, but it was anything but. "Nothing. You?"

"Can I come in?"

"In?" The detective constable swallowed. "In…?"

"There. In the room you're in. Can I come in?"

Tammi-Jo shifted her weight from foot to foot. Heather could hear them shuffling on the carpet in her brother's bedroom.

"Is this one of those times I should stand my ground?"

"No," Heather told her. "It really isn't."

With a groan, the DC stepped back, letting the door swing open. She was already babbling out an explanation when Heather entered the room. Something about being sorry, and about her putting everything back the way it was, and about how she knew it was taking liberties, but she found it a really useful tool.

Heather heard very little of it, and paid attention to less than half of that. Instead, she stared at the mass of *Post-it Notes* stuck to the wall above where the bed had been.

It was starkly similar to the wall Heather had once seen in Ace's bedroom, where the girl had laid out the details of a thirty-year investigation in a manner that, at first glance, made no sense whatsoever.

And, at second glance, was somehow even worse.

Names, times, and random words were written on the notes in colourful bubble writing. There was a drawing on one of what might have been an ironing board, but could equally have been a robotic horse of some description.

"I, um, I still had some of the stickies in my bag from the castle. They don't leave a mark, or anything, they just peel off. It's a really weak glue, so it doesn't do any damage to the walls. I mean, it's barely even glue at all. I don't even know if you can technically call it—"

"Detective Constable?"

Tammi-Jo flinched. "Yes?"

"Shut up."

Heather let her gaze hop from note to note, searching for some sort of logic that connected them, but finding none.

It wasn't how she'd have done it. It wasn't how she'd seen *anyone* do it before, in fact. But she knew exactly what this was.

"You've made a Big Board?"

"What? No!" Tammi-Jo cried, like this was an outrageous accusation. "I mean, yes. Obviously. Sort of."

Heather crossed her arms, rocked on her heels, then sucked in her bottom lip and spat it back out again.

"Right, then," she said. "In that case, you'd better take me through it."

TWENTY-FOUR

HEATHER SAT on the end of her brother's bed, watching Tammi-Jo adding yet another note to the collection on the wall.

She was still none the wiser as to what most of it meant, but writing the notes kept the DC quiet for a few moments. For those few glorious seconds, the only sound in the room was the snoring of Scott next door, which allowed Heather a bit of time to think.

Once Cathy had left with Ace—with a promise to be back by half-eight the next morning—Heather had called Marty to report the handprint next to Tony Crier's fireplace.

The DS had promised to get straight onto the SOCOs with it, to check if they were either aware of it, or had accidentally made it themselves.

He'd called back ten minutes later to say they'd responded in the negative to both. Someone was going to head out to the house to investigate further, and would report back ASAP.

Upon being given this news, Tammi-Jo had drawn a handprint on a *Post-it*, spent a full minute considering where it should go, then had stuck it to the wall a good eighteen inches away from any of the other notes.

Then, without a word of explanation, she'd peeled it off and stuck it back on upside-down.

Heather wondered what Ace would make of it all. The girl had shown the DI her own 'Wonderwall' in her bedroom, and it had been equally as bamboozling as DC Swanney's effort.

Would this one make sense to Ace? Would Tammi-Jo take one look at the Wonderwall and immediately see the pattern?

Or were they both just batshit crazy in their own unique ways?

"OK, so… Where will we start?" Tammi-Jo asked, scanning the scattered notes. If there was a pattern there, Heather couldn't even begin to see it. It was like someone had loaded all the *Post-its* into a shotgun and blasted it at the wall from three feet away.

The writing was all in jolly bubble-style, with smiley faces above some of the lowercase *i*'s. She'd written the word 'Killer' on one, but at least the smiley face on that one had the decency to look angry.

"No idea," Heather said. "You choose."

Tammi-Jo accepted this burden of responsibility with a look of surprise, then a solemn nod.

"Right. OK. Well…" She considered her options. "The Iron Woman."

"What about her?" Heather asked.

"Did she seem weird to you?"

"Everyone seems weird to me."

"OK, but, like, jumpy? Nervous?"

"She threw up in her sink," Heather reminded the detective constable.

"Yes! Is it weird that her water isn't working? Is that anything? There was water in the dog bowl, but not from the taps. Is that something? Should I put that on the wall?"

"We could just remember it. I don't think it needs to go on the wall," Heather said. "Although, I don't know what qualifies anything to—"

"I'll put it on the wall," Tammi-Jo announced.

Heather took a sip of coffee while the DC wrote out another note. She'd have preferred another bottle of cheap, weak, Eastern European lager, but she was half-thinking of taking a drive back to Mickey Buttfuck's to see if anyone was home.

Tammi-Jo slapped the new note on the wall beside the picture of the ironing board. It read 'Plumbing/Dog?' and was therefore one of the more easily decipherable ones.

"The fact she took the money tells me she's in financial bother," Heather said. "She clearly felt bad about it. Can't be cheap running that house, and if her only wage is what she takes from the ironing, it's bound to be a struggle."

"Yeah, I've got that there," Tammi-Jo said, pointing to a note with a single pound sign on it.

"Oh aye," Heather muttered into her coffee. "So you have."

"Here's what I don't get, though. She pulls up in her van to bring him his ironing. She goes to the door, it's locked, so she gets the key."

"From under the stone."

"From under the stone. Exactly. She gets the key from under the stone, unlocks the door, goes in. Then, she sees him on the stairs, checks him, calls the ambulance, stays with him for a while, then goes through to the living room to look out of the window for any sign of the paramedics arriving."

"That's what she said," Heather confirmed. "So?"

"So, she sees the money then, and she lifts it."

"Right..."

"The ambulance arrives a few minutes later."

Heather's next coffee slurp neatly conveyed her growing irritation. "I know all this. I was there when she said it. Is there a point?"

Tammi-Jo turned to the wall and gestured to it with both hands, like a conductor leading an orchestra towards its big final crescendo. "What's missing?" she asked.

"All logic and reason?" Heather guessed, her gaze flitting across the notes.

"Where's the ironing?"

Heather lowered her coffee cup.

The next word out of Heather's mouth wasn't really a question. It was verbal punctuation designed to give her brain a chance to reprimand itself for missing that detail.

"What?"

"The ironing. Two bags, she said. She was bringing them round to drop them off." Tammi-Jo shrugged and gestured to the wall again, as if the answer should be found there. "So, where are they?"

"I didn't see them in the crime scene report," Heather admitted.

"They aren't. I checked. No mention of them," Tammi-Jo said. "Not in the house, or outside it. She could have taken them away with her again, I suppose, but why would you? Especially if you took the money. If you took the money, then you'd leave the ironing. That's the transaction. Especially if you feel bad about taking the cash, which I think she really did. You take the money, you leave the bags. Right? That makes sense?"

"It does," Heather confirmed.

Of course, if Selma was telling the truth, then she'd have been badly shaken up, and probably not thinking straight. It was possible, then, that she'd have taken the bags away with her again.

Possible, but unlikely.

"Thoughts on it?" Heather prompted. "Why weren't they there?"

"Either she *did* take them away with her, or she never had them with her in the first place," Tammi-Jo reasoned. "Which would mean that whatever she was there for, it wasn't to drop off Tony's ironing."

"Which would mean she lied to us."

"Yes. It would. Which is a shame, because she seems nice. I felt quite sorry for her. Did you feel sorry for her?"

"No," Heather said. She shrugged. "Then again, I don't really feel anything for anyone."

"OK, well, I don't believe that, but whatever you say. I felt sorry for her. I don't really want her to be the killer, but the bag thing is weird. It niggled at me at the time, but it wasn't until we were back here that I realised what was bothering me. It is weird, isn't it? It's not just me."

"It's not just you," Heather confirmed. "Makes me wonder what's under that bandage."

"You don't think it's a burn?" Tammi-Jo asked.

Heather shrugged. "Halfway up the inside of her forearm? Even I'm not that shite at ironing, and I don't do it for a living. We can talk to her again tomorrow. Ask about the bags and see if we can find some way to look at the injury."

Tammi-Jo nodded, then turned the *Post-it* with the drawing of the ironing board on it sideways. Presumably, this meant something to her, but Heather chose not to ask.

"Mickey Buttfuck's place," Heather said, unilaterally deciding on the next discussion topic. "I told Marty to have Uniform keep an eye on it. As soon as anyone shows face, I want to know about it."

"Did he come back with anything? On Mickey BF I mean?"

"South London, originally. Did a six-year stretch for an incident involving the pointy side of a claw hammer and his cousin's skull."

"Ouch."

"Aye. I'd imagine so," Heather agreed. "Marty couldn't turn up any direct connection with Shuggie, but most likely drugs, or God knows what else, was flowing from one to the other at some point."

"Pretty basic house for someone high up," Tammi-Jo pointed out.

"Everything was taken off him. Proceeds of crime. He

must've been the only one of those bastards without an accountant bent enough to keep his money out of the hands of the legal system. He's skint, but seemingly trying to make a go of going straight."

"Good for him!" Tammi-Jo declared. "And good luck to him."

"I think he might've murdered Tony Crier," Heather said.

The detective constable seemed crestfallen. "Oh. Right. Well, that's disappointing. What makes you say that?"

"The handprint," Heather said.

"Aha! Wait, I've got that here!"

Tammi-Jo slapped her hand on the wall below the *Post-it* with the drawing of the handprint on it.

"There it is. Pride of place," Tammi-Jo said, standing back to admire her work.

"Why's it upside down?"

The DC shot Heather a look that bordered on the sympathetic. "Because we don't know what it means yet. Or I didn't think we did, anyway. Although, I mean, I suppose we kind of do."

"Do we?" Heather asked.

"Well, I'm guessing someone was touching the coal?"

Heather thought about the fireplace and the empty grate. "There wasn't any coal. I don't think Tony actually uses the fire. *Used* it, I mean."

"Right. Oh." Tammi-Jo looked over the entire wall, like this bit of news had rendered her entire system meaningless. Or more meaningless, anyway. "So, what does it mean, then?"

The bed gave a squeak as Heather got to her feet. "Right, there are some leaps here, but stay with me," she urged. "So, we know Tony had a telescope in his bedroom."

"Pointing into the little girl's room," Tammi-Jo said.

"Pointing into Mickey Buttfuck's back garden," Heather corrected. "Where, as we know, at least two men regularly spent time. I think Tony was watching them."

"Ah. OK. OK! So, you're saying he wasn't a paedophile?"

"No. He wasn't."

"He was gay!"

"What?" Heather shook her head. "No. I don't mean... He wasn't watching them like that. I meant he was watching them because he had suspicions about them. He reckons there's something dodgy going on, so he keeps watch. And he keeps note."

Tammi-Jo clicked her fingers. "The pen!"

"The pen," Heather confirmed. "Scene of Crime found the pen, but not the notebook it should be attached to." She began to pace back and forth, ideas fizzing and merging together in her head. "Tony watches out the back, makes note of what Mickey's up to, who he's meeting with."

"Could it have been Shuggie?"

"Doubt it. He's too high profile. If Mickey's parole officer found out, he'd be back in the jail. And Shuggie doesn't smoke these days. There were two types of fags in the garden."

"Oh! Oh! Maybe the other one? The big fat fella?"

"Gonad? No. He's got weirdly tiny feet. I don't know how he stays upright. Neither of those prints were his. And that's a point. They weren't Shuggie's either. He wears those stupid bloody cowboy boots all the time."

Tammi-Jo grimaced, disappointed. "Typical. What about...?" She leaned on the wall and drummed her fingers, staring into space as she tried to think of another suspect.

"It could be anyone. It doesn't matter right now," Heather said. "Whoever's out there with Mickey, Tony gets to watching them, making notes. They find out somehow. Mickey realises that whatever Tony has got written down could sink him."

"So he goes round one night..."

"Kicks shit out of him," Heather continued. "Probably aimed to kill him there and then, but didn't quite finish the job. But he can't find the notebook. He clears out before it's light, then goes back later and tries looking for it again."

"Up the chimney!" Tammi-Jo concluded.

Heather nodded. "That's my thinking. Ash couldn't have made the mark on the carpet. His hands were clean. Literally, I mean, not metaphorically."

Tammi-Jo's burst of excitement quickly hit a stumbling block. "How would Mickey know that we didn't have it?" she asked. "If he knew we'd been in, how would he know that we didn't find the book and take it with us? Why risk coming back to look?"

There were a couple of possible answers to that. One of them did not bode well for police corruption stats, so Heather latched onto the other.

"Maybe because no one had been round to arrest him," she said. "But if he thought it was just a matter of time, that might explain why he's cleared off."

Tammi-Jo sat heavily on the end of the bed that Heather had only recently vacated, like her legs had given out beneath her.

"Wow. So, you think it was Mickey Bumfudge? You think he's the killer?"

"I think he's pretty high up on a short list of suspects," Heather replied. "Now, all we have to do is find the bastard, but that might be easier said than done."

Heather's phone rang then, a shrill, piercing sound that made her dig frantically in the pocket of her jeans so she could silence it before it woke up the man now snoring like a petrol lawnmower next door.

DS Brompton's name filled the screen, and while it shouldn't really have come as any surprise—she'd asked him to contact her with any updates, after all—an inexplicable sense of dread filled Heather as she tapped the button to answer.

"Marty. What's up?"

The detective sergeant's tone did nothing to ease Heather's

concerns. She listened in silence, then slumped down onto the bed beside Tammi-Jo.

"Eh. Right. Aye," Heather said. She rubbed her dry, tired eyes with a finger and thumb, and it was only when she took it away that she realised her hand was shaking. "Call Ozzy. Wake the old bastard up, if you have to."

She checked her watch. Through the wall, her dad continued to snore.

"I'll be there as soon as I can."

TWENTY-FIVE

FROM WHAT SHE could see of his face, he'd been scared.

Even now, once the life had left him, and all the tension had ebbed from his muscles, his expression was still frozen in a mask of abject terror.

He'd been scared.

Then again, watching all that blood—your blood—gushing from a ragged slash across your throat, who wouldn't be?

"Patrol found him an hour ago."

Snecky's voice sounded distant and far away, like he was talking to her from the other end of a long tunnel.

"Brother-in-law reported him missing a bit before that. His wife called him in a panic. Although, he hadn't checked in at the end of his shift, so base was already aware."

He'd been on his knees, by the looks of it. Ozzy and Aiko would confirm, but from the pooling of blood beneath him, Heather guessed he'd been on all fours when his throat had been cut.

The twisting of his neck had forced the wound open. She could see the edge of it, like a second mouth, smirking slyly at her from beneath the body.

There could be other injuries, of course. She'd have to wait to find out. But judging by the blood spray, his heart had been beating when his throat had been cut, which almost certainly put that as the cause of death.

"Where's his car?" Heather asked, looking back in the direction of the community centre car park. It had been cordoned off, and a ring of high-vis vests had formed around the area, keeping back the handful of nosy bastards trying to get an eyeful of the dead cop on the ground.

"We don't know," Snecky admitted.

"What do you mean? What about tracking? How can we not know? There should be tracking."

The DCI shrugged. "Look, I'm only telling you what they've told me. Don't shoot the messenger." He covered his mouth with the back of his hand, stifling a yawn. "Where's DC Swanney, by the way? Why isn't she here?"

"She's at my place," Heather said. "I needed someone there in case my dad woke up."

"Oh, right. Is he still…?" He pointed to the side of his head, although he at least had the decency to look sympathetic.

"Aye. He's still got dementia. He's not snapped out of it yet."

"Can they do that?" Snecky asked. "Can that happen?"

The look on Heather's face answered more effectively than words ever could.

"No," Snecky mumbled. "No, I suppose not, right enough."

Heather squatted as close to the body as she dared get before the SOCOs had gone over it. From that angle, she got a better look at his face. There was blood across his forehead that seemed to come from a thin diagonal wound around two inches long. A scratch, maybe, or a slice from a razor.

There may well have been more of them, but the blood and tarmac kept them hidden for now.

Headlights swept across the area where they were gathered. Heather straightened and shielded her eyes to look, and saw

Aiko's ridiculous little electric car pulling up just ahead of the Scene of Crime van.

Heather headed over to meet the head of the SOCO team as she clambered out of the car, slammed the door, and opened the tiny, wallet-sized boot.

"Evening," Heather said.

Aiko looked up and flashed a smile that was as unconvincing as it was brief.

"I was on a date," Aiko said. "First one in how long? Six years. That's how long. Promising, too. No kids. No ex-wife. Own teeth."

"What more could you want?"

"A mouthful of dessert wouldn't have gone amiss," Aiko said.

Her accent was Glasgow to the core. This took a lot of people by surprise when they first met her, given that she was second-generation Japanese.

They were also usually taken aback by her level of confidence, given that she stood precisely five feet tall with shoes on.

"They had Arctic Roll on the pudding menu. Can you believe that? Proper Arctic Roll."

"Christ, where was it you were eating?" Heather asked her. "The 1970s?"

"Here, don't you go knocking an Arctic Roll," Aiko warned, then she ducked under the cordon tape simply by lowering her head, and nodded over to where the body lay. "This us, is it?"

"Aye," Heather confirmed. "Darryl Hartmann. Constable. He's one of ours."

"Ah, shite. Fuck." She drew in a breath. "OK. Well, we'll take care of him. Ozzy here?"

"Not yet."

Aiko tutted. "Useless old bastard. He's probably stuck in his crypt. Well, we'll sweep the area until he gets here, then focus on the body once he's done. Does he have a car? The body, I mean."

"Should have. It's missing, though," Heather said. "We're looking for it."

"OK. Well, when it turns up, I'm sure we'll hear."

She turned and beckoned to the four SOCOs disembarking from the van, then pointed to the car park and made a circular motion with her finger.

"Fingers out of our arses, guys. Alright?" she told them. "Especially you, Phil."

A thumbs-up from one of the other officers confirmed that the message had been received, then they set about getting changed into their protective paper suits.

"You know him?" Aiko asked, turning back to the DI. "He a friend of yours?"

"No. Met him a couple of times," Heather said. "But not a friend, no."

"Forgot. You don't do them, do you?" Aiko said. "Very wise. Best avoided. I hear they're a pain in the arse."

Heather managed a thin-lipped half-smile. "Aye. I have heard that right enough."

Aiko held out a hand as one of her team passed her a paper suit sealed in clear plastic, then tucked it under her arm.

"He got family?" she asked, indicating the body with another nod of her head.

Heather blew out her cheeks. "Not sure," she confessed. Snecky was walking towards her, his phone to his ear, a look on his face like he was shitting thistles. "But I've a feeling I'm about to find out."

Aiko wished her luck, then headed to the van to get changed. Snecky stopped next to Heather, and held up a finger for her to stay where she was.

"Uh-huh. Uh-huh. Yeah. Uh-huh," he said into the phone. Heather could make out a woman's voice on the other end of the line, but the words were too tinny and jumbled for her to hear the details. "No. No, of course. Uh-huh. Uh-huh. Uh-huh."

Heather crossed her arms and puffed out her cheeks, making her impatience crystal clear. Snecky raised the same index finger as before, but this time held it there like it could magically ward off her growing irritation.

"Yes. No. Uh-huh... Uh-huh. Got you. Yep. Text it through. Uh-huh. I will. Uh-huh."

He ended the call and tucked the phone into the inside pocket of his jacket.

"Thank God for that," Heather told him. "One more 'uh-huh' and I was going to put my thumbs through your eye-sockets."

"One more what?"

"One more 'uh-huh.'"

"I don't think I said that, did I?"

"You said it about forty times."

Snecky snorted in disbelief. "I *think* I'd remember if I'd—"

"It doesn't matter. What's happening?" Heather demanded.

"Oh. Right. Yeah. Someone—ideally not me, because I'm not very good at it—needs to go talk to the wife. Ex-wife. No, not... Former wife. Widow, I mean. The widow. Couldn't think of the bloody word!"

"She hasn't been told?"

"No. She's, eh, she's got a wee one, too. Year old."

Heather ran a hand down her face. "Christ."

"Aye. So, um, could you...? You know? Do the honours?"

"For her sake, aye," Heather said. "Last thing she needs is you turning up and wedging your foot in your mouth."

It was widely known on the force that Snecky wasn't great at breaking the news of a loved one's untimely passing. It was a difficult part of the job, and nobody enjoyed it, but Snecky had demonstrated an early tendency to mess it up so badly that he was spared from ever having to do it again.

He'd once asked the grieving mother of a dead nineteen-year-old if she'd known the deceased well, and had assured the heartbroken wife of a man drowned in a boating accident in the Moray Firth that there were 'plenty more fish in the sea.'

"That's probably for the best," the DCI said. "If it's any consolation, though, you won't be going on your own."

Heather didn't bother to hide her disappointment. She liked being on her own. Being on her own suited her just fine.

"Who?" she asked. "Marty?"

"No."

"Not Simon. There's no way I'm taking Simon."

Snecky shook his head. "Not from the team. It's his sergeant. He wants to come along. He's met the wife a few times."

"Right. OK. Fair enough," Heather said. She didn't like it, but she understood.

"I think you know him," Snecky said. "Wayne Gillespie. Weren't you two doing that careers fair together?"

Heather bristled at the name. The last time Heather had seen Darryl alive, he'd voiced his concerns about the behaviour of Wayne, and the influence he was having over Ash and some of the other Uniforms.

Based on their encounter at Tony's get-together in the canteen, there had been no love lost between the men.

And now, Wayne was inviting himself along to break the news of his death.

This should be interesting.

"Aye, fair enough," Heather said. She turned and headed for her car. "Ping me the address, and tell him to meet me there. And tell him that if he even thinks about knocking on that door before I get there, I'll break every bone in his body."

TWENTY-SIX

WAYNE at least had the good sense to park down the street from the house, so that Daz's wife wouldn't see the squad car lurking outside. He clocked Heather pulling in a few cars behind him, and was waiting on the pavement by the time she'd completed the manoeuvre.

"Was starting to think you weren't coming," he said, practically grunting the whole sentence at her.

"Sergeant," Heather said, acknowledging him with a quick look up and down. "Thanks for waiting."

"Aye, well. Another few minutes and I wouldn't have. You ready?"

Heather bit her tongue and counted to three before replying. "You know her? The wife?"

"Barely. Name's Jessica. They've been married about three years. Got a wee one. Girl, I think."

Heather had been hoping that there was an existing relationship there. That could sometimes soften the blow a bit.

Although, never by much.

"Fine. In that case, I'll lead," she said, setting off towards the address.

It was a Housing Association terraced house tucked away

at the back of an estate in Provanhall, in the northeast of the city, just a handful of miles from the community centre where Constable Darryl Hartmann's body had been found.

"Can't believe the fuckers did that to him," Wayne muttered as they made their way along the darkened street. Half of the streetlights were out, and those that remained cast watery orange pools onto the cracked road surface below. "Fucking animals."

"Who?" Heather asked, looking back over her shoulder. "Do you know who did it, like?"

Wayne scowled back at her. "Well, obviously not specifically, or we'd be round there right now, panning their fucking heads in."

"Placing them under arrest, you mean."

"Of course, Detective Inspector," he replied, sarcasm oozing between the syllables. "We'd be doing it all by the book, just like I hear you do."

Heather's boot scuffed on the pavement as she stopped and turned. "What's that meant to mean?"

"Oh, come on! Don't deny what you are. Own it. Be proud of it. You know the system's broken," Wayne said.

She was used to him whinging, or ranting, or throwing in a touch of bravado, but he suddenly sounded sincere and level-headed. Chillingly so.

"You see it. Same as I do. These fuckers out there, the shit they do, the shit they *get away with*." He shook his head. "It's not right. It's not fair. We've got all these rules, but what about them? What rules do they have to stick to? None. So, how can you win that game? If you stick to the rules and they don't? How do you stop them winning?"

"Easy," Heather said. She opened the gate beside them. "You don't treat it like a game."

"Oh, I know it's not a game. Don't you worry about that," Wayne spat. "Daz today. Tony yesterday. That young lad up north the day before. No, it's not a game. It's life and bloody death. That's what we're facing out there. And it's getting worse. This isn't the end of it. Daz won't be the last. You can bet your fucking boots on that.

"This shit won't end until it's ended. Until we end it. A big show of force, round up all the Neds, and the No-Marks, and the Shuggie Cowans of this world, and let every man and his dog see that we won't fucking stand for their shite anymore!"

His chest was heaving like the speech had set a fire in him.

She did her best to put it out again.

"Cute manifesto," she said. Then, with a jerk of her head, she indicated that the sergeant should lead the way up the path. "After you."

Every light was on in the front of the house, with the exception of one of the bedrooms upstairs. Although, it was covered by a pale yellow blackout blind with little pink butterflies on it, so for all Heather knew, the light was on in that room, too.

The sight of the butterflies, and the thought of the infant girl in that room, made her stomach tighten. Her only memories of her father would be hand-me-downs. Her only impression of him formed from a montage of photos, videos, and stories from those who'd been given a chance to get to know him.

"We're going to find the bastard who did this," Heather said, just before she raised a hand and knocked on the frosted glass of the front door. "We're going to do it properly, we're going to find them, and we're going to put them away."

"Cute manifesto," Wayne said. He removed his cap and tucked it under his arm. Along the hallway, a shape moved. "But who are you trying to convince, Detective Inspector? Me or you?"

The door opened before Heather could reply. A young woman—too young for a conversation like this one—stood shivering, an oversized man's cardigan wrapped around her for warmth.

Heather watched, as she'd done so many times before, as

the realisation, and the horror, and the pain kicked in.

"Hi, Jessica?" she said.

The woman in the doorway slumped sideways so her shoulder rested against the wall. A shaking hand covered her mouth, and two tears set off at the exact same moment down her cheeks.

"I'm Detective Inspector Heather Filson. Do you mind if we come in?"

Jessica's gaze flitted to Wayne. Heather couldn't see the expression on the sergeant's face, but she witnessed the reaction to it on Jessica's.

"Oh no. Oh, no, please, no!"

Another shape moved behind her. Suddenly, Ted from the canteen was there, his hands on her shoulders. He smiled kindly, though he struggled to keep his bottom lip steady.

"Hey, hey. In you come," he soothed, and Jessica clung to his arms like they were the only thing tethering her to this plane of existence, awful as it may be. "Come on, we'll get a seat."

He steered her around, mouthed to Heather for her to come in, then clocked Wayne for the first time. The sight of him made the special constable's jaw clench and his nostrils flare, but he made no comment about the sergeant's presence.

"Come on, we'll get the kettle on," Ted said, helping Jessica along the hallway.

As they passed the foot of the stairs, a sharp cry rang out from up above.

"Oh, no, no, not now," Jessica whimpered.

"It's fine. I'll get her," Ted said. "She'll have just heard the door."

Heather wiped her feet on the doormat, then stepped inside. The house's decor was simple and modern, the light grey walls of the hallway adorned with photos of Darryl, Jessica, and their daughter, all professionally taken and mounted in elegant white frames.

In what had to be the most recent, the baby looked to be around six months old. She was lying across her dad's back, her pudgy fingers messing up his hair, the woman who had now been reduced to a broken shell in her hallway lying beside them, beaming from ear to ear.

The minimalist theme continued into the living room, the neat lines of the place broken only by some scattered baby toys and a couple of well-chewed cardboard picture books.

Ted lowered his sister onto a two-seater couch, then gestured to the matching three-seater that sat at a right angle to it.

"Please."

Heather and Wayne both sat at opposite ends of the couch. The crying from upstairs was louder in this room and crackled as it came through a baby monitor on the coffee table.

Ted shot his sister a smile of apology, then tilted his head towards the door. "I'll just... Right. I'll just settle her and be back. I'll be right back."

Jessica's grip tightened on his hand, and for a moment it looked like she wouldn't let go. Couldn't let go.

But then, an anguished scream over the monitor made her fingers uncurl and her hand drop into her lap.

With a short, sharp look in Wayne's direction that made his displeasure at the sergeant's presence clear, Ted left the room and hurried up the stairs, making soft, low, *shushing* noises as he went.

Heather sat forward a little and gently cleared her throat. "Jessica, I'm really sorry to have to—"

"How did it happen?" the other woman asked. Grief was constricting her throat, but there was a 'cut the bullshit' look in her eye that Heather fully appreciated and understood.

"We don't have a lot we can tell you yet, I'm afraid. We're just running our initial..."

The crying of the baby was like a dagger to the heart. The look on her mother's face wasn't helping, either.

"It looks like he was attacked," Heather said. To hell with the platitudes. Fuck the guidelines. The woman deserved to know what had happened to her husband. "He responded to a callout. Kids causing trouble or something. It looks like someone ambushed him from behind. But, as I say, it really is early, so some of this is just speculation."

Jessica nodded. Her hands were clasped together and squeezed between her knees, like she had to keep them trapped there for their own safety.

"Was it a knife?"

It was Wayne who replied. "Yes."

Her shoulders shook. More tears broke through her now fully crumbled defences.

"He always worried about knives. You see so many of them, he always said. He was always worried someone might..."

She folded forward and buried her face in her hands, her whole body heaving with grief.

Over the baby monitor, her daughter's crying eased off a little, and a whispered lullaby floated around the room.

"Hush little baby, don't say a word..."

"Jessica," Heather began. "I promise you that we're going to—"

"Can you get out now, please?"

Heather hesitated. "I know it must be—"

Jessica's hands fell away, revealing a face that was all twisted up in rage.

"I said, get out! Get out! *Get out!*"

She snatched up a silver satin cushion from the couch and hurled it across the room. It hit yet another family photo frame, which slid down the wall and smashed on the wooden flooring.

Jessica stared mutely at the broken glass on the floor for a few moments, before a piercing, inhuman squeal rose from somewhere deep inside her. The sound of pain in its rawest, purest form.

The singing from the baby monitor stopped. Footsteps creaked overhead, and then thudded down the stairs, accompanied by a resurgence of wailing.

When Ted raced into the living room, he had a red-faced howling infant held to his chest. "What's happened? What's going on?" he demanded, and Heather noted the way he glared at Wayne, like he suspected the sergeant was responsible for whatever had kicked off in his absence.

"Nothing. We were just talking, and she got upset," Wayne said, talking as if Jessica wasn't still right there with them in the room.

"Of course she fucking *got upset*," Ted spat back. "What the hell did you think was going to happen?"

The venom in his voice made the baby cry harder still, and he fought to control his anger while he bounced her gently in his arms. Swallowing back her own grief, Jessica held out her hands for her daughter, and cooried her in close the moment Ted handed her over.

"Right, I think we're done here," Ted said. He turned to Heather, bypassing Wayne completely. "Thanks for coming, but I think you should go now. You can send a liaison."

Heather stood up. The movement made Jessica flinch and pull her baby closer to her.

Wayne placed his cap back on his head, then looked down at the woman rocking with her daughter on the couch. "I'm sorry for your loss."

"Just get out," Ted warned, and Heather could sense the anger he was fighting to contain.

The sergeant eyeballed him, then tapped the peak of his cap. "My condolences again," he said, before turning on his heel and marching along the hall.

Heather hung back for a moment. "Well, uh... I'll make sure someone comes round."

Ted nodded. "I'll see you out."

After a glance at his sister to make sure she'd be able to hold herself together for the next few moments, he followed Heather to the front door. Wayne was already out of the garden, hurrying up the street in the direction of his parked car.

"Thanks for coming," Ted said, once they reached the front step.

The November night air was bracing, and Heather tugged on the zip of her leather jacket to help fend off the worst of the cold.

"Of course," she said. "I'm just sorry we had to."

Ted nodded, but he didn't seem to be really listening. "Did he ask to come? Wayne? Was that his decision or yours?"

"His," Heather said. "Why?"

Ted narrowed his eyes and peered through the patchy darkness in the direction the sergeant had gone. The headlights of the squad car kicked in, the beams sweeping across the street as Wayne pulled out of the parking space.

"Nothing. It's probably nothing," Ted said.

He watched as the car passed. It slowed, and Wayne glowered at him through the side window, then the engine roared and he sped off out of the estate.

"Didn't seem like nothing," Heather said. "Is there something you're not telling me?"

"No. I just…" Ted sighed and rubbed his eyes with a thumb and forefinger. "Daz had talked about putting in a complaint."

"About Sergeant Gillespie?" Heather asked.

"Aye. Not sure if he got around to it. But he was worried about some of the stuff Wayne—Sergeant Gillespie—was saying."

"Why? What sort of stuff was he saying?" Heather asked, feigning ignorance.

Ted shuffled uncomfortably. "I, eh, I don't know. Not exactly. Just… I didn't really hear him saying it, so…"

"What did Darryl tell you?" Heather prompted.

Ted cringed, clearly wishing that he hadn't opened his mouth. "He's been getting some of the boys fired up. A few of them have taken to dishing out slaps to a few of the Young Teams. Throwing their weight about a bit. Again, I've not heard or seen anything. I'm just saying what Daz told me."

Heather nodded. "Anything else?"

"No. Not really."

There was more there, Heather could sense it.

"Ted, anything you can tell me…"

The special constable groaned below his breath, ran a hand down his face, then stepped out of the house and pulled the door gently closed behind him.

"Daz said Wayne seemed weirdly obsessed with Shuggie Cowan. Said it was because of Cowan that people thought they could say and do what they like. But, I mean, that's bollocks. Pardon my language."

"It's fine."

"Cowan was a big man back in the day, but he's minor league now. Isn't he?"

Heather couldn't really argue with that. Shuggie Cowan's name had once been known and feared across the whole of Central Scotland. Now, he was an old man with a janky pub, clinging to past triumphs.

He was still dangerous, aye, but he was the knackered old lion sleeping on the ground, not the hungry Alpha standing atop the rocks. You still wouldn't want to stick your head in its mouth, but it was unlikely to chase you down.

"Aye. More or less," Heather confirmed.

"But the way Wayne was talking about him, it's like he's the Devil himself. He wants to bring him down. And I don't mean arrest him." Ted held both hands up. "But that's just Daz's opinion on it all. Wayne has barely said a word to me in a year and a half, since all the stuff with his wife blew up. Not that I'm complaining."

Heather remembered something the special constable had mentioned at Tony's gathering. "You said you'd put in a complaint about him, didn't you?"

Ted nodded. "Yeah. A while back, though. Three years, maybe. Bit longer. He took a kick at a couple of homeless guys. Young lads. Probably not even out of their teens. They weren't for shifting, so he stuck the boot in. He got pulled in for it, but he denied it of course. Never heard the outcome, though he was back at work a week later, as much of an arsehole as ever. Pardon the language."

"It's fine," Heather said again. She looked along the street in the direction Wayne had driven. "Anything else you can tell me?"

"No. Sorry. That's all I know. But Daz was going to put in a formal complaint. I know that for a fact. Don't know if he'd done it yet, though."

"Did Wayne know? What Daz was planning?"

Ted shook his head. "Doubt it. I think I was the only person he'd said anything…"

Heather saw the realisation descending on him. It was a heavy thing that pulled down his face and stooped his shoulders.

"What? Was there someone else? Did someone else know that Daz was planning to report Sergeant Gillespie?"

Ted's eyes darted around, like he was looking for a way out of having to answer. "Um, I'm not…"

"Ted. If there's someone, you need to tell me. I need to know. For Daz's sake."

The special constable groaned and looked up at the under-side of the canopy that covered the step. He closed his eyes and exhaled. A faint cloud of white mist blossomed in the cold night air.

"Ash," he said, in a voice that was barely a whisper. "I think he might have mentioned it to Ash Crier."

TWENTY-SEVEN

MARTY WAS in the office when Heather called from the car. But then, of course he was.

Rain had started to fall, and the lights of the city slid past as blurs on the slick glass. The flashing blues of a fire engine tore past. Somewhere, a little further to the east, sirens wailed.

Glasgow was lively tonight. Even more so than usual.

Heather listened grimly as Marty filled her in on the latest on Darryl Hartmann's murder.

He'd been stabbed in the stomach, the blade angled deliberately upwards beneath his protective vest. Large knife, judging by the wound. The killer must've taken it away with them, because it was nowhere to be found.

As Heather had expected, he'd died from blood loss from the throat wound, though that likely only accelerated the process, the damage having already been done with the stomach injury.

"What about the forehead? There was a cut," Heather said.

Marty's intake of breath was silent, but she sensed it down the line.

"Someone wrote on him. Carved into him, I mean."

Heather tore her eyes off the road long enough to glance at the stereo. "Jesus. Saying what?"

"ACAB," Marty said.

Heather was momentarily lost for words. Eventually, she managed a muttered, "Christ," through gritted teeth. "All cops are bastards."

"The Gozer and the higher-ups are having a meltdown," Marty said, his voice lowering like he was afraid someone might be listening in. "Three of our lads in three days, all violently killed. The media's already getting in about it."

"I'll bet they are."

"They're going to have a bloody field day. And if the bams think that people are murdering polis and getting away with it…"

"Then it'll be open season," Heather concluded.

An ambulance screamed past, followed by two squad cars. She squinted at the passing light show, then watched them disappearing in her rearview mirror.

"Wild West out here tonight," she said.

"Aye, seems to be," Marty confirmed. "Load of the old Young Teams are out and about, kicking off."

Heather scowled. "Are they no' all settled down with ten kids each by this point? They're too old for that shite."

"Probably tasting blood in the water," Marty reasoned. "If they start seeing us as weak…"

Heather cut him off there. "You're starting to sound like Wayne Gillespie."

It took Marty a moment to place the name. "The sergeant?"

"Aye. I want you to look into him for me, will you? See what complaints have been lodged. Check if Darryl Hartmann ever reported him."

"Shit. Wow. OK," Marty said, immediately grasping the significance.

"In fact, Tony Crier, too. Check if Tony ever made any complaints about him, or raised concerns."

"Jesus. Right. Aye, will do. I'll get on that."

Heather checked the clock on the dash, then double-checked it against her watch. "It's nearly two o'clock in the morning, Marty. Hand this over. Go home and get some rest."

"Aye, no, I will," the detective sergeant said. "I'll just make a start on it, then pass it on."

Heather stopped at a junction, just as another fire engine went whooshing past with its blues on. The lights of the city always cast an orange glow against the low-hanging cloud, but tonight it seemed to flicker more than usual.

What the hell was going on out there?

"Right, well, I'll believe you. Thousands wouldn't," Heather told him. "I'm heading home, though. I'll bring DC Swanney in with me in the morning and we'll see where we're at."

"OK. You got time for a couple of things, though?"

"I'm still driving," Heather said. "So, aye. Are they going to keep me awake, though?"

"Maybe," Marty admitted, but then he pressed on regardless. "They found Darryl's car. It was out on the Burnhouse Industrial Estate at Whitburn. Along the M8."

"And?"

"Burned out. Looks like the tracker was faulty, or maybe deactivated back at the community centre, though that would take a bit of know-how. Aiko's lot are going to go over it, but it's a shell, so nobody's holding out much hope."

"No." Heather wriggled in her seat, trying to keep her arsecheeks awake. She still had a lot of miles left to do. "Bollocks. And I'm guessing most of the estate would've been shut?"

"When it was found anyway, aye. No saying when it got there, though. CID's rounding up numbers for everywhere now, and getting in touch. Anyone we don't get, we'll scoop up in the morning. Someone might have seen something."

"You think?" Heather asked.

Marty sounded as optimistic about their chances as she felt. "Never know, I suppose. Stranger things have happened."

"Aye. Maybe," Heather conceded. "What was the other thing?"

"The other...? Oh! Aye. Mickey Buttfuck's wife and kid flew off to Spain this morning," Marty told her. "Or yesterday morning now, I suppose. Looks like they've got a place out on the Costa del Sol."

"Course they have. What about Mickey? He not with them?"

"Not unless he's travelling under a different name. A different name than his real one, I mean. I doubt his passport says 'Mr Buttfuck' on it."

"What is his real name, anyway?" Heather asked, suddenly realising that she'd never heard it.

"You don't know?!" Despite his tiredness, Marty's excitement was palpable. "It's a belter. You ready? He's Michael Gaylord Butterworth."

"Jesus Christ," Heather muttered. "No wonder he turned to a life of crime."

"I know. I mean, I'm an openly gay man, and even I'd rip the pish out of him for that," Marty said. "Can you imagine if he went to school round here? He'd have been dead by Primary Two."

"Aye. If he was lucky."

"But, anyway, as far as we know, he's still in the country," Marty said. "We've got ANPR watching for his plates. If he pings up, we'll be the first to hear about it."

"And Uniform's watching his house?"

Marty confirmed that they were.

"Find out who it is. Make sure it's someone we trust," Heather said. She adjusted her grip on the wheel. "Something's... I don't know. It doesn't feel right."

"That'll be all the murdered polis," Marty suggested. "That sort of thing can really set you on edge, right enough."

"Aye. Maybe." She watched as another police car rushed by in the opposite direction, lights flashing and sirens screaming through the night. "But something tells me this is all going to get a whole lot worse before it gets any better."

TWENTY-EIGHT

CATHY TURNED out to be as good as her word. In fact, that was doing Ace's mum a disservice. She was better than her word. She turned up a few minutes before eight, spent a few minutes reintroducing herself to a half-awake Scott, then set about making breakfast for him while simultaneously ushering Heather and Tammi-Jo out the door.

That meant that, even with the morning traffic, they were going to arrive at HQ earlier than expected. Heather couldn't be having that, not after Snecky had given them grief for being late the day before. He'd start to think she was actually listening to him.

Instead, they took a detour via Tony Crier's house. If that notebook was still there, the place was worth another look.

They were intercepted on their way to the gate by an older constable who jumped out of his warm car, nursing a Thermos flask to his chest. Though he looked confrontational to start with, his demeanour changed when he recognised Heather. Once he'd handed over the key, and assured her that nobody had come or gone during his shift, the DI told him to go get back in his car and out of the biting, early morning cold.

He hadn't argued, and by the time Heather and Tammi-Jo were halfway up the garden path, the constable was back sipping coffee in the driver's seat.

"That must be where the Iron Woman got the key," DC Swanney remarked, as Heather unlocked the door.

She pointed down to a rounded rock at the edge of the path. The grass around it had been flattened, indicating that the stone had been moved multiple times. Anyone who was paying even the slightest bit of attention would've figured it out as a hiding place.

"Not exactly subtle," the DC said. "You can see it a mile off."

"Aye, but most people are thick," Heather reasoned. "Or, at least, they're usually not paying attention."

"That's true, I suppose. About them not paying attention, not them being thick. I mean, whoever broke in didn't notice it, obviously, since they came in through the back window."

"Aye." Heather pushed down the handle and opened the door. "Or that's what they wanted us to think."

She led the way inside, but stopped a few paces into the hall. The stairs led up to the right for two steps, then hung a sharp left turn and climbed to the floor above.

Theoretically, it would've been possible to see Tony lying on the stairs from the front door, but only if you were making a point of looking. You wouldn't be fully confronted by the sight of him unless you leaned to the right a bit, and you couldn't really do that until the door was closed.

It didn't rule out the Iron Woman's story as being true. It could well have happened exactly as she described.

But Heather had her doubts, especially as she was claiming that she'd been laden down with bags at the time.

"Where should we start looking?" Tammi-Jo asked.

Heather turned away from the stairs. "Scene of Crime'll have gone over the rooms upstairs with a fine-tooth comb. If there was anything there to find, they'd have found it," she said. "Which leaves downstairs and outside."

"Outside?"

"There's a coal bunker. It's a possibility," Heather said, though she didn't sound particularly convinced.

"If it's that important, wouldn't it be risky to keep it outside?" Tammi-Jo asked.

Heather shrugged. "If that's what he was killed for, clearly it was risky to keep it inside, too."

"Suppose. Well, I could do the inside, if you want?" Tammi-Jo said.

"What, not the manky, freezing cold bit that's covered in spiders? Very generous of you."

Tammi-Jo smiled, though it was partly a grimace. "I mean, I *can* do outside if you really want me to."

Heather rolled her eyes. "It's fine. I'll check out there. You just... I don't know. Look around."

The DC nodded happily. "I'm good at looking around. It's one of my top five skills."

Heather regarded her big beamer of a smile for a moment. The detective constable, as ever, appeared to be completely genuine.

"Well done," Heather said. She pointed towards the living room. "Start in there. Try and not break anything unless you really have to."

"Ten-four," Tammi-Jo replied, snapping off a salute. She pushed open the door beside her, and Heather set off along the hallway towards the kitchen.

She was shocked at first to see the carnage on the Linoleum floor. Broken glass and crockery lay strewn across it, along with a couple of teaspoons and a long-handled pot scourer.

The blinds, it seemed, had given up the ghost at some point, their damaged fixings giving way, allowing the whole thing to come crashing onto the worktop, scattering the dishes that had been drying on the draining board.

With the blinds down, Heather got a clear, full-on view of the back garden, and of Mickey Gaylord Butterworth's house standing beyond it. There was still no sign of movement at the ex-con's place. It looked as empty as it had the day before.

Heather crossed to the back door, let herself out, and clumped down the two stone steps until she stood on the strip of stone slabs that ran along the back of Tony's house.

The coal bunker was an ancient metal thing with a fold-up plastic lid. Rust pitted the surface around the welded joins, and a light patina of frost had patterned the sides.

The lip of the lid was blackened with coal dust, so Heather used the end of her jacket sleeve to flip it open, then shone her phone's torch inside.

There was a single layer of coal way down at the bottom, gaps visible between the lumps. Spiderwebs covered much of it, suggesting it had been quite some time since Tony had used it.

"Bollocks," Heather muttered. It had been a long shot, but it would've been a nice result to find the notebook wrapped and buried in there.

She checked around the storage bin, in the gap between it and the wall, and on the underside of the lid.

There was no space beneath the bunker to slide even a sheet of paper, so she ruled that out, too.

The rest of the garden was just grass, the tips white and rigid with November frost. Unless Tony had neatly dug up a patch, hidden the notebook, then expertly re-laid the turf, she wasn't likely to find anything else out there.

Returning to the kitchen, she closed the door, then rubbed some warmth back into her hands as she looked around.

Scene of Crime would've gone over this room, too, since it was the point of entry. Supposedly, anyway. Besides the drawers, there were no obvious hiding places. Even if Aiko's team hadn't discovered the missing notebook in here, surely whoever had broken in looking for it would've checked here first before rummaging around up the chimney?

In fact, surely they'd have checked everywhere? What was she really hoping to find here? Anything of any significance was most likely already gone.

"I think we should knock this on the head," Heather announced, trudging on through to the living room. "I doubt we're going to…"

She stopped when she saw Tammi-Jo slowly rotating in the centre of the room, her head craning up and down like she was painting the walls with her gaze.

"What *are* you doing?" Heather asked.

"I'm looking," Tammi-Jo said.

"What with, X-ray vision? The notebook's hardly likely to be sitting around in the open, is it? We'd have noticed."

Tammi-Jo continued her gradual rotation. "I'm not looking for the notebook," she said. "I mean, I am, but I'm not. I'm not right now, I mean."

Heather's brow creased in confusion. "What are you looking for, then?"

"I don't know," the DC admitted. "But there's something."

The DI put her hands on her hips and stole a glance around the room. "What are you on about?"

Tammi-Jo stopped turning and met Heather's eye. "I can't really explain it. It's just something my brain does. There's like a little light on right now telling me there's something I should be seeing."

"A little light?"

"Not actually. It just feels that way. Do you know what I mean?"

Heather shook her head. "Absolutely not."

Tammi-Jo smiled. "I think I just notice things. But I don't necessarily know I've noticed them, and then I have to think about what it is I've noticed until I realise what it is. Does that make sense?"

"Again, no. Not really," Heather told her. "So you think you've noticed something in here?"

"No."

"No? OK, now I'm really confused. What the fuck are you talking about?"

Tammi-Jo shifted her weight from foot to foot. "I don't think I've noticed something. I know I've noticed something."

"But you don't know what, or where it is?"

"Not yet. But I usually figure it out."

Heather raised an eyebrow. "Usually?"

"Nine times out of ten," Tammi-Jo replied. "Well, seven. Probably closer to seven. Maybe eight! Eight times out of ten? Could that be right?"

Heather sighed. "You sound like you've lost your mind."

"I haven't. I mean, it might sound a bit like it, I suppose, but it's true. I notice things. Like out front, with the stone that Sergeant Crier kept the key under. I noticed…"

She blinked. It was a slow peeling up and down of her eyelids, like something inside her had been forced to do a hard reset, momentarily powering her down.

"I know what it is," she declared, then she turned one-eighty and scurried quickly to the corner of the room, to where the sparkling purple geode stood mounted on its wooden plinth. She slapped the top of it. "The stone."

"What about it?"

Tammi-Jo pointed a finger up towards the ceiling, then redirected it in the direction of the floor. Heather followed it and found herself looking down at the circular wooden plinth the geode was mounted on.

"Scratches," Heather realised.

"Scratches," DC Swanney confirmed. "It's been moved. More than once."

"Shift," Heather urged, stepping past the detective constable and wrapping her arms around the big hunk of rock.

She braced her legs and then attempted to straighten them, but there was no moving the bloody thing.

"Christ, that's heavy," Heather muttered.

"Maybe tip it?" Tammi-Jo suggested. "You tip, I'll look?"

Heather didn't say a word, but walked behind the standing stone and gripped it by the opening that revealed the sparkling purple innards.

"Ready?" she asked.

Tammi-Jo knelt on the floor by the plinth and snapped on a pair of thin latex gloves that she'd taken from a sealed pack in her pocket.

"*Ready, Keptin,*" she said in a broad Russian accent. "Sorry, that was the guy from Star Trek. I've got no idea why I— Oh, we're going!"

With a grunt, Heather tilted the lump of rock towards her, creating a gap at the bottom.

"I see something!" Tammi-Jo cried.

"Hurry up and get it, then!" Heather urged, struggling with the weight.

The detective constable placed the flat of a hand on the front of the geode, helping to support it. The other shot into the gap, fumbled around for a moment, then emerged holding something carefully wrapped in a plastic carrier bag.

"Coming down!" Heather warned, then the weight of the stone became too much and it slammed back down onto the wooden base.

Its momentum rocked it back and forth, and for a moment it looked like it would be thrown off-balance. It soon settled, though, and aside from another scratch on the wood, nobody would ever know it had been moved.

Tammi-Jo was already in the process of unwrapping the bag from around the object within. Heather tapped a hand against the side of her leg impatiently, watching as the detective constable carefully unravelled the folds of plastic.

"What is it?" the DI asked when Tammi-Jo finally got the bag open.

The detective constable looked inside, stared in silence for a moment, then angled the bag towards the senior officer.

Inside, lurking at the bottom, was a small hardback notebook that was missing its matching pen.

"See?" Tammi-Jo rocked happily on her heels. "Told you I notice things."

TWENTY-NINE

ACE WURZEL WAS BEING WATCHED. She could feel it.

And, more importantly, she could see it. He wasn't exactly hiding it.

He stood near the front of the room, his hands tucked behind his back, nodding to the rest of the class as they filed past him out the door, while keeping his eyes trained on her as she finished packing everything back into its correct position in her bag.

"Ace, do you mind hanging back for a few minutes?" Mr Pearse asked her.

There was a smile packaged alongside the question, but after several missteps throughout the years, Ace had eventually worked out that questions like these from teachers weren't actually questions at all. They were orders in disguise.

She nodded curtly, put her arms through both straps of her bag, then stood by her desk waiting for the rest of the class to leave. A boy, Edward Williams, shot her a slightly worried look, before being ushered out by Mr Pearse, who closed the door behind him.

"Am I in trouble?" asked Ace, who didn't believe in beating around the bush.

Mr Pearse smiled again and perched one bum cheek on the corner of his desk. "Why would you be in trouble?"

Ace took a moment to consider this. How much did he know? Clearly, there was some reason for her being kept back. Her classwork was of a high standard, her homework had been done, and she hadn't annoyed anyone lately, at least not deliberately. So, it couldn't be any of those.

Mr Pearse wasn't just her English teacher, though, he was also her Guidance teacher. Maybe this was a pastoral issue. Maybe someone had expressed concern for her wellbeing.

Unlikely, she thought.

"I have no idea," she finally admitted. "But, I'm assuming you're not keeping me back for a personal chat."

"No."

"Because that would be wildly inappropriate."

"No, I know. I'm not—"

"Good. Because I'm really not interested."

"What? Jesus!" the teacher spluttered, rising quickly back to his feet. "I'm not... That really isn't... You were absent. Yesterday. You missed both periods in the afternoon!"

"Ah." Ace pulled on the red glasses that had been hanging from their string around her neck, and pushed them into place with the tip of a finger. "That's why you wanted to talk to me?"

"Yes! That's why I wanted to talk to you!"

"Right. Yes. That makes sense," Ace said. "Apologies, but you hear stories, don't you, about young teachers and students? I wanted to make it clear up front that I have no interest whatsoever in any sort of—"

"Neither do I!" Toby cried.

"Right. Good. Because you're romantically interested in Detective Inspector Filson."

"Because I'm not a predatory paedophile!" The teacher realised that his voice had risen sharply, and took a moment to straighten his tie while he brought it back under control. "Also, I'm not... I don't know what's given you the idea that I'm... With DI Filson. Because that's just not..."

"OK. Fine. Whatever you say. I'm not actually interested. So, I can go now?" Ace asked, gripping the straps of her bag and heading for the door.

Toby nodded and waved his hand. "Yes! You can... Wait. No. I haven't finished talking to you yet."

Ace stopped and nodded solemnly. It had been worth a try.

"Where were you?" the teacher asked. "Yesterday afternoon, where did you go? Is everything alright?"

"Everything's fine, thank you," Ace confirmed.

Toby nodded expectantly at her. "So...? Why weren't you in periods six and seven?"

Ace didn't even have to think about her answer. She'd already prepared it, just in case of this sort of scenario.

"Women's troubles," she said, so bluntly and flatly that Mr Pearse could only blink.

"Oh."

"Related to my female monthly cycle."

"Right."

"I won't go into the details."

"Please don't," the teacher said. He blew out his cheeks and sat on the corner of his desk again. "You sure that's it? It's not like you to miss classes."

"It really was a particularly heavy flow," Ace said.

"Jesus," Toby whispered. He ran a hand down his face. "If there's something else bothering you, Ace, you can talk to me. You know that, right?"

Ace hesitated, then gave a tiny nod of her head.

"If you're in trouble. If there's anything you're struggling with. If anyone is being a dick to you..."

Ace's brow furrowed, surprised by the swear word usage, however mild it may be.

"Being nasty to you, I mean."

"No. I mean, no more than usual. Less than usual. A bit. It comes and goes." She hoisted her bag a little higher up on her shoulders. "People had difficulty speaking to me before. They always have. Being kidnapped didn't exactly help matters. Not once the novelty wore off, anyway."

She took a deep breath, looked around the classroom as if searching for something, then turned her attention back to the teacher again.

"Do you mind if I ask you something?"

Toby smiled. "That's pretty much what they pay me for. Go for it."

"How do you do it?" Ace asked.

The teacher's eyebrows rose. "Do what?"

"Get people to like you. You seem to be good at it. Even this class, populated by half-wits and cretins as it is. They like you. How do you do that?"

Mr Pearse let out a little laugh. "Well, I start by not calling people half-wits or cretins."

Ace took this on board with a, "Huh." She tapped the side of her skull like she was locking it in. "And?"

"Aaaand…" Toby shrugged. "I guess just be yourself. Be honest."

Ace immediately shook her head at that. "I *really* can't see that helping. I'd say that's possibly the problem."

"You'd be surprised," Toby said. "If you're honest, if you open yourself up to people and show them the real you, you'll be surprised how they react."

Ace took another moment to consider the advice. "But what if the real you just isn't very likeable?"

"I really don't think that's something you need to worry too much about, Ace."

"Honesty, you say? Well. We'll see how that works out. Thank you for your time, Mr Pearse. I promise there'll be no further unauthorised absences from me for the foreseeable future."

The teacher smiled and got to his feet. "Good. Glad to hear it," he said.

He walked with her to the classroom door, falling into step beside her. Ace could sense there was more he wanted to say, but it was only when she reached for the door handle that he blurted it out.

"Detective Inspector Filson. You... know her, don't you?"

"I do. We're friends," Ace said. "Well, in as much as a fifteen-year-old and a thirty-six-year-old can be friends. We're not doing each other's hair or anything. Why?"

"Just..." The teacher scratched at his neck. His nails left white marks on his reddening skin. "Does she ever, you know, like, mention me? At all?"

"You?"

"Yes."

"No."

"Oh."

"Never."

"Right."

Ace may not have been particularly adept at reading facial expressions, but even she could tell he was disappointed.

"You did say I should be honest," she reminded him.

"What? Oh. Yes. Yes, of course. Well done!" He opened the door, then watched as one of the boys from his class went scurrying backwards into the corridor, his eyes wide with terror. "Edward? What are you doing?"

"Nothing, sir," Edward said, his voice rising to a squeak, then quickly collapsing back into a dull monotone. "I wasn't hanging about."

"You were hanging about, Edward. You were clearly hanging about," Toby pointed out. "Look. You're still hanging about now."

"No, sir, I was just..."

He ran a hand up and down the doorframe, nodded like it was the most impressive thing he'd ever seen.

"Smooth that," he remarked, then he clicked his fingers a few times and backed into the corridor. "So... I'll just..."

His eyes met Ace's, then he quickly looked away. The girl remained completely oblivious to it. The teacher, however, did not.

"Well, listen, since you're here, maybe you can keep Ace company over break?"

"What?" Edward spluttered. He put his clenched fists on his hips and inhaled deeply, like he was a car mechanic about to drastically over-inflate a repair bill. "I mean, I was going to sort of, like..."

He lost the thread completely, stared in silence at the teacher for a moment, then ran a hand up and down the door-frame's woodwork again.

"That's really well done."

"Ace," Toby said, guiding the girl towards the door. "I'm going to leave you in Edward's capable hands. And just, you know, remember what we spoke about. OK?"

Ace nodded. "I will. Thank you for your time."

She tucked her thumbs in under the straps of her bag and stepped out of the classroom. Toby watched through a narrowing gap as she and Edward shuffled away together, then closed the door to allow them their privacy.

"So... So, so, so," Edward said. He clicked his fingers again and slapped the side of one hand against the palm of the other. "Were you in trouble?"

"Not really," Ace said. Then, remembering the teacher's advice, she admitted, "A bit."

"Was it because you left school at lunchtime?"

"Yes. How did you know that?"

Edward's cheeks stung red. "What? Oh. I just... I think I might have seen you leaving. Hawkeye asked where you were in Maths, but I didn't say anything. I wouldn't."

"Thank you. I appreciate that," Ace said. Their feet scuffed along the vinyl floor in near-perfect step with one another.

"Are you, em...? What are you...?" Edward narrowed his eyes and looked up, like his mind had just gone completely blank on him. "What was it I was going to say again?" he muttered.

"I have no idea," Ace told him.

"Ha! No! I mean, you're not a mind reader!" Edward said. He grimaced at the thought, then swallowed hard. "Thank God."

"Why *thank God*?" Ace asked. "What were you thinking that you didn't want me to know about? This isn't a trick, is it?"

"What?"

"You're not going to lock me in a cupboard or throw me down the stairs?"

"No!"

"Or put dog faeces in my bag?"

"No! Why would I put dog shit in your bag?!"

Ace's eyes narrowed. "You tell me."

They turned a corner and parted to let a first-year go sprinting past, then remained on opposite sides of the corridor while a couple of furious third-years went thundering after him.

Once the chase had progressed deeper into the school, they set off walking again.

"I'm just... I was thinking that maybe, I don't know, if you're not busy, or whatever..."

The redness of Edward's cheeks had been replaced by a pale, pallid grey now. Whatever he was building up to, it was taking a lot out of him.

He gulped down a giant breath, then exhaled the next sentence in one big puff.

"I thought maybe you might want to go bowling. Or something."

Ace stopped walking. "Bowling?"

"Or something," Edward reiterated. He danced from foot to foot, clicking his fingers in a frantic, frenzied rhythm.

"Stop doing that," Ace told him, pointing to his hands.

Edward did as he was told. "Sorry," he said. "I fidget when I'm nervous."

Ace's eyes narrowed behind her red-framed glasses. "Why are you nervous?"

Edward's fingers almost started clicking again, but he stopped himself in the nick of time. "Well, you know, because I'm asking you out."

"Bowling."

"Or something."

Ace pushed her glasses higher up the bridge of her nose with the tip of a pinkie finger.

"Lawn or ten pin?"

Edward tilted an ear towards her like he hadn't quite heard. "Sorry?"

"Bowling. Lawn or ten pin?"

The boy beside her looked pained by the question. "Ten pin? Or the other one, if you prefer. I'm not that fussed."

Ace looked along the corridor, then up at the ceiling, before finally turning her attention back to Edward.

"No," she said.

"No?" Edward squeaked.

"I mean, it doesn't sound awful. I'm potentially interested. But I can't right now. I'm in the middle of an investigation," Ace said.

"For *Crime De La Crime*?"

Ace hesitated. "You listen to my podcast?"

"Of course."

"Good. Huh. Well, yes. For that," Ace said. "Also, there's something I need to do, too."

"What is it?" Edward asked.

Ace took off her glasses and let them dangle around her neck. "I need to be honest with someone," she announced. She started walking again. "Next Tuesday."

"What?"

"Assuming I'm not in jail."

Edward frowned, hurrying to keep up with her. "I don't understand. What do you mean?"

"Bowling. Ten pin or lawn? I don't mind which one, either. Lawn's quieter, but you don't get the bumpers at the side, and it might be raining. And everyone's over fifty. And I don't know the rules, though I could look them up, I suppose, if it came to it."

She stopped abruptly again and thrust her hand out to him. He stared at it in disbelief, not quite sure what he was meant to do with it.

"Do we have a deal?" Ace asked.

"Uh, yeah." Edward took the offered hand and shook it. "It's a date!" He cringed at the sound of the words coming out of his mouth. "I mean... unless it's not. Is it?"

"A date?" Ace continued to shake his hand, her arm pumping up and down like it was powered by pistons. "Yes," she conceded, after some thought. "Yes, I suppose it is."

THIRTY

HEATHER HAD BEEN RIGHT about the notebook. Tony Crier hadn't been leering into a little girl's bedroom window, he'd been gathering evidence on two individuals meeting in the garden that backed onto his.

There were dates and times. No names, but the initials B and G appeared in more or less every entry, and some question marks that suggested other people had occasionally attended whom Tony couldn't identify.

The entries themselves weren't exactly crammed full of useful information, though. The bedroom window was too far away from the neighbouring garden for Tony to be able to hear anything, and based on some of the gibberish he'd written down, lipreading hadn't been one of the sergeant's strong points.

He'd added asterisks before and after any 'quotes' and stressed after each one that they were mostly guesswork.

Tammi-Jo had read the entries out loud while Heather had driven up the road to Glasgow. From what they could gather, the relationship between B and G was not always amicable. There had been pushing, shoving, and even a couple of slaps, mostly from B, though G had lost the rag a few times, too.

Unlike B, who seemed to express his anger physically, G was a shouter. It was through one of these more vocal outbursts that Tony was able to hear the one snippet of conversation that he seemed certain of.

"You fucking need me a lot more than I need you," G had bellowed. "If Cowan finds out about this, you're way more fucked than I am."

B had moved quickly to calm him down, and it was then, when B had been looking around to see if anyone had heard, that Tony had been spotted.

That entry was dated two days before Tony's death. It was the last one in the book.

Now, standing in the Incident Room, Snecky peered down at the notebook's pages. Simon leaned over the DCI's shoulder, his lips moving faintly as he read Tony's neat handwriting.

"Who's B?" Snecky asked, still skimming over the pages.

"We don't know," Heather admitted. "Butterworth, maybe. As in Mickey."

"Or Buttfuck," Simon suggested, with a smirk that suggested he just wanted to say something rude in the office without fear of repercussion. "Also, as in Mickey."

"And G?" Snecky wondered aloud.

Heather shrugged. "Not sure."

"Graham?" DC Wolfe guessed.

"Who's Graham?" Heather asked.

"Dunno. It's a G name though, isn't it?"

Marty looked up from his desk just long enough to mumble, "There's no arguing with that logic," then he went back to tapping away at his computer keyboard.

Heather decided just to put it out there. "Gillespie."

It took Snecky a moment to catch up.

"What, yon sergeant fella?"

"Wayne Gillespie, aye," Heather said. "If it's Butterworth, then Tony was using surname initials."

"Graham's a surname," Simon muttered.

Heather gritted her teeth long enough to count to five, then continued.

"I can't prove it yet, it's just a feeling, but I think he's involved. I don't know if he killed Tony, but I think he knows who did."

Snecky grimaced. "That's quite a claim. I mean, that's huge. What are you basing that on?"

"Nothing. Yet," Heather admitted. "I just—"

"You feel it," Snecky said, his nostrils flaring like the words offended him.

"Yes. I feel it."

"Facts trump feelings," Simon said. It came out of him like it was some automated response that had been programmed in back at the factory that had shat him out.

"You can't just go throwing that sort of accusation around," Snecky warned. "You need evidence." He picked up the notebook. "And this? This isn't it. This tells us nothing. A couple of people got into a few arguments in a garden. Whoop-de-doo. Lock them up and throw away the key. Except, no, wait, we can't, because we don't actually know who they are, do we?"

"One's got to be Mickey," Heather protested.

"No. It doesn't *have* to be. It might be. There's a very good chance that it could be. But it doesn't *have* to be anyone."

"It, uh, it does make sense," Tammi-Jo ventured.

Snecky spun to face her, and his bluster melted away in the crystal blue pools of her eyes. He lowered himself onto the edge of his desk and pinched his chin, like a professor considering some new thesis.

"Go on," he urged.

Heather rolled her eyes, then dropped into the seat beside Marty and crossed her arms.

"Well, I mean, it's DI Filson's theory, but it makes sense. Mickey's out back, talking to someone, making plans for some sort of, like, shenanigans."

"Sexual shenanigans?" DC Wolfe asked, waggling his unkempt eyebrows.

"Jesus Christ, Simon," Heather spat. "Put a sock in it, eh?"

Marty leaned a little closer to her. "Makes a change from him putting a sock *on* it," he whispered, and—juvenile as it was—Heather couldn't help but smirk at the comment.

"Criminal shenanigans," Tammi-Jo said. "He's out back with this G, whoever it is, and he's up to no good. He spots Sergeant Crier—we know he did, because it says so in the final entry—and then he comes round a couple of days later, and beats him up."

"No."

To the DC's surprise, it was Heather herself who objected.

"No? But that's pretty much exactly what you said last night."

"I know, but I didn't have the timings then. And there's something we forgot. The girl's window. The whole paedo thing. Going to Shuggie and asking for help."

Tammi-Jo shuffled her weight from one foot to the other, considering this. "He wanted to try scaring Sergeant Crier off first. But, no, that can't be it, because he didn't give it time to see if it worked. The sergeant was killed soon after Stevie went round."

"Gonad," Heather translated, when Snecky and Simon both showed their confusion. "And he lied. To Shuggie, I mean," the DI continued. "Mickey didn't tell Shuggie that he'd been spotted getting up to no good by a copper, he told him his daughter was being spied on by a nonce."

"Why lie?" Tammi-Jo asked. "If they're friends, why not just tell him the truth?"

Heather's phone rang. She checked the screen, saw the name 'Nancy Drew,' and swiped to reject the call.

"Because he couldn't. Because he was hiding something," Heather reasoned.

Tammi-Jo was pacing back and forth now, making everyone's head swing left and right to follow her. She pressed her fingers to her temples like she was channelling some sort of psychic energy.

"In the notes," Snecky said, flipping through the pages of the book. "Didn't it say something about...?"

"'If Cowan finds out about this, you're way more effed than I am,'" Tammi-Jo recited from memory. "But he didn't say 'effed.' He said the other one."

"Fucked," Simon said, in what was very possibly his most useful contribution to the entire conversation so far.

"So, why get him involved?" Marty wondered.

Tammi-Jo stopped pacing with an abrupt click of her heels. She and Heather both came to the same conclusion at the same time.

"He was setting him up!"

Heather's phone buzzed on the table beside it. She silenced it again, then leapt to her feet.

"He wants us to think Shuggie had something to do with Tony's death," Heather realised. "But he doesn't count on Shuggie sending Gonad, the one man who couldn't possibly have clambered in through the kitchen window."

She ran a hand through her hair. The build-up of grease felt slick between her fingers.

There was still something else. Something she was missing.

"Gonad got a kicking," she said. "He wouldn't tell us who from, but I think it was polis that did it."

"They must've thought he'd done it," Snecky said.

"Or they were trying to make it look like he did," Heather countered.

Snecky folded his arms and sniffed. "Well, if that's true. If it was some of our lot that did it, then they're lucky they didn't start a bloody war."

Heather blinked. A shape was forming in her head. It was still too faint and blurry for her to be able to see it properly, but it was in there somewhere, shifting and sharpening with every new piece of information.

"They did. Or, I don't know, they are. That's what they're trying to do." The DI let out a short, sharp laugh. "Fuck. He told me himself. He told me what he was doing."

"Who, Cowan?" Snecky asked.

Heather shook her head. "Wayne. Last night. He went on about rounding up the Shuggie Cowan's of the world, like he was going to personally execute him in George Square."

"Pretty good place for an execution," Simon said. He took a bite of a banana he had produced from somewhere. "Like, a firing squad or something." He chewed thoughtfully. "Hanging, maybe."

Heather ignored him, as did everyone else.

"So, Wayne's working with Mickey. Mickey wants to bring Cowan down so he can step into his shoes."

"I thought they were friends?" Snecky said. He pointed to Tammi-Jo, who was back pacing again. "She said they were friends."

"They're not friends," Heather replied. "Guys like that don't have friends. Shuggie said he was doing Mickey a favour, repaying him for some old slight or something. Christ knows what. But that's not how Mickey plans on being repaid. He's out to get his own back."

"By setting him up for murdering a police officer?" Snecky asked, sounding sceptical about the whole thing. "Even if Cowan did do it, there's no evidence. It doesn't help Mickey's plan."

"But it's an excuse for us to come down on Cowan like a tonne of bricks," Heather explained. "Our boys go in heavy, his lot retaliate, it escalates and escalates, and then suddenly we're at war."

"And Mickey Buttfuck slides in!" Marty said.

Heather grimaced. "I mean, I'd rather you hadn't said it like that, but aye. It's all a power grab. This whole thing is so Mickey can move in on Cowan's territory."

She turned back to the DCI. He flinched and visibly braced himself like he was expecting the worst.

"I want to bring Wayne Gillespie in," Heather said. "I want to pull him in for questioning."

Snecky groaned and rubbed at his forehead, a growing stress headache visible in the lines of his face.

"There's still not enough. It's all speculation. And Uniform's already on edge, we don't need this kicking off. There were running battles in the streets last night. They're having a rough time of it out there. It's like someone put something in the water."

"The way it's going, I bet our lot started it," Heather said. "They're on the warpath out there, and Wayne's driving it."

"Again, speculation," Snecky said.

"Then let me talk to him," Heather urged. "Let me and Marty bring him in here and question him under caution."

Snecky considered the request.

But not for long.

"No. Not yet. We need more."

Heather snatched up the notebook and stabbed a finger against the front page. "G. Gillespie. He's a smoker. There were fags in Mickey's back garden. He practically told me he was planning on taking Cowan down. No, he *literally* told me. To my face! And Daz, Darryl, was going to complain about him."

"Jesus! You're putting him down for Constable Hartmann's murder, too?" the DCI cried. "These are huge accusations, Detective Inspector. Huge. You need more evidence. Or *some* evidence, at least."

Heather had already turned away, and was addressing DS Brompton. "Marty, was there a complaint put in by Daz? Against Wayne?"

Marty smiled thinly, but shook his head. "No. Nothing."

Snecky leaned back on the desk, his face a picture of smug superiority.

"That doesn't mean anything," Heather insisted. "In fact, if he hadn't put in the complaint, but Wayne knew he was going to, then all the more reason to kill him!"

"Right. And I suppose Wayne *somehow* knew this, did he? He'd *somehow* got word that Darryl was planning to—"

"Yes."

That took the wind from the DCI's sails a bit. "Did he?"

"Ash knew. Darryl had told him, and he and Wayne seem to be..." Heather's face fell. "Oh, God."

"What? What now?" Snecky asked.

"The book. The notebook. That's what I was missing."

There was some consensus from the rest of the team that they had no idea what she was on about.

"Mickey spotted Tony watching them. We know that. It's written down. But I couldn't figure out how they knew about the notebook to come looking for it. What if Ash told them? What if he's in on it?"

Snecky pinched the bridge of his nose. "Jesus. Are you seriously saying Ash Crier murdered his own father?"

"No. I'm not saying that," Heather said, though she didn't sound sure. "I'm just saying maybe he'd mentioned something. Maybe he didn't even realise what it was he was saying. But if he tells Wayne that his old man's been keeping notes about something suspicious he's seen, it wouldn't take a genius to put two and two together."

"We could bring Ash in," Marty suggested. "See what he's saying."

"That might give us enough to bring in Sergeant Gillespie."

Heather thought back to her last encounter with Ash Crier. He hadn't been in a particularly talkative mood then. The one topic he had expressed any interest in chatting about, she'd very much like to avoid.

But what were her options? Snecky wasn't going to let her

pull Wayne in without more evidence, and she couldn't think of another way of getting anything concrete on the sergeant.

Her phone rang.

Nancy Drew.

She swiped it away absent-mindedly.

"Do you need to take that?" Snecky asked. "They seem determined."

"It's nothing," Heather said. She nodded. "Let's get Ash in. See what he has to say for himself."

"Hold up," Marty announced. He leaned in closer to the screen and scrolled his mouse wheel, his eyes darting from side to side as he read. "I think I might've just found Mickey Buttfuck."

"What? Where?"

Marty looked up from his screen. "Somewhere you're not going to believe."

THIRTY-ONE

HEATHER FINALLY RELENTED JUST as she was pulling the Audi onto the street where *The Pig & Bicycle* stood. She stabbed the green button on her phone screen, gave the call a second to connect, then said, "Jesus Christ, what?"

"You're a very difficult person to get hold of, Officer," Ace Wurzel said. The note of reprimand in her voice was unmissable. "I've tried calling you several times."

Heather braked so hard that Tammi-Jo had to brace herself against the dash.

"Tell me about it," Heather said. "I've been busy."

"On the case? Anything you can share on the record?" Ace asked.

"No. What do you want?"

Heather shut off the engine, glanced at the pub, then up at the mostly abandoned flats across the road from it.

"I have a confession," Ace said after a pause.

"OK. Can it wait?"

"Preferably not. I'd like to get it off my chest."

Heather sighed, and looked across at Tammi-Jo. The DC had no idea what was being asked of her, so she just shrugged and raised her eyebrows, and hoped that covered it.

"Fine. Go. But be quick," Heather urged, studying the front of the pub again.

The heavy wooden double doors were closed, but there were lights on upstairs. Possibly downstairs, too, though the boarded-up window made it impossible to tell.

"OK. Here goes," Ace said. She took a breath. "Yesterday, for the purposes of my own investigation, I gained entry to the home of the late Sergeant Crier."

Heather shut her eyes for a moment, and tightened her grip on the steering wheel. "After I specifically told you not to?"

"No. Before then," Ace admitted. "I was considering telling you last night, but then you said you were going to put me in prison. And, well, I don't enjoy the thought of that, so I didn't tell you. But you should know. It's important."

"Did you touch anything?" Heather asked.

"*I* didn't, no."

The emphasis made Heather's ears prick up. "You didn't. But someone else did?"

"Well deduced, Officer," Ace said. "There was someone there when I entered the house. That's another reason I'm telling you, because if I'm arrested, I'd like you to be there."

Heather stared at the stereo like she could somehow read the girl's facial expression over the airwaves.

"Why would you be arrested?" she asked.

"Well, because it was a policeman who was there. He was looking for something up the chimney."

Both Heather and Tammi-Jo's seats creaked as they leaned forward at the same time.

"Right. I see," Heather said. "A policeman was looking for something up the chimney?"

"Correct. That's literally what I just said."

Heather gripped the wheel. Held her breath. "Would you recognise him? If I showed you some photos, would you recognise him?"

"Oh, there's no need for that, Officer," Ace said. "I already recognised him."

"You did? What? How?"

"Well, it was your colleague, wasn't it?" Ace said. "It was your colleague from the careers fair. The one who clearly hated children."

Heather shot Tammi-Jo a sideways look, and mouthed, "Wayne." The detective constable's mouth formed a little circle of surprise.

"Right, and you're sure?" Heather asked. "It was definitely him?"

"Yes. I'm certain. If you could talk to him and apologise on my behalf, that would be very much appreciated. I accept that what I did was wrong, but I'd still rather not go to prison, if it can possibly be avoided."

"You're not going to prison," Heather assured her.

"Well. That's a relief," Ace said. "I was worried how my mother was going to take it, having a jailbird for a daughter. Also, I want to go to university, so incarceration was certainly going to make that more challenging."

"But I will need you to make a statement," the DI told her. "Just saying exactly what you told me."

"I can do that," Ace said. "In the meantime, I'll continue my investigation for the podcast."

"No. No, don't do that."

"I'll be careful. I'm just going to go step-by-step through the events of the morning when Sergeant Crier's body was discovered. I have a few leads that—"

"No! Don't. I mean it," Heather said. "Just stay out of trouble."

There was a long pause, then an, "Ugh. Fine. I'll stay out of trouble." She perked up as a thought struck her. "Oh, and there was one other thing, Officer. Unrelated, but I thought you should know."

"What is it?"

"It appears that my theory is correct," Ace declared.

"And what theory's this now?"

"It would seem that our mutual acquaintance, Mr Pearse, is *very* interested in you. Romantically, I mean. He didn't say as much, but even I could read his expression, and that's saying something, believe me."

From the passenger seat, Tammi-Jo made a solid attempt at whistling a '*wooot-wooo,*' before a glare from Heather shut that shit down.

"Don't care," Heather said, turning back to the stereo. "Stay out of trouble. In fact, go to my house. Your mum's there, anyway. Wait to hear from me. If anyone from the police turns up looking for you, you call me right away, OK? You don't go with them."

"You want me to resist arrest?"

"If that's what it comes to, then aye. Preferably just run. Is that clear?"

Ace didn't sound entirely convinced. "Very well, Officer. But, for your information, I've recorded this entire call, so if I end up behind bars as a result of your instructions, please rest assured that I'll be taking you down with me."

THIRTY-TWO

TAMMI-JO HADN'T BEEN happy about the orders to stay in the car, but she'd eventually agreed on the understanding that, at the first sign of trouble, she'd call for backup and then come rushing in. And that she couldn't guarantee it would be in that order.

Heather had accepted the terms, then headed over to *The Pig & Bicycle* and hammered on the door until someone had opened up.

He was a big lad—one of Shuggie's fuckwits—but bright enough not to try and stop Heather striding past him. She heard voices up above as she passed the foot of the stairs, then continued through into the downstairs bar to find Shuggie wedged into his usual corner.

"Bloody hell. Maybe I should be getting you your own key," Cowan said. "You're here that often."

"Not through choice, Shuggie," Heather told him. She stopped a couple of feet from his table and watched as he sized her up.

"You look on edge," he told her.

"Aye, you can say that again," Heather snapped. "Michael Butterworth. Mickey Buttfuck."

"What about him?"

"Where is he?"

Shuggie shrugged his big, rounded shoulders. "Beats me. Have you tried his house?"

"Why are you protecting him?" the DI demanded.

"Protecting him? Me? I'm not protecting him," Shuggie said.

"You said you owed him a favour."

Cowan pulled an exaggerated frown. "Did I say that?"

"Don't piss me about, Shuggie. What's the story?"

Cowan held her gaze for several seconds, then sniffed, scrunched up his nose, and shrugged. "He ended up getting a bit more mixed up in a job of mine than either of us had planned. Did a stretch for it. Kept his mouth shut, though. Which is what you want sometimes, isn't it?" he asked.

He raised his dyed eyebrows, though he needn't have bothered. His meaning was already clear.

"People who'll help you with your dirty work, and not breathe a word to anyone. That's someone you can depend on. Someone who goes above and beyond like that? Gets you out of a bind? That's the sort of person you'll feel compelled to do a favour for."

"What favour did you do for him?" Heather probed.

"Like I told you, we had a wee word with Sergeant Crier. Just that, though. Just a word. Nothing more. Man to man. Well, man to nonce."

"Tony wasn't a nonce, Shuggie. He wasn't watching the girl. He was watching her father."

Shuggie crossed his arms, saying nothing.

"And do you know what Mickey was doing when Tony was watching him?"

"I'm sure you're going to enlighten me."

"He was plotting," Heather said. "Against you."

Not a muscle of Shuggie's face moved. Not a millimetre. "Against me?"

"Aye. See, it turns out that Mickey wasn't happy with you doing him a wee favour. Mickey wanted more than that. No, sorry, he *wants* more than that. He's playing you, Shuggie. He's trying to either set you up, or kill you off."

Cowan shook his head. "Bollocks. He wouldn't. He wouldn't fucking dare, for a start, but no, he wouldn't do that."

Heather leaned down so the knuckles of her clenched fists rested on the gangster's table.

"I'm going to ask you again, Shuggie. Do you know where Mickey is right now?"

Cowan drummed his fingers on the table a few times, then shook his head. "No."

"Well, you must be getting sloppy in your old age. Because guess what, Shuggie? I do know where he is," Heather said. She tilted her head back in the direction of the door. "He's out there. Across the road. He only went and rented himself a flat directly overlooking this place. Looking right in your upstairs window. Right down on your front door."

Shuggie adjusted his bulk on the bench seat, then glanced past the detective inspector to the frosted glass of the door. The window was still barricaded by the big wooden board on the outside, though Heather couldn't see any damaged glass on the inside.

"Risky," he grunted.

"Risky?"

"Them flats are a death trap. Full of asbestos. Wiring's ancient and pretty much fucked. It's a miracle they've not gone up before now."

"I'm going to bring him in, Shuggie," Heather told him. "I wanted to make sure you weren't going to get in the way of that."

"We've all got our jobs to do, Detective Inspector," he said, after a moment's thought. "Tell you what, I'll leave you free to do yours, if you don't get in the way of mine. How's that sound?"

Heather snorted out a laugh that lasted all of half a second. "No promises."

"No? Shame. Well, in that case, I'll settle for you bringing all your wee lapdogs to heel."

Heather frowned. "Meaning?"

"Meaning all them twats in uniform you've got running about stirring up shite," Shuggie spat back. "Going after my boys. Not just them, though. Anyone who looks at them the wrong way. Anyone who doesn't scrape and bow to them. Those lads had better watch themselves. The good people of Glasgow aren't renowned for their tolerance towards arseholes. And especially not jumped-up pricks in flat caps and high-vis vests."

He smiled, but it was a cold, ruthless thing that made the skin on Heather's front feel like it was trying to crawl its way around to her back.

"I warned you, didn't I? If they didn't calm down, things were going to kick off. If it's a war you wanted, I said, it's a war you'd get."

"Nobody wants a war, Shuggie. That's what I'm trying to avoid. And that starts with me bringing Mickey Buttfuck in for questioning."

Shuggie sucked in his bloated bottom lip, chewed on it, then spat it back out again. "Well, like I said, Detective Inspector, far be it from me to get in the way of you doing your job."

A clattering of movement at Heather's back made her turn. She half-expected to find an angry knot of Shuggie's guys lurking there, waiting to block her path, so was instead surprised to find a wide-eyed, slightly breathless DC Swanney.

"What are you doing here?" Heather demanded. "I told you to wait in the car."

Tammi-Jo shook her head, and shot a nervous glance back over her shoulder at the slowly closing door. "It's him. He's coming. He's coming here."

Heather frowned. "Who? Mickey Buttfuck?"

"No. No, not him," Tammi-Jo said. The door fully closed with a firm, solemn *clack*. "Sergeant Gillespie."

"Wayne?"

Heather's gaze flitted to the boarded-up window. The glass was completely undamaged. There was no reason, as far as she could tell, for the wooden barricade. The thought niggled at her, but it would have to wait.

"Wayne's coming here?"

"Yeah," Tammi-Jo said. She glanced back over her shoulder again. "And he's not alone."

There was no time to ask anything more. The inner doors to the pub *squeaked* as they were pulled violently open, revealing a squad of Uniforms gathered in the corridor. Eight. Ten, maybe. They were too densely packed to easily count.

And at the front, leading the way, flanked by a constable on either side, was Sergeant Wayne Gillespie.

He didn't look surprised to see Heather there. Quite the opposite, in fact. His expression barely flickered to register her presence, like her being there had been some grim inevitability.

"Sergeant Gillespie. What are you doing here?" Heather demanded.

"Funny. I was about to ask you the same thing, Detective Inspector Filson."

The Uniforms filed in and fanned out behind their leader. Heather spotted Ash in the front row, a couple of men along from Wayne.

They all bore broadly similar looks of disdain on their faces, though some more confidently than others. Wayne's was etched in stone. Ash's was pretty close. A few of the younger constables looked less certain, though. They'd come here to confront a bad guy, and instead, they were facing a Detective Inspector, and a royally pissed-off one at that.

"Tell you what I'm going to do," Heather announced. "I'm

going to do you all a favour and pretend this didn't happen. I'm going to let you all walk out of here right now, and get back to what you're supposed to be doing."

"This is what we're supposed to be doing," Ash hissed, taking a step forward like he was readying himself to lunge. "This is exactly what we're supposed to be doing. Taking down fuckers like him."

From the corner of her eye, Heather saw Tammi-Jo slipping off her shoes, and adjusting her stance. The positioning of her feet wasn't wildly different to how she'd been standing before, but Heather could read the signs of a woman getting ready to start hoofing some men in the bollocks.

"Taking them down?" Heather let out a burst of derisory laughter. "Who is it you think you are, Ash? Starsky or Hutch? In fact, sorry. That reference is probably before your time, since you're literally a fucking child."

"Come on, now. No need for name-calling, Heather," Wayne said, and his smirk curled the DI's fingers into fists.

"It's Detective Inspector," she reminded him.

The smirk went nowhere. "No point in standing on formality, is there? We're all friends here. You're one of us. And you're good mates with him, too!" Wayne's gaze flitted, just briefly, to the gangster in the corner. "You're just that affable, aren't you? You're everyone's pal. Even cold-blooded murderers."

His smile fell away completely. The air around him seemed to crackle. The other men, sensing this, hardened their resolve, the lines of their faces drawing themselves darker and heavier.

"Move," he said, with a jerk of his head. "He's coming with us."

Shuggie chuckled. It sounded like rocks scraping together at the back of his throat. "Good luck with that, son."

"Shuggie, shut the fuck up," Heather warned, keeping her gaze fixed on Wayne and his small army of constables.

"Oof. Lover's tiff?" the sergeant asked. "I'm not going to ask you again, Heather. Move."

"You heard him," Ash added. "Step aside."

A couple of other constables mumbled their agreement.

Feet shuffled. Knuckles cracked. The ring of Uniforms tightened around them. If she didn't de-escalate this, it was about to get very ugly.

"You'll all lose your jobs over this," Heather told them. "Is that what you want?"

"Maybe," Wayne said, answering for them. Nobody seemed quick to object. "If the job is ignoring bastards like this, letting them do what they want, then we don't want it. We signed up to take these fuckers off the street, not to hang out in their pubs with them, chatting away like best pals."

He ran his tongue around the inside of his mouth, like he was searching for food. As he did, his smile returned.

"Not making secret wee pacts together to help one another out."

The floorboard beneath Heather's feet creaked as her weight shifted. What did he know? How much had he found out?

"We're here on official police business," Heather said.

The boarded-up window caught her eye for a moment. There wasn't a scratch on the glass. She pushed the thought away, and focused her attention on the more pressing problem.

She could take out her phone and call this in, but that might kick it all off. Wayne had got these guys all fired up. She could practically smell the surging adrenaline and raging testosterone. It was a powder keg. One wrong move and someone was getting their head cracked open.

Calming things down was the only option open to her.

Unfortunately, a moment later, the option was taken away.

The doors that the Uniforms had piled in through opened again, revealing a six-strong squad of Shuggie's guys. They carried pool cues and beer bottles, and had clearly ventured down from upstairs to find out what all the noise was about.

Around half of the Uniforms turned to face them, hurriedly grasping for their batons.

This was not good.

"Wait!" Heather barked. "Everyone just keep the heid! Stay calm. There's no need for this to get any worse."

"Oh, I think there is," Shuggie said, hauling himself to his feet. He eyeballed Wayne, matching the sergeant's level of disdain. "These cheeky fucks think they can march in here to my pub and throw their weight around, do they? Accuse me of all sorts without a shred of fucking evidence." He looked along their ranks, and three or four constables almost jumped right out of their skins when he roared, "Is that what you fucking think, is it?"

"You hear that, Heather?" Wayne asked. "You hear your pal threatening us like that? You just going to stand there, are you? Take his side?"

"I'm not taking anyone's side. You're both arseholes," Heather shot back. "Shuggie, you sit on your arse. Wayne, you fuck off."

"Naw," Shuggie grunted.

"No," Wayne replied.

"Last chance," Heather warned. She aimed that at the rest of the Uniforms. If they left, Wayne would have no choice but to beat a retreat. "Go now, and I don't mention this to anyone. Don't, and you're all off the Force. No jobs. No pensions. Nothing."

"We won't have nothing." Ash's voice was a flat monotone, and Heather knew right then that there'd be no getting through to him. "We'll have the knowledge that we did the right thing."

"The right thing?" Heather laughed again at that. It made Ash's jaw clench and his fingernails dig deeper into his palms. "Is that what you call it? Grassing up your own dad? Getting him and poor Daz killed?"

She watched him blink. A chink in his armour.

"What's that meant to mean?" Ash demanded.

"Don't listen to her, son," Wayne warned. "She's playing head games."

"Ha. Aye. That's what you'd want him to think, right enough," the DI continued. "See, you're asking what I'm doing here hanging out with a known criminal, but I could ask you the same, Wayne, couldn't I? I could ask about you and Mickey Buttfuck."

Silence. On the surface, the sergeant's expression didn't change. But there was something going on deeper down. Something shifting in the strata below.

He swallowed, and Heather knew then that she had him.

"One thing I don't understand, Sergeant," she said. "When you and the convicted felon Michael Butterworth were having your secret meetings out the back of his place, did you know that Sergeant Crier's house directly overlooked his garden? Seems like a hell of an oversight."

Ash shot Wayne a fleeting sideways look, his eyebrows dipping in confusion.

"What's she talking about?"

"Nothing, son. I told you. Head games," Wayne replied. "Just women and their head games. You know what they're like."

"We found the notebook that you were looking for, Wayne," Heather said. This time, the flicker of worry made it all the way to the surface. "That handprint on the floor, Ash? In front of the fireplace? That was Wayne here. He was looking for the notes your dad was keeping on the comings and goings of the house out back. I take it you mentioned that to Sergeant Gillespie?"

Ash was deflating before her eyes. He shook his head, trying to deny all the little pieces that were no doubt now clicking together in his head.

"No. No, it wasn't real, though," Ash said. "He was just... He was bored. He was just people-watching. We all joked about it a bit. About him trying to relive the glory days. There wasn't anything actually going on, or...? Sarge? This is bollocks, isn't it?"

"Load of old bollocks, son," Wayne said, but a few of the other constables were looking at him differently now. His power was fading. "Absolute fantasy stuff."

Heather shook her head. "Come on now, Wayne. Don't sell yourself short," she told him. "This whole thing has been planned out from the start. Your pal Mickey wanted to move in on Shuggie's territory here, but before that, he needed to weaken him. Take out a few of his guys. Get them killed, locked up, didn't really matter. Long as they were off the board.

"What did he offer you, exactly? Money?" Heather wrinkled her nose. "Nah. Can't see that being your thing. Power, then. Or fame, maybe. You'd get to be the guy who took down the once-great Shuggie Cowan."

"Here. Less of the fucking 'once,'" Cowan objected.

"Even if it was true, which it isn't, what would be wrong with that?" Wayne asked. "Getting rid of the likes of him is what we're meant to be doing."

"But you wouldn't be getting rid of *the likes* of him, would you? You'd be getting rid of him specifically, and letting someone else step right in to fill the gap."

Wayne could only snort. He had no more responses to offer. Heather decided it was time to go in for the kill.

"But you needed a reason to escalate, didn't you? You needed to galvanise your wee gang here. Convince them to overstep the mark. Tony's death couldn't have come at a better time for you, eh?"

Wayne's jaw clenched. "Don't you dare."

"When you found out that Tony had been spying on you, keeping notes, did you see it as a problem or as an opportunity?" Heather pressed. "Much-loved local bobby, beaten to death in his own home. Arrange for Shuggie's boys to be seen in the area, and boom, suddenly all the fuckwits are out for blood and flocking to your cause."

She looked around at the assembled constables. The few who were still facing her, and not keeping their eyes on Shuggie's guys, avoided her gaze.

"That's you lot, by the way," she stressed. "You're the fuckwits, in case there was any confusion."

"This is all nonsense," Wayne drawled. "Don't listen to her, boys. Block her out."

"Well, tell you what, why don't we hear it straight from the horse's mouth?" Heather suggested. "Mickey's right across the road. We could bring him over, see how the chemistry is between you two. Two good pals like you, we're bound to see it."

"I told you about Daz," Ash muttered. His eyes had been searching the floor, but now turned on the uniformed sergeant. "I told you he was going to complain about you. About all of us."

"It's head games, Ashley," Wayne barked. "Ignore them. Block her out."

"Two dead polis," Heather said. "*All Cops Are Bastards* carved into one. Gets you fired up, doesn't it? Gets the blood pumping. Makes you angry. Makes you scared. And angry, scared people can be made to do some pretty stupid things. Like throwing away their careers. Risking arrest. Taking the law into their own hands."

"I didn't kill them," Wayne said. He finally looked at Ash, who was glaring at him through angry, red-ringed eyes. "I didn't."

"Well, I'm sure between us we can get to the bottom of it all," Heather said. She drew in a slow breath. "Wayne Gillespie, I'm arresting you on suspicion of the murders of Sergeant Tony Crier, and Constable Darryl Hartmann."

She held a hand out to Ash. After a moment, his cuffs were

placed in her open palm. Heather gave him a grateful nod, then handed the cuffs over to Tammi-Jo.

"Will you do the honours, Detective Constable Swanney?" she asked. "Then get this bastard out of my sight."

———

A few minutes later, after she'd encouraged the constables to all piss off, and sent Tammi-Jo off to the car with the hand-cuffed Wayne Gillespie, Heather strode through the knot of black-clad hardmen, rapped the fibreglass pig on the nose, and then was met by the smell of burning when she stepped outside.

DC Swanney stood in the middle of the street, talking urgently into her phone. A few people had emerged from the neighbouring cafes and coffee shops, and were all pointing or taking photos of the flames that leapt from the window of one of the flats across the street.

The grubby white paint on the building's frontage was already blackened and blistered. From inside the flat, there came the crash of a ceiling coming down.

Though she hadn't heard him approaching, Heather wasn't in the least bit surprised when Shuggie spoke from right beside her.

"Oof. God, would you look at that? That is unfortunate," he said. "Told you the electrics in that place were a death trap."

Heather turned to look at him, but was distracted by the boarded-up window. A barricade, not to anyone breaking the glass, but to one specific person looking through it.

"You knew," Heather realised. "You knew he was there. You knew what he was up to."

Shuggie frowned. It was an exaggerated thing, like he was a character in a pantomime.

"I don't know what you could possibly mean, Detective Inspector," he said. He looked up at the burning flat, the flames stretching towards the sky like they were trying to escape their own heat. "My condolences to anyone who might have been in there."

He sniffed the air, savouring the smell of the smoke and the stoor. Then, without another word, he stepped back inside *The Pig & Bicycle*, and quietly closed the door.

THIRTY-THREE

HEATHER HAD ALMOST MADE it all the way to the interview room without incident. Sure, there had been some staring from passing Uniforms when she'd led the hand-cuffed Sergeant Gillespie across the car park and into the building.

There had been whispers and muttering as she and Tammi-Jo had checked him in. Nobody had actively tried to intercept them, though, until they were just a few feet from the interview room door.

"Detective Inspector."

The Gozer's voice was like a rumble of distant thunder. Heather turned to find him standing along the corridor, a cup of coffee in one hand, a briefcase in the other. He looked her up and down, let his gaze linger on the captive sergeant for a moment, then jerked his head towards the door he'd just come through.

"A word."

"Be right there, sir," Heather said, fighting to keep the dismay off her face. She instructed Tammi-Jo to take Wayne into the interview room, then set off along the corridor in reluctant pursuit of Detective Superintendent MacKenzie.

She caught up with him in the next corridor. He didn't look happy, but she felt confident she could win him round.

Usually, a move like this—arresting a fellow officer—would have to go through the higher-ups. Circumstances had made that impossible, though. She reckoned, depending on what side of the bed the Gozer had climbed out of, she could make him understand that.

Her confidence waned, however, when Snecky came striding around a corner and picked up the pace when he saw them. His face was arranged in its usual expression—fifty percent smug superiority, fifty percent clueless as to what was going on. The ratio changed from time to time, but those two elements were always somewhere in the mix.

"What the hell's the story here?" the Gozer demanded. "Why do you have a sergeant in handcuffs?"

Snecky stopped beside them, but neither the Detective Superintendent nor the Detective Inspector acknowledged his arrival.

Instead, Heather explained her theory on how Sergeant Wayne Gillespie was connected to the murders of Tony Crier and Darryl Hartmann. She told him about the possible connection to the ex-con, Mickey Butterworth, and about Wayne's attempts to storm Shuggie Cowan's place with a squad of uniformed constables.

"What evidence do you have?" the Gozer demanded.

Heather was hoping he wouldn't ask that. "He's repeatedly mentioned in the notes Tony Crier kept," she said, which wasn't necessarily *not* true.

"By name?"

Damn.

"By his initial," Heather admitted.

"Initial? Or initials?"

When Heather hesitated, Snecky answered for her. "The letter G."

The Gozer's eyes closed. "For Christ's sake," he whispered,

then he sprang fully back to life again. "Tell me that's not all, DI Filson. Tell me there's more than that."

Heather thought about mentioning the handprint on the floor, but that would mean telling him about Ace involving herself in the crime scene, and she'd rather not do that yet. She was a witness, and if any of Wayne's more loyal followers got wind of that, she could be in trouble.

"I was there when he entered Cowan's pub, sir," Heather said.

"He's a bloody police sergeant! Shuggie Cowan's an ex-con and a current dodgy fucker. If Sergeant Gillespie went there in an official capacity, then I fail to see the problem. And I certainly don't see why he should be bloody paraded through the station in cuffs!"

"He wasn't there in an official capacity, sir," Heather protested. "He was there to start shit. He's working with Butterworth."

"You *think* he is! You don't *know*."

"Well, that's why I want to interview him!" Heather snapped back.

"Watch your tone, Detective Inspector," the Gozer warned. "First and only warning."

Snecky swallowed. "Uh, maybe I could just interject, sir?"

Heather groaned.

Christ. Here we go.

"Oh, by all means, Samuel. I'm assuming you didn't authorise this?"

Snecky pressed his lips together until they became a single thin line across his face. He drew in a few breaths through his nose, like he was preparing to jump into ice-cold water, then nodded.

"I did, sir, yes."

The Detective Superintendent frowned. "What?"

"What?" Heather muttered.

"DI Filson came to me earlier laying out her list of concerns,

and whilst none of them individually was satisfactorily
concrete enough to take action on, taken together, I felt that it
was appropriate to—"

"Jesus. Alright, alright, I don't need a bloody monologue,"
the Gozer told him. "My tea's already getting cold."

He sighed heavily and looked at them both in turn. When
he spoke again, there was a weary resignation to his tone.

"I'm going to get so much grief about this. You two have
ruined my day, I hope you both know that."

"Sorry, sir," Snecky said. "That wasn't our intention."

The Gozer didn't acknowledge the apology, and instead
continued to glower at Heather. "So, you'd better get something from him. This had better be bloody worthwhile, or so
help me God, I'll wring both your necks. Is that clear?"

"Got it, sir," Heather confirmed. "I'm going to break him.
Don't worry."

"I don't want to know," the Det Supt replied. He strode past
them, sloshing tea onto the floor. "Just get me a result that'll
keep the Assistant Chief Constable from hauling me over the
coals."

"We will, sir!" Snecky confirmed. "You can bet your boots
on it, we'll be sure to—"

The door at the far end of the corridor slammed behind the
Detective Superintendent.

"Oh. He's gone," Snecky said.

"What was that for?" Heather asked. She was eyeing him
with suspicion, like he might be some sort of impostor.

"What was what for?"

"The support," Heather said.

"I'm always supportive!" the DCI protested.

Heather just looked at him with her eyebrows raised until
he tutted and relented.

"Fine. OK. Something came up. Something... weird."

"About Wayne?"

Snecky nodded. "Yes. Another connection."

The door that the Gozer had gone through opened again. This time, it was DC Swanney who appeared. Heather practically felt Snecky's pulse quicken at the sight of her.

"He's in the interview room," Tammi-Jo said. "He's saying some pretty mean stuff about you. Really quite nasty." She took out her notebook as she scurried over to join them. "I wrote some of it down. Do you want me to read any of it out to you?"

Heather almost declined, but then reconsidered. "Aye. I want to hear you reading it out."

Tammi-Jo shook her head emphatically, then thrust the notebook towards the DI. "Well, I can't. You'll have to read it."

"Wait, what's this?" Snecky asked.

Heather rolled her eyes. "She refuses to swear."

"What, in this job?" the DCI snorted.

"I've never met anyone I felt really deserved it," Tammi-Jo explained.

The explanation only added to Snecky's already evident confusion. "What?" he said again. "In *this* job?"

Heather waved the notebook away. "It's fine. I can probably guess most of it," she said, then she turned back to Snecky. "What's the new info, then? What's come up?"

Snecky looked up and down the corridor in both directions, then beckoned for the other two detectives to lean in closer.

"His wife," the DCI said in a low, secretive voice.

He leaned back again and nodded, like this was all the information they required.

"Whose wife?" Tammi-Jo whispered.

"What about her?" Heather asked.

Snecky tutted again. He kept his mouth mostly still as he spoke, like he was worried about rogue lipreaders ratting him out.

"Wayne's wife. Or ex-wife. Or soon-to-be-ex-wife. Or whatever she is."

"What about her?" Heather asked again.

The Detective Chief Inspector looked exasperated, like they should have figured it out themselves by now.

"It's her, isn't it?" he mumbled. "She's the one who found him. She's the one who found Sergeant Crier."

Tammi-Jo gasped.

Heather swore.

"Fuck! You mean…?"

"Yes!" Snecky said, nodding solemnly. "Wayne Gillespie's ex is the Iron Woman."

"That means…" Tammi-Jo began, before almost immediately running out of steam. "What does that mean? Does that mean something? I mean, it's a coincidence, sure, but it feels like… You know?"

"Go get her," Heather told the detective constable. "She's seen you. She knows you. Bring her in."

Snecky looked between them both. "You think she's involved?"

"I don't know," Heather admitted. "But the bags. She didn't leave the bags. That doesn't make sense. And she's got an injury. On her arm. We need to look at it."

"If you think she might be involved, you should take backup."

"He's right," Heather agreed.

"That's going to freak her out," Tammi-Jo reasoned. "And, to be honest, the encounters I've had with Uniform down here haven't exactly filled me with confidence. She's one woman. She seems nice. I can get her to come with me. I'd feel more comfortable going on my own."

Snecky jumped in before Heather had a chance to think it over.

"Fine. Just be careful. If anything seems off, you get out of there, alright?" He put a hand on her shoulder and gazed deeply into her eyes. "We're not losing you, DC Swanney."

"Um, OK. Good?" Tammi-Jo said, then she knocked his arm

away in her frantic scramble to catch the keys that Heather tossed to her.

"Like he said, be careful," the DI instructed.

"You're letting me take your car?" Tammi-Jo asked, her eyes wide with wonder. She looked at the keys in awe, like they were some sort of magical talisman. "You're actually letting me take your actual car?"

Heather frowned. "Uh, that was the plan. Why?"

Tammi-Jo's fist tightened around the keys, and she shoved them into her pocket. "DCI Logan *never* let me drive his car!"

"Wait. Why? Why didn't he let you drive his car?" Heather asked, but the DC was already rushing along the corridor, shooting a smile back over her shoulder.

"Don't worry about a thing," she chirped. "I'll bring it back in one piece as soon as I can."

"Why did you feel the need to specify 'in one piece'?" Heather called after her, but the detective constable had already skipped on out the door. She turned to Snecky. "Why would she say it like that?"

"She's clumsy as fuck," Snecky said, with a rare level of directness. "We never used to let her drive anything in Aberdeen. And that's basically one street that runs straight through. If the car comes back in *any* number of pieces, you'll be doing well."

Heather grimaced. Technically, it wasn't her car, it was the Force's, but she'd grown quite attached to it. "She'll be fine. I'm sure it'll be fine," she muttered. "I need to go in and talk to Wayne. Is Marty free?"

Snecky shook his head. "Nope. He's digging up some more dirt on Sergeant Gillespie for us. He's going to bring us anything he finds."

Heather didn't like that word—us—particularly when Snecky was the one using it.

"What are you saying?" she asked.

The DCI straightened his shoulders and lifted his head.

"I'm saying, Detective Inspector, that you and I are going to have ourselves some double team action!"

The phrase hung there in the air between them like a bad smell.

"But not, you know, in any sort of sexual sense," Snecky added. And then, slouching and lowering his head again, he scurried off in the direction of the interview rooms.

THIRTY-FOUR

WAYNE SAT FORWARD in his chair, shoulders rounded, hands clasped together, eyeballing Heather while she made the necessary introductions for the recording.

"And, for the benefit of the record, Mr Gillespie has declined all offers of legal or police staff representation. Can you confirm that's correct, Mr Gillespie?"

Wayne sniffed. It was a deep, burbling noise that spoke of long-standing sinus problems. "It's Sergeant," he corrected. "It's Sergeant Gillespie, not mister."

Sitting across the table from him, Heather shook her head curtly. "Not today, it isn't. Can you confirm that you—"

"Aye. Fine. I don't want anyone in. I don't need them. This is all a load of shite."

"Which bit?" Heather asked. "You palling around with Michael Butterworth, or you murdering two serving officers?"

"Both," Wayne told her.

Heather winced. Snecky, who sat beside her, mirrored the movement just a moment later.

"That's unfortunate, Wayne," Heather told him. "See, we've got quite a bit of evidence regarding your relationship with Michael Butterworth. That bit's rock solid. We know that's true.

So, you denying that? Well, that just makes you look like a liar, doesn't it? And if you're lying about you and Mickey, it makes me think you're lying about the rest of it, too."

She pursed her lips in a thin smile and raised her eyebrows. It almost looked like an apology.

"You can see what I'm saying, surely?"

"You haven't got anything. It's bollocks."

Heather let out a slow, weary-sounding sigh. "You can't really believe that? Surely? I mean, you were literally hanging out in the man's garden in full view of a serving police officer. A good man, too. Straight as an arrow. He kept detailed notes about you. DCI Grant, would you...?"

Snecky took his cue, pulled a sheet of paper from the folder in front of him, and read, "'You fucking need me a lot more than I need you. If Cowan finds out about this, you're way more fucked than I am.'"

He glanced at Heather, then sat back again, looking quite pleased with himself. He'd been given a juicy role in proceedings, and felt confident that he'd pulled it off with some aplomb.

"Ring any bells, Wayne?" Heather asked.

Wayne shook his head, but she'd seen the worry in his eyes. The realisation of quite how much trouble he was in.

"That's alright," Heather told him. "See, despite the 'electrical fault' in the building, Mickey made it out in one piece. He'll be in hospital for a few days—smoke inhalation—but he's already made it very clear that he's willing to talk."

"He's alive?" Wayne asked, and that worry deepened all the more.

"He is. For now. But, well, between you and me, he's a bit worried what Shuggie might do to him. He's had a narrow escape. He's keen to avoid it getting any narrower, if you know what I mean?"

The DI sat back and folded her arms. Snecky did the same.

"In my experience—probably yours, too—that means he's

going to sing for his supper. He's going to tell us *everything* if he thinks it'll keep him and his family safe. See, making plans in your garden to overthrow an elderly gangster doesn't actually carry a prison sentence. It's not actually a crime.

"But, if he can convince us his life's in danger, then we'll have to protect him. If he wants to convince us, though, then he's going to have to tell us everything. What was discussed. Who with and when. He'll tell us all of it. And you can bet he's going to be painting himself in the best possible light."

She let that sink in for a moment. Across the table, Wayne rubbed at his wedding finger, like the spot where the ring had been was itching.

"And where will that leave you, Wayne?" the DI asked. "You'll be playing catch-up, having to deal with the fallout of whatever he tells us. You'll be on the back foot. That's not a great place to be when you're staring down the barrel of life imprisonment."

"Do you know what they do to us lot in jail, Wayne?" Snecky asked.

One of Heather's eyes twitched, annoyed by this interjection. It didn't hurt her cause, though. Wayne's face turned a rather alarming shade of grey as he gave the question some thought.

"This is your chance to get ahead of the story, Wayne," Heather said, smiling like she was doing him a favour. "This is your chance to tell us your side of things before Mickey Buttfuck pins the whole thing on you. And believe me, if he does— if he convinces everyone that it was all your idea to move in on Shuggie's turf—then prison will be a dream compared to what Cowan will do to you."

She sat back in her chair again and shrugged.

"We'd do our best to protect you, of course, but you know yourself, Wayne, there's some crooked bastards on the force these days. You just don't know who you can trust. So, let's start with the easy ones. You and Mickey. What was that all about?"

"I didn't kill anyone," the sergeant protested.

Heather held a hand up to stop him. "I'm delighted to hear that, Wayne. I can't wait until we sort that out. But we're getting ahead of ourselves." She crossed her arms again. "You and Mickey. All your discussions in the garden. Tell me about them."

Wayne chewed on his bottom lip and stared down at his hands. He'd picked at the skin at the top of his thumb, and blood now dotted the bottom corner of the nail. He stared at it like it was the most fascinating thing he'd ever seen, even as he answered the question.

"It was just talk."

Heather swallowed back her elation. She had the bastard.

"About?"

Wayne shrugged. "Nothing to start with. I, eh, I pulled him over one day. One of his taillights was out. Didn't know who he was. Seemed an alright guy, though. I let him off with a warning, and he, eh, he thanked me for it."

"Thanked? Or rewarded?" Heather asked.

Wayne continued to study the smear of blood on his nail. He scraped his bottom teeth across his top lip. "Couple of hundred quid," he admitted. He looked up then, his gaze darting imploringly between the detectives. "I wouldn't have touched it, but he was... I don't know. He seemed to get it. What it's like."

"How do you mean?" Heather pressed.

"I mean, like..." Wayne sighed. "That it's tough. The job. The shit we put up with. He mentioned Cowan, and how fuckers like that live the high life while half the Force can't pay their electricity bills. It was like he was reading my mind. You know what I mean? Like he'd tapped into something."

He blew out his cheeks, shook his head, then ran both hands backwards through his hair.

"Next thing I know, I've got two hundred quid in my pocket, and I'm arranging to meet him a few days later."

"At his house?"

"Not at first. Back end of nowhere. I'd looked him up by that point, so I knew about his previous. I should've stayed away, but he got it. Ex-con or not, he understood how I was feeling. How I *still* fucking feel," he said, his attitude rallying for a moment, before collapsing from under him again. "And when he started talking about how we should take Cowan down, I was on board. Because no other bastard was doing anything about him. Were they, Heather?"

"It's Detective Inspector Filson," she corrected.

Across the table, Wayne sneered. "Not today, it isn't. If I'm not a sergeant, then you're not my senior officer. And anyway, like you said, Heather, talking about overthrowing an elderly gangster in someone's garden isn't a crime."

"Taking bribes is," Snecky pointed out.

"One bribe. And aye, it was a mistake. I shouldn't have done it. And I'm sure you'll both make sure I'm punished to the full extent of the law for it. But I didn't kill Tony. I didn't kill Darryl. They were good lads. Both of them. Honest, hard-working guys. Tony had cancer, for Christ's sake. He only had a few months left."

He must've seen the surprise on Heather's face because his smirk became a full-blown grin.

"Oh, aye. I knew about that. Ash told me and a few of his pals that Tony was dying. So, why would I risk everything by killing him? And then not even kill him? You think I'd just beat an old man half to death, then walk away and leave him lying there, knowing that, if he pulled through, he'd be able to identify me? What sort of idiot do you take me for?"

Snecky shifted in his seat, suddenly uncomfortable.

"Maybe you thought he was dead," the DCI ventured.

"Maybe? That's what you're going to try to nail me with, is it? A *maybe*?" Wayne grunted. "It's no fucking wonder the

Force is in the state it's in, with clowns like you running the show."

"You were in Tony's living room," Heather said, going for the jugular. "After his death. You entered his house, and searched the premises, looking for the notes you knew he'd been keeping."

"No, I didn't."

"We've got an eyewitness who can place you at the scene," Heather told him. "And despite your best efforts to clean it up, Scene of Crime were able to get your prints from the sooty black hand mark you left."

Wayne scowled. "Off a carpet? Aye, sure they fucking did."

This time, Heather allowed just a little of the elation to show. Wayne must've seen it, because the colour that had started returning to his face all drained away again.

"Who said anything about a carpet?" the DI asked. She turned to Snecky, letting him share in the moment. "Did you mention a carpet, DCI Grant?"

"No, Detective Inspector," he replied. "I didn't mention a carpet. Or a rug."

"Well—"

"Or any kind of flooring," Snecky concluded.

Heather gave it a second to make sure he was done this time, then continued.

"Well, then how on Earth would Mr Gillespie know where the handprint was if neither of us mentioned it?"

Wayne's mouth moved up and down, but the only sounds that came out were some barely audible squeaks and a few clicks from lips that had suddenly gone dry.

Heather sighed, shook her head, then closed over her folder.

"What are you doing?" Wayne managed to ask, as the DI got to her feet, and indicated that Snecky should do the same. "Where are you going?"

"To talk to Mickey," Heather said.

Panic flared behind the sergeant's eyes. "What, now?"

"Aye. You're just pissing us about, so we'll see what he has to say. Should be enlightening. DCI Grant, do me a favour and officially suspend the interview will you?" Heather shot the sergeant a look of disdain. "I've already wasted more than enough of my evening on Mr Gillespie."

———

Ace's hands were doing quite a lot of talking. They were usually quite passive, conversation-wise, but her passion for her subject matter meant they were really getting into the swing of things.

The movements were still quite stilted, and she came across a bit like a malfunctioning robot as she paced back and forth, vocally airing her grievances.

"She treats me like I'm a child. And, OK, yes, fine, I *am* a child, technically, but I'm also a journalist. A podcast journalist, which is arguably the most significant kind, particularly in the true crime genre.

"I appreciate that she wants to keep me safe, but I ask you, did Delia D'Ambra ever sit on the side lines? Did Payne Lindsey ever shy away from danger while pursuing a lead? What would Sarah Koenig say if she could see me hiding away here, rather than heading out there to follow up my leads? Hmm?"

She stopped pacing long enough to stare at the old man sitting in the armchair, slurping tomato soup from a shaky spoon. Half of it had missed his mouth and was coating his chin, but he didn't seem to mind.

"Sorry," he said. "Who are you, again?"

Ace pointed to him. "Yes! Exactly! She'd question my right to call myself a true crime podcaster. She'd strip me of my podcasting badge. If there was such a thing."

She began to pace again. Heather's dad watched her over the rim of his spoon.

"Thankfully, there isn't, because I'd be so ashamed I'd have no choice but to hand it in to… I don't know. Whoever administered the scheme."

She shook her head. She was letting herself get bogged down by the details. Details were important, of course, but the details of the case, not of a fictional podcasting regulatory and licensing scheme that she had just dreamed up.

Although, it might be worth coming back to that at a later date.

"I shouldn't have told her my plans. I should have kept them to myself. That way, she couldn't have stopped me," Ace continued to rant. "Now, though, my hands are tied. She's expressly forbidden me from…"

The girl stopped pacing. Her mind raced, replaying the conversation she'd had with the DI earlier on the phone.

Had she told her not to investigate? She'd told her to stay out of trouble, yes, but those weren't necessarily the same thing, were they? She could gather material for *Crime De La Crime* without getting into danger, couldn't she?

Granted, that might not be following the spirit of the law— or of the angrily muttered instruction, in this case—but technically it adhered to the letter of it.

Technically, she wouldn't be disobeying a direct order, she'd simply be finding a loophole around it.

"What would DI Filson do?" she asked.

Scott slurped on his soup, but that was fine, she wasn't asking him. She already knew the answer.

She'd speak to just one person. She'd tick just one thing off her list. She'd pop round, have a quick chat, and be back before anyone noticed she was gone.

The person she wanted to speak to lived a couple of miles out of town. Her mum was upstairs getting a bath ready for

Heather's father, and there was no way she'd drive out there, anyway.

The first thing she'd have to do, then, would be to find a bike. Her dad's old one was in the shed back home, so she could take that.

The second thing she'd have to do would be to learn how to ride a bike. She could check YouTube while she walked back to the house. It couldn't be that difficult. She'd seen some of the boys from her class racing around no-handed, and half of them could barely spell their own names.

Then again, that was hardly their fault. Especially poor Jaxon.

Ace's hands fell back to her sides, like they'd worn themselves out. She nodded.

"Yes," she announced. "I think this is going to work! But you can't tell anyone. You can't say a word."

Heather's dad stopped slurping his soup. His eyes, which had become distant and unfocused, sharpened a little.

"Can't say a word about what?" he asked, his mouth forming a gummy, uncertain sort of smile.

Ace pointed to him again. "Yes! Exactly." She tapped the side of her nose. "This is between you and me!"

THIRTY-FIVE

HEATHER LANDED HEAVILY in her chair, ran a hand through her greasy hair, and caught a whiff of her armpit. It had been a long, stressful day, and even longer since she'd last had a shower. She should probably tackle that at some point.

"How's it going?" Marty asked.

Heather made a weighing motion. "Giving him a chance to stew. He's admitted to being on the take, and to hanging out with Mickey Buttfuck. Denies being in the house, though, and he's adamant that he didn't kill anyone."

"Bugger. Didn't just break down and admit the whole thing, then?"

"Sadly not," Heather said. She looked up as Snecky entered the Incident Room, and immediately worked out why he looked so confused.

"So… Michael Butterworth's alive and in the hospital then, is he?" the DCI asked. "Nobody told me."

"Oh, God, no. He's dead. Burned alive," Heather replied. "But, the longer we can keep that fact from Wayne, the better chance we've got of him spilling his guts to us. Self-preservation's a pretty effective motivator."

"Who's the witness?" Snecky asked. "You said there was an

eyewitness who could place him in the house. Was that bit true?"

"It was, aye," Heather replied, though she was a little cagey about it. "I'd rather not involve them yet, though."

"But they exist?" Snecky pressed. "You can at least say that?"

"They exist. They saw him in the living room with his hand up the chimney. They'll testify to that, if it comes to it, but I'm hoping Wayne breaks before then."

"You didn't bring up his wife," Snecky said. "How come?"

"I'm building up to it," Heather told him. "We'll let him stew for a bit, then go back in. We'll use his wife then, see how he reacts."

She rotated her chair until she was facing Marty again.

"What about Tony's complaint? Did you find anything?"

Marty shook his head. "Not on Wayne, no."

"Damn. That would've been something else we could've used," Heather said. She frowned at the slightly odd phrasing of Marty's reply. "What do you mean 'not on Wayne'? Had Tony complained about someone else?"

"Uh, yeah. Eighteen months back or so," Marty said. He shrugged. "Some special constable."

"Oh. Right."

Heather started to turn away again, but then stopped.

"Wait," she said, gripping the arms of her chair. "What special constable?"

———

Tammi-Jo listened to the echo of the doorbell, and wrapped her arms around herself to fend off some of the cold. Night was settling across the house and the surrounding fields, a carpet of black squeezing down on an underlay of inky blue, compressing it until, soon, nothing but absolute darkness would remain.

Though she was barely fifty yards from the road, she could no longer see it. The only light came from the house beside her, a couple of lamps burning in two of the rooms. The curtains had been drawn, so she couldn't tell if anyone was inside, but no light spilled out through the gap at the bottom of the garage door, so it didn't seem that Selma, the Iron Woman, was working.

Tammi-Jo tapped her feet and made a series of tuneless *popping* sounds through her pursed lips while she waited for a response from inside.

Not that she waited long. Patience wasn't one of the DC's strong points.

She rang the bell again, and this time heard movement from inside. An exhale of anticipation bloomed as a cloud of white vapour. She gave her arms one final warming rub, then fixed on her best and brightest smile for the woman who came to the door.

At least, that was the plan.

A man in police uniform stared back at her from the doorway, the light from behind him casting his face into deep pockets of shadow.

"Uh, Detective Constable... Swanney, wasn't it? Like the song. About the river."

Tammi-Jo blinked. Then, because her brain still hadn't caught up, she blinked again.

"Um, yes. Yes, that's me," she said. She realised her smile had fallen away, so she worked to reattach it. "What are you doing here?"

The door creaked as Special Constable Ted Campbell inched it wider. "Funny," he said, leaning an arm on the frame. "I was about to ask you the same thing..."

———

Riding a bike was not as simple as the video tutorials made it look. In fact, Ace was starting to think that the whole thing was some sort of practical joke. Riding a bike, she had come to conclude, was impossible.

Getting the bike out of the shed had been the first challenge. There had been spiders involved, and quite a lot of dust. Her dad had left it when he'd moved out, and while her mum had used it a few times over the years, it had spent most of its time jammed at the back of the shed, partly hidden by an ever-growing wall of half-empty paint pots and assorted bits of junk.

It had taken her several minutes to free the bicycle, and a few more to stick all the stuff she'd had to take out of the shed back in.

At that point, she assumed that the hard part was done. The videos she'd watched on the walk back to her house had made riding a bike look straightforward.

Climb on. Aim the front wheel in roughly the direction you wanted to go. Pedal.

And, ideally, don't fall off.

That was the gist of it, and though she'd mastered the first two steps, the third was proving impossible. She was pedalling. She was definitely pedalling. Her legs were flailing around in circles, knees pumping, but the only movement from the bike was a slow sideways topple that eventually forced her to throw out a leg to save herself from crashing to the ground.

This couldn't be right. Clearly, something was missing.

Crossing her arms, Ace surveyed the bike lying on the ground. She had no memory of it as having once been her father's. In fact, she had very few memories of him at all. She felt no emotional attachment to the dirty metal frame on the path. It was an object that had been in her shed, nothing more.

And yet...

She wasn't going to let it defeat her. She wasn't going to let it win.

She had a job to do. She had an interview to conduct and a podcast to produce.

Ace resisted an urge to give the bike a kick. It wasn't the bike's fault, after all. It had been cast aside by her father, just like she had. Forgotten. Overlooked.

It just needed some care and attention, that was all.

She squeezed the tyres. The rubber compressed easily beneath her thumb. She turned a pedal by hand. The chain, hanging limply, didn't move.

"Right, then," Ace announced into the gloom of her back garden.

Then she took out her phone, searched for a video on bike repair for beginners, and set to work.

THIRTY-SIX

TAMMI-JO'S BRAIN was a whirlwind of thoughts, ideas, questions, worries, and the theme tune to *Baywatch*, which was playing on a loop for some reason. They all crashed together, leaving her momentarily struck dumb as she sorted through the wreckage.

Finally, she was able to isolate and vocalise a single question.

"What are you doing here?"

It felt familiar. She'd already asked it, she realised, but she hadn't been given an answer.

Why was he here? What did this mean? It meant something. It had to.

He was wearing his Special Constable uniform, which for all intents and purposes looked just like the standard constable's getup.

Had he been sent to assist? Was that why he was here? If so, then why was he already in the house? And...

"Where's Selma?" Tammi-Jo asked, the question suddenly feeling too pressing to keep inside.

Ted smiled. "Which one do you want me to answer first?"

"Both," the DC said. She looked back over her shoulder.

There were no other cars in the drive besides Heather's Audi and the Iron Woman's van. "Why are you here?"

"Because I live here," he replied.

"Wait. What? You live here?" Tammi-Jo pointed to the ground at her feet. "Here? In this house? With Selma?"

"Sometimes, yeah. I stay over a few nights a week. It's not too serious, though. Just a bit of fun. We're free to see other people," Ted said, and the way his gaze flitted up and down made it clear that he would be very open to seeing the detective constable. "It started out as just business—the ironing company was my idea—but… Well. Things progressed."

"Right. OK. Well…"

He shouldn't be in uniform. You didn't wear your uniform home. It was against the rules. She looked down and saw herself reflected in the mirror-like surface of the special constable's boots.

Even from that angle, she looked confused.

"Is Selma in?" she asked.

Ted shook his head. "No. She's nipped out," he said. The door gave a mouse-like *squeak* as he pushed it open a little wider. "Do you want to come in and wait for her? She won't be long."

The light was on in the hallway behind him, but a room at the far end was in near-total darkness. It made the DC think of creepy caves in old fairy tales. Of lurking dangers in ancient tombs.

"Uh, no. No, it's fine," she said.

"You sure? I could make tea. Although,"—he grinned playfully and pointed to her—"you don't like tea, do you? Milk!"

Tammi-Jo could only nod and pull together a smile that she hoped didn't veer too far into being a grimace.

How did he know that? Had she mentioned it during the one and only time they'd met? She didn't think so.

"I'm trying to cut back," she said, already retreating. He

looked disappointed, but didn't move to follow. "Just have her give me a ring, will you?"

"You didn't give me your number," Ted pointed out.

"Just get her to call 101 and ask for me."

Ted chuckled. "Can't blame a guy for trying!" he said. "But, yes, don't worry. I'll tell her. Thanks for coming. Sorry you missed her."

She didn't turn away from him until she was close to the Audi. She clambered inside, locked the door, then patted at her pockets until she found her phone.

Halfway through dialling Heather's number, she looked up at the house. The front door stood open, but the doorway was empty.

A flash of movement beside her made her turn. She hissed and threw her hands up in front of her face as fragments of glass exploded into the car.

The door *clunked* as it was unlocked. Fingers wormed through her hair, then tightened, sending a shockwave of pain through her scalp.

Grabbing the wrist, she dug her fingernails in, and savoured the sharp cry of pain from the man in the special constable uniform.

But then, an impact. Hard. Fast. It drove against the side of her jaw and snapped her head around.

She was torn from the car. The ground raced up to meet her. The sudden impact stole the breath from her body.

And the last thing Tammi-Jo Swanney saw before unconsciousness descended was her terrified reflection in the shiny black surface of an immaculately polished boot.

———

"Come on. Talk to me," Heather urged. "What does it say?"

She stood across the desk from Marty, one hand gripping

the top of his computer monitor like she was about to wrench it away from him and hurl it against the wall.

It wasn't entirely out of the question.

DS Brompton's eyes darted left and right, while his index finger scrolled his mouse wheel, searching for the details of the report. Snecky was pacing back and forth behind DI Filson, gripping his hair like he was scared his head was going to fall off.

"I vouched for you. I said I backed you on this!" the DCI muttered. "You've got the wrong guy!"

"He's still on the take," Heather hissed. "We were right to bring him in. Now stop pacing, you're putting me on edge."

"I'm putting *you* on edge?!" Snecky wailed. "Do you have any idea how much shite I'm going to be in once the Gozer—"

"Got it," Marty announced. "The complaint was about Theodore Campbell. Ted. He applied for a full constable gig in February last year."

"He said he didn't want to be a full-timer," Heather said.

"Aye, well, he's full of shit. He applied, but he was knocked back."

"Why?"

Marty's gaze crept upwards until it met hers. "Tony Crier put in a written recommendation that he shouldn't get the job."

"Jesus. What was the reason?"

Marty scanned the screen in front of him. "He said he knew Ted personally, through his son. That'll be Ash, I'm assuming. Says he always found him to be a bit unstable. Prone to wild mood swings and violence. Vindictive, manipulative, carried grudges. Tony thought it was too big a risk, making him a full constable." Marty winced as he continued to read. "Bloody hell. Tony reckoned Ted killed Ash's dog when they were kids, but he could never prove it."

DC Wolfe lifted his head so it could be seen above the screen of his computer.

"Bastard!" he announced. "You don't kill the dog. People,

aye, fine. I mean, not fine, obviously. Don't do that, either, ideally. But don't kill the dog!"

Snecky stopped pacing. "God. So, what are we saying now, then? This Ted guy killed Sergeant Crier?"

"I mean, he's got a motive," Marty said.

"Thin, though," Heather said.

Marty shrugged. "Messed up his career. Not that thin."

"Aye, over a year ago. Nearly two years ago," Heather countered. "Why now? What prompted this?"

"He could've just been biding his time. It would've been too obvious if he'd done it right after Tony had put in the complaint."

Heather grimaced. "Still not feeling it. There had to be some other reason for… Shit. Wait. They knew. He told them."

"Who told who what?" Snecky asked.

"Ash. Wayne said that he'd told a few of his friends that Tony was dying."

Marty sat up straighter. "So, Ted finds out that Tony's not got much time left…"

"And realises that he needs to move fast," Heather finished.

"What's the point in that?" asked DC Wolfe. "If he was dying, anyway?"

"It wasn't about him being dead, it was about him being punished. Dying of cancer would be unfortunate for Tony—"

"That's a bloody understatement," Snecky muttered.

"But it wouldn't be revenge for Ted," Heather concluded. "If he wanted to get his own back, then that wouldn't count. It wouldn't be enough."

She turned around and stabbed a finger at DC Wolfe. The forcefulness of it almost made Simon topple backwards out of his chair.

"You. I want his address. Find out where he lives, then get round there. Check with the liaison at his sister's house, see if he's still there. If he isn't, find out where he went. If he's on duty, I want to know where."

Simon wrote in his notepad.

"Check... with... liaison..."

He shook his pen, licked the end, then scribbled on the page and tutted.

"Anyone got a spare pen?"

"For God's sake." Marty tutted. He tossed a pen across the desk, and Simon juggled it for a few frantic seconds before finally catching it.

"Cheers."

"That's a point. What about Darryl?" Snecky asked Heather. "Constable Hartmann? That's Ted's brother-in-law, isn't it? They're mates. I mean, Darryl stood up for Ted when Wayne was giving him grief at Tony's wee gathering thing. I somehow doubt that Ted's turned around and said, 'Thanks very much for that,' and then killed him!"

"Maybe. I don't know," Heather admitted. "I don't know enough about him. I just know he's lied to us, that he had good reason to hate Tony." She clicked her fingers. "Wait. He's got a business. He mentioned that."

"Doing what?" Snecky asked.

"Don't know," Heather admitted. She turned to Marty, but the detective sergeant's fingers were already flying across the keyboard. "Got him. He's on the Companies House database. Says there's one linked limited company. Hang on."

He clicked a link and impatiently tapped his fingers on the mouse buttons while he waited for the page to load.

When it did, his jaw all but fell open. Heather stared at the screen, then took a shuffled step back, a hand covering her mouth.

"Holy shit!" Marty said.

"What?" Snecky asked, sidling in front of Heather to give him a clearer view of the screen. "What is it? What are we looking at?"

He followed the detective sergeant's finger. His eyes

narrowed while he searched the screen, then suddenly blew up wide in disbelief.

"Holy shit!" he cried, echoing Marty's reaction. He turned to look back over his shoulder at DI Filson standing behind him.

But DI Filson was already gone.

THIRTY-SEVEN

ONLY ONE OF Tammi-Jo's eyes was willing to open. The other felt glued shut and sticky, and it refused to do as she asked.

There was a cold roughness against her cheek. The way it prickled reminded her of the time back in primary school when she'd been blootered in the face with a football at near point-blank range. She'd had just enough time to turn her head before the *Mitre* had made impact, and though her quick reactions had saved her from a broken nose, her cheek had burned bright red for days.

There was the same prickling sensation on her skin, but there was a coldness this time, too. It radiated up through her flesh and took root in the bones of her cheeks.

Give her the football any day.

She was looking at a stack of washing that had toppled from a basket and lay scattered on the floor. Everything was sideways, though, and her brain was taking longer than it should to figure out which way was up.

A sharp pain in her wrists chose that moment to introduce itself. A duller one in her shoulders throbbed as if in reply.

Her hands were tied behind her back, two lines of thin plastic digging trenches in her flesh.

She was in the garage. Though she couldn't see much of it, she knew where she was because the place was filled with the same pine-fresh scent as earlier. There was still a hint of stale vomit hanging in the air, too.

And, though she couldn't yet place it, something else. Something familiar.

Tammi-Jo lifted her head, grimaced through the pain it brought, then heaved herself up into a sitting position. Her legs had been tied together at the ankles and knees, and it was only when she was semi-upright that she became awake enough to notice the gag across her mouth.

Her eyes met those of Selma Baird. The Iron Woman huddled in soiled underwear against the side wall, her wrists tied to a metal hook by a length of climbing rope. The cold coming up through the concrete floor was chilling her, making her whole body shiver.

The bandage on her arm had peeled off. She'd been telling the truth about the burn. A perfect imprint of the plate of an iron marked her flesh, all the little ridges and dots clearly visible.

Selma's face was one big slick of snot and tears. The dog bowl that Tammi-Jo had spotted earlier lay upturned just beyond the reach of her feet, a puddle drying on the stone floor and pooling beneath one of the rubber tiles.

Unlike the detective constable, Selma wasn't gagged, but her breathing was too erratic for her to be able to speak, and all she could do when she saw Tammi-Jo was awake was to issue a shrill warning, "*Shhh.*"

It occurred to Tammi-Jo then that she could see. She'd been aware that she could see since opening her eye, of course, but the significance of it was only now filtering through.

A standing lamp stood at the back of the garage, a bare bulb casting a sickly orange glow across the unfinished floor and walls.

That was good. Being able to see was a bonus.

Although, that really depended on what it was she was going to be looking at. It didn't take a big leap of deduction for her to conclude it was unlikely to be anything pleasant.

The garage door was closed. The window at the far end of the room showed only darkness beyond it. The three metal bars across it made sense now. Their purpose had never been to keep anyone out.

The gag was pulled tight, wedged between her teeth and knotted at the back of her head, so her mouth movements were limited. She managed to make a few inquisitive noises, but even those faint sounds launched Selma into full-scale panic.

"P-please, don't. Don't," the Iron Woman whispered. "He'll get angry. Don't make him angry. Please. Please."

"You should listen to her."

Ted's voice was frighteningly close. Selma let out a yelp then shrunk back, pressing herself against the wall, shocked to see him standing there in full uniform by the door that led into the house.

He entered with a relaxed, nonchalant sort of gait, brushing his hands against one another like he was cleaning off some dust. He yawned, but made no attempt to cover his big, wide-open mouth.

"Sorry. Lot of late nights lately."

He stopped in front of Tammi-Jo, so he was standing over her. He playfully nudged her feet with his own, like they were two lovers playing footsies under a dinner table.

"And sorry about the, you know,"—he gestured at her bindings—"all this. I shouldn't have hit you like that. I panicked. I just... I just panicked." He bumped the toe of a boot against the side of her shoe and smiled hopefully. "Forgive me?"

Behind him, Selma summoned the courage to get out a whisper. "T-Ted, please."

The special constable's face fell. He drew a deep breath in through his nose, looked up at the ceiling. "Will you please just *shut the fuck up?!*"

The sentence started normally, then escalated into a roar that rolled around the inside of the garage.

His smile rushed back to his face, but it was a desperate, fragile thing. He rolled his eyes at Tammi-Jo. "She won't give me peace," he said. "Always giving it that."

He brought up a hand and flapped the fingers and thumb open and closed like they were the mouth of some nagging puppet.

"*Meemeemeemee!* That's what she's like," Ted said. He laughed and winked at the detective constable, as if the other woman wasn't right there in the room. "Just *meemeemeemeemee* all the fucking time. And I'm so fucking sick of it. I used to blame Wayne for cheating on her. For sleeping around. But Christ, what choice did the poor bastard have, listening to that all fucking day?"

He rounded on the captive Selma. She screwed up her eyes and turned her head away, bracing herself for pain.

Ted didn't strike her, though. He just stood there in silence, listening to her stifled sobs, waiting until the fear of the unknown became so great that she had to open her eyes to find out what was taking so long.

"I think we're over, Selma," he told her. "Honestly, I think we were over a while ago, we just didn't want to admit it to ourselves. It was fun while it lasted, though. Eh?"

Tammi-Jo and Selma both watched him as he walked towards the back of the garage, squatted down, and slid a plastic toolbox out from under a bench.

"I know what you're thinking, DC Swanney. 'How come that bitch doesn't have to wear a gag, but I do?' That's an easy one to answer."

He opened the lid of the box, and when he stood up, a claw hammer hung limply by his side.

"Trust," Ted said. He pointed with the hammer at Selma. "See, I know for a fact that she's not going to call for help. She wouldn't dare. She knows what'd happen. But you? It's different. You and me, we're still in that Honeymoon period. Still dancing around one another."

He bounced from foot to foot, twisting his hips slightly, like he was getting ready to rumba.

"You can feel it, can't you? The electricity between us. The chemistry. Neither of us quite knowing what to say. How to act with one another. It's exciting. But it's dangerous, too. Because I don't know if you'll scream for help the second I take that gag off you. I just don't have a clue. Not that anyone would hear you out here, but still."

He lightly tapped the head of the hammer against his chin while gazing at the detective constable through narrowed, thoughtful eyes.

"So, here's what we're going to do," he announced. "In a second, I'm going to take that gag off you. That way, you and me will be able to have a little chat. But, fair warning, if you scream, or shout for help, or say any mean things, then I'm going to take the claw part of this hammer, and I'm going to put it through one of her eye sockets."

Selma whimpered. Ted's smirk suggested he enjoyed the anxious little squeak she made.

"Just one. The left one," he said. "And I'm going to leave it there. I'll just leave it in there. Hanging out. Do you understand what I'm saying? Nod if you do."

Tammi-Jo glanced across at the trembling, terrified Selma. The Iron Woman's heels were bleeding, her bare feet having been scraped across the concrete floor.

"I need to know you understand," Ted told her.

Tammi-Jo tore her gaze away from Selma, and forced herself to look up at the special constable standing above her.

Slowly, deliberately, she nodded.

"Good. And do you believe me? That I'll do it. Do you believe I'll put this hammer through her eye?"

Tammi-Jo swallowed as best she could behind the gag. She dipped her head again.

"Fantastic!" Ted cried, with a manic sort of cheerfulness that felt completely out of place. "I'm so glad we understand each other."

He squatted in front of her and leaned in until his face was only a few inches from hers. The tip of his tongue flitted between his lips as he studied her. The back of his hand brushed up and down one of her cheeks.

"Because," he murmured, moving closer, breathing her in. "I am so looking forward to the two of us getting to know each other."

———

Ace whooped.

She had never whooped before, but it felt like an appropriate first time to do so.

It was very possible that she wasn't actually going all that fast, but she felt like she was riding on the back of a rocket ship, the lights of the houses lining the streets blurring as they streaked past like stars.

This must be what flying was like, she thought, albeit without the whole business of actually being in mid-air. It was exhilarating.

For a moment, she contemplated taking her hands off the handlebars and thrusting them into the air, but common sense alerted her to the fact that she'd almost certainly die, and she continued to cling on to the rubber grips for dear life.

Because, as well as being exhilarating, it was also quite, quite terrifying.

But it would all be worth it. She had her podcasting equipment in her backpack, a route plotted out on her phone, and a head crammed full of questions.

With front wheel wobbling, bike lights blazing, and legs pumping nineteen to the dozen, Ace pressed on out of town, headed north on the road to Kilmaurs.

THIRTY-EIGHT

TAMMI-JO DIDN'T SCREAM. She didn't dare. Ted was passing the hammer from hand to hand as he stood above her, twirling it around, and generally doing everything he could to keep it at the forefront of the detective constable's mind.

He hadn't made any move to act on his threat yet, but something about his demeanour—everything about his demeanour—made her believe that he would.

Selma clearly believed it, too. She had tucked her head in so it was pressed against her knees, and her body shook with silent, stifled sobs.

"So, I probably owe you an explanation," Ted said. "About" —he gestured around with the hammer—"all this. About everything."

Tammi-Jo swallowed, steadying herself. "I'd appreciate that, Ted," she told him.

"You're going to judge me. I know you are. Everyone does."

"I won't," the DC assured him. "No judgement. I'll just listen."

Ted breathed that thought in. "I'd like that," he said. "I don't believe you, but I like you, so I'm going to take a chance and pretend I do. I'm going to put myself out there."

His voice cracked, and he looked away for a moment. When he turned back, there were tears in his eyes. "I'm not well," he said. He tapped the side of the hammer against his head. "Up here. I'm not well."

"I'm sorry," Tammi-Jo replied. "I'm really sorry to hear that, Ted."

His expression changed for the better whenever she mentioned his name. That was good. She'd keep doing that. It was one of the things you got told early on in training—learn the names of the people you were dealing with, and use them. Form a connection. Build trust.

There was a lot of other advice, too. Useful stuff on how to deal with situations not dissimilar to this one.

She really wished she could remember some of it.

"I do things. Things I don't really mean to do. Things that aren't really me," he said.

"It's OK," Tammi-Jo assured him. "We all make mistakes."

He wiped an eye on his uniform sleeve. "You think so?"

"I do. I really do. Everyone knows it. We all do it," the detective constable replied. "Like this, this is a mistake. But we can sort it out. It's not too far gone yet. We can deal with this between us. We can fix it."

"You mean that?" Ted whispered.

"Yes. I mean it," Tammi-Jo said.

Ted knelt in front of her, placing one knee down on the ground, then the other. He put a hand on the side of her face and smiled kindly.

"My God, that just makes this all so much harder," he groaned, before planting a big kiss on her forehead and standing up again. "You see, when I was next door, when you were still sleeping, I was thinking about how I can get out of this. I knew that you knew. When I saw you on the step. I could see it in your eyes that you'd figured it all out. So, while you were knocked out, I was trying to think of some way to tidy all this up. Some way to put everything back to normal. Like a reset button. Boom. Fix everything."

He spun the hammer around again, twisting the handle, then opening his hand just enough to let it rotate a couple of times before his grip tightened again.

"But you can't undo this sort of thing, can you? You can't just rewind and put the genie back in the bottle. You know what I did. I know you know. I just don't know how much you know, or who else knows. So, that's what I need you to tell me, DC Swanney-like-the-river."

Tammi-Jo saw two possible paths opening up before her. In one, she kept trying to talk him down, to convince him they could still get past this, that he could still avoid prison, or whatever it was he was worried about. That path involved assuring him that she was on his side, and making him believe they were going to work all this out together.

The other path was a rockier one. Take that route, and she'd have to convince him that backup was already on the way, that everyone knew everything, and that he was going to get caught, so he may as well hand himself in and hope that the judge was in a lenient mood.

Neither option was perfect.

Neither option was true.

"You know I killed them, yeah?" he asked, which forced her to take the second path. "Course you do. You already know I killed them."

"We do. We know. Everyone's looking for you, Ted. And they know where I am."

He didn't appear to care about this, just about getting across his side of the story.

"But do you know *why* I did it?" he demanded.

"No. But you can tell me," the DC told him, deciding that a combination of paths one and two might open up a whole new road to salvation. "Like I said, Ted, I want to listen. But we need to be quick. The others are on the way. They're going to be here soon, and if I'm going to help you, I need to know everything."

Ted nodded slowly. "You're right. No, you are. You're right. I need to explain myself." He took a breath, then let it out again. "They were a pair of pricks." He smirked down at her. "How's that for a motive? They were a couple of jumped-up, self-important arseholes who deserved what they got."

Midway through the sentence, his smile twisted itself into a bitter, angry sneer. His knuckles whitened as he tightened his grip on the hammer.

"Did you know Tony stopped me getting into the police? Just flat out told them I wasn't suitable. Can you believe that?!"

Tammi-Jo could very much believe that, but she tried her best to look disappointed on his behalf.

"He's always had it in for me. Called me vindictive. Called me cruel. Said I was unhinged. All because he thinks I killed his dog, which was bollocks, because I love dogs. Even that yappy wee prick of a thing. Even when Ash wanted to play with it all the time instead of me. I still wouldn't have hurt it! But, oh no, big Tony still thinks I killed it. Or he still thought I killed it," Ted corrected. He grinned, like he'd just cracked a brilliant joke. "Probably not so much now, eh?"

He let out a sharp burst of laughter that echoed shrilly around the garage, and made Selma bury her face further into her knees.

"Found out he was dying last week. And, I don't know, I got angry. I'd been holding it in for ages, thinking about what I wanted to do to him, but I never had the nerve to actually do it," Ted explained. "And then, when I heard, I was like, why should he get to just pop off without paying for what he did? How does he get to ruin my life, and then just die of cancer like a normal person? How's that fair?"

Tammi-Jo chose not to answer the question.

"So, you killed him?"

"So, I leathered fuck out of him," Ted corrected. He pointed with the hammer at the cowering Selma. "Then this useless bitch was meant to come round and make sure he was dead. I wanted her to see him. To see *me*. To see exactly what I'm capable of."

He rounded on the Iron Woman, bent low, and spoke to her in a slow, raised voice.

"But she couldn't fucking do that, could she? She couldn't follow one simple instruction."

"Sorry, sorry, I'm s-sorry," Selma whispered.

"Hey. Hey, shh. It's OK," Ted said, his voice suddenly filled with kindness and care. "Babe. Don't worry about it. Look at me. Look at me."

It was clear that Selma didn't want to look at him, but nor did she want to incur his wrath. Shaking, sniffling, she raised her head an inch or two so she could peer at him over the tops of her knees.

He slapped her, his arm swinging at her out of nowhere, the flat of his hand connecting hard with the top of her head. She cried out and tucked her head in again, the sound of his laughter ringing in both women's ears.

"I helped her set all this up, by the way. This was all my idea. I told her that her husband was shagging some tart, and then I set her up in business so she could try and scrape together a bit of money. And how does she repay me? By being a useless fucking bitch!"

"What about Darryl?" Tammi-Jo asked, trying to draw his attention away from the Iron Woman and back to her. "Why did you kill him?"

Ted's nose crinkled up at mention of his late brother-in-law's name. "Daz was a dick. Acted like the nice guy, but he wasn't. Not really. Used to throw his weight about a bit. And Jess, she put up with it, because that's what our old man used to do. Can you believe she's greeting her eyes out over him? I mean… what?! Like mother, like daughter. Fucking doormats, the pair of them. Clearly runs in the family."

Tammi-Jo felt it best not to point out the irony of what Ted was saying. Then again, even if she'd wanted to, she didn't think she could break through his rant.

"And did you see how he tried to humiliate me at Tony's do? How he told Wayne to let me in like I couldn't do that on my own? Like I was too weak to stand up for myself? Not so weak now, am I?

"And, do you know what? It was easy. I built up the idea of killing Tony in my head for months before I did it. With Daz, it was just like"—he clicked his fingers—"that. I just knew I was going to do it, and so I did. I knew where he was. I phoned in an anonymous call for some neds acting up nearby, and I waited." He shrugged. "It was easy. It didn't even feel like anything. It was like, meh. Yep. That's done. Then, I ditched his car. Job done."

He smiled sadly down at the detective constable, then let out a slow, solemn sigh.

"It's going to be more difficult with you, though. Her? No. Couldn't give a fuck. But you. I thought we had something. I thought we clicked. Did you feel that?"

"I did," Tammi-Jo said, and it wasn't even a lie. Back at the station, she'd liked him. He'd seemed awkward, and nice, and a little bit funny. She liked that in a person. "I thought we got on really well."

Ted threw his hands into the air in exasperation. The one clutching the hammer swung back down more quickly than the other.

"See? Argh! That just makes it worse! I knew it, though. I knew it. I could feel it. Fuck!"

He tossed the hammer aside. It landed with a *clunk* on the concrete floor.

"It's really unfair," he said. "On both of us."

He walked towards the back of the garage, and seemed to

be headed for the door. Tammi-Jo looked across at Selma. The Iron Woman's bonds were snagged over the hook on the wall, but they weren't attached to it. She could simply lift her arms to unhook them.

Tammi-Jo glared meaningfully at the hook, then down at the hammer on the floor. It took Selma a moment to realise what she was getting at, then she hurriedly shook her head and buried her face back into her knees.

So much for that plan.

There was a sloshing sound, then the smell that Tammi-Jo had vaguely recognised from earlier grew suddenly, over-whelmingly stronger.

Panic flared in her chest. She struggled against her ropes, but they were too strong, too tight.

She watched, motionless, as a puddle of petrol ebbed across the concrete floor.

"This was the solution I came up with," Ted announced, swinging a jerry can around and flinging fuel across the stacks of washing. "Wipe the slate clean. Start again. Cleanse this whole place with fire, and nobody will know I was here."

"They know, Ted," Tammi-Jo told him. "They already know. This is just making it worse."

"Don't lie," he said in a teasing voice. He stopped pouring petrol on everything long enough to wag a finger at her. "If they knew what I've done, and they knew I was here, they wouldn't have sent you on your own. It'd be a sea of Uniforms out there. Wayne Gillespie would have kicked my door in."

"He's been arrested!" Tammi-Jo cried. "Sergeant Gillespie. We arrested him. He was on the take."

Ted set down the petrol can and clutched at his head. "Fuu-uuuck!" he cried. "Really? Bloody hell. I didn't see that coming! I mean, I knew he was an arsehole, but *crooked*? Jesus Christ. Makes you sick. You can't even trust the fucking police these days!"

He looked around, and made a gesture to indicate the extent of the building they were currently in.

"Mind you, shouldn't really come as a surprise. You seen this place? How the fuck does a sergeant afford this? And it wasn't this clueless bitch. All she knows how to do is iron and fuck things up."

The toe of his boot stamped down on the floor just inches from Selma's bare feet. She jumped and pulled them in closer to her, but didn't dare utter a sound.

Ted shook his head like he was deeply disappointed. "Know what? I'm glad I'm not a full constable. I don't want to be part of an organisation that promotes people like that." He picked up the canister again. "I've got morals."

He started to slosh more petrol across the clothes, then a sudden sound from inside the house made him stop.

A series of bells chimed in a grandiose, self-important sort of way.

The door. Someone was at the door.

Ted set down the can and grabbed for the hammer, pointing it at Tammi-Jo before she could say a word. He knelt in front of her, put her gag back in her mouth, then placed a finger to his lips, indicating that she should keep quiet.

The doorbell rang again. When Ted stood up, there was a wet patch of petrol on one of his knees.

"Shit," he muttered, brushing it down.

Then, with a warning look at both women, he headed for the internal door, and closed and locked it behind him.

Tammi-Jo held her breath. Over the sound of her crashing heartbeat, she heard Ted jogging along the hallway of the house.

"Alright, alright, hold your horses!" he cried, jovially. "I'm just coming!"

———

The door opened, spilling light out from the hallway onto the darkened front step, and onto the face of the teenage girl standing there with a microphone in her hand.

"Um, you aren't Selma Baird," Ace announced, as if this would be news to the man.

"No. Well spotted," the man in the police uniform replied. "Sorry, who are you?"

"I'm Ace Wurzel. The Crime De La Crime podcast? I'm covering the murder of Sergeant Tony Crier."

"Oh. You are, are you?" The constable glanced into the darkness behind her, then ramped up his smile. "She's just through in the living room. Do you want to come in?"

Ace hesitated. Aside from the hallway, most of the house seemed to be in darkness.

The police officer was smiling, which was generally a positive thing. But there was something about this particular smile that she didn't like. As someone who had never quite mastered the knack of pretending to smile, and had several years of school photographs as evidence of that fact, she could identify the similarly afflicted a mile away.

This man wasn't smiling. Not really. He just wanted her to think that he was.

DI Filson's warning had been very clear. Don't trust anyone, even the police. Especially the police, in fact.

"Uh, no. Thank you. I'll come back another time."

"It's fine," Ted insisted. "She's just right inside. She'll be happy to talk to you."

"No. It's quite alright," Ace insisted, backing away. "It can wait."

Ted sighed. "OK. Well, at least let me drive you home. It's dark. It's late. Did you walk all the way out here?"

"I took my bike," Ace said, though she immediately wished that she hadn't told him that. The less he knew about her, the better. "I should get going."

The officer regarded her in silence for a moment, then shrugged. "OK. Just be careful."

"I will," Ace said, keeping her eye on him while she fumbled in the darkness to find where she'd abandoned her bike.

With a wave, he retreated back inside the house, closing the door behind him. Ace breathed out a cloud of white mist, then unhooked her bag from her shoulders and hurriedly stuffed her microphone back inside.

———

Tammi-Jo and Selma both tensed when Ted came barging back into the garage. He splashed through the petrol puddle and hurried to the side of the roll-up door, where a narrow gap allowed him to peer out into the darkness.

"Go on. Go on, piss off," he muttered, staring out. "Just keep going."

Outside, just a few feet away, Ace clumsily swung her leg over the frame of the bike, and played footsie with the pedals like she couldn't quite remember how they worked.

She finally managed to co-ordinate both feet with the rest of her body, and set off away from the house along the drive.

"That's it," Ted whispered. "Off you—"

The next word caught in his throat when the girl stopped the bike beside the parked Audi. It wasn't a particularly graceful stop, and it ended with her almost firing herself over the handlebars.

Once steadied, she looked at the car's open window, then down at the fragments of broken glass on the ground beside it.

Finally, she looked back in the direction of the house. Of the garage. Of, he would've sworn, Ted himself.

"Oh, no. Shit, shit, shit!"

He turned for the door. Ran. Vanished for a moment, then reappeared.

A lighter ignited. An apology was muttered. Then, a plastic container filled with neatly pressed jeans and t-shirts erupted into flame.

Through her gag, through her tears, and the blackening smoke, Tammi-Jo managed to shriek a single shrill word.

"Run!"

THIRTY-NINE

ACE RAN, the bike abandoned somewhere far behind her, her feet too clumsy to operate the pedals in such a moment of high stress.

The darkness around her was absolute. The ground beneath her feet was rough and uneven. She'd started running back down the drive, but then an engine had fired up, and she knew her pursuer would have the advantage on level roads.

She'd swung a hurried left and plunged into a field, the frozen mud crunching beneath her feet, her trainers snagging in the iced-up tangle of grass and weeds.

At first, when the Audi had gone revving along the driveway, she'd thought she'd escaped unseen. But then, with a crunching of tyres on gravel, the car had swung towards her, its full-beam headlights blinding her as they zeroed in.

She zig-zagged, weaving left and right, trying to stay out of the lights, even if it meant she couldn't see the ground in front of her. Turning was her only advantage. Turning was the only way she could stay ahead of the vehicle. Turning was her only chance of staying alive.

But turning—and running—took energy.

And Ace Wurzel's energy—and time—were rapidly running out.

The Audi bounced across the pockmarked surface of the field, arcing around until the light hit her again like a prison yard's spotlights.

She turned. Again. Back towards the house this time, and to the smoke rolling up from its roof.

Chest heaving, lungs burning, breath rasping in her throat, and an engine roaring angrily behind her, Ace stumbled onwards into the dark.

———

Flames crackled and licked at the garage walls, blistering the cheap paint, layering the ceiling in a cloud of choking black smoke.

Tammi-Jo coughed behind her gag, her eyes screwed tightly shut against the smoke and the heat, the ropes burning her wrists as she fought to get free.

Selma coughed too, a dry, chesty rattle that suggested damage was already being done.

DC Swanney forced her eyes open, and through the tears saw that the other woman hadn't moved. Her hands were still slung over the hook, her mouth uncovered, her feet untied.

Through the rag across her mouth, and her own barking cough, Tammi-Jo urged Selma to move. To get up. To get them both out of there.

But all the Iron Woman would do was shake her head and bury her face between her bare knees. Death, it seemed—even this death—was a lesser evil than getting on Ted Campbell's bad side.

She wasn't going to do anything to help them. If Tammi-Jo wanted out of this, she'd have to figure it out herself.

Wriggling, she managed to get herself up onto her knees. Back in the day, when she'd been training regularly, she'd be able to jump up from that position onto the flats of her feet without any real effort.

But that was three or four years ago, she hadn't been trapped in a burning building, and her feet hadn't been tied together at the time.

Still, if ever there was a motivator, it was the columns of flame that moved to surround her. The side door was already impossible to get to, which left only the roll-up door at the front of the garage.

How she was going to open that with her hands tied behind her back, she didn't know.

But first things first.

Lowering her weight so she was sitting on her heels, Tammi-Jo steeled herself, steadied herself, braced herself, then jumped.

Her momentum propelled her into the air just enough for her to whip her knees up, bringing her feet out from under her.

She'd have made it, too, if it hadn't been for her shoes. The toe of the left one caught, slowing the movement of her legs just enough that she couldn't plant her weight properly. She crashed down, her shoulder and the side of her head landing hard in a puddle of acrid-smelling petrol.

Reflected flames danced across its surface, a mirror image of the burning ceiling above.

Despite the smell of the fuel, the air down there felt clearer. Cleaner. Tammi-Jo decided to rest for a moment. Just a moment. That was all she needed. Just long enough to get her breath back.

She'd try again. She would. But it was just so hot and hard to breathe. She just needed a second or two. That was all.

A metallic *bang* snapped her eyes open. She choked on the suddenly soaking rag, the taste of petrol seeping into her mouth.

"Hello! Hello! Is anyone in there?!"

DI Filson! It was DI Filson!

Tears streaming, Tammi-Jo forced herself up onto her knees. She tried to shout, but the gag and the smoke and the petrol made it impossible to do anything but choke and cough.

There was a final shout of, "Hello?!" from outside, then some muttered swearing, and the sound of retreating footsteps.

"N-no," the detective constable managed to sob, then a burst of flame from the back of the room knocked her sideways onto the floor.

Outside, an engine came to life. Over the crackling of the flames, Tammi-Jo heard a gearstick give a crunch.

And then, the world erupted into noise and movement, as the nose of a police car came crashing in through the front door and stopped mere inches from the detective constable's head.

The incoming rush of air fanned the flames, ramping up the heat. It was blistering, coming from everywhere, from every direction, all-consuming. There was nothing Tammi-Jo could do to fight it. Nothing she could do but surrender.

And then, hands were grabbing at her. Pulling at her. Hauling on her. Dragging her across the floor.

The cold was like an angel's kiss against her skin, dulling the pain, clearing her head. The gag was pulled down, and she vomited onto the gravel. Her eyes stung as she forced them open. The blue light of a single police car flashed across the front of the house, as if fighting back against the roaring orange flames.

From inside the garage, she heard an angry shout.

"Stop fighting me, you silly bitch! I need to get you out."

After a moment, a screaming, writhing Selma landed heavily on the ground beside Tammi-Jo, her bare skin blackened by soot and smoke.

The ropes binding the DC's hands were untied, and Tammi-Jo couldn't fight back a throaty sob when Heather shuffled around into her view.

"You alright?" the DI asked.

"Ace," Tammi-Jo wheezed.

"You don't fucking look it," Heather told her.

The DC shook her head. "No," she said through her scorched throat. She pointed off across the field to where the taillights of a vehicle bounced up and down on the uneven ground. "Ace."

Heather's face fell. She caught a glimpse of a distant running figure silhouetted against headlights.

"Oh," she groaned. "Shit."

FORTY

THE MUSCLES in Ace's legs were screaming. The muscles in the rest of her body weren't exactly celebrating, either, but the legs were leading the protests.

She couldn't keep this up for much longer. She'd rolled an ankle a few right angles ago, and pain went ricocheting through her every time that foot made contact with the ground.

There was a police car back at the house, its lights flashing, but it had made no move towards her, and every time she tried to run towards it, the twin beams of the headlights behind her seemed to immediately lock on, forcing her to change direction again.

She felt like she was getting closer to the house, but at a rate that meant it would probably take her a good half hour to get within spitting distance.

There was no way she could keep running for half an hour. Even half a minute felt like an impossible dream right then.

Besides, even if she did make it to the house, who was to say she could trust whoever had pulled up in the car? There was a good chance that the driver of that car was in cahoots with the driver of the one currently charging up behind her.

Cahoots was a good word, she thought, though she immediately concluded that it probably wasn't the best time to dwell on it.

A ditch appeared out of nowhere. She just got the sense of the world falling away a few paces ahead of her, and then she was falling, tumbling down a short incline, then slamming against the opposite side of the V-shaped hole.

Lights blinded her before she could move. Soil slid down on her as the front of the Audi cleared the gap and then smashed, nose-first, into the ground right above her head.

Frantically, Ace scrambled out from under the vehicle, grasping and clawing at roots and weeds as she heaved herself back up onto level ground.

She looked back over her shoulder at the car as she limped on, and saw its airbags had deployed upon impact. Any hope that the driver had been injured in the crash soon evaporated, though.

The driver's side door was flung open. The man in the police uniform slid out of the Audi, and disappeared into the ditch.

Ace stood watching, sucking in air, giving her body a few seconds to recover.

And then, like something from a zombie horror movie, a hand appeared above the top of the ditch, the splayed fingers digging into the dirt.

His head appeared next, shrouded by a ring of white mist from the hot breath swirling down his nostrils.

Ace saw the other hand come up, a claw hammer clutched in its grip.

She set off, limping, towards the house. It was her only chance. Whoever was there, whatever was waiting for her, reaching it was her only hope.

But her ankle, and her legs, had other ideas. The next step brought agony. Her other leg, too weak to react, gave out, and Ace sprawled headlong onto the hardened, frosty mud.

She tried to launch herself upright again, but her body

wasn't listening. Instead, all she could do was roll onto her back and frantically kick backwards across the ground as the man in the police uniform raced towards her.

The blazing light from the burning house picked out the fury on his face and glinted off the metal head of the hammer as he drew it back, raised it high, readied to swing it down.

And then, a shadow exploded from the darkness. The charging police officer seemed to vanish, as if the night itself had opened its jaws and swallowed him whole.

Ace raised her head and looked around, then saw him lying several feet away on his side, a figure dressed in black pinning him down, the glow of the fire dancing across the semi-reflective surface of a leather jacket.

Sprawled there, on the cold hard ground, Ace let out a long sigh of relief, then allowed her head to drop back onto the frosty grass.

A few feet away, over the sound of a man being forced face down into the mud, Detective Inspector Heather Filson hissed, "Gotcha!"

———

Heather was the only one walking properly when they arrived back at the burning house. Ace's aching legs and sprained ankle had turned into a painful waddle, and from a distance, it looked like she was straddling the back of a small, invisible horse.

Special Constable Campbell's sideways impact with the frosty ground had done damage to one of his knees, and Heather had quite deliberately done damage to various other parts of him once she'd seen the state of her car.

His cheeks, chin, and forehead were all grazed, and blood trickled from one of his nostrils. Heather had been sure she'd heard a rib break when she'd slammed him onto the ground. In an ideal world, it would be more than one.

He hobbled along with his hands cuffed behind him, mumbling incoherent complaints below his breath. Heather gripped him by the upper arm, her fingernails digging into his flesh whenever she wanted him to speed up, slow down, or alter direction, or just whenever she fancied it.

The house was done for, the flames now leaping outwards through most of the windows, and stretching up through the partially collapsed roof towards the stars overhead. Burning embers rose into the cold November sky, carried on a cushion of heat.

The police car had been reversed out of the garage mouth, and now sat parked a little further down the drive. Heather could see Selma Baird huddled under a blanket in the back. Alive. Unharmed, though?

Time would tell.

"So, in hindsight..." Ace began, but a look from Heather silenced her before she could go any further.

Clearly, things were still too raw. Apologies and explanations would have to wait.

Heather pointed to the parked police car, and ordered Ace to go wait by it while she called for backup.

Before she could punch in the number, though, Ted twisted free of her grip with a cry of triumph. He lashed out with a foot, driving it into her stomach. As she staggered, he turned towards the burning garage.

The reversing car had pulled the rest of the door down, leaving a rectangular opening that was filled with black smoke and orange flames, like the open mouth of some terrible, terrifying dragon.

"You're not going to take me alive!" the special constable screeched, launching himself towards the fire, hobbling with as much speed as he could muster.

"Hey, Ted!"

A hand whipped out directly in his path. A karate chop connected with his throat. The upper half of his body stopped, but the lower half failed to get the memo. His legs bicycled in thin air for a moment as he went horizontal, then he crashed down onto his back, cracked the back of his head against a rock, and gazed, dazed and winded, at the smoke-drenched stars above.

A footstep crunched on gravel. A woman with the face of an angel appeared above him, staring down.

"Go fuck yourself," Tammi-Jo told him.

And then, a pattern of dancing darkness turned his vision into a long, narrow tunnel, and concussion dragged him downwards into a cold and haunted sleep.

FORTY-ONE

THE SMELL of bacon enticed Heather to finally open her eyes. She rolled over in bed, checked the clock, and groaned when she eventually figured out that the number on there started with an eight.

Less than two hours of sleep. That wasn't healthy.

Then again, nor were most of her habits. Or, for that matter, her career choices.

Everything ached as she swung her legs out of bed. She wriggled her toes when she realised she still had her socks on. In fact—she looked down at herself—yep, she was still fully clothed.

Obviously, taking the time to get undressed had proven to be one step too far. At least she'd taken her boots off, although Christ alone knew where they were.

It had been a long night. Marty had come out with a squad of Uniforms and taken Ted in for questioning. The fire brigade had done what they could to salvage the house, while paramedics had taken Tammi-Jo and Selma Blair to hospital to be checked over. They'd both been kept in for observation, though Tammi-Jo had largely seemed fine.

The same couldn't be said for the Iron Woman. She'd barely

said a word, and had wailed and screamed so much when the paramedics tried to look her over that they'd been forced to sedate her.

Heather could only guess at what Ted had put her through.

She *could* guess, but she really didn't want to.

It would all come out in time. The special constable was safely under lock and key and wasn't going anywhere. They already had enough to put him away for years. Once he confessed to the murders on tape—and he would, Heather knew his type—he'd be banged up for life.

Maybe he and Wayne Gillespie would end up sharing a prison cell somewhere. Although, frustratingly, any custodial sentence for the sergeant was likely to be a fleeting one.

Giving up on finding her boots, Heather followed the smell of bacon down the stairs.

At least, she hoped she was smelling bacon. She still had the stench of smoke wedged in her sinuses somewhere, so there was a chance that the bacon aroma was some cruel nasal hallucination brought on by that.

Thankfully, it wasn't a mirage, and Heather opened the kitchen door just in time to see a shaky hand tip three crispy rashers from a spatula onto a roll with an obscene amount of butter smeared across its innards.

"Touchdown!" Scott cried. He turned to Cathy, who had been standing immediately behind him, and patted her enthusiastically on the shoulder. The big beamer of a smile on his face made most of Heather's grogginess fade away. "Houston, we don't have a problem!"

He looked towards the door and uncertainty crept across his face like the shadow of some dark, brooding cloud.

But then the smile returned, and he pointed excitedly at the plate on the counter. "Heather! Look! Did you see that?"

Heather stifled a yawn and smiled back at him. "I did. Nice work, Auld Yin!"

Scott grabbed for the kettle, which was almost to the boil.

"Will I do tea?"

Thankfully, Cathy moved quickly to intercept, blocking him before he could do himself, and possibly everyone else in the kitchen, a mischief.

"I'll do the tea. You give Heather her roll."

Scott's face fell. "Wait, is that no' my roll? Am I not getting a roll?"

"You already had two!" Cathy reminded him.

"Oh. Did I?"

Heather's dad gazed forlornly at the bacon buttie. She sighed and nudged the plate towards him. "Knock yourself out, Auld Yin."

His eyes lit up with delight. He made a show of licking his lips and patting his stomach, then he picked up the roll and, after a moment's thought, tore it in two.

"There you go, pet," he said, handing the notably smaller half to Heather. "You look like you could do with a feed."

"Half a feed," Heather corrected.

Scott shoved his half roll in his mouth, then let out a giggle that made both Heather and Cathy snort with laughter.

"What are you like?" Cathy asked him.

She poured mugs of tea for all of them, then used Scott's like a carrot on a stick to lure him to the living room.

By the time she returned, Heather was sitting on the kitchen worktop, her tea swapped out for a big mug of strong instant coffee.

Cathy picked up her own cup, took a sip, then started to load the dirty breakfast dishes in the sink. "You're really going to have to stop saving my daughter's life," she said, then she looked back over her shoulder and winced. "That came out wrong. Please don't stop doing that. I meant she's going to have to stop getting herself in situations where her life needs saving."

Heather nodded. "Don't worry, I got it. And aye, that would be ideal." She took a hit of her coffee. "How is she?"

"Surprisingly, she's fine. Or, as far as I can tell, anyway. No saying what'll come out in the next few days, but today, she's insisting she's good. She even insisted that she's going to school. Against my better judgement, I should add." Cathy sighed and shook her head. "Stubborn wee cow."

"She's resilient," Heather said. "But keep an eye on her. I'll need to talk to her later. They wanted to take a statement last night, but I told them it could wait."

"Thank you," Cathy said.

Heather shrugged. "I was just lucky I got there in time."

"Not for saving her. Though, thank you for that, obviously! For looking out for her. For being her friend."

"Oh."

Unable to think of anything more to add, Heather looked down into the dark pool of her coffee.

"She was planning on riding her dad's old bike to school," Cathy said, turning back to the sink and squeezing in some *Fairy Liquid*. "Apparently, she rides a bike now. She couldn't yesterday, and now she does."

Heather chuckled. "Like I said, resilient." She swirled her coffee around. "Anyway, I thought we agreed to not thank each other?"

"Ha. Yes, we did, didn't we? But then you went and saved her life all over again, so I think I get an exemption for that one."

"That's fair, I suppose," Heather conceded. "But in that case, thank you for staying with my dad last night."

"You're very welcome."

There was a knock at the front door. Cathy fixed Heather with a smile. "I believe that's going to be for you."

———

"Good morning, Officer. It's nice to see you up and about. I see you're wearing yesterday's clothes."

Heather leaned an arm on the doorframe and slurped from her coffee. "Yep," she confirmed. "I see you aren't."

Ace looked down at her Kilmarnock Academy uniform, then made a show of adjusting her clip-on tie. "Well spotted. You'd make quite the detective."

"Cheers. I'll give that some thought," Heather said.

The girl drew herself up to her full height. "I wanted to apologise. I know you enjoy hearing this, so I'm going to say it. You were right."

"I'm always right," Heather replied. She swigged another mouthful of coffee. "But what was I right about this time?"

"I shouldn't have gone investigating on my own like that. It was reckless, it was dangerous, and it could have ended very badly had you not turned up."

Heather tilted her head from side to side. "I'd add that it was idiotic, but go on."

"Yes. Well, quite," Ace said. "The point is, I have learned my lesson. Crime De La Crime is obviously an important journalistic outlet."

"Obviously."

"But it's not worth losing my life over."

"No," Heather agreed.

"Although, I did recently hit twenty subscribers."

Heather let out a low, impressed-sounding whistle, the sarcasm of which completely went over the girl's head.

"Thank you. It was a landmark moment."

"Shame they're going to be disappointed."

Ace looked confused by the comment. "I'm sorry?"

"Your subscribers. They're going to be disappointed that you're stopping the podcast."

The girl let out a snort. "Stopping the podcast?! Stopping Crime De La Crime? Now, just when it's building momentum? Are you mad?"

Heather stopped with her mug halfway to her mouth. "What? Didn't you just say...?"

"I'm not stopping the podcast, Officer!"

"Detective Inspector," Heather corrected.

"I'm expanding it. The danger wasn't in the investigations, it was in carrying them out on my own. As of today, I am no longer flying solo!"

Before Heather could ask, Ace turned on her heel and pointed a little way along the street. A smaller sandy-haired boy stood sheepishly by the gate of a neighbouring house, holding onto the handlebars of a battered old bicycle.

He blushed so forcefully when Heather looked at him that his whole head lit up like a warning beacon.

"That's Edward. He's my new partner. You might say we're in *cahoots*," Ace explained, and she appeared to take particular pleasure from that last word. "We actually thought about changing the podcast name to Partners in Crime, but, well, it's not as good a name, so we didn't."

"Makes sense," Heather agreed.

She looked over at Edward again. He immediately looked up to the sky like there was something going on up there that was terribly interesting.

"That your dad's bike?" she asked.

Ace followed her gaze, let it linger there for a second, then turned back. There was a smile on her face that Heather couldn't quite decipher.

"No," Ace said. She drew in a breath, like she was savouring the moment. "It's mine."

Heather tilted her mug in a toast to the girl. "Good for you, Nancy Drew."

"I'm going to attempt to give Edward"—she formed quote marks in the air with her fingers—"'a backie.' I suspect it won't end well, but it will be a learning experience, if nothing else."

Heather looked from the girl to the boy, then back again. "Yeah," she said. For once, she didn't even bother to hide her genuine delight. "I'm sure the two of you will figure something out."

FORTY-TWO

DC SWANNEY WAS STANDING by her bed, dressed like a cow, when Heather rocked up at the hospital.

It took the DI a moment to understand what she was looking at, then eventually realised that Tammi-Jo was wearing a bovine-themed onesie with big black patches, a swinging tail, and a pocket on the front shaped like a set of udders.

Heather chose not to give the younger woman the satisfaction of mentioning it.

"You're alive, then."

"Yep! Very much so!" Tammi-Jo confirmed in a voice that still had a bit of a croak to it. Her tail swished happily as she rummaged around in the chunky plastic bedside drawer. "I'm sure I had sweets in here, though. A nurse got me some from the wee shop last night."

Heather pointed to an empty bag of *Rowntree's Fruit Pastilles* on the floor beside the bed. "That them?"

Tammi-Jo stared blankly down at the bag for a minute, then nodded. "Ah. Yeah. That's them. Forgot I ate them all. Bum."

Heather smirked. "Back to not swearing, then?"

"Saving it for special occasions," the DC replied. She sat on the bed, which made her udders all bunch up. "They're letting me out later today. The only treatment they've given me is some ice cream. Three little tubs. It's great in here. I mean, they were all vanilla, but still, it's a classic for a reason, isn't it? Do you like vanilla?"

Heather shrugged. "I have no real opinion."

Tammi-Jo rolled her eyes. "You're such a liar. Of course you have an opinion. Do you or do you not like vanilla ice cream?"

Heather tutted. "I mean... I wouldn't choose it."

"Well, not if there was other stuff, obviously!" Tammi-Jo cried. An old woman in the bed opposite grumbled in her sleep, and the detective constable lowered her voice again. "No one would choose it if there was other stuff. But do you like it?"

"God! Aye! I don't mind."

"There! That wasn't so difficult, was it?"

Heather rolled her eyes, sighed, then said what she'd driven all this way to say.

"The Muppet Christmas Carol."

Tammi-Jo blinked, confused, then sat up straighter, her whole face lighting up with joy.

"Me and my mum used to watch it," Heather said. "It was our thing we did on Christmas Eve."

"No way! No way!" Tammi-Jo was on her feet now, udders and tail jiggling excitedly. "That's my favourite, too! We can watch it together! We can get popcorn and hot chocolate. No! Hot chocolate with popcorn in it! Oh! That can be our thing!"

"What do you mean?"

"Like, our police thing. Our special partner thing."

Heather shook her head. "We're not partners, and we don't need a thing."

"We do need a thing. And we've got a thing!" the DC insisted.

She clapped her hands together, and the woman in the bed opposite muttered a, "Shut the fuck up!"

Tammi-Jo was too fixated on DI Filson to hear her.

"The Muppet Christmas Carol. That's our thing!"

Heather snorted. "Oh, aye. Because that's going to strike fear into the hearts of criminals everywhere, isn't it? 'Watch oot lads, here come thae two lassies who like the fuckin' Muppets. Better turn wirselves in.'"

Tammi-Jo put her clenched fists on her hips. "Do you think that could happen?"

Heather hesitated. Not for the first time, she was unsure if the detective constable was taking the piss. "No," she eventually said. "I don't."

"No. Probably not. But we might fill them with Christmas spirit and they might just, you know, give up crime."

This had to be an act. It had to be. Nobody was this nice. Nobody was this naïve. Nobody who worked for Police Scotland, at any rate.

"Aye, well. We'll see," Heather said.

She bit her lip, hesitant to say the next part, even though she knew it was the right thing to do. The decent thing.

And, even though, deep down—way deep—some small part of her relished the thought of it.

"Listen, you're going to need someone keeping on you for a bit," the DI said. "If you want—no pressure, obviously, it's no skin off my nose—but if you want, you can use Stewie's room for a bit."

"I can stay?!"

"For a bit," Heather stressed. "Just until you get somewhere sorted."

Tammi-Jo let out a banshee-like squeal and lunged. Instinctively, Heather swung with an elbow, clouting the detective constable on the side of the head.

"Shit! Sorry."

Tammi-Jo's smile remained locked in place. "My fault! Only fair. Should've remembered what happened last time!"

She rubbed her ear, then held a hand out for the detective inspector to shake.

"I would be delighted to accept your offer of accommodation, DI Filson."

"Temporary accommodation," Heather stressed, but Tammi-Jo just smiled as they shook on the deal.

Then, she reached into her udder, pulled out a Fruit Pastille, and popped it in her mouth.

"Knew I'd kept some somewhere," she said. "You want one?"

Heather scrunched up her face at the thought of it, looked down at the bulging udders, then sighed.

"Ah, what the hell?" she said, holding out a hand. "But if you give me a black one, I'll rip off your tail."

———

Twenty minutes later, Heather sat in the multi-storey car park of Glasgow Royal Infirmary. The unmarked BMW she'd borrowed from the carpool was five years older than her Audi, smelled of stale smoke, and had crumbs all over the carpets.

So, at least it didn't feel entirely unfamiliar.

It was barely ten in the morning, and she'd already made some headway on her To Do List. Aye, there was still a host of interviews to have with Ted Campbell, Wayne Gillespie, and Selma Baird—assuming she was ready to talk—plus everything else that would be involved in building the cases against both men.

Wayne wouldn't be her problem for long. Assuming Marty had pulled another all-nighter, all their evidence and information on him would be ready to hand over, along with Sergeant Gillespie himself. He was about to become someone else's problem.

Ted wouldn't be so easy, of course. That one would land on the MIT's shoulders, which meant that she'd end up bearing the brunt of it.

But that was fine. That was right.

And besides, she could always dump the donkey work on DC Wolfe.

Before that, though, there was another matter to attend to.

She took out her wallet and removed the business card that Tammi-Jo had found down the side of the bed in Stewie's room.

The eye-shaped logo of the nightclub seemed to stare defiantly at her, like it was daring her, taunting her.

She didn't dwell too long on it, and instead just turned it over, took out her phone, and began to punch in the digits of the mobile number that had been scribbled on the back in red ink.

There was a moment of hesitation before she hit the button to dial, her thumb hovering above the screen, a thousand thoughts crashing through her head, but none of them solid enough for her to hold on to.

"Fuck it," she muttered, then her thumb touched down, and she brought the phone to her ear.

At first, there was nothing. An empty void of electronic silence.

And then, to her surprise, the ringing started. She'd told herself the number wouldn't be active, deliberately dampening her expectations.

But now, it was ringing.

And now, there was a click.

And now, there was a voice.

"Hello?"

A woman. An accent. That was all Heather could get from the one word.

"Uh, hi. Sorry, who is this?"

A pause.

"Who is this?" the woman countered.

Russian? Young. Twenties, maybe. Sounded a little slurred. Drunk?

"I'm, eh, I'm looking for Stewie. Stewart Filson," Heather said.

A pause.

Longer this time.

Heather glanced at the screen to check if the line had dropped.

The seconds ticked up, counting the silence.

She was about to try again, when the voice returned.

No, not *the* voice. A different one. A man this time, with the same accent as the woman before him.

"Good luck," he said.

And then, with a click, the line went dead.

ALSO AVAILABLE

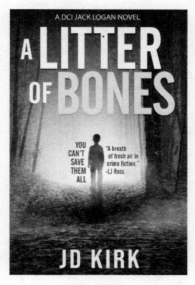

A Litter of Bones

Meet DCI Jack Logan in the first bestselling book from JD Kirk.

JOIN THE JD KIRK VIP CLUB

Want access to an exclusive image gallery showing locations from JD's books? Join the free JD Kirk VIP Club today, and as well as the photo gallery you'll get regular emails containing free short stories, members-only video content, and all the latest news about the author and his novels.

JDKirk.com/VIP

(Did we mention that it's free...?)

ABOUT THE AUTHOR

JD Kirk is the author of the million-selling DCI Jack Logan Scottish crime fiction series, set in the Highlands.

He also doesn't exist, and is in fact the pen name of award-winning former children's author and comic book writer, Barry Hutchison. Didn't see that coming, did you?

Both JD and Barry live in Fort William, where they share a house, wife, children, and two pets. You can find out more at JDKirk.com or at Facebook.com/jdkirkbooks.

417